MW01254022

THE MAN WHO MARRIED A REDHEAD

A novel

By Paul Naintre

To Monica & John,
Our Dear Friends,
From Nancy & Paul

To my beautiful mermaid, Jena di Bella Luna,
amore vero mio per sempre.

To Bridie Enright my lovely Mother,
and to my great Father, Vittorio Naintre.
Grazie Tanto.

Copyright © 2009 Paul Naintre. All rights reserved.

Ferrari is a registered trademark of Ferrari NA and Ferrari S.p.A.

This book is a work of fiction. All events are products of the author's
imagination.

My thanks to the PR department of Ferrari S.p.A. for permitting me to
use the great Enzo Ferrari's name in fictitious events throughout this
book.

ISBN: 978-0-557-08134-9

Contents:

1: BLACK GREASY GOLD.

The battered, old truck careened down the mountainside. Worn out tie rods and springs made it veer and bounce wildly in all directions. The gold bars, smeared with black axle grease, mud, and sand, hidden in the spare wheel carriers, bounced up and down with each jolt. Stefano fought with the steering wheel to stay on the narrow track. The cab sweltered, but the tropical heat didn't bother Stefano, or his best friend Billy Joe, because they were feeling really pleased with themselves, singing as loud as they could: "She'll be coming round the mountain when she comes!

She'll be wearing pink pajamas, wearing pink pajamas, wearing pink pajamas when she comes! Singing I Yi Yippee Yippee Yai…….." They made up their own words and yelled them out.

They had good reason to be pleased. After months of digging tunnels inside the mountain, they had found a vast seam of gold.

They had shuddered and shook in their boots, touching the yellow gold gently; afraid it would disappear in front of their eyes. They dug into the gold seam, removing huge solid chunks, not knowing or caring if it was night or day outside. Hour after hour they worked, hands red raw, jeans ripped from top to bottom, shirts in tatters, hair full of gold dust, glittering in the light of their oil lamps.

Only when all went dark as their lamps ran out of oil, did they stop digging. Leaning against each other back to back, exhausted, they fell asleep. Billy Joe woke first then shook Stefano awake. They struck matches and stared incredibly at their fortune, burning their fingers as the flame ate the matches and seared into the skin. They knew they should leave the gold and go out into the fresh air, but were afraid to leave, in case someone else came and stole it, so they sat in the dark, discussing what to do. The discovery of the gold had given them a fever and only after they felt the rats biting them, did they finally decide to leave the gold for a short time. They crawled back through the tunnel they had dug, until at last they saw a speck of daylight; then scrambled with renewed energy towards that tiny bit of light.

They burst out of the tunnel, breathing in huge gulps of fresh air. In the hot midday sun they danced together, like drunken people, arms around each other, yelling and screaming in their fever. They danced so hard and so fast they fell over and rolled halfway down a ravine. Had they rolled ten foot more, they would have rolled over a ledge and been seriously injured in the long fall to the bottom of the ravine. But the gods were smiling on them and they stopped short of the ledge and lay in the hot sunshine, clasped together like two lovers.

Now, two days later, with as much of the gold as they could carry down the tunnel broken into rough bars, and wedged into the spare wheel carriers, they were on their way to the Recife docks to find a freighter to Genoa.

Suddenly, a loud bang went off somewhere ahead of the truck and the windscreen shattered. Stefano shouted, "Bandits!", as he saw two men with rifles firing at them from up ahead. A third man appeared off to the right, firing and hitting the cab of the truck.

Billy Joe reached for the shotgun behind his seat, pointed it up the track and loosed off a shot. One of the men seemed to dance in the air as the heavy gauge cartridge hit him in the chest. Stefano braked and the truck slowed. Billy Joe fired again and another of the men staggered and fell backwards. Stefano stopped the truck and reached behind the seat for the second shotgun.

A bullet zinged by his ear and ricocheted off the cabin wall. Stefano aimed and fired at the man to the right, just as he fired at the truck.

Billy Joe's scream of pain stunned Stefano who jerked around to see him clutching his chest. Blood poured from between his fingers. His mouth opened as he tried to speak, but blood frothed out instead of words.

Stefano jumped out of the cab, lifted Billy Joe out and sat him up against a tree. Gasping for breath, choking in his own blood, Billy Joe pulled Stefano close and whispered through the gurgling blood, "I'm done for, my friend. Promise me you will use the gold to find your beautiful redhead, marry her, and give her a kiss for me!"

"I promise! But first I must get you to a hospital."

Stefano leaned over to lift his friend up, but saw the light go out from Billy Joe's eyes and his body went limp. He was gone.

Stefano let out a huge sob. His body shuddered with emotion and the realization that his best friend had left the earth. He looked up at the sky and howled.

The sun blazed down on the shimmering, sandy road. The scorpion skittered along, searching for food. The vibration sensor at the tip of its leftmost leg detected movement from two mounds of living flesh. The scorpion changed direction and headed towards them, pincers outstretched. Finding shade underneath one of the mounds, it burrowed into the sand to wait for an unsuspecting insect to pass by.

Suddenly, one of the mounds of flesh started to fall onto the scorpion, which quickly raised its tail in defense and injected a deadly stream of venom. The mound of flesh never felt the scorpion's sting, for it had taken its last breath seconds before.

2: LOVE AT FIRST SIGHT.

Stefano stood on the balcony watching the lizard basking in the early sunlight.

It reminded him of the scorpion he had found under Billy Joe's body when he lifted him up to bury him.

He wished Billy Joe could have been here today to be his Best Man.

Memories of his friend's last words brought tears to his eyes.

He would marry his beautiful redhead today and keep his promise to Billy Joe.

The wedding would be at noon in Maranello, a small town in Northern Italy, where the bride was born. The priest would perform the ceremony; then they would leave on their honeymoon to travel by road to Rome and Naples, then up to Genoa by ferry.

His bride would wear red. The most beautiful red, he thought. The most succulent red… no, not succulent, ….sexy red, no, wrong again… fiery luscious, hot red, like no other red imaginable.

Stefano was in his early thirties, with a dark complexion and black, wavy hair, down to his collar. A strange person really, not one of your everyday stereotypes, always seeking ways to make life more interesting, even in the most mundane tasks that all men must do to put bread on the table. Luck was with him, along with a firm sense of reality, which invariably caused him to land on his feet.

So here he was, in a comfortable hotel in Northern Italy surrounded by mountains, to wed his beautiful redhead at noon today, May 24th, 1987.

The telephone rang inside the room; he walked in and picked it up.

"Hello, this is Stefano."

"Signore, would you like to order breakfast to your room?" The girl's voice was fresh and pleasant sounding, her Italian accent coming through clearly.

"Grazie, Signorina, I would like toast, marmalade and coffee please."

"I bring to your room in ten minutes, Signore." The telephone clicked as she rang off. Stefano put down the telephone and went into the bathroom.

He took off his dressing gown and stepped into the blue marble tiled shower, set the tap to warm and turned it on. The water came out as smooth as oil, and he soaped and lathered himself with the fine soap and shampoo provided by the hotel. Bracing himself, he turned the tap to cold. The freezing water jolted him. Twenty seconds later he was out of the shower wrapped in a hotel bathrobe. A few seconds later he heard a gentle knock on the outside door.

"Just coming," he called. He ran a comb through his hair and checked his robe in the mirror. I can smell the coffee, he thought. Opening the door, he was stunned by the lovely sight that met his eyes!

In front of him stood a young lady in a black silk dress with a white apron around her waist, carefully balancing a silver tray on her right hand level with her shoulder.

A mass of black hair framed her face. She looked at Stefano and her face lit with just the hint of a smile. The prettiest smile he had ever seen.

Her smiling eyes looked into his as she said, "Your breakfast, Signore."

Stefano's heart beat wildly as the most pleasant sensation he had ever experienced rushed through his body. He knew he was drowning in delight looking into her gorgeous brown eyes. An angel; he told himself, as another passionate wave swept deep inside his soul!

"Mi Scusi, Signore," Her full red lips parted as she looked at him, mystified.

He realized he was blocking the doorway and that she wished to come in and put the tray down, but he was frozen as if in a dream. Again he heard, "Mi Scusi, Signore." This time her voice had a soft touch of shyness in it.

Abruptly, his normal senses returning, he backed into the room profusely apologizing for being so rude. She came into the room and very professionally swung the silver tray down and placed it upon the table.

"Signorina, please, please, forgive me. When I looked into your beautiful eyes, my heart just went wild. I was sure you were an angel from Heaven."

"Please, Signore, do not jest, I am not an angel of any sort, only a hotel maid bringing you the breakfast you ordered."

With that, she turned on her heel and marched out of the door, her thick black hair floating around her like a lion's mane; her silk dress highlighting the beautiful curves of her body.

He stood in the same place for at least two minutes overcome by very strange feelings. This is crazy, he thought, what do I do now? I must find out her name and ask her to my wedding!

He shouted aloud, "I am in love, I really am in love!"

He recalled the smile in her warm brown eyes, so full of tenderness. The passionate aura coming from her which had made his heart beat wildly. And it was still beating wildly! He could feel it even now beating with tremendous force in his chest! He remembered her thick black mane of hair, and the way she filled her dress out very evenly with soft curves from her neck to her bosom, all the way down to her shapely legs.

What should I do? he asked himself. He poured a cup of coffee and spread butter on his toast, all the while thinking how to ask her to his wedding, so that he could get to know her. The wedding! I nearly forgot, he thought. Today at noon he was to marry his beautiful redheaded bride.

"I must pull myself together," he said aloud. He spread the thick orange marmalade on the toast and began to eat. The telephone rang, startling him. The piece of toast in his mouth didn't want to go down. He chewed it quickly and reached for the phone.

"Hello," he said, still trying to consume the piece of toast.

A man's voice on the other end said, "Good Morning, Signore Gapucci?

"Yes, who is this?"

"My name is Alberto Fostanelli, I am from the Maranello Limousine Service. I would like to know what time to pick you up, Signore."

"Please pick me up at 11.30… no wait! Exactly how long does it take to drive to our destination?"

"Fourteen minutes from the time you enter my limousine," replied Alberto, "I timed it yesterday." He spoke with confidence and Stefano was reassured.

"I shall be in the hotel lobby at 11.30, precisely."

"Si, Signore, I will meet you there." With that, Alberto hung up.

Stefano went to the wardrobe, and put on the clothes he had bought for the wedding: navy blue shirt and trousers, blue socks and dark blue Italian shoes.

"My God, I am lucky, so very lucky, and today I will wed the redhead of my dreams." He chuckled aloud and strode through the French doors to the outside patio. The cool mountain air was intoxicating, the view stupendous. He walked towards the low wall at the edge of the patio and stared into the distance. His back was to the door, so he did not see the young maid come into the suite. When she tapped on the doorframe, he jumped and turned around. "Oh! Signorina, you startled me," he exclaimed with a smile.

She said, "Scusi Signore, may I take your breakfast tray if you are finished?"

He could not reply, just stood smiling at her.

The wind blew hard for an instant pushing her beautiful black hair flat back against her head, exposing exquisite high cheekbones and the softness of her throat and neck. The wind died down again and her hair swung forward again, veiling her face with wisps of hair.

Now I am behaving like a schoolboy! he thought. What is the matter with me? He knew inwardly that it was because two magnificent occurrences were happening on the same day, one that he had planned for six months and one that was totally unexpected; this warm blooded young woman standing four feet away from him had stolen his heart.

Stefano's mind swirled as he sought words to express what he was feeling this very instant. If I tell her that I have fallen in love with her at first sight she will laugh at me, or call the manager or the police. He decided to brave that possibility, his Italian amorous bloodline overcoming the rationale by which he normally lived.

"Please, Signorina, sit down with me here." He gestured to the sofa next to his chair. "I have something very important to tell you. Do not be afraid, I beg of you." After this he went silent, trying to determine her reaction, hoping fervently that she would not turn on her heel and disappear again. The young woman looked at him incredulously, her large brown eyes wary.

She must think I am some lecherous salesman trying to lure her into a cheap affair, or some crazy madman who is so conceited, he thinks all women will fall instantly in love with him.

"Signore, I don't wish to be impolite, but you are embarrassing me." She spoke softly. "I am the maid for this floor, I am learning the hotel business. Even though my father owns this hotel, I still must understand all of the tasks involved in running a hotel so that one day I can take over when my father retires... now I must go, I only came to clear away your breakfast tray, I should not be talking to the guests." She turned to go into the room.

"Please Signorina, one second, before you go: please don't think I'm crazy, but I must tell you that I have fallen in love with you!"

She looked at him incredulously, trying to determine if he was serious.

Before she could say anything, Stefano continued, "I have a favor to ask, no two favors actually. Today at 12 noon I am to be married to a gorgeous redhead. At 11.30 a limousine is coming here to pick me up. I would be very pleased if you would come to my wedding as my maid of honor. This is my first request. My second request is that you come to the reception, it will be held here in the hotel at 2 this afternoon. Only a few people are coming and I don't know any of them personally, they are all from the bride's side of the family. Please don't say no, you will enjoy it, I promise! I think you will find it the most unusual wedding you have ever seen!"

She looked at him and smiled. "You must be really crazy, Signore, I don't know you and also I must work today, I cannot just take off whenever I feel like it, my father would have a fit."

Stefano's heart pounded. She had smiled, there was hope!

"Let me speak with your father, when he hears what I have to say, he will understand and will surely say yes you can go."

"No, Signore, I cannot, and now I must go." She picked up the silver tray and left the suite, once again carefully balancing the tray on her right hand. As the door swung shut behind her, Stefano wondered how he could get her to come to his wedding.

The young lady's name was Lucia. She stood in the drawing room in a private part of the hotel that her father used as his office. Her father, Luigi Constanetti, sat at his huge desk, his eyes closed, deep in thought. A full minute passed before he spoke. "My dear Lucia, tell me again about this man."

"Well father, he seems respectable, dresses well, and has nice hair. He seemed very attracted to me, and even said he had fallen in love with me, but then he asked me to come to his wedding as his maid of honor. I can't understand him at all, why would he do such a thing?"

"Sounds like a strange fellow indeed. Let me see if there is any information in his confirmation file." Luigi opened the lower front right drawer of his desk to reveal an indexed set of folders. "What suite was it, my dear?"

"Suite 26," replied Lucia.

"Ah, here we are, Suite 26 for the month of May, 1987." Luigi took out the typewritten sheet containing the confirmation of the current tenant. "Signore Stefano Gapucci, confirmed via the American Express travel agency six months ago, one large suite for one week. He particularly asked for the best available, cost was no object."

Luigi's eyes widened as he read the sheet. "Here is a very interesting request…a large secure garage to be made available, accessible only by him, containing no other vehicles."

"Why is that strange?" asked Lucia.

"Well, I remember when he checked in, I asked him for his car registration and he said, "I have no car, I took a taxi from the airport"."

Luigi thought for a second and said, "Maybe he plans on renting a car, although why he would bother paying extra for a garage for a rental car is beyond me."

Lucia walked over to the window and looked down over the valley. "I would so like to go to a wedding, Father, it has been ages since I have been out of the hotel and I am bored to say the least. And you never know, it might be fun."

"Where is this wedding, Lucia? Is it in the church on the mountainside or the one in the town?"

"I never gave him a chance to tell me, I told him my father would not let me go and that he, being a stranger, I couldn't drop what I was doing and come to his wedding."

"If your mother were alive she could have accompanied you, but you cannot go alone with this stranger, I could not allow it. You were right to tell him your father would forbid you. So there is an end to it, run along now and leave me to finish my bookkeeping for today. Soon it will be lunch time and I must discuss the menu with Chef Maretti."

"Very well, Father, I wasn't really that set on going anyway, but it was such a strange request that I had to talk to you about it. Now let's forget it and I will get back to my work. I have nearly three more months to work as a maid before I can begin my stint at the front desk as we agreed."

"My dear, one day, when I retire, this hotel will be yours to run as you wish. I only want you to learn all the ins and outs of the business firsthand so that you will truly know all of the problems that can come up, and you will be knowledgeable enough to manage them. Stay for a while and have a glass of wine with your Papa."

Luigi opened another one of the desk drawers and took out a bottle of wine that was half full. From another drawer he took two crystal wineglasses, removed the cork from the wine bottle and poured them each a generous portion. He handed one of the glasses to Lucia and held his own glass up.

"Salut, my dear, let us drink to your beauty, I am a very lucky father to have such a beautiful daughter…you look so like your mother, God rest her soul." Luigi clinked his glass against Lucia's, and smiled with great pride at his beloved daughter.

Stefano had made up his mind. He would go down to the front desk, find out her name, find her father and ask his permission to take her to the wedding. The least he can say is no, thought Stefano. He put on a navy blue jacket and took his wallet and room key from the bedside table drawer. His eye caught the time on the little brass clock that sat on the table.

Damn! Ten o'clock already. He left the suite and looked up and down the hallway to see if the young lady was around. No such luck! he thought. He hurried down the wide staircase and entered the lobby. No one was behind the front desk so he gave the little brass bell a light tap and it pealed with a curiously high note. A few moments passed and a tall man, dressed in an elegant black dress suit with tails, appeared from a side door.

"May I be of assistance, Sir?" the tall man asked with a confident smile.

"Yes, my name is Stefano Gapucci, I am staying in suite number twenty six. I had the great fortune of having my breakfast delivered to me in my room by an exceptionally sweet young lady and I need to speak with her again. I wonder if you could tell me her name and where I could find her or her father."

Stefano thought the man might react negatively, but instead the man in the tails smiled again and said, "You are in luck today, Sir. The young lady in question is Lucia and I am her father, Luigi Constanetti, also the owner of this hotel. How can I help you?"

"I have only seen Lucia fleetingly, for two brief moments, but both times I felt as if my blood vessels would burst. I was struck as if by a magic spell. An aura of tranquility and goodness surround her and I was overcome with a deep desire to tell her that my heart was pounding from the first moment I saw her. Never in my life has such a thing happened to me. This is why I asked her to come to my wedding as my maid of honor. I wish to get to know her better and for her to get to know me. I am sure that you must think me absurd, but a man must do what he believes in and I have summoned up the courage to speak my mind to you and Lucia, so that you will both know that I am an honorable man with the best intentions. If there is another man who has already stolen her heart, then tell me so and I will depart in anguish, but at least content that she is happy, if you tell me so." Stefano stood now silent and awaited Signore Constanetti's reply. He did not have to wait long.

"What of this wedding you speak of? How can you be so attracted to my daughter and make such overtures about how she enchants you, when on the same day you say you are to be married? How can you do such a thing?"

"Signore, this marriage is not what you think. I swore myself to secrecy that I would never divulge my bride's relationship to me with anybody until after the ceremony. One thing I promise you, there is no other woman involved, nor man for that matter. All I am doing is marrying a dream, but it is not a flesh and blood person that I am marrying. You will laugh when Lucia tells you about it after the wedding. Please allow her to come as my maid of honor. I assure you that I will treat her with the utmost respect."

Luigi stared at Stefano trying to understand what he had just heard. "I am totally bewildered…how can you talk of marrying someone that is not of flesh and blood? Surely you must be mixed up in the head! Tell me who you are marrying, and why, and if I am not satisfied with your response, then I will request that you leave my hotel immediately and never bother my daughter again!"

Stefano thought rapidly, What can I say to convince him without breaking my pledge of secrecy? "Signore, I am a man of honor, I ask you to trust me. Also, I have an idea that I am sure you will agree to. My limousine will be here at 11:30. It is now…" Stefano glanced at his watch, "…five minutes past ten. If you will permit me to be so bold, I would like Lucia to come as my maid of honor and yourself as my best man. There is plenty of room in my limousine and you can be chaperone to Lucia. I am sure that once you see my bride, all will be revealed. More I cannot divulge. Please say you will come!"

"You are a strange man indeed, Stefano Gapucci, but your tale intrigues me, so I will talk to Lucia and see if she wants to go. I will call you in your suite at 10:30 precisely, to inform you of our decision." Luigi turned on his heel and went to his private office.

Stefano was happy. I have done all I could, he said to himself. Back in his room, he poured himself a Gin and Tonic from the drink cabinet and took his drink out onto the balcony.

Memories of exciting times digging for gold with his old friend Billy Joe came flooding back to him. He relived the moment when Billy

Joe made him promise to find and marry the beautiful redhead, and the terrible sadness he felt when Billy Joe died.

He raised his glass in the air and silently made a toast, "To Billy Joe, to my bride, and to Lucia who I have fallen in love with." He drained his glass and looked at his watch. It showed 10:25. "Oh well, five more minutes will decide my fate."

The telephone rang. Stefano ran into the suite and picked up the receiver. "Hello, this is Stefano Gapucci." He waited for the reply praying it was Luigi with good news, but it wasn't.

"Hello, Stefano, my name is Anna Capello, I work as a consultant for the Cabrini Agency, and I am responsible for planning your unusual wedding today. I apologize for not calling you earlier, but I had a few last minute arrangements that required smoothing out. However, now everything is ready just as you requested…" She paused. "You will be here today at 12 noon?"

"Yes, Anna, I will be there. I am looking forward to it." Stefano looked at his watch, it showed 10:30. What if Luigi is trying to call! he thought.

"I will be in the main square when you arrive, your chauffeur Alberto will point me out to you… it is all arranged," said Anna.

Stefano felt himself warming to her voice; it was very feminine, with a gorgeous Italian accent. "Very well, Anna, see you soon." He replaced the receiver into the cradle hoping it would ring again, but it sat there, silent. "Ring, why don't you?" Stefano said aloud, worried now that he might have missed Luigi's call. He sat down in the leather armchair.

The telephone rang, Stefano picked up the receiver. "Hello…" he said rather nervously.

"Ah, Stefano, this is Luigi Constanetti. My daughter and I have discussed your proposal and although it is rather short notice, we accept your invitation to come to your wedding. It is not every day that we get to attend a joyous occasion.   Lucia is busy changing now, so we will meet you in the lobby at 11:25 as you requested. Ciao! Stefano"

"Ciao! Luigi." Stefano was ecstatic. He could hardly contain himself and shouted aloud as he put the phone down. "Lucia! My true love Lucia! Thank you for saying yes!"

3: THE WEDDING.

At precisely 11:20, Alberto slid the Cadillac limousine into the parking area in front of the Bella Montagna hotel. Truly a beautiful piece of architecture, thought Alberto, as he gazed up at the hotel. Its splendor was really magnificent; the whole exterior cast in blue and white veined marble blocks, built like a small fortress nestling in the lap of the massive mountains that soared behind it. Alberto opened the limousine door and stepped out into the mild sunshine. He walked slowly up the sweeping marble staircase that led to the hotel foyer. The doorman, Eugenio, clad in a dark blue tuxedo and matching top hat, greeted him warmly,

"Ciao, Alberto, come sta?"

"Molto bene, grazie, Eugenio, e lei?" replied Alberto.

"Bene, bene, Buon giorno!"

Alberto had known Eugenio for many years, first at the tiny hotel in the town square and now for the last seven years here at the mountain hotel.

"You are picking up Signore Gapucci?" asked Eugenio.

"Yes, do you know him? What is he like?" questioned Alberto.

"All I know is that he has asked Lucia to be the maid of honor at his wedding today, also I heard that Don Luigi himself will be accompanying Lucia. That really is strange. He rarely leaves the hotel for social occasions; this must be very special to him."

At that moment Stefano entered the hotel lobby, walked over to the cashier's office, introduced himself to Maria, the young cashier, and asked for his four leather satchels to be brought from the safe. Maria typed in a code on the security monitor sitting on her desk. The rear wall made of steel slid upwards to expose a large walk-in safe.

Marcello, the assistant manager, heard the safe wall rise and came over from his desk to help. He smiled at Maria and asked, "What are we looking for?"

"Four leather satchels for Signore Gapucci," said Maria. She found them easily and went to lift one. "Oh!" she exclaimed loudly. 'This is too heavy for me to lift…here you try this one, Marcello."

Marcello examined the satchels, which were made of black leather, about one foot square in size with extremely strong looking handles. Each one had a small but strong looking padlock through the steel hasp to keep out curious eyes. He turned one of the satchels over with difficulty and examined the underside. "Ah ha!" exclaimed Marcello, "Just as I thought, there are small wheels attached to each satchel…all we have to do is keep them upright and pull them along." He grasped the handles of the satchel and rolled it out of the safe. He did the same for the other three satchels. Maria typed in the code to drop the steel wall, which slid soundlessly down into place.

"I wonder what is in the satchels?" said Maria. "What do you think Marcello?"

Marcello shook his head. "Who knows, my sweet? Could be dumb-bells or gold ingots, but they are well and truly padlocked, so we will probably never know." Maria and Marcello rolled all four satchels into the lobby where Maria had Stefano sign a receipt and asked him what he would like done with them, now that they were out of the safe.

"Please have the bellboy take them out to my limousine," said Stefano, smiling at Maria and taking in her attractive bosom which was ever so neatly contained beneath her black silk dress suit.

"Certainly, Signore Gapucci," said Maria with a slight blush, acknowledging Stefano's appraisal of her anatomy. She beckoned to Pietro, the head bell boy, to come over and requested him in a quick burst of Italian to take the satchels out to the car. Maria was dying to ask Signore Gapucci what was in them, but her years of training under Don Luigi forbade her to. As he had always said, "The guest has every right to privacy while he or she is in our hotel and we must maintain that principle."

Pietro wheeled over an ornate brass baggage cart and loaded the four satchels onto it, groaning at the weight of each satchel. Being young and curious he immediately made a comment that there must be dumb-bells or cast iron in the satchels. Marcello hushed him to be quiet and take the satchels to the limousine.

As Pietro completed the loading of the satchels onto the cart, Luigi and Lucia came into the foyer. Luigi was resplendent in a dark blue suit and mirror shined shoes. Alongside him stood Lucia, wearing a peach colored dress, which was just tight enough to show off her magnificent full figure.

Stefano saw Lucia and his heart started pounding again. "Lucia…may I call you Lucia? You look positively adorable in that dress. I am so very proud that you and your father consented to come, you have made me truly happy."

Lucia blushed and said, "Signore, you must save your compliments for your wife-to-be." She followed Pietro through the double doors and stood in the morning sunshine, looking very relaxed, a flit of a smile on her face as she looked down over the valley.

Pietro wheeled the cart down the slope next to the marble staircase and stopped by the rear of the huge limousine. Alberto pulled a small transceiver from his inside pocket and aimed it at the trunk of the Cadillac. He pushed a button and the lid of the trunk rose smoothly upwards, reached its open position, and stopped.

"Mama Mia! It never fails to amaze me when I see you do that. It's like magic. Can I do it once, please Alberto?" Alberto gave Pietro the transceiver and showed him the two buttons to push, one for opening and the other for closing the trunk. Pietro aimed at the trunk and pressed the button on the transceiver, but the trunk lid did not move. He pressed again several times, but nothing happened.

Alberto said, "Try the other button I showed you."

Pietro nodded and looked down at the transceiver. "Oh! Oh! Which was the other one?" The transceiver looked back at him, its twelve buttons glistening in the sunshine. He remembered that it might have been 3 and 4, but he wasn't sure. He pressed number 4. A whining hum came from the Cadillac, the rear sliding roof slid slowly open. Pietro gulped and pressed number 3, now the right side window lowered itself. Pietro noticed Alberto staring at him. That's good, he is still smiling! thought Pietro.

He decided to experiment and pressed 1, then 2, then 3 all the way to 12. The Cadillac came alive in a world of its own, the trunk lid was finally rising, it rose to its full extent, then started to go back down again; all of the six windows were going up, down, up, down; the front and rear sliding roofs were opening and closing, opening and closing. Pietro looked at Alberto. "How do I stop it?" he shouted.

Alberto started to laugh and his whole frame shook with merriment. He was a heavyset man of 300 pounds from all of the pasta his wife had cooked for him over the years, and his huge belly was writhing under his shirt as he kept on laughing. Then Pietro started to laugh. Alberto and Pietro were mesmerized by the sight of the Cadillac whining and huffing, as the remote controlled options played out their functions simultaneously. All of a sudden, a loud screaming noise emitted from the limousine. The alarm system had finally caught on that all was not well and decided of its own accord to alert the world with its high-pitched screaming siren. Alberto stopped laughing, grabbed the transceiver from Pietro's hand and frantically pushed the reset button on the side of the transceiver. The siren stopped along with all of the other electrical gadgets.

"Wow! Yipppee!" shouted Pietro. "That was fun!" Again he burst out laughing. Alberto didn't have the heart to chastise him and instead smiled and laughed with Pietro.

"My boy," said Alberto, catching his breath, "You are funny...never have I seen this poor car doing do many circus tricks at one time." He wiped the tears from his eyes with his handkerchief, then gently adjusted all of the Cadillac's windows and roofs with the transceiver. Now that the trunk lid was open and stayed so, Pietro started to lift one of the leather satchels off of the cart. Alberto saw that it was really heavy. "Here, let me help you!" he said, and together the slim young man and the huge old man loaded the four satchels into the trunk, joking about the weight.

Alberto closed the lid and clapped his hands together. "Bellissimo!" he cried.

Pietro smiled at Alberto, then wheeled the cart slowly up the incline, back towards the hotel. He stopped halfway up, turned and gave Alberto a stiff army style salute with his hand. "Thank you, Alberto, that was great fun." Alberto gave him a friendly wave in return and Pietro continued up the incline, pushing the ornate brass cart ahead of him.

Luigi took his daughter's arm and they walked slowly down the marble staircase towards the limousine. Halfway down the staircase, Lucia turned and called back to Stefano who was daydreaming again, admiring Lucia's walk from behind. "Signore Gapucci, come now or you will be late for your wedding!" She was smiling all the while, knowing he had been watching her walk in the tight dress.

Stefano caught up with Lucia and Luigi. "Lucia, I have two more huge favors to ask you; please call me Stefano, it would make me so happy, and if you would take my arm I would be so honored."

Lucia looked across at her father, then said to Stefano, "Today I will call you Stefano, but tomorrow it must be Signore Gapucci again." Stefano and Luigi both smiled at her reply and Lucia looked from one to the other and couldn't help herself. A magnificent smile lit up her whole face. She took Stefano's arm, and with Luigi on her right and Stefano on her left, they walked slowly down the wide marble staircase.

Stefano was so ecstatically happy, arm in arm with Lucia, he nearly fainted. As they came up to the limousine, Alberto proudly opened the doors for them. "Buon Giorno, Lucia, Buon Giorno Luigi, Buon Giorno, Signore Gapucci." he said.

"Please, Alberto, today we call him Stefano," said Lucia laughing aloud.

"Si, Signorina, as you wish. Buon giorno, Stefano."

"Buon giorno, Alberto," replied Stefano.

The three settled into the soft leather seats as Alberto closed the rear door, got into the driver's seat and started the engine. "Please, there is a bottle of champagne on ice in the drink compartment... please help yourselves, per favore!"

Luigi opened the drink compartment, took out three crystal glasses and placed them on the little table. Then he took the champagne bottle from the ice bucket and eased out the cork in a very professional manner. Bam! The cork hit the roof, but before any champagne could be spilt, he deftly poured it into the three crystal glasses. He passed one glass to Lucia and one to Stefano. Then Luigi raised his glass. "A toast to Stefano on his wedding day!' said Luigi. Lucia raised her glass and sipped the bubbling champagne.
"One more toast," said Stefano, 'to Luigi and his beautiful daughter Lucia, my friends forever!" He raised his glass. "Salute!"

"Salute!" said Lucia and Luigi, joining in the spirit and smiling at Stefano, this funny man who was getting married. Alberto opened the rear sun roof and took off slowly down the winding road towards the town.

The sirens screamed their message to the heavens; quite a musical but extremely penetrating noise. Six policemen on Ducati motorcycles led the two black Alfa Romeo police cars up the road towards the hotel. Six more police motorcycles followed behind. The sirens became overpoweringly loud even inside the limousine, so Alberto pulled over onto the grass verge and stopped. The cavalcade of Polizia came around the bend and surrounded the limousine.

"What is happening, Alberto?" said Lucia. "It can't be for driving too fast, you were only going slowly, I will vouch for you."

"I don't know, Signorina. There are so many policemen!" A look of concern showed on his face and he lowered his window as one of the police officers approached his limousine.

"Buon giorno, Signore," said the policeman with a smile.

"Buon giorno, how can I help you?" asked Alberto.

"Is your passenger Signore Stefano Gapucci?" asked the policeman, peering into the limousine.

"I am Stefano Gapucci, what can I do for you?" said Stefano.

"The Mayor heard of your generous donation to the Maranello Children's School from Anna at the Cabrini Agency. He asked us to escort you into the town. I apologize for not calling you in advance, but we only heard about it one hour ago and we spent the time washing our vehicles and changing into our parade uniforms. I trust you will accept our offer of an escort, Signore?"

"I am deeply honored to have such a splendid escort, Signore !" said Stefano.

"Very well, Signore, we too are proud to be your escort on your wedding day!" said the police officer. He asked Alberto for directions to the wedding, then asked him to drive behind the first six motorcycles and follow them. The police officer went off to give the destination to the lead motorcyclists, then went back to his black Alfa Romeo, climbed in, beeped his horn once and the motorcyclists started their engines and neatly, two by two, pulled out into the road.

Alberto took up his station behind the first six motorcycles and the long cavalcade began to wind its way down the road to Maranello. A continuous scream of sirens started again, but now Alberto was happy; he grinned and honked his horn and said to his passengers, "What a spectacle! For once I don't get no ticket. Today, God is good to me. You must be very highly regarded by the Mayor, Signore."

"The donation was my way of thanking the town of Maranello for nurturing my beautiful bride who was born here; I wanted to give the town something back, so that when I leave with my beautiful redhead, I will be content to know that I have helped a little with my donation to the school."

"You are a strange man, Signore," said Luigi to Stefano. "Who is this redheaded woman you are marrying? Please tell me her name."

"Soon you will see, Luigi, and I will have the pleasure of watching the expression on your face when you see her, for she is as beautiful as Lucia, but in a different way. I have loved her from afar for a long time and prayed for this day to come, to make my dream come true. With Lucia as my maid of honor as well, let me say I am the happiest man alive and I am deeply thankful that you permitted Lucia to attend the ceremony."

Lucia looked at her father, then at Stefano. "How can you speak of me making you a happy man on your wedding day? Soon you will be married to this beautiful redhead of whom you speak, and I will be remaining in Maranello long after you have departed. As my father said, you a strange person indeed, but because we love weddings, Father and I are pleased to attend the ceremony. We want to see what sort of beautiful redhead surrounded by mystery you are marrying."

The sun came out from behind the clouds as the motorcade turned into Via Veneto, the main street of Maranello. The people of the town came out of their shops and houses when they heard the shrill shrieking of the police escort. Both sides of the street were decked out in large tubs of colorful flowers set every fifty metres.

As they reached the Town Hall, the motorcade slowed to a crawl as the Maranello town band, in all its finery, marched ahead of them. The first row of five young men dressed in blue and white uniforms beat their snare drums in a fast staccato that bounced off the walls of the street. They were led by a strikingly pretty young lady also in a blue and white jacket and tall Grenadier's hat, but instead of trousers she wore blue tights that seemed molded to her legs and thighs, and her feet were encased in short blue leather boots. She marched with athletic ease, her beautiful long legs lifting high in the air, giving the impression of a prancing young mare. The young town boys whistled loudly as she passed by, trying to get her attention, but she ignored them all, concentrating on twirling her silver baton high in the air. One young man, braver than the rest, picked a red flower from one of the tubs and calmly walked out in front of her with his offering. Without pausing she smiled, neatly side-stepped by him and continued her elegant march.

The atmosphere in the town was exciting, as more and more people thronged the pavement of the Via Veneto, heads craning to see the parade; fathers had their little children on their shoulders to get a good view.

"What is the parade for?" the young children asked their parents.

"It is for a special wedding between a young man and his lady love from Maranello," they replied.

"Who is the lady love, Papa?" said one little girl to her father.

"We don't know yet, it is a secret," replied her father.

Indeed, only a handful of privileged people in the town knew who the bride was and they chuckled to themselves in a knowing way when asked by their friends if they knew who it was.

The band turned left, into the main square of Maranello, where flowers were everywhere, adorning each lamp post in a mass of color.

A twenty-five foot long table stood in the middle of the square covered by a magnificent white lace embroidered tablecloth. On the ends of the table were huge baskets of flowers and in the center were rows and rows of plates, stacked with delicious looking sandwiches and cakes. Large bottles of champagne were placed along the table, each bottle surrounded by a dozen long-stemmed crystal glasses and large glass bowls full of fresh lemonade for the children. To the right of the table stood two arches made of thin strips of wood, each ten feet high and ten feet wide adorned with red and white carnations. Joining the arches was a huge piece of white silk, easily twenty feet in length and eight feet wide.

To the right of the arches stood a low structure about eighteen feet long and seven feet wide, covered in white satin. It looked like a stage but no-one was standing on it.

Under the arches stood three imposing figures; a priest dressed in a green chasuble robe holding a golden staff. To his left stood the Mayor of Maranello, Signore Bravarrone, wearing a silk tunic of blue and gold, a blue tricorn hat with a huge white curling ostrich feather attached to it, and a long pair of shiny black leather boots. Next to him, stood a tall, distinguished looking gentleman in a beautifully cut black dress suit, a white ruffled shirt and brilliant red tie. His hair was greying and swept back off of his face, you could not see his eyes because he wore a pair of steel sunglasses with dark blue lenses.

The band marched up to the arches led by the pretty young lady in the tall Grenadier's hat. The young lady stopped the band and lined everybody up next to the three men, as the police motorcade, sirens still shrieking, rolled past. When the limousine came abreast of the arches, it stopped and the mayor stepped forward and opened the rear door. Lucia stepped out of the limousine into the warm sunshine, followed by Luigi and Stefano.

"Lucia, you are so beautiful!" said Stefano, overcome again by this gorgeous young woman, whose black hair glistened in the sunlight, and who made his heart pound whenever he looked in her eyes.

"Don't be silly!" cried Lucia, "Please save your compliments for your bride-to-be! Has she arrived yet or do you think she will keep you waiting?"

Stefano smiled but did not reply.

Luigi said, "Stefano, you selected a strange place for wedding, why not a church?"

"Ah," said Stefano with a merry chuckle and a twinkle in his eye. "Soon you will see my reasons, but first I would like you to meet some very special people."

He introduced Luigi and Lucia to the mayor and the priest.

Before he could introduce them to the distinguished looking gentleman in the black suit, a young lady with long flowing hair the color of golden corn came up to Stefano and held out her hand. "Hello Stefano, I am Anna Capello from the Cabrini Agency. I trust everything is to your satisfaction so far?"

"Anna, you have done a marvelous job, couldn't be better." He smiled and grasped her hand with both of his, leaned forward and brushed her cheek with his lips.

Anna blushed and said, "You are very welcome, Signore, it is not every day that we have the occasion to deck the town in such color, many thanks to you."

Luigi and Lucia looked long at Anna. Eventually Luigi said, "My dear, you have chosen well. Signore Gapucci will make you a grand husband, I am sure."

"Oh dear! It is not I who am fortunate enough to marry Stefano today... I only arranged the flowers and wedding procedure." Anna giggled slightly and went on to say, "His bride is the most astonishing redhead you have ever seen." Anna giggled again.

"We cannot wait to see this redhead; does she not have a name?" asked Luigi.

"Ah, yes indeed, she does have a name," said the tall man wearing the dark blue sunglasses standing next to the priest. "Allow me to introduce myself, I am the bride's Godfather, Enzo Ferrari, and I will be giving her away. Soon you will see the beautiful redhead of which Anna spoke."

Luigi said, "Buon Giorno Signore Ferrari, I am Luigi Constanetti and this is my daughter Lucia. It is a great pleasure to meet you." Luigi and Lucia shook hands with Enzo.

Anna turned to the crowd which had gathered in front of them.

"Signora e Signore, the Maranello School choir would like to sing a happy song of welcome to Signore Stefano and his bride-to-be." The crowd cheered as the choir filed out from behind the arch. They sang a beautiful children's song about lambs, hillsides and sunshine. As the final words were sung, the girls curtseyed, the boys bowed and the crowd cheered.

Anna motioned to the bandleader. "Now is the time," she called. The band broke into the age-old music of "Here Comes the Bride," and the crowd looked around expectantly for the bride. Some were thinking it was Lucia, but she stood very still, herself wondering where the bride could be.

Suddenly, the fierce growl of a tiger exploded into the square, startling the crowd. The growl came again, ever more ferocious. The crowd looked around expecting to see a live tiger appear.

Two young men in black tuxedos, standing near the arch, lifted one end of the white satin cloth from the long stage-like structure.

Out of the structure emerged the fastest road car in the world, a Ferrari Testarossa with voluptuous curves and fiery red paintwork.

Low and sleek, she moved forward an inch at a time towards Stefano. The roar of the tiger came from the perfectly tuned exhausts as the driver revved the twelve-cylinder engine.

Anna spoke into the microphone. "Signora e Signore, I present to you the bride, Signorina Ferrari Testarossa!"

The crowd cheered in amazement as the magnificent machine glided next to Stefano. The door opened and out came the tall man dressed in black with the dark blue sunglasses. He moved closer to Stefano, drew himself up to his full height and spoke in crisp, clear Italian, requiring no microphone. "Signora e Signore, today is a special day in my life, for today I am honored to be the Godfather of the bride."

The Mayor spoke into the microphone. "Dear townspeople of Maranello, we gather here today to witness the marriage of Stefano Gapucci to this Ferrari Testarossa." The crowd audibly sighed in wonderment. "I shall now ask Signore Capulini, our priest, to conduct the ceremony."

The Mayor handed the microphone to the priest who took it and began to intone the sacred words of matrimony. "Do you, Stefano Gapucci, take this Ferrari Testarossa to be your lawful wedded wife, to love and to cherish, in sickness and in health until death do you part?"

Solemnly, Stefano, head held high, replied, "I do."

The priest turned to the tall man. "As Godfather of the bride — as she cannot speak for herself — will you, Enzo Ferrari, speak for her?"

"I will," said Enzo.

"Will you, Ferrari Testarossa, take this man, Stefano Gapucci, to be your lawful wedded husband, to love and to cherish, in sickness and in health until death do you part?"

Enzo replied, "On behalf of my Goddaughter Testarossa, I do."

The priest intoned, "I now pronounce you husband and wife, you may kiss the bride!" Stefano went down on his knees and kissed the prancing horse image on the bonnet of the Testarossa. The crowd cheered and the children threw flower petals into the air, showering Stefano and the Testarossa.

Luigi shook Stefano's hand, "Congratulations, Stefano. Now I understand about your bride being a Redhead. Testarossa in Italian means Redhead! It all becomes clear when you put Ferrari in front of it."

Lucia smiled at Stefano, "I wish you much joy with your new bride, Stefano!"

Stefano laughed, "Now you know my secret, may I kiss my Maid of Honor?"

Lucia smiled again and nodded. Stefano kissed her lightly, once on each cheek, then unable to contain himself, brushed her lips with his own. To his amazement, Lucia did not step back and slap him, instead she leaned forward, kissed him on the lips and in a low gentle voice said, "Stefano, I like you...you are a strange man, rather weird I think, but you certainly do exciting things and I love your new bride, she is truly beautiful!"

"Nothing on earth is as beautiful as you, Lucia! My heart pounds when I look at you, your beauty sets me on fire! Please may I hold your hand?" said Stefano, relieved that he had finally spoken his true feelings and that she had not rejected him. Lucia held out her hand, Stefano took both of her hands and kissed first one and then the other then sighed loudly in his happiness. Lucia smiled, happy, too, that this strange young man expressed his true feelings in such a gentle way.

The Mayor spoke into the microphone, "People of Maranello, today is a special day for our school children. Stefano has given a gift to the Maranello School of $50,000 as a dowry to his bride and to further the education of our children." The crowd roared and whistled its appreciation. "With this money, we can buy new school books and organize more school trips so that the children can see more of our wonderful Italian countryside." The Mayor paused, turned to Stefano and continued, "Stefano Gapucci, the people of Maranello thank you for your generosity!" The crowd clapped and calls of "Speech! Speech!" were shouted.

Stefano let go of Lucia's hands and went over to Alberto. "Signore, please get one of the satchels from the limousine."

Alberto nodded and went to the rear of the Cadillac, opened the trunk, lifted out one of the leather satchels and wheeled it over to Stefano who knelt down and unlocked the satchel with a small key. All eyes were upon him as he opened the zipper and reached inside. He held up an oblong object that looked like a small loaf of bread but shone brightly in the sunshine.

"My friends, this is a solid gold bar from the Banque De Suisse in Zurich. It weighs 500 grams and at the current exchange rate is worth $5,000. In this satchel are nine more bars like this one. I hereby donate this satchel and its contents to the Maranello School." Stefano turned and gave the gold bar to the Mayor.

Loud cheering from the crowd broke out and the band began to play.

"Please take a glass of champagne and we will toast your health," said the Mayor, stepping towards the long table and pouring champagne for Stefano, while the two young men in tuxedos poured for the rest of the group. The crowd then lined up for champagne and lemonade and soon everyone had a full glass.

Enzo took the microphone from the Mayor and spoke into it, "Friends of Maranello, it is a very proud day for the Ferrari Factory. We are proud to give our Redhead to Stefano in this unusual marriage…my heart goes out to him for his sincerity and generosity to the town. Let us make a toast," he held his glass aloft, "To Stefano Gapucci and his bride, who was made with special love, care and attention here in Maranello. Long may they share happiness together! Salute!" With that said, Enzo raised his glass and toasted Stefano, then drained his glass and smiled.

The townspeople followed suit, "To Stefano and his new bride!" they shouted merrily. A festive atmosphere filled the town square with all the people smiling and laughing.

Stefano spoke into the microphone. "Signora e Signore and all your beautiful children, I would like to share a story with you as to why I married the Testarossa and why I donated the gold to the Maranello school. Many years ago my father, Enrico Gapucci, attended school here in Maranello. After leaving school he was proud to be offered a job as a test driver for Enzo. He always remembered the day when Enzo opened the Ferrari factory and how the band played and a fiesta was laid out for all of the townspeople, and how since that day, every car that Enzo manufactured was more powerful than the previous one."

"My father taught me to drive go-karts and Formula 3 racing cars. I won many races and saved my wages in a bank, until I had enough to buy a used Ferrari. Just as I was about to make the deal, the bank went broke because of bad investments and all my money was gone. I couldn't believe it." The crowd whispered their understanding of the pain that Stefano must have gone through, shaking their heads and sighing.

"I went to a bar to drown my sorrows and met a fellow named Billy Joe who spoke of gold, lots of gold…more than any man could wish for. He told me of a place in South America where he had worked as a surveyor, and where gold had been dug out of the mountains. The company that mined the gold took it all out of the mountain by trucks, and devoured the landscape until nothing was left but lifeless shale. Then they fired all of the workers including Billy Joe and closed down the operation.

"I asked Billy Joe a simple question. Could there be any more gold left in that region? Billy Joe sipped his Pernod and told me he was sure that within a ten mile radius there would be more to find. I said to him, 'Let's go there and find it!" To me it seemed ridiculously simple!

"Billy Joe smiled and said, "Why not!"

"We sold everything we owned to raise a little money and the next day took a merchant ship from Genoa to Recife. There we bought an old truck, a tent, two shotguns to hunt with, and pickaxes and shovels to dig with. Then we drove into the mountains to look for gold."

"After months of searching, Billy Joe and I had great luck and found a vast seam of gold inside a mountain. We broke the gold into rough bars, smeared it with grease, mud and sand and hid it in our old truck's spare wheel carriers. Our plan was to drive to the Recife docks and get a ship to transport us and the truck back to Genoa, but on the way bandits attacked us and Billy Joe was shot in the chest. Just before he died, he made me promise to use the gold to find my beautiful redhead, marry her, and give her a kiss from him.

So today I am in Maranello seeing a fiesta, as my father once did and finally achieving my dream of having my own Ferrari Testarossa. But instead of just buying her, I came to take her as my bride to keep my promise to Billy Joe. I met with Enzo at his factory six months ago and set this date for the wedding. Now I will keep the second part of my promise to Billy Joe." Stefano went down on his knees and said to the Testarossa: "Bella Signorina Testarossa, I give you this kiss from my best friend Billy Joe who cannot be here today." Stefano kissed the prancing horse image on the bonnet of the Testarossa for the second time today. Again the crowd cheered and the children threw flower petals into the air, showering Stefano and the Testarossa.

Stefano stood up and spoke again to the townspeople, "I donated the gold to the school because of my father's — God rest his soul — love of this town. Thank you all for making it such a wonderful occasion!"

The crowd roared its approval, calling him a lucky man and wishing Stefano "Buona Fortuna" with his new redheaded bride.

Stefano moved closer to Enzo and spoke quietly, "Signore, I must thank you for this day and the time has come to pay my debt. I have two more satchels of gold amounting to $100,000 as the balance I owe you; can I have Alberto drive to your factory and put the gold into your safe?"

"Surely, my boy," said Enzo, "I will have one of my men escort him. Also, I would like to take you and your bride for a spin on our test track so you can get used to her before you take her on the road."

"Fantastico!" said Stefano. "One moment, Signore, while I tell Lucia and Luigi." Stefano spoke to Lucia and Luigi and asked them to ride with Alberto to the Ferrari factory office where he would meet them. They smiled and agreed. Stefano then asked Alberto to take Lucia and Luigi, and deliver the two satchels to the Ferrari office. "Please take the last satchel back to the hotel and have them put it in the safe for me."

Alberto nodded and ushered Luigi and Lucia towards his limousine, where he courteously opened the doors for them in his usual gentlemanly fashion.

Stefano spoke one last time into the microphone, "Dear friends of Maranello, thank you for coming to my wedding. Please stay awhile and enjoy the food, champagne and lemonade." The crowd cheered and began to partake of the food and drink on the long table.

"Come, Stefano, come and meet your new bride," said Enzo, taking hold of Stefano's arm and steering him towards the redhead. On their way, Stefano in passing thanked Anna, the Mayor and the priest for making his day such a happy one.

"God go with you my son," said the priest. Anna just smiled and Stefano blew her a kiss.

"Thank you on behalf of the school children, Stefano, I shall see to it that your donation is wisely used," said the Mayor, shaking Stefano's hand with great gusto.

Stefano walked towards his new bride with great happiness in his heart, and with Enzo watching carefully, he tucked his fingers underneath the top of the huge air vent which curves inwards along the side of the Testarossa and found the door handle which he squeezed gently towards him. The beautiful red sculpted door clicked open and swung outwards.

Enzo smiled and said, "Now you have opened the door to her heart!" Stefano laughed, stepped over the sill, grasped the pillar with his left hand and slid deftly down into the soft leather seat.

"Bravo!" congratulated Enzo. "You did that well. You are a true bridegroom." Enzo walked to the other side of the redhead and entered in the same fashion as Stefano.

Stefano looked around the interior of his new bride, taking in the soft tan leather that wrapped all around them and gave off a sensational smell. "She is so beautiful!" He leaned forward and gently kissed the prancing horse image on the center of the steering wheel.

"Gentlemen, start your engines," whispered Enzo. "Let's see how your bride behaves." Stefano turned the key on the right hand side of the steering column and the flat twelve cylinder caught immediately. The redhead began to vibrate in beautiful motion. Incredible unleashed power sounds came from the engine as Stefano gently revved it with his foot on the accelerator pedal. Stefano revved it to 1500 rpm and listened to the symphony of power coming from the engine just behind his head.

"Oh my sweetheart!" cried Stefano, "you are all I ever thought you would be and more." Again he kissed the prancing horse.

"Stop kissing it and let's go," said Enzo with a wide smile on his face, pleased to see another human being so in love with his thoroughbred. Little did Stefano know that Enzo felt exactly the same loving feeling each time he sat in a Testarossa.

Stefano studied the gear lever noting the way first gear was back and to the left and opposite reverse, second gear was over and up, third was back opposite second, fourth over and up to the right again and finally, fifth was a direct straight back pull opposite fourth gear.

He was mentally ready. Here goes, he thought. Stefano pressed down on the light clutch, moved the gear lever down and back to first gear, released the handbrake, eased up on the clutch and pressed the accelerator gently. The redhead started to move slowly through the path the crowd had opened up. The band began to play the Wedding March. As the redheaded bride purred gustily towards the street, the music came in through the redhead's open windows and mingled with the sound of the engine. Stefano eased down on the clutch and rolled to a stop at the entrance to the main street.

"Go left for 500 metres, then turn left again into the Racing department area," said Enzo. Stefano pressed the accelerator and simultaneously eased up on the clutch while turning the steering wheel with its three alloy spokes to the left. The redhead lunged forward. Even in low gear the tremendous sense of flowing power registered in Stefano's head. Smiling, he changed into second gear; it clicked as it hit the gate and Stefano let up the clutch and again pressed on the accelerator. He felt the massive power of the engine kick in as he wound up the revs slightly. Almost instantly he was approaching the entrance Enzo had mentioned, he glanced at the speedometer, which showed 45 mph. Wow! Stefano thought. Lucky the street is empty, I need to remember to keep the speed down when I am in town in the future. He turned neatly in through the gates of the Racing Department, where the guard on the gate saluted with a smile, as he saw Enzo.

"Go straight past the building on your left and pull up at the entrance to the track. I need to open the security gate myself, because the rest of the guards are in the square celebrating with their families," said Enzo. Stefano did as directed and eased to a stop in front of the blue steel gates. Enzo got out of the car, inserted a plastic card into the card reader on the gate post, typed in his security code, and as the gate swung open, got back into the redhead.

"Now we need to put on the seat belts if you wish to drive at speed," said Enzo, pulling his seat belt across and latching it into place. Stefano did the same, then selected first gear, eased up on the clutch and moved towards the massive oval track, which was wide enough for four cars side by side. It stretched as far as the eye could see before turning left into the first corner.

"It's roughly a figure eight with two straights, each about a mile in length. Let's take one circuit around slowly so you can get the feel of it and the redhead can warm up," Enzo suggested.

Stefano needed no second bidding. He said, "Ok! Here we go!" and gently accelerated until he was actually on the track. Once there, he quickly changed up to second, gunned the redhead gently again and then changed up to third. He glanced at the speedometer. "Unbelievable power!" he cried to Enzo. "Already 80 miles per hour and growling like a tiger!" Stefano pressed the accelerator again and the mighty redhead surged forward to 95 mph. Stefano deftly changed up to fourth gear, enjoying the sheer power. The beautiful bride soared down the track, its twelve-cylinder engine roaring now like an enraged tiger, defying the pull of gravity, demanding to be free.

"You handle your bride well, I am pleased. I do believe she is falling in love with you because she likes the way you handle her," said Enzo, smiling widely again. Almost immediately, they were coming up on the first turn. Stefano double-declutched and smoothly clicked the gear lever from fourth to third, the revs rose to 4500 rpm as the engine braked; Stefano steered into the corner and then accelerated again, steadying at about 80 mph to pull out of the figure eight into the next straight.

"Now you can take it to 120 mph if you wish on this straight," said Enzo. Stefano again accelerated to 95 mph and changed up to fourth, as the gear lever clicked into position, he pressed down on the accelerator and a giant hand pushed the bride forward instantaneously to 120 mph.

"Bellisimo!" sighed Stefano. They soon came up the next figure eight turn and again Stefano steered neatly around it in fourth gear at around 80 mph, then again they were back on the straight.

Enzo said, "You are handling her so well! If you would like to take her up to 150 mph, now is your chance!"

Stefano gunned the accelerator to 110 mph, then changed up to fifth and pressed down again on the accelerator, the bride surged forward past 120, 130, 140 to 150 mph. Stefano noted the revs were at only 5500 and eased off of the accelerator, enjoying the thrill of driving at high speed in his gorgeous thundering new bride. He listened to the roar of the flat twelve-cylinder engine behind him, its exquisite machinery not even close to laboring at this speed.

"She will do about 180 mph maximum; this track is a little short for that, but great for 170 mph," said Enzo.

Stefano glanced across and noted Enzo's smile and relaxed sitting position. Inwardly, Stefano was very proud that he could drive the great Enzo's redhead at this speed with Enzo sitting next to him, confident that Stefano was in full control of the car. They drove in silence, both listening to the deep-throated growl coming from the twelve cylinder redhead two feet behind their heads. It emanated a remarkable sound of perfection in a machine in motion, particularly so when Stefano executed his double-declutching while changing down from fifth to fourth when the revs would climb to 7000 rpm for an instant as Stefano made the swift gear change, then again from fourth to third for the sharp corners of the figure eight track. When he accelerated out of the curves there was no body roll due to the superb suspension and the huge Michelin rear tires which gripped the racetrack like superglue.

Suddenly, a vision of Lucia appeared in Stefano's mind and a strange warm feeling engulfed him. He blinked and shook his head in order to concentrate on driving his new bride, but the vision stayed with him of Lucia's beautifully sculpted features, her thick head of glistening blue-black hair and her deep brown eyes. He knew that he was totally and absolutely in love with her, not just because she was beautiful in his eyes, but because of the tremendous glow that he felt whenever he saw her. Stefano decided he must see her as soon as possible and ask her to marry him. He knew that it would be difficult, perhaps impossible to convince her that he was truly in love with her after such a short time, but he swore to himself to do his utmost to win her heart.

Stefano eased up on the accelerator and coasted down the straight to the point where they had joined the track. He swiftly changed down from fifth to fourth then again to third, allowing the engine to brake gently to bring the speed down to 70 mph. He steered towards the exit slowing to 45 mph, changing down again from third to second gear, then eased the redhead off of the track at a gentle 30 mph onto the roadway leading to the main street.

"The entrance to the factory is directly opposite," said Enzo. Stefano pulled the redhead to a brief stop at the street entrance, checked for oncoming traffic and drove the redhead across the street and through the Ferrari factory gates, which were open and manned by a security guard sitting in a steel cubicle. The guard saluted as Stefano drove past him towards the parking area where he could see Alberto's limousine. He neatly slid into a parking slot next to the limousine, slipped the gear lever into neutral and applied the handbrake that was situated to his left between the door and his seat. The flat twelve-cylinder engine purred as if it was immensely content. Stefano turned the ignition key to the off position and silence came from behind his head.

"The lady tiger is sleeping," said Stefano.

"She likes the way you handle her, I believe she feels that the marriage has now been consummated and she has a first new lover," said Enzo, smiling broadly.

"I am proud to have such a beautiful bride, Signore! I will truly love her until the day I die! She is magnificent!" said Stefano.

"I, too, am proud that you love her so much, Stefano. It makes me a very happy man. Now let us go and join your friends; also, I have someone special that I wish to introduce you to," said Enzo.

They both got out of the bride and softly closed the doors. Stefano stepped back and ran his eyes over the flawless red paintwork that shone so vividly as if it were alive. "Like the reddest lipstick applied to the most beautiful mouth in the world," murmured Stefano.

Enzo heard his comment. "My friend, it took more than five years to develop that color in the Pininfarina factory…I could see the color I wanted to achieve in my mind and explained it to the painters, but it proved very elusive and then finally, one day the head of the paint department called me at five in the morning at my home. All he said was, "Bellissimo, Bellissimo." and I knew then he had found the color I had told him about, the gorgeous red tinted with a hue of orange that finally comes out as this color, "Rossa." Today the color is made by a secret formula and every time I see it, it fills me with a special pride to gaze on a living artwork that I created in my mind."

Stefano listened quietly and knew that he was fortunate enough to be in the company of a true genius. Enzo and Stefano walked through the large glass doors into the foyer of the Ferrari Factory customer reception area. Stefano looked around and smiled. On the walls he saw marvelous paintings and beautiful photographs, depicting the different models of Ferrari cars built over the years. Across the foyer he saw Lucia, standing next to her father. She was talking to a well-groomed man who was explaining a photograph of a lifesize twelve-cylinder engine. Stefano's heart pounded; to his eyes Lucia was so beautiful, her stance erect and graceful, and she was full bodied, filling her dress with incredible chique.

She glanced in Stefano's direction and a hint of a smile lit up her face. Her black hair shone in the sunlight streaming in from the vast skylight high above her head. Stefano walked slowly over to her and stood quietly, waiting for an opportune moment to speak to her, for an idea had suddenly come to him.

Enzo approached the three of them and gracefully interrupted Lucia's conversation by saying, "Ah, Signore Rossi, I see you are entertaining our guest, Lucia." He bowed towards Lucia. "I would like you to meet the young man responsible for this festive day in the history of Ferrari! May I introduce Signore Stefano Gapucci, who today married his blushing bride in the Town Square. Stefano, this is Ingegnere Maurizio Rossi of the Experimental department. He and his two colleagues, Dottore Ingegnere Angelo Bellei of the Project department and Ingegnere Nicola Materazzi of the Engine department were principally responsible for developing your bride."

Stefano shook hands with Maurizio. "A great pleasure to meet you, Signore, I am a truly lucky man to have such a thoroughbred beauty for my wife."

Maurizio chuckled. "Stefano, I have seen many strange things in my life, but I have never heard of a man who married an automobile, even if she is a blushing Testarossa. Tell me, how did you arrive at such a decision?"

"Ah Signore, it was such an easy decision," Stefano replied. "Whenever I see my Testarossa's voluptuous curves and her fiery red paintwork glistening in the sun, my heart pounds with pleasure and my soul lights up. Every time I open her door and get inside her I feel a glow like the very first time a love affair begins. I know deep inside me that I must always drive her with passion, precision, and respect. When I start her engine, she bursts into life with a magnificent growl, telling me she is giving me her heart. After I have warmed her up so that all of her fluids are warm, I press down on the clutch, engage first gear, lift up on the clutch and press on the accelerator. She surges away like a raging tiger. My heart pounds with love for her. This is why I married her. I hope I have answered your question?"

"Bravo! Signore, it is splendid to hear such praise for our creation, I too am always awed by the tremendous power of our illustrious redhead. She is so like the prancing horse, a wild untamed beast, at her best at 7000 revolutions per minute on a winding country road with no other traffic in sight. I like to get up at 3 in the morning and drive for two hours as fast as I can, leaning back in the seat and just letting the engine noise play to me, you know? Like some people love opera, I love the sound of a perfectly tuned Testarossa at 140 miles per hour. I drive home again and crawl into bed, full of dreams and inspiration."

Lucia turned to Stefano and asked, "What was it like, Stefano, to drive your dream car on the track?"

"It was very special, Lucia, I really enjoyed it. Would you like to come for a spin on the track? I will drive very carefully, we can just drive a few laps and you will see what I mean. Please say yes?"

"He has the touch of a master. I was impressed by his skill and timing," said Enzo. "Stefano drove with perfect confidence, so I am sure he will look after you while you are in the car. Go on, have some fun! I will talk to your father, so he doesn't get worried, off you go!"

Stefano needed no second bidding, he took Lucia's hand, and even as she was hesitating slightly, he led her to the door and into the parking area. Lucia looked at the Testarossa, smiled and said, "Even though it is parked, it looks sleek and powerful and the color is perfecto!"

Stefano opened the passenger door for Lucia and demonstrated the easy way to get in. Lucia laughed. "You are so proud of your car, you have driven it for 15 minutes and already you show it off so well." She settled back in the seat and buckled her seat belt. "Mama Mia! The leather smells so gorgeous!"

Stefano watched her sitting in the seat; he could not take his eyes off of her. "Lucia, you sitting there makes the car perfect. Today I am the happiest man on earth...I am so happy I could cry!"

"Don't be so silly, Stefano," chided Lucia. "You hardly know me and I think you are happy because you now have the most splendid car in the world. Come on, get in and show me how it goes around the track."

Stefano didn't know what to say. How can I tell her I love her so much? he thought. She won't believe me, but it is true. He walked around the car, opened the door, got in, buckled his seat belt and started the engine.

"Oh, oh!" chuckled Lucia, "The engine, she growls like a hungry tiger."

Stefano reversed out of the parking slot and putting it into first gear, headed for the gate. He noticed that the guard was staring at Lucia in amazement. Stefano braked at the street entrance and looked across at Lucia who was busy admiring all the gauges and the interior. She looks like an angel from heaven, thought Stefano, All men must see her as I see her. Like the Madonna, she shines like a star in the middle of the night.

He drove carefully across the road into the test track lane, past the Racing Department building and out onto the track. He changed into second gear with a click and accelerated briefly to 50 mph.

Lucia shrieked gleefully, "Wow! What a car, it goes so quickly."

Stefano laughed and gently pressed the accelerator again, the Testarossa roared its symphony and took off to about 80 mph, at which point Stefano nimbly changed up to third gear and spurted to 100 mph. Then at nearly 7000 revs per minute, he changed perfectly into fourth gear. "How do you like 100 mph?" he asked Lucia.

"Fantastico! How fast can it go?" asked Lucia.

"It's been road tested at 180 mph, but on this track, you can only do 170 mph because the curves come up so fast." Even as he said it, he approached the first curve, revved the engine, double-declutched and changed down to third gear, slowing the redhead to 85 mph.

"It doesn't lean in the curves at all, it sits on the ground like a spider," said Lucia, laughing. Stefano sat stiff and proud, guiding the large car around the curve until he was in the apex, then accelerated briskly out of the curve onto the straight, revving up to 5500 rpm, changing up into fourth gear at 105 mph, then pressing the accelerator hard. The redhead surged down the straight till the speedometer showed 150 mph with the revs showing 5000 rpm on the rev counter.

Lucia gasped, "Such power! I never imagined it could be so much fun, the engine, she is singing and growling at the same time. Oh! Stefano, you have married a real racing car, it is so unbelievably fast! I love your redhead!"

Stefano listened to Lucia extolling the beauty of the car and the speed, which it attained so effortlessly. He loved the way her words were so heavily accented with the Italian lilt.

"How would you like to take a trip with me and this gorgeous redhead?" he asked her. "I am planning to take a trip to Rome, then to Naples, and then by car ferry up to Genoa, where we could drive to Switzerland, putting the redhead on a train to go through the Simplon Tunnel. We can stay in Lausanne at a house I have rented there. It's about a two week trip if we take it easy, and we would stay at some really peaceful little hotels that I have booked in advance, I would call ahead and book you your own room at each one so you could have privacy at night. What do you say? Please say yes! I love your company and we could have great fun together, see all the sights and even take turns driving 'this real racing car' as you call it. I would love every minute of it. I know it sounds mad but again I have to say it, Lucia, when I opened the door of my hotel room this morning and saw you for the first time, my heart flipped over and told me that I had fallen head over heels in love with you!"

After that long speech, Stefano fell quiet and concentrated on driving his new bride, slowing down to a more sedate speed. Now I have done it, he thought furiously, she will never believe me and will only think I am trying to get her into my bed. Maybe I should have taken it a bit slower. Then again he had told the truth; it must be worth something to tell her now how he really felt, rather than try and hide his feelings and leave the hotel, wishing he had asked her to come with him. He glanced across and caught the flicker of a smile on Lucia's beautiful face. She is considering it, I know, Oh please, God, let her say yes....

Stefano continued to drive, waiting patiently to hear Lucia's reply. The redheaded engine growled and purred as he accelerated out of the curve at the top of the track. The sound of the engine diminished in Stefano's ears as Lucia replied.

"Stefano, what can I say? I have known you for such a short time, only a few hours and we have only spoken for a few minutes really during that time. We don't know each other at all. I am sure you are an honorable man, but I could not agree to take off with you for a two week holiday at such short notice." Lucia smiled and continued, "Even though it would be fun indeed to drive through Italy and Switzerland in this beautiful new car."

Stefano had a feeling of sadness in his voice when he spoke. "Lucia, I have lived a strange life, not always happy, sometimes very sad times, but from the moment I saw you I wanted to tell you that my heart actually stopped for a second, then burst into motion with the most glorious pounding. Then the warmest feeling came over me. It was like I had known you in a past life…I tried to figure out what happened and all I can come up with is that it was truly love at first sight…not physical, although I think you are the prettiest girl in the whole wide world, but it was more than that, it was like a spiritual emotion. I only pray that you will take me seriously and let me prove to you, in any way I can, that I am serious." Stefano concentrated once more on his driving, slowing the redhead to a crawl as he left the track and headed back towards the factory.

Lucia leaned back in her seat, visibly shocked. "Stefano, never in my life has any man said such beautiful words to me. I think now I believe what you felt. I can be honest and tell you that I liked you also when I first saw you, but I have led a fairly sheltered life and never allowed myself to show any emotion with strange men that I didn't know, especially guests in the hotel. My father taught me, when I was much younger, to keep my distance with both my body language and my facial expressions so that men would not try and take advantage of me. I know he was right, because he has kept me safe and honorable throughout my life. I have had a few boyfriends and once I nearly got engaged, but his wife turned up out of the blue and accused me of being a wanton husband snatcher. Are you married, Stefano?"

"No, Lucia. I, too, have been close to being engaged a few times, but never did I feel that I was in love enough to marry." He laughed quietly. "That is not quite true, I did get married today, but I guess that was different."

Lucia suddenly cried out. Stefano stamped on the brakes and the redhead stopped immediately. "What is wrong, Lucia ? Are you all right?"

Lucia laughed and said, "Oh I am sorry, I meant to say turn the car around and go back to the track. I didn't mean to startle you, but I was so excited."

Stefano smiled. "You like driving around the track? That is okay, let's go back and drive as long as you like." He gently accelerated and swung the car around and headed back towards the track.

"You misunderstand me," said Lucia. "It is I who would like to drive your car on the track, if you would let me?"

"Of course I will, Lucia, it would be a great honor for this beautiful car to be driven by such a beautiful woman."

"You compliment me so much I am not sure if you are sincere, Stefano," Lucia said, blushing. "But it is good to my ears, so don't stop."

Stefano felt so happy to hear Lucia say those words, he was ecstatic. "Lucia, my heart is the one doing the talking, I truly am very proud and so happy that you came along with me today, I only hope that you will change your mind and come to Switzerland with me." Stefano pulled out on the track and stopped the redhead, put the gear lever in neutral and pulled on the hand brake. "Okay, Lucia, let's change places, it is time for you to show me how young Italian ladies drive." Stefano opened the door and went around to the passenger side and opened the door for Lucia.

"Grazie," said Lucia as she eased her dress over the sill and stood up.

"Prego!" said Stefano, smiling at Lucia.

Lucia went around to the driver's side and got inside.

Stefano got into the passenger's side and watched Lucia prepare to drive the redhead. Lucia removed her high heel shoes and moved the seat forward until she felt comfortable, then closed the door and fastened her seat belt. The redhead purred at idle, Lucia pressed down on the clutch, moved the gear lever into first gear, let the hand brake off, then pressed the accelerator. The redhead pulled crisply away. Almost immediately Lucia changed into second gear, pressed down on the accelerator again and Stefano felt his body press into the seat as they gathered speed. Lucia drove remarkably well, Stefano was impressed. She changed into third gear with a distinct professional click and the car was soon doing 85 mph at 5000 rpms. Lucia gunned the accelerator again, waited till the revs were at 7000, and deftly slid the gear lever into fourth gear, again with an audible click. The speedometer showed 105 mph and climbing steadily. The engine sounded like a jet turbo with a low growl in the background; such a glorious sound! Stefano closed his eyes and listened to the mechanical symphony of the magnificent redhead. The car was in the middle of the straight portion of the track, maintaining a line close to the left. Suddenly a louder noise became evident to Stefano and he opened his eyes and looked around.

"Whoosh!" The sound came from an object fast overtaking them; a red dart, even lower than the redhead shot past them on right doing about 170 mph. One instant it was there and the next it was gone, as way ahead of them brake lights gleamed as it slowed to take the top turn.

"Madre Mio!" exclaimed Lucia. "What the hell was that?"

"It looked like another Ferrari, but I have never seen one quite like that," said Stefano.

"If they want to play, then let's play," said Lucia, "I will try and catch them." She pushed the accelerator to the floor and the redhead roared forward to 135 mph. She changed up to fifth gear and floored the accelerator again. When they came into the start of the curve at 155 mph, Stefano glanced across at Lucia. She showed no fear whatsoever as she changed down to fourth, braked for the first turn, took it at 120 mph, then changed down to third, braked again and took the redhead into the hairpin at 95 mph. The redhead behaved immaculately, with no tailspin or frontal slide, as if it was glued to the track. Lucia gunned the redhead out of the final curve and accelerated up to 120 mph in third gear. She changed up to fourth at 7000 rpms on the gauge, and the speedometer needle swung towards 150 mph. Now on the straight, Lucia changed up to fifth gear and pushed the accelerator to the floor again. The 12-cylinder redhead actually seemed to have unlimited power. It surged forward effortlessly, the speedometer now showing 175 mph as Lucia steered the car, both hands at the quarter to three position.

The other red car was now losing distance, as the redhead started to close the gap.   One hundred yards, fifty yards, ten yards until it was level with the other car. Stefano looked at the speedometer: incredulously, it was showing 180 mph at 5500 revs per minute! Both cars were neck and neck. Stefano looked across at the driver. Enzo raised a hand and waved. Next to Enzo in the passenger seat sat someone who, at first, Stefano could not make out. Then Lucia pulled ahead slightly.

"Lucia! It's Enzo and your father!"

Lucia let out a little yell. He looked across at her and she was laughing. Stefano was amazed. "What a woman!"

Lucia gently slowed the car down, stepping on the brakes and deftly changing down from fifth to fourth. The speedometer now showed 135 mph, then fourth to third with rpms at 5500. She braked harder and brought the redhead down to 80 mph. She drove the car off of the track and quickly slowed to 50 mph, then 30 mph and finally stopped next to the Racing Department building. The redhead purred in neutral as Lucia let the engine cool, then she switched it off.

"Wow!" she said, "La Bella Macchina! What a fantastic car!"

"What a driver!" said Stefano. "Where did you learn to drive like that?"

"I have a little Alfa Romeo at home that I occasionally take out in the early morning, to see how fast it can go. It never went more than 120 mph, but it taught me well how to drive with 5 gears and get the most power out of each gear without blowing up the engine," said Lucia.

"Did you realize that you had this redhead at 180 mph back there?" said Stefano, interested in what Lucia's reply would be.

"Of course," said Lucia. "But this car can do it with ease. The engine is powerful, the steering is perfect, and the suspension seems to sink lower the faster it goes. It was utterly breathtaking! Thank you, Stefano, for letting me drive your redheaded bride. I have made up my mind, I would like to come with you to Switzerland. We will have fun and see the sights of Rome, Naples and Genoa. Of course I must get permission from my father first though! If he allows me to go, then we go." She looked at Stefano with a twinkle in her eye.

Stefano's face lit up with a broad smile. "Oh yes, Lucia, I want you to come with me now more than ever. We can take turns driving this incredible machine and laugh all the way to Switzerland."

Lucia drove slowly back to the Ferrari factory and parked across from the main entrance. She switched off the engine and applied the parking brake. Stefano was just about to get out of the redhead and open the door for Lucia when with an incredible "Whoosh!", the other Ferrari slid into the parking place next to them.

Enzo got out and walked around to the driver's side of the redhead. He stood, frozen in amazement, when he saw it was not Stefano, but Lucia in the driver's seat.

"Lucia! Was it you out there on the track? I wasn't quite sure whether I saw you or Stefano driving. I mentioned it to your father, but he laughed and said that it would be impossible; you could never drive that fast. I came over to congratulate Stefano on his driving ability, but now I will congratulate you, my dear. You have broken the test track record for a Testarossa, I was showing 180 mph when you came up alongside me."

Luigi got out of the other Ferrari and came around to stand next to Enzo. "Lucia, my darling! Enzo was right, it was you driving! But how did you do it? Do you know how fast you were going?"

Lucia giggled and rose from the Testarossa gracefully. "Papa, you are so funny. You know I always drive the Alfa at top speed, so why should I not drive the Testarossa in the same way? Such a beautiful car begs me to drive it faster and faster. When Enzo overtook us, I could not resist the challenge. I enjoyed it immensely!"

Stefano came and stood next to Lucia. "She is a really cool-headed driver. She changes gear like no one I have ever seen. I think Lucia was born to drive redheads at top speed…she does it so well, without fear, but with the utmost skill."

"I agree," said Enzo. "Only the best drivers can achieve such a speed on such a small track. Now I really do have a serious problem." He looked up at the sky and, for the first time removed his darkly shaded sunglasses.

"What do you mean, Enzo? What problem has Lucia caused?" said Luigi.

"No, my friend, I explained myself badly. She is not the problem. You see, I was ready to ask Stefano if he would drive for me in the Le Mans 24 hour race, but now I would like to ask both Lucia and Stefano to race for me. I am concerned it will sadden you if she accepts. What do you say?"

Luigi sighed, and Lucia looked at him and showed her concern. "Oh, Papa, please do not be worried for me. I would like to accept Enzo's fantastic offer, but I know how worried you would be, so I am going to say thank you, but no thank you to Enzo." Lucia turned to Enzo and said, "Thank you for the chance, but I will have to say no. I hope you will understand, but I would like to see Stefano drive in the Le Mans. When is it?"

"It is in three weeks, my dear, and yes, I would like Stefano to drive for me. I was impressed with his skill today in handling the Testarosssa. He has a natural talent that is a rare gift, and he's a born racing car driver. What do you say Stefano?"

"Enzo, I would be proud to drive for you and I am really excited, but I have promised Lucia to take her with me to Switzerland on a two week trip, starting tomorrow. So as long as I can still do that and prepare for the race, I say yes please! Si, Grazie!" The chance of a lifetime, Stefano thought. I have always wanted to drive in a real road race in a Ferrari, but the opportunity has never shown up before. Now I will have my chance.

Luigi was in shock. "Everything is moving so fast. First Enzo asks my daughter to drive for him in the Le Mans, and thank God, she said no. But now I hear she is off to Switzerland for two weeks with a young man she only met this morning, and this is the first I hear of it. But I am not going to stand in Lucia's way if this is what she wants to do."

"Papa! Thank you." Lucia took his hand and kissed it. "Stefano is going to be a perfect gentleman and book us into separate rooms in the places we stay and he is going to let me drive his Testarossa, only a bit slower, I am sure. We leave for Roma tomorrow, if you say you are sure it's okay, Papa."

Luigi nodded his head. "If that is what you really want, my lovely daughter, what can I say? But to you," he turned to Stefano, "I say, look after my daughter, she is my most treasured possession!"

"I will, Signore, you may be sure, I think of her as the most precious person in the world and I will see no harm comes to her," said Stefano.

"This calls for a celebration!" exclaimed Enzo. "Come inside my friends and we will taste a glass of the finest champagne." Enzo ushered them into the customer lounge and went off to arrange for the champagne.

Stefano, Lucia and Luigi looked at the prototype Ferrari engines on display while waiting for Enzo to return. "I never knew how much engineering it takes to make an engine," said Luigi, looking at a model of an 8-cylinder engine which had been neatly cut in half to show all of the working parts.

"That is my new prototype, the heart of the F40, which we drove just now, Luigi.

This is the engine with which I hope to win the Le Mans. It has seven hundred and sixty horse power." Enzo stood with a small lacquered tray in his hand and on it sat four exquisite champagne flutes. He offered one to Lucia, who accepted with a smile, and then gave one each to Luigi and Stefano.

Enzo took the last one, put the tray down on a nearby table and turned to the little group. "My friends, today is indeed a special day. First, I was honored to be the Godfather of the bride at the wedding, then I find I have two of the fastest drivers ever on my race track, one of whom is not only the fastest, but also the prettiest young lady I have had the pleasure to meet in a very long time. Then, finally, I got to drive my F40 at high speed for the first time with Luigi, who I have been wanting to meet for a long time, since I have been many times a visitor to his beautiful hotel, where the chef creates such tasty Italian delicacies."

Luigi said, "Enzo, it is my pleasure. I much enjoyed the wedding ceremony, even though it was rather unusual to see a mechanical bride, but a very attractive bride at that. I've always thought your cars were gorgeous, like wild women, but when you drove on the track today I felt the whole car come to life, with that magnificent engine producing so much tremendous power. If I were a few years younger, I would most certainly buy one, if I could afford it."

Lucia laughed aloud, "Papa, you are so funny. You are not that old and you could afford one I am sure! How much does an F40 cost, Enzo?"

Enzo turned to Lucia. "Well, my dear, I sold the first three for $500,000 each. You would never guess what one of them has done with his F40!"

"What did he do?" asked Stefano.

"Well," said Enzo, "he had his whole living room torn out and the floor rebuilt so that the F40 would be sunken into it. Apparently, you can still get into the car, but it will never be driven on a real road. The owner has cocktail parties and all the guests sit on cushions around the F40, admiring it and discussing how it would be to drive. Occasionally, one of the especially honored guests is allowed to sit in the F40, but that's about as far as it goes…no ignition key, no benzini, no power."

Luigi said, "Yes, I also read an article once that described your cars as the ultimate perfection in art. It said that art lovers are buying your cars as investments, for their value and for their beauty. Whereas before one might spend half a million dollars on a Renoir painting, nowadays it is more sophisticated to invest in a beautiful Ferrari, with all of its parts intact, just waiting for the owner to get in, start the engine and go. Seeing the Testarossa today up close, I can believe why they want to do that. It is such a superbly designed piece of art, I congratulate you, Signore."

Luigi looked at his wristwatch, a slim gold Peugeot with a brown leather strap. "Well, my friends, I must return to the hotel, it is nearly 2:00 o'clock and if I recall correctly, you, my friend," he pointed to Stefano and grinned, "have a wedding reception at my hotel, although how you intend to get your bride into the reception room is going to be interesting."

"Ah, Luigi, my redhead will be honeymooning inside your garage for the rest of the day. Maybe I can find a Bugatti to keep her company on her wedding night," said Stefano.

Enzo laughed, "You are a strange man, Stefano, but I like you. I will send instructions on the Le Mans to the hotel tonight. I must depart soon as well, I think I need a rest after all the excitement." Enzo turned to Lucia. "My dear, it was truly a pleasure to meet you and I thank you once again for setting a new track record with Stefano's Testarossa. If you would ever like to drive my F40, please let me know and I will be delighted to be your passenger."

"Oh, Enzo," said Stefano, "I still owe you for my bride, I have two satchels of gold ingots out in the limousine as promised. They total $100,000, the balance of our agreement. Would you care to take charge of them now?"

"Come on then," said Enzo. "This is the first time I have been paid in gold for one of my cars." They all trooped out into the foyer and Stefano located Alberto who was standing next to the two satchels on the floor, reading a brochure on Ferrari racing cars. Stefano, with Alberto's assistance, lifted the two satchels, one at a time onto the desk in front of them.

Stefano opened both satchels and took out an ingot. "The Swiss bank seal indicates the weight and you will find the current exchange rate to be more than adequate per ounce."

"I believe you, my friend." Enzo requested the Director and his assistant to lock the gold in the safe and write Stefano a receipt. "If you ever need anything for your bride, let me know and I will take care of it, wherever you are in the world." Enzo smiled, took Lucia's hand in both of his and gave it a gentle kiss. "Goodbye, my dear, I hope we meet again soon, Ciao." He shook hands with Luigi and Stefano and then departed from the foyer to his own private office.

Luigi turned to Lucia. "Well, my dear, today has been nothing but surprises for me. Will you be coming back with me to the hotel, or are you going to drive with Stefano?" His tone was one of sadness. He now realized that his daughter was being gently romanced by someone he hardly knew and who was succeeding on all fronts.

"Oh Papa! Please don't be sad." Lucia knew her father well and was concerned that he was worried about her hasty decision to drive to Rome and Switzerland with Stefano. "Stefano and I will have fun on the trip and it's only for two weeks. Then I will come back and everything will be the same, you will see."

Even as she said this, Lucia knew that things might change for both her and her father. She was very happy inside that Stefano had been so open with her about his feelings. Could it be true that he really fell in love with me at first sight? Or could it just be a tale that he tells all the girls he meets? She pondered about this for an instant then decided that she had two weeks to get to know Stefano better. With that decision made, she answered her father's original question.

"You go back with Alberto, Papa, and I will drive back with Stefano. We will meet at the reception where I will mix you your favorite drink and make you a tasty snack. And if you get tired, I will tuck you up for an afternoon nap. What do you say to that?"

Luigi smiled and nodded. He realized that he had better not try and convince Lucia that her decision might be too hasty and that she should give it some further thought. I am getting old, thought Luigi. Lucia is young and carefree and the holiday will do her good, regardless of how it might end. "Very well, my girl, I will see you and Stefano back at the hotel."

He turned to Stefano. "Please, Stefano, take care of my daughter, she is so very precious to me. There was a time when I would have said there is no possibility of taking her on a two week holiday, that you would have to court her here for at least six months first. and only then might I consider it. But I see she is so happy about the idea, so I will not stand in her way." Luigi shook hands with Stefano, kissed Lucia gently on both cheeks and said to Alberto, "Come, Alberto, take me back to the hotel and we will both have a taste of a cognac that I save for special occasions."

Alberto nodded, and he and Luigi left the foyer and went outside to the Cadillac.

Stefano looked at Lucia and Lucia looked back at him. Her eyes twinkled and Stefano could not resist the urge to kiss her. He stepped forward, took Lucia in his arms and gave her a passionate kiss on the lips. Lucia melted in his arms, clasped Stefano to her and kissed him back. It was a long kiss, full of fire and emotion, as if laying a seal of bonding between them. Slowly they ended the kiss, then Stefano stepped back and devoured Lucia with his eyes. She returned his gaze with her own and studied Stefano carefully, taking in his hair, his face, his nose and ears. She liked what she saw. Lucia felt very peaceful standing here with Stefano; she had no more doubts that he really loved her with tremendous passion. Certainly, he was a man of spirit and had an adventurous air about him. She liked his tender kisses and the passionate kiss they had just shared. She felt happy inside and astonishingly alive; not for a long time had she felt so alive.

Neither spoke a word, lest they break the spell they had cast. Stefano took Lucia's hand and led her to the door. Outside, they walked hand in hand to the Testarossa, where Stefano opened the door for Lucia and gently helped her take her place in the plush tan leather seat. He reached over to get the seat belt and buckled it close across her chest. brushing his lips against her hair. He could not resist moving his lips to hers and stealing a soft kiss, before he got in and started the engine. The silence was broken by the lusty sound of the redhead's twelve cylinder engine bursting into life. Stefano revved the engine to 3000 rpms, and listened intently. It was as if an orchestra was playing the 1812 overture. The chassis of the redhead vibrated ever so slightly, as Stefano eased off of the throttle, and then it tensioned again as he revved it again, to hear the wonderful sound. Lucia was listening too, mesmerized by the magnificent whirring, growling and throaty roar of the redhead's engine and exhaust. She relived the feeling of ecstasy while driving this red-painted beauty at high speed and felt incredibly happy.

Stefano selected first gear, revved the engine slightly and let in the clutch. The huge rear tyres bit into the asphalt and the redhead moved forward towards the factory gates.

Two lines of mechanics, dressed in blue overalls with the Ferrari insignia emblazoned on their breast pockets, stood on either side of the gates. Each mechanic held an Italian flag on a white stick four feet high, tilted at an angle to meet their counterpart, so that an arch of flags was formed. They cheered and waved as Stefano and Lucia slowly passed through the arch. "Buon Viaggio!" They shouted.

Stefano blipped the horn as he passed through the arch. He waved and Lucia smiled, and waved too. Stefano shouted through the open window, "Grazie mille! Viva La Italia!" The two lines of mechanics watched proudly as Stefano navigated the magnificent car to the street, slowed at the curb, then with a burst of speed, swung sharply to the left and accelerated swiftly away towards the road that led to the hotel.

As they passed the town square, the townspeople were still eating and drinking from the long table, festivities still in evidence. The band, spying the redhead, broke into "Here comes the Bride," and the crowd roared their approval. Stefano blipped his horn again and waved and smiled. Soon they were past the square, heading for the winding road that led up to the hotel. Stefano drove fast up the hill, enjoying the curves, occasionally unleashing a little extra power as he turned a sharp bend and saw that the road was clear, the redhead responding superbly, eager for more, its engine singing and growling.

When they reached the drive leading to the hotel, Stefano asked Lucia which way to the garages. She pointed right and Stefano steered the car past the hotel to a group of buildings standing about 100 yards from the hotel. He pulled the car to a stop and Lucia said, "The first garage is yours; I will go and get the key." She gave Stefano a kiss on the cheek, got out and walked quickly off towards the hotel main entrance.

Stefano sat in his car, quivering slightly with the realization that he had attained two of his most important dreams today. He could hardly believe it. He thought about Lucia, how she smiled and how she laughed. He remembered the deep kiss at the factory, how her lips were soft and moist and how it felt to hug her close to him and feel her hugging him in return. He was truly in love with her and he knew that she liked him, otherwise she would never have let him kiss her so passionately, and she had returned his kiss with what seemed like fervent desire, which had so surprised him.

He got out of the car and looked at the garage; it was a large building made of stone slabs, painted light blue, that the sun had mellowed over the years, with an arch over the huge double doors that were locked by a large metal bar with a padlock at one end. More like a church than a garage, a fitting place for my bride to spend her first night, thought Stefano.

He snapped out of his thoughts as Lucia came into view carrying a large bunch of keys on a ring. "Here we are," she said, choosing the largest key. Inserting it into the padlock, she turned the key and the well-oiled lock opened easily. Stefano moved forward to help her, taking the padlock off of the hasp. Pulling the bar opened the doors to reveal a huge chamber with tiny windows up near the roof. As he pulled the doors wide open, the sunshine lit up the interior. The garage was about 30 feet long and wide enough to take two large cars side by side, spotlessly clean, with workbenches on either side and a huge electric hoist for removing engines from cars for service and repair.

"We don't use this one very often, as we keep our own cars in another garage around the back of the hotel. Most of the guests just park in the car park or have the valet park their car for them in the underground parking area," said Lucia.

"You have an underground parking area, too?" said Stefano in surprise. "Did your father have that built at the same time as the hotel?"

"No." Lucia giggled. "The hotel is over 300 years old, it was originally owned by an Italian Count whose family sold it to my grandfather many years ago. My father had it restored about ten years ago to make it into a hotel, and the underground parking area is actually part of a catacomb of caves that extend under the grounds."

"I thought it might be old, but not that old," said Stefano. "It is a very beautiful hotel, you are very lucky to have such a fine piece of property. How foolish of me to think that your father had it built."

"I can see I will have to teach you the little I know about Italian history when we are in Rome," laughed Lucia, her large brown eyes making fun of him.

"I look forward to that indeed," said Stefano.

"Can I drive your bride into the honeymoon suite?" asked Lucia.

"Of course you may, but first I would like to kiss you again. I haven't recovered from our kiss at the factory yet and I don't want to." Stefano pulled Lucia to him and passionately kissed her warm full lips.

Lucia kissed him back and sighed, resting her head on his chest. "Stefano, you kiss like a hot fire." She hugged him close. They parted and she went to the redhead, got in and started the engine. She pressed the clutch, selected first gear with a click and drove the redhead into the centre of the huge garage. She put the gear lever in neutral and revved the engine slightly causing the huge 12 cylinder engine's exhaust to echo against the walls with a gorgeous throaty roar of power. Lucia turned off the engine and sat in the seat looking at the fabulous interior with its bright red speedometer and rev counter increments etched onto the black dials. "She is superb, everything is so well designed, I love it!" she cried, getting out, she ran her hand along its exquisite sculpted lines, running from the massive air ducts in the doors, up to the sleek shoulders. "Stefano, let me see the engine, please. I need to see exactly what makes that beautiful sound and tremendous power."

Stefano reached for the chrome lever by the driver's seat, emblazoned with a prancing horse, that released the engine compartment cover. He lifted the cover and they gazed at the powerhouse of the engine.

"Why do you call it a redhead? Is it because of the red paint on the top of the engine?" asked Lucia.

"No, the famous redheads are actually here on the sides," said Stefano, pointing to the brightly painted red camshaft covers on either side of the engine, each with six bright red spark plug leads connecting to the spark plugs. Above the camshaft covers sat the huge intake manifolds, six on either side made of aluminum; on top of each manifold the flat ridged area was painted bright red, and the raised lettering read Ferrari Testarossa.

"This is called a Flat 12 engine because the six cylinders on either side are horizontally opposed, which is a very unusual and very powerful racing design. The engine has a capacity of 5 litres, outputting 390 horsepower at 6300 revolutions per minute," Stefano explained to Lucia.

"How do you know all this technical stuff?" asked Lucia, shaking her head in admiration.

"Well, I did quite a lot of research before selecting my bride-to-be," replied Stefano, laughing.

"How fast will she go?" asked Lucia.

"Actually, the rated speed is 180 miles per hour," said Stefano.

"Tell me something, Stefano, where does the luggage fit in the car? If I am to travel for two weeks I must bring some clothes, but I don't see anywhere to put any luggage. Oh dear, maybe I won't be able to come after all." Lucia was genuinely concerned.

Stefano shook his head and laughed once more. "No problem, see here..." He leaned inside the car and pulled on the other chrome lever and the bonnet opened. Nestled inside the carpeted compartment were three tan leather suitcases. Stefano lifted one out to show Lucia. "You see, these are specially designed to fit in this area, they will hold your dresses and bathing suit and whatever else you would like to bring." Indeed, the suitcases were splendid and Lucia's eyes lit up as she touched the soft leather.

"Oh, they have the same prancing horse design as the motif on the steering wheel, and they feel exquisite, so soft and supple; now I feel better." Lucia unzipped the long slim case and saw that inside there were hanging compartments with wooden hangers and pockets for shoes and accessories.

"Also, there are three more small cases behind the seats, they are all custom made to fit the Testarossa, by Maurice Sichedoni of the world famous Modena Leather Factory. Enzo thinks of everything," said Stefano. He lifted the three small cases from behind the seats and stood them on the ground; then he took the other two long cases from the front compartment and closed the bonnet, which shut with a solid click. "Now you have plenty of room," said Stefano. "I will take one long one and one small one and you can have the rest to pack your clothes for our trip tomorrow." He closed and locked the doors to his bride and helped Lucia carry the cases out into the sunshine.

"Sleep well, my darling, tomorrow you will get some exercise," Stefano said to the Redhead as he closed and locked the garage doors, then pocketed the key. "Now Lucia, let's you and I go and have a drink to celebrate." He gathered up the cases and they walked to the hotel main entrance.

Pietro, the valet, smiled at Stefano and Lucia as they came in through the double doors of the hotel. "Signore Gapucci, allow me to take your beautiful cases up to your room." He took the cases from Stefano and placed them on a luggage cart. "They are very beautiful indeed," said Pietro. "Never in my life have I touched such soft leather… and what a color! Mama Mia! You are a very lucky man, Signore." Pietro stroked one of the bags as if it were a cat. "One day, Signore, I will save my money and buy a leather case just like this. Then I will walk around the town and show everyone I know. They will feel it and I will tell them it is just the same as the case that Signore Gapucci has, the best in the world."

When Stefano looked at Pietro's face, he realized that Pietro was being sincere and that he did indeed consider the case to be the best in the world. "I hope you get your wish someday," said Stefano. "I agree they are very well made and you are right, the color is most extraordinary, such a rich tan. By the way, the cases came as a set with my new car that I just married. I think Enzo gave them to me as a wedding present."

"Enzo! You met the great Enzo Ferrari, who is my all time most favorite person in the world? His cars are so gorgeous and so powerful, ah Mama Mia!" Pietro sighed passionately.

"Please take two large and two small cases to Signorina Lucia's room and one large and one small case to my room, Pietro," said Stefano.

Pietro smiled and replied, "Immediately, Signore." He placed the case he was holding on the luggage cart and wheeled it away, humming an old Italian opera melody, "La Donna e Mobile."

"He is quite a charmer and has a good taste for quality. What do you think Lucia?" said Stefano.

"Oh, Pietro is quite a comedian, although sometimes unintentionally, but he has been here many years. He is a bit of a scatterbrain at times, but a sweet scatterbrain. He is like you. He spends all of his money on books about Ferraris, some in English and German, also. I think he just looks at the photographs in those. But the ones in Italian, I've heard he can quote word for word from the text on every Ferrari ever made. I am really surprised that he didn't ask you to show him your Testarossa. Perhaps he went off to do some studying on it and he will catch us tomorrow, before we go." Lucia smiled at Stefano who stood and stared at her, not seeming to listen, but transfixed as if in a dream. "Stefano, you are staring at me again and I know you weren't listening. What are you thinking about?"

Stefano came out of his trance. "Every time I look at you, I feel my blood pounding and the warmest feeling flows through me. When you speak, I hear your voice and it makes me so happy, it is the strangest thing. I am so proud to be with you, I want to shout to the world that you are my love!"

"Oh, Stefano you are so weird! The funny thing is that you are so sincere, but I like what you say and I, too, am happy. Let's go and find some maps so you can show me the routes. I am longing to drive your bride again. It was so exciting today, I really enjoyed it."

At the front desk, Lucia found some maps of Italy in the travel stand. Sinking into the luxurious softness of the huge tan leather sofa, Stefano unfolded the map of Italy and asked Lucia which routes she would prefer, fast autostradas or small back roads.

Lucia replied, "Let's start out with small back roads and see how it goes. It will be great fun whatever way we go, I'm sure." They studied the map and settled on a coastal route that, although small and winding, would miss most of the commercial traffic and just pass through small villages, avoiding the centre of large towns. The route started in Maranello and headed South to Modena then to Zocca, through Lucca, and on to the coastal city of Pisa. From there they planned to stay the night in Castagneto Carducci, a little way beyond Livorno. The following day they would drive along the coast to Scansano, then on to Santa Marinella, and finally into Roma. The total distance was around 310 miles.

Stefano made a few notes on the map to remind himself of the route and then jumped up and beckoned to Lucia. "Come, let us have a drink to toast our holiday in advance." They went through the lounge into the bar and sat on the barstools. A waiter with a white shirt and a red sash around his waist came bustling over. "Ah! Signorina Lucia, you look so beautiful today, what can I get you and your friend to drink?" he asked.

"Buon giorno, Silvio, allow me to introduce my friend Stefano. I have no idea what I would like to drink, maybe a small anis?"

"One anis coming up Signorina, and for you Stefano, what is your pleasure?" Stefano asked for a gin and tonic with a slice of lemon.

"Do you have a preference for the gin, Signore?" asked Silvio.

"Gordon's gin, Grazie," replied Stefano.

Silvio prepared the drinks and brought them over.

"I wish to congratulate Signore, I heard you were married today in Maranello!"

"Word travels fast," said Stefano.

"Such a beautiful bride I was told," said Silvio with a smile.

"Yes, she is beautiful, I am very lucky. My friend, allow me to buy you a drink to celebrate my good fortune, what will you have?"

Silvio replied he would join Stefano with a house white wine. When Silvio had poured his wine, Stefano called out, "A toast to my new bride." He raised his glass and all three said, "Salute!".

Stefano sipped his gin and tonic, enjoying the comfort of the bar and just being next to Lucia.

He looked across at her and said, "How is your drink? Is it good?"

Lucia took a sip and nodded, "It is very good, not too strong, but interesting. I like the minty taste of anis, it is so different from all the brandy and whiskey. I can't drink those at all, but this I like."

At that moment pretty fair-haired girl entered the bar and headed in Stefano's direction. Stefano saw her coming and remembered her as the cashier Maria from the hotel.

"Signore Gapucci, I have been looking everywhere for you. Did you forget you have a wedding reception at 2 o'clock?"

"Oh dear, Maria! I completely forgot, here we are sitting in the bar and missing the reception." Stefano looked at his watch. "It's 2:30, is anyone still at the reception?" he asked.

"Si, Signore, the Mayor and the school teachers have all come to see you and to thank you again for the donation to the school…also some of the engineers from the Ferrari factory want to meet you. They won't mind if you are a little late, won't you come and join them? They are in the banquet room called Caesar. I am sure Signorina Lucia will show you where it is when you are ready. I will go there now and tell them you are coming." Maria turned and left the bar. The way she walked, unconsciously swaying her magnificent body, attracted Silvio.

"Mama Mia! Such a woman, how you say, beautiful? Bella bella donna, capiche, Stefano?"

"Si," said Stefano, "she is indeed beautiful."

Silvio put on his black suit jacket, checked his tie in the mirror, hurriedly pulled out a comb and combed his dark red hair back, then took off in pursuit of Maria.

Lucia smiled at Stefano, who could not resist leaning over and kissing her soft lips. "Oh, Stefano! You are such a romantic, you must be careful not to inspire all the men you meet to chase after beautiful women, because sometimes, the woman may be married and the Italian husband will surely kill any suitor!"

Stefano laughed and kissed Lucia again, this time with such tremendous passion that his barstool rocked and he nearly fell off of it in his fervor.

"Come, Stefano, let's go to the reception. Your guests will be tired of waiting and will all go home if you don't go now."

Stefano stood up and helped Lucia down from the barstool. He held her hand in the air and gestured like a matador, "Aprez vous, Mademoiselle, mon cheri!" Lucia looked at Stefano and smiled again.

They left the bar and Lucia took him to the banquet room named after Julius Caesar. The room was not as full as Stefano had feared, only about a dozen people were standing around, chatting to each other with drinks in their hand. The banquet table was full of delicacies, most of which had hardly been touched. As Stefano and Lucia entered they were immediately noticed by the Mayor who raised his glass and beckoned them to join him.

"Signora e Signore, a toast to Signor Stefano Gapucci for his generosity to our little town and to our school children. It is not every day we are so fortunate." The Mayor raised his glass and looked around at the small ensemble.

"To Signore Gapucci!" Everybody raised their glasses, "Salute!" They cheered.

A waiter brought a silver tray of champagne flutes to Lucia and Stefano.

Stefano cleared his throat and spoke. "Signora e Signore, I wish to propose a toast to the people of Maranello for making the wedding such a happy occasion. The town was dressed up so nicely with all of the flowers, the band played with great gusto, and the children sang beautifully. Although I was a little afraid that the townspeople would laugh at me for marrying a Ferrari Testarossa, they did not show anything but understanding and good wishes. My heart goes out to you all. Salute!" Stefano raised his glass and sipped his champagne.

"Signore Gapucci…" A tall grey-haired, distinguished gentleman in a stunningly tailored double breasted suit held out his hand to Stefano. "Allow me to introduce myself, I am Constantino Feruzzi. Enzo asked that I and my colleagues Vittore and Enrico attend your reception on behalf of the Ferrari Factory. We three are design engineers and we work for Signore Materazzi, who I believe you met today at the factory."

Stefano shook hands with Constantino and replied, "Buon Giorno, Signore Ferruzzi, it is my pleasure to meet you." Stefano shook hands also with Vittore and Enrico.

"Please Signore, call me Constantino. We are pleased and somewhat amazed at what you did today. We have heard that in the business of exotic cars one always finds eccentric people, but you stand in a class of one, I think," said Constantino with a broad smile. "You are the first man to actually marry a Testarossa with a priest to conduct the ceremony that we know about. You must truly love your Testarossa!"

Stefano smiled and said, "Indeed I do, Constantino. I love her for her beauty, but most of all because she is a passionate beast with an engine that growls like a tiger, roars with power and comes alive when driven at high speed."

"Bravo, Signore; we admire your courage and your lust for life. Enzo told us you drove the Testarossa with fire in your heart on the track and we wanted to congratulate you."
 Constantino, Vittore and Enrico clicked glasses with Stefano and said, "Salute!"

Stefano said, "I am being very rude, permit me to introduce my very best friend and maid of honor, Signorina Lucia Constanetti. Lucia has the new honor of owning the Ferrari test track record of 180 miles per hour in my redhead. She drives with passion and I am madly in love with her." Lucia blushed and shook hands with the three engineers who were overcome with her spirit and her beautiful Italian features.

"Signorina Lucia, please tell us how you felt driving the Testarossa at such high speed. How did it handle, were you frightened?" asked Enrico. "We are really interested because it is not every day that we meet such a lovely young lady who can handle such a powerful car on a race track."

Stefano stood to one side as Lucia explained the thrill of driving the big Testarossa. The three engineers hung on her every word. Stefano watched as Lucia told them about her little red Alfa Romeo that she drove and how it had prepared her for the Testarossa. He looked at her features, deep brown expressive, alert eyes set above high cheekbones, her pretty nose which suited her face so well, and her soft lips that were so full. Just observing her, Stefano felt a mixture of love, admiration and desire.

Lucia continued to explain her feelings for Italian cars and gesticulated with passion how she hated automatic transmissions, and would only drive a car with a clutch and gear lever. "I was lucky my father taught me to drive in his very old Maserati. He still has it, but doesn't drive it very often. Mostly he drives a car with automatic transmission. I sometimes tell him to fix up the Maserati and get rid of the other car, but he hasn't done it yet."

Vittore asked Lucia about her reactions to the redhead's heavy clutch and, as she replied, a young lady approached Stefano and caught his eye. "Hello Signore Gapucci, my name is Christina Veroni. I am the headmistress of the Maranello school and I would like to personally thank you for your donation to our school. I wish to assure you that the money will be used wisely for the benefit of the school children."

"It was my pleasure, Signora. I felt it was the least I could do in return for my good fortune in being able to come here and marry my very own Testarossa. I hope you don't think I am crazy," said Stefano.

"Strange, but not crazy. Every person on the earth should be allowed to achieve their fantasies if they don't harm anyone else."

Signora Christina's logic made Stefano feel better about himself; he had been secretly concerned about going through with the wedding. But it was true, he thought, if you want to do something as unusual as marrying a car, you must do it if you have the courage.

Christina explained some of her ideas on how to make the best use of his donation. "Trips to a farm that has horses, cows and sheep is on the top of my list. I think outings are very beneficial to the children, they teach the children a lot about life they don't see very much of in the town. I also will put some by to send some of our junior teachers to some seminars that have been designed to teach using new concepts. Up till now we could only get that information from the library and I have great belief in trying out new concepts in addition to the basic foundation of math, Italian history, reading and writing and science, of course. I hope you agree with my plans? Yes?"

Stefano nodded in agreement.

"You are a kind man, Signore. Not too many people in the world would make such a gift to our school. We are very lucky." Stefano felt proud that he had made the donation. Even though he knew his funds would not last forever, he knew they would help a little.

"It was a pleasure meeting you, Signora, Please say thank you from me to the school choir and the band for making today such a festive one."

Christina introduced Stefano to a few of her teacher friends she had bought along. Stefano chatted for a while, then politely excused himself. He turned and looked for Lucia who was still chatting to the engineers. He walked over and tapped her on the shoulder.

"Mi Scusi, Signori, I would like to now take this young lady for a walk."

Smiling, but a little begrudging, the three engineers shook hands again with Lucia and Stefano and bade them, "Buona Fortuna!"

Stefano waited for an opportune moment then moved to the centre of the room and tapped his glass with a spoon. He tapped his glass a few times again, looked around to make sure he had everyone's attention, then said in a calm voice, "Signore e Signori, we are leaving now, but before we leave I would like to thank you all for coming today. It has been a great pleasure to meet and talk to you all. Thank you again."

The small group clapped and wished Stefano good luck with his new bride.

"Molto bene, grazie," replied Stefano. He took Lucia's hand and left the banquet room.

Outside, Lucia whispered to Stefano, "I know what we could do now, if you like?"

"What's that?" Stefano asked.

"I will take you and show you my little red Alfa Romeo. It's not as glamorous as your stunning redhead, but it has been good to me and I am very proud of it."

"Let's go, I would love to see it," said Stefano. They went out of the hotel and walked towards the garages at the rear of the hotel.

Stopping outside one of the garages, Lucia took a key from her purse and opened the garage door. Stefano pulled it open and smiled as he saw the Alfa. "Well, it is certainly a beautiful color, bright red and so clean. Who washes it to keep it so sparkling?"

"I do, of course, I wash it about once a week and polish it every so often." Lucia opened the driver's door. "Here, Stefano, get in and see how it feels." Stefano sat in the Alfa and looked around. In front of him was a wood-rimmed steering wheel with aluminum spokes, and the Alfa logo right in the middle.

He grasped the wheel. "Feels great," he said. "I can just see you screaming around the road bends in this." He looked at the dashboard which had twin pods, one for the rev counter and one for the 140 mph speedometer. "What year is this Alfa, Lucia?" he asked.

"It's a 1974, I have had it for many years now; it is getting old, but runs perfectly and it is my pride and joy." Lucia got into the passenger seat and explained the car to Stefano. "Its all original and I have driven it about 18,000 miles. Not so many long trips, but many short ones," Lucia told him. Stefano looked at the gear shift lever that stuck nearly straight out rather than straight up as in most cars. It was set in a soft leather pouch with a long chrome lever. Atop of the lever was a beautiful piece of white ebony with the shift pattern indented on it.

"I would love to take it for a spin. Do you trust me?" said Stefano.

"Of course I trust you, silly, didn't you trust me with your redhead? The least I can do is to let you drive my little Alfa," said Lucia.

She took the ignition key from her purse and handed it to Stefano, who inserted the key into the ignition, checked that the gear lever was in neutral by pushing it from side to side, then turned the ignition key and started the engine. The little Alfa caught immediately and gave out a pleasant little roar as all 4 cylinders caught.

"I guess we should let it warm up a bit first," said Stefano. "I will reverse it out and you can show me the engine while it warms up." He pressed down on the clutch, put the gear lever into reverse, let the clutch up gently and the Alfa rolled backwards out into the sunshine. Stefano braked, put the gear lever in neutral and set the hand brake. He got out of the car. Lucia reached in and pulled the bonnet latch, then walked around to the front of the Alfa and lifted the bonnet.

Stefano whistled. "Wow! That is a clean engine. Who on earth keeps it that clean?" he asked.

"I have Alfa do all of the oil and filter changes, but I polish everything in the engine compartment whenever I have spare time," said Lucia proudly. The twin camshaft cover shone in the sunlight, no dirt or oil was present anywhere. Stefano could see that Lucia really loved her little Alfa Romeo.

"For a 1974 model, it looks just like new," said Stefano. "You really look after it well."

"I really enjoy cleaning and polishing the whole car, that way I can see any oil leaks and I can get them fixed before they do any damage."

"Good principle," said Stefano. "You can polish the redhead whenever you feel like it." This he said jokingly, but Lucia took it seriously.

"If I owned such a car I would keep it in the house and be forever polishing it and admiring it, but for me the Alfa is my pride and joy." She looked at the water temperature gauge on the dashboard, which was showing that the Alfa engine was now warm and ready to drive. "Let's go," said Lucia. She closed the hood and went around to the passenger side again, reached in and undid the clamps which held the convertible top in place, pulled the top back and folded it neatly into its storage place behind the tiny rear compartment.

Stefano got into the driver's side and closed the door. They fastened their seat belts and Stefano pressed the clutch, put the gear lever into reverse, and turned the car around to point towards the road. Stefano shifted into first gear, eased up on the clutch, revved the engine and the Alfa took off briskly. Then Stefano swiftly changed into second gear, passed the hotel entrance and turned right onto the main drive heading for the road. The Alfa Romeo Spider 2000 Veloce surged forward as Stefano pressed down on the accelerator, giving it plenty of fuel.

"It's a great car, with a beautiful clutch, and the gear lever is in the best place possible," said Stefano, as he made the change from second gear to third at about 40 mph. They drove down the hill towards the town and the Spider hugged the road on the bends, growling to go faster as Stefano accelerated out of the bends. When they reached the junction at the bottom of the hill where the road went left to Maranello, Lucia shouted to Stefano to go right and give it some stick. Stefano nodded, swung right and accelerated again and soon they were doing 65 mph in third with the rev counter at 4000 rpms. Stefano changed into fourth gear and roared into the bend which drifted to the right into a tight turn. The wind in their hair, the couple laughed out aloud as the little Alfa hurtled out of the curve onto a straight piece of road. Stefano hit the accelerator and the Alfa screamed up the road at 80 miles per hour. Stefano shouted over the wind, "This is just as much fun as the redhead, I love it!" Lucia sat relaxed in her seat, proud of her Alfa Romeo zooming down the leafy lanes in the glorious sunshine.

Lucia directed Stefano to turn off the main road to a winding narrow lane that kept going up and up until they finally crested the summit of a small mountain that was well over 3000 feet above the little town of Maranello. Stefano turned off the engine, set the hand brake and they sat in silence, exhilarated by the spectacular view. They could see for many miles into the distance. Down below them was the town and beyond that, fields and occasional small factories, many of them producing racing parts for Ferrari. Further in the distance were the foothills leading up to more mountains. The scenery was beautiful and the day was still warm; even the wind was not blowing hard, just a gentle breeze.

Stefano looked at Lucia and Lucia gazed back into his eyes. Stefano leaned over and kissed her, first a gentle kiss, then more passionately. He put his arm around her shoulders and hugged her to him. He was truly a man in love, besieged by passion. They kissed again for several minutes, each feeling the love of the other through their warm lips. They came up for air and Lucia suggested they walk for a little bit to stretch their legs. They got out of the Alfa and followed a tiny path that led downwards through a maze of low bushes. The air was fresh and Lucia breathed deeply. Stefano watched her sucking in the air and enjoying it, so he, too, started to breathe deeply, mimicking Lucia.

He flapped his arms and ran on the spot, as his face reddened and Lucia laughed at his efforts.

"You look so funny, Stefano, like a windmill." She laughed again, and taking Stefano's hand, they jumped up and down together, laughing and having a great time.

Stefano walked to a small tree and did a neat handstand, ending upside down with his legs leaning against the tree, his weight supported by his hands. "Come and give me a kiss, Lucia," he said.

Lucia bent down and kissed him softly on his upside down lips. "You are crazy, Stefano," she said.

"Yes," said Stefano, "I am crazy about you and so very happy too." His hands gave in and he tumbled to the ground. He picked himself up and brushed the bits of leaves and twigs from his clothes. Lucia laughed and ran into the bushes and Stefano took off after her. He caught up with her very quickly and grabbed her around the waist. They fell softly to a heap in the lush wild grass. Stefano rolled Lucia over until she was on top of him and gazed into her huge brown eyes.

"Tell me about yourself, Lucia, tell me about when you were a little girl and how you grew up into such a beautiful woman!"

Lucia gazed back at him. "Well, I remember when I was six we had a big dog, a German Shepherd, who was my best friend for many, many years. He was always with me, playing and leaping about full of energy…everywhere I went, he would come too. His name was Prinzi and he was huge. He slept in my room at night and when I went to school, he would follow me all the way to the school gate, and when I went in he would turn around and go back home and sit in the garden until two o'clock, when he would again come to the school and sit outside the gate and wait for me. Then we would run quickly back home together and get biscuits from Momma and play in the garden.

"My friends would come and play in the garden, too, and Prinzi would sit and watch as we skipped or swung on the little swing my father had put up on a tree. Prinzi was always there. When I was sixteen years old and I started to go out with boys, Prinzi would bark at them ferociously, just like he was jealous whenever they came to the house. Then when I was seventeen, my father and mother said I had to go to a school for girls in Rome to study. I kissed Prinzi good-bye and my father took me to the train station in the car. Prinzi wanted to come too, but my father had said Prinzi could not come, as my father had business friends he had to meet in town the same day. We got into the car and Prinzi started howling and barking and running round and round the car, so that my father could not drive away. My father got out of the car and tied Prinzi to a long piece of rope that was fixed to the fence, and then we drove off.

"The station was about ten miles away and my father drove very fast so that we would be sure to catch the train. When we got there, I got out of the car and Prinzi came bounding up the road and leapt into my arms and knocked me over, licking my face and barking with affection. He had followed the car all the way, and to this day, we don't understand how he could have run so fast, but he did. He must have broken the rope fixed to the fence straight away and just followed the car to the station. After a great deal of fuss, my father shut Prinzi in the car, but the window was open and he jumped straight out again. My father was very frustrated and worried I would miss the train, so he closed the windows in the car and we both managed to get Prinzi back in again. Prinzi howled but couldn't get out. I started to cry and my father took me into the station, bought a ticket, put me on the train and kissed me good-bye.

"I never saw Prinzi again. My father told me he drove home and tied Prinzi up with two very strong ropes to the tree in the garden, but Prinzi didn't try and get away again. He howled and howled for three days and three nights and then one morning my mother went into my bedroom to see if Prinzi was there and found him dead under my blanket. They called the vet, but it was too late. The vet said he could find no physical reason why Prinzi died, that it could only have been from a broken heart, after I left for college. My mother and father buried Prinzi in the back garden and kept his death a secret from me for the whole term, afraid that the news would tear me apart.

"I found out when I came home again for Christmas holidays. I got off of the train and I knew something was wrong when I saw my mother's and father's faces. I looked around for Prinzi and didn't see him. I rushed out of the station to the car, but he was not in the car. I asked my mother and father where Prinzi was and they told me he had gone to doggy heaven. I cried and cried all the way home and all over Christmas until my face swelled up so badly, my mother had to take me to the doctor. The doctor told my mother to buy a new dog for me but I said no, that I would cry no more, but I did not want another dog, at least not yet."

Lucia sat up; her eyes were moist as she told the sad story to Stefano. Stefano held her close to make her feel better.

"He must have loved you very much," said Stefano, "as much as I love you, for if I were to lose you now, I, too, would die of a broken heart."

Lucia looked up at Stefano and saw that he was serious. She did not know what to say, but she knew that she, too, was very happy being with Stefano, in a way that she had never been with any other boy or man before.

"I have never told the story about Prinzi to anyone before, not even to my closest friends, but I felt comfortable telling you about it," Lucia confessed.

"Well, Lucia, that was such a sad story. Let's walk a little, then we will drive back to the hotel in your sweet little Alfa, go straight to the bar and celebrate...not celebrate my marriage, but celebrate our meeting each other and loving each other." Stefano grinned. "What do you say?"

"Good idea," said Lucia, "Let's do that." She gave Stefano a little kiss on his nose then got up, brushed down her dress, and put out her hand to help Stefano up. They walked in the late afternoon sunshine, taking in the glorious view and the sweet fresh air. They made their way back to the car and Stefano asked Lucia to drive.

"I like watching you drive...you do it so well and you enjoy it so much, it makes me so happy!"

Lucia smiled, "Okay, I will drive, but a bit slower than I did in your Redhead." They got into the Alfa, put on their seatbelts and closed the doors. Lucia started the engine, slid the gear lever into reverse and backed the Alfa round to point to the road. She deftly put the gear lever into first gear, revved the engine and accelerated briskly, then changing up to second gear, she floored the accelerator and the little red Alfa roared off down the mountain.

Stefano leaned back in his seat; relaxed and comfortable as Lucia steered the Alfa down the twisty lane towards Maranello. She drove with total control, braking into the bends and accelerating out of them with tremendous nerve and concentration. The Alfa's engine loved to rev and the rev counter occasionally swung round to 5000 rpm out of the bends at 70 miles per hour. A short time later, Lucia drove the Alfa into her garage, applied the brakes, put the gear lever into neutral and switched off the engine.

"I love your little Alfa Romeo as much as my Redhead. It goes fast and is great fun and it suits you perfectly," said Stefano, stretching out his hand and blowing a kiss to Lucia.

"Come Stefano," said Lucia with a smile, opening her door to get out. "Let's get that drink and celebrate."

They walked to the hotel front entrance hand in hand, laughing and joking, excited about their trip tomorrow, the sad episode of Lucia's tale on the mountain forgotten as if it had never happened. They were a stunning couple, not because of their looks or their clothes, but because they were so obviously in love and showed it in their walk and their expressions, their faces flushed and smiling as if they were on a honeymoon without a care in the world.

Pietro met them at the door, gesturing them in with a flourishing bow, his arm spread out welcoming them. They laughed and thanked him for graciousness and as they went past, Pietro called to Lucia in a humble tone, "Signorina Lucia, I have a great favor to ask."

Lucia paused and looked at Stefano, "I know what he is going to ask. He wants to see your new bride," she whispered.

Pietro came closer and said, "Mi Scusi, Signorina e Signore, I have thought and thought how could I be of service to you and suddenly an idea came into my head."

"Tell us your idea then, Pietro," said Lucia softly.

Pietro felt the blood rushing to his head and even though his mouth opened, no words came out, he tried again, but still no words came.

"Pietro, what is the matter, why don't you say anything?" said Lucia.

Pietro summoned all of his courage. "I would like to sleep tonight, next to the Signore's bride, what do you say?" The last words came out very loud and Pietro, realizing this, spoke more softly. "All my life, I save pictures of the Testarossa…every day I read little pieces of information about the car. I always wanted to look at one close up. Then one day a man from the bank came to the hotel in a red Testarossa and asked me to park it and look after it for him. I nodded and took the keys from him, but I was too afraid to get in the car in case I damage something. I just stood there for two hours, making sure no one touched this beautiful red beast. Finally, the owner came back, gave me a handsome tip and drove off. That night, I cried and cried, unable to sleep, feeling so foolish that I had missed my one opportunity to drive the car that I had dreamed of driving for so many years."

"I know the feeling, Pietro," said Stefano, smiling, "I, too, always wanted to own a Testarossa, to sit in it, turn the engine on and listen to those magnificent 12 cylinders growling in anticipation of being let loose on a fast road. But for many years I was unable to fulfill my dream, until one day, after a lot of tortuous, hot work in a mine in South America, my friend and I came across a seam of gold, so vast we could not believe it!

If you wish to sleep next to my bride tonight, then please do so and I will know how you feel. For it is not just a car, but a beautiful Italian sculpture that has a 12 cylinder beating heart; a glorious piece of artwork hand built by proud Italians."

"Bravo! Bravo!" shouted Pietro, then embarrassed he looked around, "Grazie, Signore Gapucci, you have made me the happiest man on earth, I will guard your bride with my life, I will even bring my shotgun to defend your bride!"

"But Pietro, you cannot sleep on the cold concrete floor in the garage and the Testarossa doesn't have enough space to sleep in…what will you do?" said Lucia with real concern in her voice.

"Ah, Signorina Lucia, already I think of that in case the Signore he say yes. I will borrow a cot bed from the hotel, you know the spare beds that fold up and have little wheels on so that they can be pushed into the room for large families. I will ask your father if I can rent one for the night, I am sure he will say it is okay. Please Signorina, do not worry for me, because tonight I will be the luckiest, happiest man in all of Italy."

"Pietro, you are a man who knows what he wants and I am happy for you, so happy that I have made a decision. You can not only sleep next to my bride, but you can take her for a short spin, what do you say?"

Pietro's mouth fell open, he was visibly stunned. "You mean it, Signore? You mean I can sit in the Testarossa and turn the key and listen to the beautiful engine and drive it up the road? Very, very carefully, I assure you. I am a good driver, Signore, the best in the world. Every day I park the customers' cars, but never, never did I park a Ferrari Testarossa. Maybe I can't drive it, what do you think, Signorina Lucia?"

"I will come with you in the car, Pietro, and you will feel calm and happy and drive perfectly, I am sure," said Lucia with a smile.

"Uno momento, per favore, I come back in about five seconds," said Pietro, 'then I get to drive the car, yes?"

"Whenever you are ready, Pietro, we will wait for you," said Stefano.

"I just tell my friends in the hotel, they will be so happy for me, uno momento, please." Pietro rushed into the main foyer of the hotel, stopping to tell each of the staff what he was about to do.

"He looks so happy, Lucia. Can he really drive well?" asked Stefano.

"Yes, he is a good driver and I have known him since he came here six years ago. He has a very kind heart and is just crazy about Ferraris."

Pietro came back, bowed graciously and said, "Signore e Signorina, I am ready to fulfill my passion, it is still okay?"

"Certainly, Pietro, let's go and do it. When you come back I can take Lucia for that drink I promised her."

They went out of the hotel again, back towards the garages. Pietro was hopping and skipping like a little boy, amazed at his good fortune. Stefano unlocked the padlock on the garage door and Pietro pulled both doors wide open.

"Oh Mama Mia, she is a beauty!" he exclaimed. Stefano gave him the key and opened the passenger door for Lucia. She got in and buckled her seat belt. Stefano gave her a kiss and closed the door. Pietro got in the driver's side put on his seat belt and put the key in the ignition. He closed his door, said a prayer and made the sign of the cross, then turned the key and the Redhead immediately fired into life, the dramatic roar of its lusty exhaust booming inside the garage as the 12 cylinders responded to Pietro's foot on the accelerator. He reversed the Redhead out of the garage then pulled to a stop and put the gear lever in neutral waiting for the engine to warm up.

Stefano looked around, the whole staff had come to see Pietro achieve his dream. They stood silent, listening to the Redhead, in awe of the glistening red, low slung wide racing body that sat in front of them. Pietro sat calmly at the wheel smiling to himself, taking in the beautifully finished tan leather interior and the low growl of the engine that emanated two feet behind his head. The temperature needle slowly moved up to the middle mark, indicating to Pietro that the engine was now warm enough to drive. He pressed the clutch down and pulled the gear lever into first gear, gave a thumbs up sign to Stefano and took off very smoothly. Accelerating gently, he changed into second gear and pressed the accelerator, and within a second he was gone, out of sight, heading for the open road. The small crowd of hotel staff oohed and awed as he pulled by them, grinning from ear to ear, waving profusely.

Lucia looked across at Pietro. He was obviously very excited, lost in his own world, achieving his dream. She watched the way he drove the Testarossa. He sat very rigid, his hands at quarter to three on the steering wheel. Occasionally, he would take his right hand off the wheel and change gear up to third and back to second as he negotiated the turns on the winding road. He was thoroughly enjoying himself, although at the same time being very attentive to the rear view mirror and craning his neck sometimes, to try and see what was around a bend in case a car or bicycle was coming the other way. If nothing was there he would accelerate ferociously out of the bend and then slow down and repeat the maneuver for the next bend. The Redhead's flat 12-cylinder engine sang like an express train.

Lucia leaned back and listened as the huge engine made its own music. She sighed. Now I know what Stefano meant when he says he is in love with the Redhead, she thought. The engine produced the most incredibly exciting sounds as it revved up and down. She listened carefully to the exhaust note which sometimes growled in low bass coming into a corner, then increased into a wonderful howl as the car accelerated out of the bends. Lucia looked again at Pietro. He handled the car perfectly, with no sign of stress or nervousness now he that he was used to its power. They roared down the road towards the junction to Maranello where Pietro braked gently, stopped at the junction and looked carefully up and down the road.

"Nothing coming," he said. He pressed the clutch down, eased the gear lever into first gear with a neat click, then with a gentle touch of the accelerator he did a U-turn that had them back on the road up to the hotel. He changed up to second gear and gunned the Redhead, which took off like a bullet. He drove fast and accurately up the hill and pulled into the hotel area, slowing to a crawl as he passed the staff, who all waved and smiled at him. He drove a few more yards to where Stefano stood waiting, stopped the car, put the gear lever into neutral, set the hand brake and turned off the engine, all in one fluid motion. He got out of the car and rushed around to the passenger side to open the door for Lucia. She got out and thanked him.

Pietro rushed up to Stefano and held out his hand. Stefano shook his hand and Pietro said, "Signore e Signorina, I thank you from the bottom of my heart…your bride is just as I thought it would be, but even more powerful and more wonderful than anything else in the world. Grazie tanto!"

"You are very welcome, Pietro. I am extremely glad you enjoyed my bride, she was built just for people like us, who love to drive and respect the incredible power of the engine."

"She drive just like a jet plane, howling and singing at the same time. She stick to the road like a racing car; she is indeed the most beautiful car in all the world. Signore, I am very happy man now. Mama Mia! What a car!" Pietro laughed and smiled. "Now I can tell my friends that I drove a real Testarossa. They won't believe me, but I will know in my heart and that is good enough for me. Tonight I will take care of your bride while she sleeps, Signore. You can trust Pietro, I promise you."

"Well, Pietro, why don't you drive her into the garage and tuck her up for the night?" said Stefano.

Pietro didn't need to be asked twice; he got back into the car, started the engine and sat there mesmerized, listening to the engine. He suddenly realized where he was again and deftly pressed the clutch, put the gear lever into first gear with a distinct click, let the hand-brake off and eased the Redhead forward into the garage. Then he took it out of gear, applied the hand-brake and switched off the engine. He sat there with his hands on the wheel, staring at the dials and the magnificent seats covered in soft leather.

"Bella, Bella, Buona Notte," he said to the car.

Pietro got out, locked the doors and handed the keys to Stefano saying, "Here Signore Stefano, you must keep the keys to your Redhead just in case a fierce lust comes over me in the night and I might not be able to stop myself from taking her for a drive." Pietro's eyes twinkled. "Just a joking, maybe."

Stefano smiled saying. "No Pietro, you keep the keys to the car. The key to the garage is in the padlock, my bride is now all your responsibility until tomorrow morning when we leave. I know you will look after her."

"I will, Signore, you can trust me. I would marry her, too, if she was mine, then I would sleep every night next to her and every day I would polish her beautiful body until she gleamed in the dark."

"Okay, see you tomorrow morning then, Pietro." Stefano took Lucia's hand and they set off for the hotel. The rest of the hotel staff who were still standing outside went to Pietro and congratulated him and Pietro, overcome by emotion, wept real tears of joy.

Stefano and Lucia entered the hotel and went to sit in the bar. This time a young waitress came over and asked Lucia what she would like to drink. Lucia thought for a moment and asked for a Margarita. Stefano laughed, then ordered the Margarita and a gin and tonic for himself.

"Why did you laugh when I asked for a Margarita, Stefano?" asked Lucia.

"When you were thinking about what to drink, I thought to myself, Lucia will order white wine or Pernod, but I guessed wrong and laughed because it surprised me," said Stefano. "I am glad that I was wrong, your taste becomes you. Margaritas are fun drinks, interesting with the salt on the rim of the glass and Tequila from Mexico. I would never have thought of you drinking Tequila. Where did you learn that?"

"When I was in school in Switzerland, my classmates and I went out for dinner once and we dared each other to order one unusual drink each, so I looked at all of the bottles of spirits behind the bar and I liked the name Tequila. When I ordered it the waiter explained about the Margarita with the salt and then when he brought it, it tasted delicious. I haven't had one since then, so I thought, tonight is a special occasion, so the Margarita came into my head."

Stefano leaned across and kissed Lucia on the cheek. She kissed him back and they moved closer together into the middle of the soft sofa. The waitress set the drinks on the table in front of them, together with a dish of cashews, peanuts and raisins.

Stefano raised his glass and Lucia raised hers and they clinked them together. "To the woman I love, to you Lucia, salute!"

Lucia smiled. "Salute, Stefano, you are a very strange man, but I think I am starting to fall in love with you."

Stefano, overwhelmed with joy, leaned across and kissed Lucia on the lips and said softly, "My darling Lucia, I am yours forever."

Stefano and Lucia snuggled together closer and embraced on the sofa, their arms wrapped around each other, their lips pressed together in exquisite passion. Neither wanting to end the kisses, they came up for air only after several minutes, then went straight back to doing it again.

A discrete cough was heard, a pause and it was repeated. Stefano looked up from kissing Lucia to see a strange man standing beside the sofa. "Mi Scusi, Signore, are you Stefano Gapucci?" asked the man.

"Yes, I am Stefano Gapucci, what can I do for you?" asked Stefano.

"Signore Enzo Ferrari asked me to deliver these documents to you, Signore." The man opened the dark red leather briefcase he was carrying and pulled out a sheaf of papers. "My name is Homer Stenzini, pleased to meet you, Signore." The man held out his hand and Stefano shook it. "Do you mind if I sit down, I apologize for interrupting, but I won't take long I assure you."

"Please, sit down, Homer, allow me to introduce my sweetheart, Lucia."

"Ah! Signorina Lucia, my heart goes out to you. Enzo told me how you drove today, incredibly fast around the racetrack. I am honored to meet you." Lucia held out her hand and Homer took it in his and bent to kiss it. "I will tell all of my friends back at the Ferrari Racing Department that I have kissed the hand of the beautiful Signorina who now owns the fastest time around the track in a Testarossa!"

Homer sat down and set the papers on the table in front of him. "Firstly, Signore, these papers signify your ownership of your Testarossa as well as the receipt showing it is paid in full. Then there is a special bonus from Enzo, a year's insurance for you, your passengers and your car.

"That's very kind of Enzo," said Stefano.

"He had his reasons, Signore and here they are." Homer pulled out two Ferrari red T-shirts and two caps, each with the Ferrari Prancing Horse logo emblazoned on them. "Plus two passes to the pits at Le Mans for three weeks from today, one in your name and one in Signorina Lucia's name." He showed them a large white card with the words "Ferrari Pit Pass" embossed in brilliant red. "When you arrive at the track, put that card in your windscreen and show the security guard your passes. They will direct you to the Ferrari pit area. Lastly, here is a map of the Le Mans circuit showing all the turns and straights…each one is marked with the maximum speed it has ever been driven, so you can study it and prepare for the race."

"Well," said Stefano, "it looks like Enzo was deadly serious about us driving for him in the Le Mans Grand Prix."

Homer looked across at Stefano. "Enzo was extremely impressed with your driving today. He is certain that you have the skill to win in the Le Mans and I know that he has never been mistaken yet. He only asks the best drivers in the world to drive for him, Signore. I have one last request. I need to know your measurements so that we can make up some racing overalls for you to drive in." Homer took out a little notebook and pen and wrote down the approximate measurements of Stefano and Lucia, which they both gave him in answer to his questions. Having completed his task, Homer put all of the documents back into the red leather briefcase, snapped the catch shut and handed it to Stefano. "Yours to keep, Signore, see you in three weeks in Le Mans. Until then Ciao, Signorina Lucia e Signore Stefano, Buona Fortuna!" Homer rose, bowed gracefully and departed as silently as he had appeared.

"Mama Mia!" giggled Lucia. "Stefano! You and I are going to drive at Le Mans! This is incredible!"

"You really want to drive in a real racing car in the Le Mans Grand Prix?" exclaimed Stefano. "I thought you promised your father you wouldn't be driving."

"Well, now I must ask Papa to let me un-promise," said Lucia.

Stefano raised his glass. "I toast to winning the Le Mans Grand Prix...what do you say, Lucia?"

Lucia breathed deeply and reached for her Margarita. "Salute! We will win at Le Mans! Where is Le Mans, Stefano?"

Stefano laughed. "It is about 128 miles Southwest of Paris, so we could drive to Paris first and stay in my little house for a few days, then drive to Le Mans for the race, then drive South to Nice and relax by the seaside."

"But that means we will be away for more than three weeks, maybe four. My father will be furious. He has such great plans for me and I do help him out a lot in running the hotel. He teaches me a lot of things during the course of a day." Lucia sipped her Margarita, "I think I had better go and talk to him, otherwise he will be surprised and upset if I just call him in two weeks and say I will be gone for two more weeks." Lucia stood up.

Stefano tugged at her dress. "Lucia, I want to be totally honest with you. Darling, I want to marry you, I want you to be my wife, whenever you are ready. Let's get married."

Lucia sat down again. "Stefano, I have known you for only a few hours and, yes, I also would like to marry you, but my father, he would say, wait for a while before you make such a decision. But I will tell him we love each other and want to get married and see what he says. Is that all right with you, my love?"

Stefano nodded. "It is fine with me, whenever you are ready I will marry you and we can live wherever you want to…here in Maranello or in Paris or in Nice, or all three at different times of the year."

Lucia stood up again, she bent over and kissed Stefano hard on the lips. "Now I will go and find my father and tell him our news." Lucia rushed off towards the main foyer of the hotel.

Stefano leaned back in the sofa and thought about the day, so many things had happened, all of them good. He thought to himself how lucky he was, first to find the gold, then to achieve his first dream of marrying his Redhead, then finally to meet Lucia who he knew would make him happy forever. What more can a man born on earth possibly want from life? he thought. He sipped his gin and tonic, relaxed and carefree.

Luigi Constanetti was livid. He had just listened to his one and only daughter tell him that she was going to marry Stefano Gapucci, not ask him, but tell him! He could not believe his ears. He sat in his chair at his desk thinking how he should react, what he should advise her. "Don't get angry," he told himself. "You will just drive her away into the arms of this young cockerel who flaunts his way into the good books of the whole town by making a public donation to the school. Then he takes my daughter out in his brand new Ferrari and impresses her with it, letting her drive it, and so fast!" Even Enzo had been astonished by the speed that she drove. My God! thought Luigi, She could have been killed driving at that speed. What a fool I was to take her to that mock wedding! Luigi forced himself to be calm. He looked across at Lucia who sat in the chair opposite, waiting for his response to her declaration of love.

How beautiful she looks, just like her mother, God rest her soul. Luigi's mind traveled back to the days when Lucia's mother, Isabella, was alive. He was entranced by the resemblance of Lucia to her mother. His mind recalled the time when Isabella sat in that same chair, her jet black hair curling down over her shoulders, advising Luigi how to react when Lucia was going out on her first date at sixteen.

"Luigi be calm," Isabella had said. 'This boy Tomaso is a good boy. We have all known him and his family for many years. He is a good clean Italian boy, very smart, always well dressed. They are only going to a dance in the town and he has promised he will bring Lucia back by 11:30 sharp when the dance ends."

"Yes, but to go and come back on a motorcycle! What if he drinks too much and drives off of the road! What will you say then, Isabella!"

"Luigi, he told me he won't drink, he just wants to dance with Lucia and have a good time. You must let her grow up; all girls must go on a first date sometime. If you say she can't go, after I said I would talk to you on her behalf. She will never ask us again, she will just go anyway and you will never know with whom. So now you must be sensible and tell her that you love her and that she is the most precious person in the whole world to both of us. Tell her that she can go and her face will light up in the prettiest smile you have ever seen."

Luigi had listened to Isabella then and had to agree her words made common sense. He had afterwards gone to Lucia's room and knocked gently on the door.

"Come in, Papa," Lucia called, knowing her father's knock. Luigi went in and stood silently, uncertain how to begin. "Did Mama ask you for me, Papa? Did she tell you that Tomaso wants to take me out dancing tonight?"

Luigi nodded, his face solemn.

Lucia looked closely at her father. She sensed that he was uncomfortable, that he wanted to say something to her, but the words would not come. Tell me, Papa, that it's all right, that I can go. Please, Papa, tell me!"

Luigi looked at her and knew that it would be as Isabella said. If he said no, Lucia would cry and be sad and would close the door to him on future occasions. He was a strong-minded man, but he loved his little Lucia so much. "Sure you can go, my little flower, enjoy yourself and have fun. I want you to be happy. Just be careful and tell Tomaso I said he must drive his motorcycle with caution, no speeding around the corners!"

Lucia's face broke into the most beautiful wondrous smile, just as Isabella had said it would. She jumped up and rushed to him and he held his arms open and clasped her to him as she reached him.

"Papa! You have made me so happy, I was afraid you were going to say no."

"Your mother is very sensible. She loves you as much as I do, but she understands we cannot forbid you to go out with boys. Maybe I could, but I can't keep you a prisoner, so go and have a good time and be back by 11:30 on the dot."

Luigi smiled in remembrance of that evening, how he left Lucia's room and heard the loud sound of the Moto-Guzzi on the gravel outside. Tomaso was early. Who wouldn't be for such a beautiful girl as my Lucia?

"Papa, what are you thinking about? You seem so very far away. Are you all right?" Luigi jolted back into the present, ten years later. Now Isabella was gone and here was his grown up daughter who wants to get married. "Lucia…" His words faltered and the vision of Isabella came so strongly to him that he could almost feel her presence in the room.

"Yes, Papa, I am here, you are acting so strangely, I am concerned about you." Lucia got up and came around the desk and stood next to her father and felt his forehead. "You don't have a fever, thank God." Lucia took her father's hand in hers. "Papa, you know I love you most of all in the world, and I know I must sound crazy to say I want to marry a man I have known for only a day. But something happened today, I don't know exactly when, just that I feel so happy when I am with Stefano. I think he truly loves me, too. He told me that he fell in love with me this morning when I took up the breakfast to his room. That sounds crazy, but I believe him, he is a very sincere person. Marrying the Ferrari was something he had to do. His friend who was shot, made him promise to use the gold from the mine to find her and marry her. It wasn't just a whim. He really loves the car and today, when I drove it, I knew just how he felt. The beauty of the car and the sound it makes when it is going fast is unbelievable, just like an orchestra!"

Luigi looked up at his daughter, her face glowing with happiness, and the vision of Isabella came back to him and he knew she had won again. "Listen to me, my child, I only want you to be happy and, if you truly feel in your heart that Stefano is the right man for you, then I am not going to stand in your way. I am your father and I will always be here for you as long as my health lasts, you know that?" Lucia nodded and kissed him on the forehead. "Why not do this…take your vacation with Stefano and, at the end of two weeks, make your final decision. If you still want to marry him, call me and let me know. Then I will set up the wedding arrangements and you can come back to Maranello and get married in the church. What do you say to the idea?"

"Papa, I must be honest with you. I feel passion for Stefano — you know what I mean — when we kiss I feel very passionate. I don't want to wait two weeks. Besides I must be a virgin to get married in church and I may not be a virgin for much longer."

Luigi was shocked! Again the anger arose in him but he fought against it. She is being truthful, he thought, Who would go away for two weeks with the man they are love in with, then get married in white at the church? That would be blasphemy.

"Lucia, your life and your happiness is the most important thing in my life. If you want to get married to Stefano, then do so. I would like to come to the wedding, but if you get married before then, while you are on holiday, let me know and I will send you the biggest telegram and the biggest bunch of flowers that I can find." Luigi smiled and Lucia kissed him on the forehead again.

"Oh, thank you. Papa! You are the world's best Papa!" Lucia hugged him to her and Luigi felt her happiness gushing over him. "I must go and tell Stefano the good news!" Lucia rushed out of the room. Luigi sat in shock, amazed at how fast things had happened today.

Lucia went back to the bar where Stefano was waiting patiently. She sat down on the sofa next to Stefano, but didn't say anything.

"What did your father say?" asked Stefano.

Lucia smiled. "He wants me to be happy. He said if we really and truly love each other enough to want to get married, then we should do it whenever we want to do it. He wanted us to wait two weeks first, but I explained to him that we may not want to wait that long." Lucia leaned over and kissed Stefano on the lips. "Oh, Stefano, how much do you love me?"

"I know that what happened today is a miracle, that we should meet and fall in love. Some people would say that it is not possible, but we know that it is and it happened. I am so very happy that I found you and I want to be with you always. That is how much I love you!" said Stefano.

While Stefano was professing his love for Lucia, Luigi was being cautious. He had run his hotel conservatively as a business for many years, so his first basic instinct was to verify that Stefano was who he said he was and not some criminal evading the law. Luigi took out his private telephone book from his desk drawer, opened it and looked through the entries he had made over the years. He found the entry he was looking for, placed the book on the desk and reached for the telephone. He dialed the number he had selected and it rang, once, twice, three times, then on the fourth ring a deep Italian male voice answered, "Chief Inspector Mazetti, speaking."

"Giampaolo, Luigi here, Come sta?"

"Bene Grazie, Luigi, e lei?"

"Bene grazie, my friend, I have a favor to ask you."

"What can I do for you, Luigi?" asked Giampaolo.

"You remember my daughter, Lucia?"

"Indeed I do, Luigi. How could I forget such a beautiful girl? Is she well? I hope nothing has happened to her."

"No, Giampaolo, she is very well indeed, It's just that she met someone today and has fallen head over heels in love with him and now she wants to marry him, all in one day would you believe it?"

"Si Luigi, it happens sometimes. I remember the night you met Isabella, God rest her soul, you came straight to my house after taking her out dancing just once and told me how you had met the woman of your dreams. Two weeks later you were married and off on your honeymoon!" chuckled Giampaolo.

"You are correct, Giampaolo, I had forgotten. It was so many years ago, such a happy time," said Luigi.

"So, you want me to check him out? Okay! What is his name and what city does he come from?" asked Giampaolo.

"It may be difficult. His name is Stefano Gapucci. He is here in Italy to collect his new Ferrari, in fact he got married to it today, would you believe, by a priest no less, with Enzo giving away the bride," said Luigi.

"I heard about that, but I didn't know you were involved, Luigi."

"He saw Lucia in the morning and came down to ask me if Lucia could be his Maid of Honor. I agreed, and now he wants to marry her and she wants to marry him, so I think to myself, call your old friend, Giampaolo, check him out just in case, so that is why I called you."

"You did the right thing, tell me where does he live?" asked Giampaolo.

"He lives some of the time in Paris and Switzerland, too, I think. He has money, real gold, which he got from a mine in South America. How can you trace such a person from here in Italy?"

"No problem, Luigi. I will call my friends at Interpol, and they will check him out from top to bottom in a very short time. Leave it with me and I will get back to you as soon as I get a reply," said Giampaolo.

"Giampaolo, you are marvelous, how can I repay you?"

"Don't worry about that now, I get back to you soon. Ciao, old friend." Giampaolo hung up.

Luigi put the telephone down and leaned back in his chair, he felt better, more relaxed. Well, at least I am trying to protect Lucia, just in case Stefano is an escaped confidence trickster, although how I could explain that to Lucia if he were, I don't know, it would break her heart. I hope he is not, that's all. Luigi closed his eyes and dreamed of his Isabella. She was smiling again. He snored softly with a smile lighting up his face.

Lucia and Stefano finished their drinks, and the Margarita had obviously gone to Lucia's head, because she was feeling decidedly merry. "Come to my room, Stefano, and help me pick out the clothes I should take on the trip." Lucia got up and playfully pulled Stefano's hand forcing him to get up.

Stefano laughed, "Okay! Okay! I am coming!"

Lucia led him by the hand out of the bar towards the back of the hotel. They went down a long corridor which had a sign reading "Hotel Employees Only." At the end of the corridor, outside one of the doors, Lucia rummaged in her handbag looking for her keys. She found the one she was looking for and inserted it into the lock; the door opened and Lucia pulled Stefano inside.

Stefano looked around the huge room, his eyes taking in the black leather sofa that looked incredibly soft with its massive wide cushioning that only Italian leather artists know how to make. The floor was covered in white Flokati longhaired rugs. In front of the sofa was a long table, its glass top resting on the back of a black full-sized panther magnificently carved out of wood, which appeared to be poised to spring on its prey. The lower half of the walls were painted blue and the upper half white, making an interesting contrast. Each of the three walls had a different hanging print framed in glass; one a desert scene of vivid oranges and reds, showed blue cacti rising up out of the desert's sandy floor. On another wall hung a print of a farmland scene with a lake and fir trees. A young girl, dressed in a white bodice and long blue dress was sitting on a fence looking out over the lake. The third wall had a print of a native American Indian in full war paint, holding a large round leather shield and sitting astride a white pony. Three feathers were in his headband, which was tightly wound around his head; his long blue-black hair hung to his shoulders. He gripped a long spear in his right hand as he rode off to war.

Stefano stared at the three prints in turn, each more interesting than the last, so much so that he couldn't take his eyes off of them. Below the prints were low white bookcases filled with books in Italian and French, some fiction, some autobiographies of famous women. An Alfa Romeo service manual proudly occupied a place of honor next to a book about the life of Alberto Ascari, world champion Ferrari racing driver.

Stefano turned to the window and looked out at the breath-taking view of the valley below, tinged with red as the final rays of the sun reflected off the little lake, surrounded by a ring of pine trees. The mountains rose in the distance and the whole scene was massive yet incredibly peaceful.

"Come, Stefano, you sit out on the balcony while I make us some coffee." Lucia opened the double French doors and beckoned Stefano to follow. Stefano walked across the room and stepped out through the French doors onto an immense wooden balcony that stretched at least twenty feet in each direction and was about eight feet wide. Along the balcony were a pair of chaise lounges, and comfortable looking lounge chairs next to a wooden table.

Stefano went to lean over the balcony. Just as he moved, a deep growl came from behind him. He turned and saw a large wolf staring at him, still emitting a menacing growl. The wolf watched Stefano, as if daring him to move. Stefano said, "Down, boy! Good boy!"

The wolf moved closer, its huge fangs visible as it licked its lips and began to growl more ferociously.

Lucia called to the wolf, "Sheba, stop that this minute! Come and say hello to my friend, Stefano."

The wolf moved closer to Stefano, sniffing him up and down with her big black wet nose.

"Don't worry, she is always like this until she gets to know you. Let her sniff and soon she will lose interest and leave you alone, you will see."

Stefano wasn't quite sure, as the wolf was still growling from deep in her belly. She circled Stefano warily, all the time sniffing him. Stefano stood motionless. A minute passed and the wolf gave a wide yawn and wandered off up the deck, found a place she liked, curled up and put her huge head between her thick paws, still watching Stefano, but no longer growling. Stefano felt better. Perhaps it had already eaten, he thought.

"Is it a real wolf?" asked Stefano. "It has the silver color and the fangs of a wolf. Is it yours, Lucia?"

"It's a real wolf. I found her when she was a tiny cub, wandering around alone in the forest just over there beyond the lake." Lucia pointed out a heavily wooded area way down in the valley. "I sat next to her for hours to see if her mother would find her, but she didn't come. When it started to get dark I didn't know what to do. I decided to leave her there in the woods and started to walk home, but the little cub followed me every step of the way. I brought her into the hotel and into my room and made a bed for her out of some old bedclothes. I put down a bowl of water and some Marie tea biscuits on a plate and the little cub ate the biscuits, drank the water, curled up on the bedclothes, and went to sleep. I went to seek advice from my father. At first he said no, that a wolf cub could never be tame and that I was to take it back to the forest first thing in the morning, to where I found it, and let it go. He was sure the mother was close by.

"We discussed it some more and he could see that I wanted to keep the little cub, so he called the vet for advice. The vet told my father a strange story. Two nights earlier some sheep on the mountainside were attacked by two big silver wolves. The shepherd took his shotgun and shot at both of the wolves, because they had killed six of his sheep in that week. When the shepherd went to check if the wolves were dead, he saw a little wolf cub running about 20 or 30 yards away. The shepherd said he aimed the 12-gauge shotgun just in front of the little cub so that it would run into the pellets as he fired, but when he pulled the trigger the shotgun did not go off. It was then that he remembered that he had already fired both barrels at the big wolves and had forgotten to reload. He reloaded, and chased after the cub with his sheepdog, but they lost track of the little cub down by the lake. He went back to the two big silver wolves he had slain and examined them. One was a big male and the other was a very large female. He remembered that her chest, legs and paws were as big or even bigger than the male's."

"So the vet thought that the cub you found was the same cub that ran from the shepherd?" Stefano asked.

"Yes," said Lucia, "he was fairly certain, as wolves haven't been seen in this area for quite a few years. The shepherd had taken both wolves' carcasses to the vet for disposal, and the vet asked my father to bring the cub down to his surgery for examination. So we took the cub down in the station wagon. The vet compared the cub to the dead female wolf and was immediately certain that it was her cub. The silver coat was identical, even down to the tiny black tip on the end of both tails.

But what really convinced the vet was that the rear hind toenails on both the mother and the cub were pink, yet all the other toenails on the front legs were black. The cub was healthy, but the vet said he had never heard of a wolf brought up like a dog before, but since the cub was so young, it might be possible. So we brought her back to the hotel and into my room and she went straight back to the bed I had made for her and fell asleep. I kept her, took her for walks every day, fed her dog food and here she is fully grown."

Stefano sat on the lounge chair and looked closely at Sheba. She had a thick silver coat which puffed up around her neck and chest; her front legs were thick solid muscle with huge paws, her ears were erect, her face slightly darker than her silver coat, except for rings of silver around her golden yellow and deep brown eyes. Her snout was wide and long with a black nose. The wolf's chest was massive and Stefano estimated that she must weigh well over 130 pounds.

"Watch this," said Lucia. "Howl, Sheba!" The huge wolf sat on its rear, lifted its head straight up and let out a blood-curdling long howl, which was so loud that it echoed back from the valley. The wolf howled again. It was a most unusual sound, Stefano thought, almost as if it was calling to all the other wolves in the world.

"That's enough, Sheba, good girl," said Lucia, as she patted the wolf's head. Sheba responded by leaning against her leg in a gesture of affection, then walked off, found a place in the setting sun, lay down, stretched out on her side, and closed her eyes.

Stefano stood up, still watching Sheba. The wolf opened one eye to observe Stefano, decided he wasn't a threat to Lucia, closed its eye and went back to sleep.

"Who will look after Sheba while you are away?" asked Stefano.

"The Chef has two sons who play with Sheba most of the day. I am sure they will be more than happy to look after her, but I must remember to ask Chef if it is agreeable with him, too. Wait here, Stefano, when the coffee is ready make us both a cup and I will be back in a moment." Lucia left the balcony and went to see the Chef.

Stefano went back inside the living room and found the kitchen. He poured the cappuccino into two cups, then took them out to the balcony and placed them on the table near the lounge chairs. He chose the lounge chair furthest from the wolf, who had woken up and was watching him carefully. Stefano lifted the cappuccino cup to his lips and tasted the hot liquid. It was delicious. He took another sip of cappuccino and leaned back in his chair, his eyes taking in the majestic view. He smiled to himself, thinking about Lucia walking home with the little wolf cub following her. The cub had good taste, thought Stefano.

Stefano looked across at the large silver wolf that had just risen to its feet and was eyeing Stefano again, licking its lips. "Stay!" said Stefano. The wolf took no notice and approached Stefano.

Suddenly Stefano had an idea...he spoke to the wolf in the same tone of voice that Lucia had used. "Sheba, howl, Sheba." The wolf stopped its approach, sat on its haunches, arched its neck back, opened its jaws and began to howl solemnly.

Stefano laughed, feeling momentarily relieved. The wolf, as if it knew it had been tricked, stopped howling and came forward towards Stefano again.

Lucia entered the balcony, coming between the wolf and Stefano. "Naughty girl, Sheba, go and sit down," said Lucia in a stern voice. The wolf shook its mane, turned around, and went back to the other end of the deck.

Stefano breathed a sigh of relief. "Whew! I really thought she was going to attack me," he said.

"Sheba has never attacked anyone" said Lucia, concern in her voice, "She was just warning you. My father and I took her to a special dog training school last year and she was trained the same way as a police dog. She won't attack until given the command, but when she does, she exhibits extreme violence and doesn't stop until the person she is attacking lies still on the ground." Sheba pricked her ears up when Lucia said the word attack and growled at Stefano menacingly.

"She was also trained to warn, which is what she was doing when I came in, but she won't attack unless I or my father give the command. She really is very docile, except she gets a little wary in unfamiliar situations. I have an idea…"

Lucia took Stefano's hand and led him into the kitchen. She opened the fridge and took out a large raw steak and put it on a plate. "Now, Stefano, take the plate and call Sheba. I want you two to be friends and maybe this will help. When she comes, hold out your hand and say 'shake'. When she lifts her paw, take it in your hand."

Stefano felt nervous, but called Sheba and the wolf came into the kitchen. Stefano hesitantly held out his right hand and said, "Shake, Sheba." Sheba warily sat on her haunches, looking first at Lucia, then at Stefano. Finally, she lifted her paw. Stefano grasped the huge paw in his hand and shook it once. The wolf's eyes were on the plate of meat.

Stefano put the plate on the floor and the wolf immediately took the meat in its jaws, chewed it to little pieces and swallowed it.

Sheba looked up at Stefano. "Friends, Sheba?" he asked. He held his hand out bravely and Sheba licked it once and settled down on the floor.

"Now Stefano, give her a belly rub and she will trust you for life!" said Lucia. Stefano knelt down and stroked the big wolf's chest and belly. The wolf began to purr like a big cat and rolled on its back, its legs straight up in the air.

"Good girl, Sheba," said Stefano, continuing to stroke the wolf, which eventually closed its eyes and went to sleep still purring softly.

"I think she could tell I am in love with you and she was just jealous," said Stefano. He stood up and took Lucia in his arms and kissed her passionately on the lips. Lucia returned his kiss with fervor and soon they were both breathing heavily. The wolf started to howl. Lucia said, "Sh! Sheba, be a good girl!" Sheba stopped howling and lay down again, watching Stefano holding Lucia close and kissing her soft neck.

A loud knock on the door interrupted them. Lucia broke off her kissing and cuddling with Stefano. "That must be the Chef's sons come to collect Sheba. I must go and let them in." She gave Stefano a quick peck on the cheek and went to open the door.

"Buon Giorno, Signorina Lucia!" The two young curly-headed boys spoke in unison. "Sheba!" called one of the boys. "Dove e il, Sheba?" asked the other. The wolf got to her feet quickly and scampered into the living room, obviously pleased to see her playmates, her tail wagging just like a dog. The two boys made a fuss over Sheba and she responded with enthusiasm, jumping up against them. "No Sheba! No jumping!" shouted Lucia above the din.

Sheba stopped jumping and looked mournfully at Lucia.

"Come on, you silly wolf, let's get your lead." Lucia fetched the thick leather lead and fitted the chain end deftly over Sheba's head, handing the end of the lead to the younger boy.

The elder boy had spotted Stefano coming from the kitchen. "Buon Giorno, Signore, I saw your car just now when Pietro took it for a drive. It is so beautiful, Signore, so beautiful, one day when I grow up I want a car just like that!"

Stefano came into the living room, "Yes, it is indeed a beautiful car, how do you call it?" asked Stefano, eager to hear what the little boy would say.

"La Bella Macchina is what we call it or La Bella Testarossa," said the elder boy laughing.

"And what are your names, young fellows?" asked Stefano.

Lucia answered for them. "They are called Romulus and Remus after the famous founders of Rome, brought up by, would you believe, a silver wolf? At least that is what they say in the history books."

"Most fitting," said Stefano, looking down at Sheba, "No wonder she likes you two, you are aptly named to look after a big wolf!"

The boys laughed.

"Chef Mazetti is a true Roman, but my father heard of his culinary reputation, so he made him an offer he couldn't refuse and now Chef has been with us for many years here in Maranello. He loves to cook for the hotel patrons," Lucia explained. "He lives for his cooking, his wife and these boys. Now off you two go and look after Sheba well for me, as I know you will!"

The two boys with their ancient Roman names laughed and pulled Sheba out the door. Sheba loved it as she knew they would play with her in the woods by the hotel until it got dark, as they did everyday. "Arrivederci, Signorina Lucia, Arrivederci, Signore," the boys called and then they were gone and the room returned to its peacefulness.

Lucia closed the door and straightened out the Flokati rugs which Sheba had sent flying in all directions, in her joy to play with the boys. "Ah!" said Lucia, "Peace at last, come, let us drink another Cappuccino, then you can help me pack, Stefano."

Lucia prepared the coffee and the two sat on the sofa talking about the trip tomorrow and what they would need to take. Then Lucia changed into a denim jacket and jeans with the vivid red Ferrari T-shirt outlining her splendid figure. "Will I do?" asked Lucia.

Stefano was stunned, it was the first time he had seen Lucia in such casual clothes, and she filled them with such grace, Stefano found it difficult to breathe. "My God, Lucia, you are so incredibly gorgeous, those jeans look like you poured yourself into them and your bottom is quite exquisite!"

Stefano could not resist giving her a cuddle and they ended up lying on top of the thick Flokati rugs, kissing and caressing each other. Stefano felt a tremendous desire to make love to Lucia, but he held back, knowing that the time would come and it would be when they both wanted it, not when Lucia was still tipsy from the strong Tequila. They lay on the rugs breathing heavily, the warmth of their body heat gluing them together. Neither moved, not wanting to break the magic that they both felt was molding their lives and drawing them closer and closer together. The sun finally set and the room became dark as they lay in each other's arms.

Lucia whispered to Stefano, "Help me pack and we can take the case to the car and say goodnight to Pietro." Stefano grunted, unwilling to move, so comfortable lying with Lucia on the soft rugs. After a few minutes, Lucia kissed Stefano and rose from the floor and felt for the lamp switch next to the sofa. A soft white light came from two blue and white china lamps and Stefano decided to get up, too. They spent the next hour and a half giggling and squabbling about what Lucia should pack. Eventually, the tan leather Ferrari case was filled to the brim.

"Lucia, this will never fit in the Testarossa," said Stefano. Lucia put her finger to Stefano's lips. "Sssh, Stefano, it will fit, you will see, let's take it down and try it."

4: EVERY DOG HAS ITS DAY

Stefano took the case and they left the apartment, went out through the hotel doors and turned towards the garage.

"That's strange," said Lucia, 'there is no light over the garage."

Glass crunched under her foot.

"Something is wrong, Stefano!" Fear crept into her voice. "Look over there!"

Stefano looked, and in the darkness, made out the shape of a large furniture van parked beyond the garages. "Stay here, Lucia. I will go and see if Pietro is okay," he said. He moved slowly towards the garage in which the Redhead was parked. He felt the hasp on the door…no padlock!

He knocked softly on the door. "Pietro!" he called, "Are you in there?"

Suddenly the door sprang open, knocking Stefano to the ground. A bright light shone in his eyes and a gruff voice shouted. Stefano, stunned by the force of the door hitting his shoulder, tried to look beyond the bright light, but couldn't make out anything. He groaned as two large arms wrapped around his midriff and lifted him up. He struggled to free himself, but the strength of whoever was lifting him was awesome, like a vice. He kicked out and tried to grasp his attacker, but no avail. His stomach was being squeezed against his backbone as the huge person threw him through the garage door, and he ended up crumpled against the rear bumper of the Redhead.

A foot was placed on his chest and the weight nearly caused Stefano to pass out. He gasped for breath, wheezing and coughing, his body trying to react against the massive pressure. He vaguely heard a stifled scream and saw Lucia being dragged inside the garage, her fingers trying to hold onto the door jamb, her mouth covered by a man's hand, one arm completely around her waist. She struggled violently, but the man succeeded in dragging her inside.

A third man stood in the doorway, looking out. Satisfied no one else was out there, he pulled the door shut and put the inside bar across it. The weight on Stefano's chest increased, and he looked up at his attacker who was shouting at him. Stefano could make no sense of the words. The weight lifted off his chest and tremendous stabs of pain shot through his shoulder and chest. His lungs pulled in air in huge gasps, as he tried to pull himself to a sitting position to see what was going on.

Stefano grimaced in horror as he saw Pietro lying naked on the concrete floor in front of the Redhead. His face was swollen beyond recognition, his back and sides were covered in ugly red welts, and under his head was a pool of blood. He was either dead or unconscious, as he made no movement. Stefano looked up at his attacker. The man above him was very fat, a brute of a man, bulging in all directions out of the filthy grey overalls that he wore. At least 350 pounds, thought Stefano. The man's arms were like a gorilla's and his neck veins bulged as he again stepped on Stefano, this time on his stomach. The weight caused Stefano to wretch and the vomit flew in all directions.

A black nylon stocking was pulled over the man's head, resulting in grotesque facial features squashed under the nylon.

The second man had Lucia in a headlock. As she tried to struggle free, she bit his arm. He uttered a loud cry and shook Lucia violently, tightening his grip around her neck. The third man who was not much larger than a midget, and dressed in a cheap black and white pin-striped suit, held a rope and wound it around Lucia's neck, then threaded it through the wooden slats that covered that area of the wall. He mumbled to the man holding Lucia. The man let go of her neck as the midget pulled on the rope and hoisted her up against the wall, the rope tightly around her throat.

Stefano was pulled to his feet by both his attacker and the second man, who punched him hard in the stomach. Stefano bent double. A massive pain shot through his neck as his attacker dealt him a wicked rabbit punch. They lifted Stefano bodily and threw him against the wall. The midget, satisfied that Lucia was well and truly tied to the wooden slats, turned his attention to Stefano, and picking up another length of rope, wound it around Stefano's neck and tied him to the wooden slats in the same manner as Lucia. Stefano tried to kick the midget, but even as he kicked, the second man kneed him viciously in the groin. Stefano's kick still managed to connect and the midget let out a scream and swore loudly.
He wound the rope around the wooden slats and pinned Stefano's legs so he was powerless to move.

Finally the knots were tied and tested and the three thugs surveyed the sorry couple. They spoke very fast. Stefano could not understand everything they said as they spoke in some colloquial slang that he had never heard before. Stefano stared at them. The first two were big and fat, both over six foot, wearing heavy work boots. The midget was obviously the boss, as he was wearing a ridiculous pin-striped suit and platform shoes.

The midget pulled out a rusty looking automatic from his inside pocket and pointed it at Lucia. He moved towards her and spoke quietly. He laughed and the other two laughed, also. Stefano tried to free himself, but as soon as he moved, the largest man kicked him again in the groin. He saw a red haze and then blackness, as he passed out.

When Stefano came to a few minutes later, he turned his head towards Lucia who was on his left. The midget was pulling at Lucia's belt that held her jeans up. "Stop!" pleaded Stefano, as loud as he could. The midget turned and shouted back at him in the strange slang.

"You can have my gold and the car, but only if you leave her alone!", shouted Stefano. All three thugs laughed loudly. The midget turned towards Lucia and spoke a few sentences to her in rapid slang about amore. Stefano heard his intentions and shouted again. "I will get a satchel of gold from the hotel and bring it here if you will let her go … there is much more gold in Zurich, and you can have it all if you just leave her alone."

The midget muttered, "Get the gold from the hotel, bring it here and don't call the police. We will take the car and both of you to Zurich, and there you will give us all of the gold and we will let you go."

"He is lying. Stefano, he will kill us both once he has the gold. Don't do it Stefano!" Lucia cried.

"I have no choice…set me free and I will get the gold I have in the hotel safe," said Stefano to the midget.

The midget picked up a crowbar from the bench and put the end against Lucia's stomach and pushed. Lucia screamed and one of the men slapped her hard across the face

The midget whispered, "Go now, you have five minutes. If you call the police or don't come back within five minutes, we will take her with us and kill her."

Stefano said, "Si Signore," to the midget and nodded his head rapidly, trying to indicate that he would do whatever they wanted.

The fat thug untied the rope holding Stefano to the wooden slats. The midget picked up a rag, spat on it and rubbed it up and down Stefano's face. "Vada," he said, "Cinque minuutia, no polizi, no caribinerra, Capisce?" he shouted at Stefano.

"Capisce," said Stefano. The first big thug took the bar off of the door and pushed Stefano towards it. Stefano halted and called out over his shoulder in English, "Lucia, I will bring Sheba back with the gold, when I call your name, tell Sheba to attack as loud as you can!" Stefano didn't know if Lucia had understood, but he never got a second chance.

The big man pushed him viciously through the door, pointing at his watch, "Cinque minuutia! Vada!"

Stefano was now on the outside and the door closed behind him. Stefano trembled violently. He was free and his precious Lucia was trapped in there with three crazy men. Panicked, Stefano staggered blindly towards the hotel, his mind racing. He reached the main door and burst into the foyer, running straight into a well-dressed elderly couple who were on their way out. The elderly man let out a stream of Italian curses. Stefano apologized profusely, "Mi Scusi!" he blurted out as he rushed past them. The couple looked at him as if he was a maniac and he realized he must look a terrible sight.

He continued running and reached the front desk. "Where is Signore Constanetti? It is an emergency!"

The man behind the desk said, "He is in his office, Signore, but he cannot be disturbed, can I help you?"

"Yes, I am Stefano Gapucci. I need you to get my leather satchel out of the safe! Hurry man, it is a matter of life and death! Capisce?"

"Si, Signore," said the clerk, "I will do it now." The clerk was flustered. "First can I see some identification, Signore Gapucci?"

"I have no time, get the satchel and put it on a baggage cart, then call the police, tell them to bring guns!" shouted Stefano.

Now the clerk was really flustered. "But Signore, I need to see some identification."

At that moment, Luigi appeared. Stefano saw him and said, "Thank God!"

Luigi said, "What has happened Stefano, have you had an accident? Where is my daughter, Lucia?"

Stefano grasped Luigi's arm and pulled him to the end of the registration desk where the clerk could not overhear. "Luigi, your daughter is a hostage in the garage. Three violent thugs are in there now. They want the gold in the safe and they want more gold from my bank in Zurich! They gave me five minutes to get the gold from the safe, or they will take Lucia and the car and kill her after they get away. They said if I get the gold, then they will let her go, but I don't believe them!"

Luigi turned white in the face, then bright red, comprehending what Stefano had just told him. "We must storm the garage and rescue her, save her at any cost. Why are you not there fighting for her life? Are you a gutless coward?"

Stefano groaned, "Luigi, I have a plan, not a brilliant plan, but a plan, nevertheless!"

"Tell me your plan," said Luigi.

"First get the clerk to get the gold from the safe and put it on a baggage cart so I can wheel it to the garage fast! Second, I need the wolf, Sheba. I have told Lucia to shout "Attack!" when I return and call her name. With luck, Sheba can give me a chance to rescue Lucia. It is a small chance but the only one I can think of. Third, you must call the police, tell them there are three thugs in the garage, two have filthy grey overalls and stocking masks, the third is a midget, dressed in a cheap black and white pin striped suit. They have violently beaten Pietro, Lucia and myself and one has a Luger pistol along with a crowbar! They will stop at nothing to get what they want; they are crazy, violent killers! Now, where is the wolf? Tell me, I am wasting time, they are molesting Lucia even as I speak!" As Stefano gasped all this out, Luigi's mind was working feverishly to think how he could help Stefano rescue Lucia.

"I have a gun." he said. "You must take it and shoot each one of them."

Luigi motioned to the clerk to open the door of the safe. When it was open, he unlocked a safe deposit box with his key and took out a cloth bundle. He opened the bundle and gave the black oily gun to Stefano. It was a short-nosed Smith and Wesson .38 revolver. "It has five rounds, make each one count!" said Luigi. "Stefano, you must save my daughter!" Luigi pointed to the black leather satchel inside the safe and shouted to the astonished clerk, "Get that satchel and put it on a baggage cart, take it out the front and wait for Stefano! Hurry, man!"

"Si, Signore Luigi!" said the clerk, trembling. He went to the satchel and lifting it by the handles carried it out of the safe as fast as he could, then fetched a baggage cart, put the satchel on it and ran towards the front door. Stefano watched, his mind trying to calculate how much time he had left.

"Where is the wolf? Take me to it now, Luigi! It is our only hope to end this madness and violence!"

"Come!" said Luigi, as he turned towards the rear of the hotel and began running. Stefano followed him. They reached a door near Lucia's apartment and Luigi banged on it. Immediately, a loud howling was heard and the door was opened by a neat little Italian woman, obviously the mother of the two little boys who were hanging onto her skirts and staring up at Luigi and Stefano.

"Quick, Teresa! Get Sheba and bring her here, get her lead, too! Quickly!
Please!"

"Mama Mia, Luigi! What is the matter? You look ill, what has happened?"

"No time to explain, Teresa, I will tell you later, just get Sheba. Now! Then lock your door and keep your boys inside after we have gone. There are criminals in the garage area!" said Luigi in a strained voice.

Teresa moved fast and brought Sheba to the door, the chain and lead already around Sheba's thick, furry neck. Stefano grabbed the lead from Teresa and started to run up the hall towards the main entrance. He shouted over his shoulder, "Luigi! Call the police! Hurry!"

Luigi followed Stefano who ran across the lobby. By now, a crowd of people had gathered, having heard the commotion and shouting from inside the restaurant.

Stefano shouted, "Mi Scusi! Mi Scusi!" and burst through them, with Sheba following. Stefano crashed through the doors and took hold of the baggage trolley from the clerk. "Go inside and lock the doors! Don't let anyone in or out till the police come! Do it, man!" Stefano was gulping for air; his chest still felt crushed, not fully recovered from the tremendous weight it had endured.

He turned the baggage trolley towards the garage area and started to run, nearly tripping over on the lead as the wolf overtook him, in what it thought was a run around the hotel grounds. Stefano recovered his balance and raced towards the garage door. He realized he was clutching the revolver, and he slowed and tried to cock it, but the pull on the leash by the wolf prevented him.

"Stop! Sheba!" he cried aloud. The wolf stopped abruptly and Stefano ran right into her. He managed to stop and using both hands, cocked the revolver. He moved forward again until he was outside the door to the garage. Stefano put the cocked gun in his waistband, bent down and removed Sheba's chain from around her neck as silently as he could. He laid it on the ground away from the door. He whispered to the wolf, "Warn! Sheba!"

The big silver wolf went into its menacing position, haunches down, its fur raised, its chest touching the ground. She began to let out a low growl and her eyes glittered brightly in the thin sliver of light that shone through a gap in the door. Stefano put his fingers to his lips. "Ssh! Sheba! Ssh!" The wolf cut her growl instantly, as if she understood.

Stefano stood up and took a deep breath, his aching chest reminding him of the violent people behind that door. He pulled the baggage trolley in front of Sheba and banged on the door. It opened a crack and the big fat thug looked out at Stefano and the trolley, then up and down the garage parking area to see if anyone else was there. He saw no one, and satisfied, his eyes dropped to the satchel sitting on the trolley. He made a sneering noise and opened the door wider, his eyes now watching Stefano to see if he had a weapon. Again satisfied, he opened the door so wide it hit the edge of the trolley which let out a loud metallic ringing sound, as the door rebounded off of it.

Stefano looked inside the garage, his eyes taking in the terrible scene. His mind froze in horror. Lucia was still tied to the wooden slats, but now she had been pulled down much lower.

Stefano moved forward towards Lucia, as the first thug moved to block his path. Stefano yelled, "Lucia!" as loud as he could.

Lucia half sobbed, half cried out, "Attack! Sheba, Attack!" The cry was stifled as the midget put his left hand over Lucia's mouth and screamed at her to be quiet.

The wolf lunged upwards and forwards, knocking both Stefano and the first thug to the ground, her 150-pound body flew through the air. Even as he fell, Stefano saw the massive wolf, jaws wide open, flying straight towards the midget. The second thug saw the wolf and raised the Luger. He pressed the trigger point blank at the wolf's stomach even as it was in the air. The gun clicked, but no bullet came out. The midget turned and saw the wolf leaping at him, just as the wolf ploughed into him. Her jaws clamped down on his exposed throat and bright red blood spurted high in the air as Sheba's teeth sunk into the midget's jugular vein. A terrible crunching sound was heard as the wolf, still in mid-air, bit deep into the midget's neck bones. The midget, covered in his own blood, hit the concrete floor with a loud smack and the back of his head cracked like an egg.

The second thug reacted quickly. He advanced towards the wolf and struck her hard on the back with the Luger. Sheba winced in pain and ripped her jaws loose from the now dead midget, then did an amazing sideways leap, followed by a complete turnaround in mid-air. With jaws open again, she bit deep into the face of the second thug, who tried to fight her off, his arms flailing to no avail. With killer instincts aroused, and the smell and taste of fresh blood, Sheba attacked in a frenzy. She bit deeper into the face of the second thug, her paws scratching wildly at his chest and belly. The wolf's massive teeth caught in the thug's eye sockets and he screamed in terror. Then her sheer weight pulled the big man down and she continued to rip his face off.

While this was happening, Stefano tried to get to his feet. He made it to his knees and frantically tried to get the revolver out of his waistband, but the third thug, big though he was, was quicker, and managed to get to his feet before Stefano could remove the revolver. Realizing that he had Stefano at his mercy, the man lashed out a ferocious kick with his heavy boot that smashed into Stefano like a sledgehammer. He fell backwards, lost his balance, and landed with his legs trapped behind him, totally out of breath, his side aching from the vicious kick. The thug picked up the crowbar and lifted it high in the air, preparing to swing it at Stefano's skull.

The sound of the 12 bore shotgun blast was incredibly loud in the confines of the garage. The huge thug was lifted up in the air and flew over Stefano's head as the force of the twin barrels blew a hole the size of a dinner plate in his back. He ended up slumped against the garage door, crumpled in a heap.

Stefano lifted his head and gazed wearily at the scene. Sheba was still gnawing on the second thug's head, her jaws covered in bright red fresh blood and bits of bone and hair. Stefano focused his eyes and looked to his right and saw a bruised and naked Pietro in a sitting position in the far corner, the 12 bore shotgun still smoking as he held the stock close to his chest, his fingers still squeezing both triggers.

Stefano vomited, his whole body shook as a long stream of liquid poured out of his mouth onto the concrete floor, splattering his trouser legs. He retched again and again, his nose blocked up as the vomit forced its way into his breathing passages. Finally, his stomach empty, Stefano rolled over away from the vomit and, pushing his hands hard against the floor, tried to get up. But his muscles would not take the weight and he started to shake violently again, the pain in his side nearly causing him to pass out. He made a superhuman effort and this time made it to his knees, his head bent, vomit still dripping from his nose and mouth. He was unable to see because the force of his vomiting had made his eyes water badly.

He tried again to get to his feet, and with knees shaking, finally stood up and slowly turned in Lucia's direction, or where he thought she was. He banged into the wall and realized he was somehow going in the wrong direction. He wiped his face with the tail of his shirt that was sticking out of his trousers. Now he could see a little better and he turned away from the wall.

He saw Lucia, her head lolling to one side, still tied to the wooden slats. For one awful moment he thought she was dead, but even as he watched, he could see her chest was heaving, barely able to breathe because the weight of her body caused the rope around her neck to cut off the air. Stefano staggered over to her, treading warily behind Sheba who was still engrossed in gnawing on the thug's head. Stefano nearly made it to Lucia, but just as he was about to get close, his legs failed him and he fell on top of the wolf who gave out a loud yelp of surprise and turned on Stefano, her jaws wide open, ready to attack.

"Sheba, no Sheba," Stefano whispered, his speech slurred. "Don't bite me, please." The wolf, her neck fur covered in blood, stared at Stefano, trying to determine if he was friend or enemy. She growled nervously, unsure of the situation. Stefano forced himself to get up again, praying that Sheba would not attack him. He turned towards Lucia and started to undo the rope holding her to the wooden slats. Lucia moaned and lifted her head, and her eyes met Stefano's. Stefano smiled and Lucia smiled wearily back at him. She tried to hold out her arms, but the rope was still tight around her. Stefano tried again to undo the knots in the oily rope. He loosened the first knot and pulled frantically at the second knot until it too came loose, he then unwound the rope from around Lucia, first from her neck, then from her arms and legs.

As he pulled the rope free from her, she fell forward and collapsed in his arms. He lowered her gently to the ground, cradling her head in his arms, saying, "Thank God, you are alive, my sweet." He kissed the top of her head gently. Stefano felt Sheba's hot breath on the back, then felt the strangest thing. The wolf was licking the side of his face very slowly and very carefully in long sweeps of her tongue. It was as if she knew that Stefano was helping Lucia, not hurting her.

Sirens wailed in the distance. Stefano looked down at Lucia. He tore off a clean part of his shirt tail and softly patted her face to remove some of the grime and wetness from her face where the blood from the thug's jugular vein had spurted over her.

Stefano felt a tap on his shoulder and turned around to see Pietro, his face a mass of bruises, looking at him. "Pietro, my friend, you saved our lives, he would have killed us all with that crowbar."

"Signorina Lucia, is she alive?" asked Pietro through his smashed lips.

Stefano leaned his head against Lucia's chest and heard the beating of her heart. He nodded. "Yes, Pietro, she is still alive, thanks to you and Sheba."

Pietro cried out, "Thank God, Thank God, she is alive, I thought she had died when she collapsed on top of you."

"No, Pietro, she passed out because the rope was pulling on her throat and the weight of her body stopped the air…but see, she breathes." The two men looked down at Lucia, as her chest rose and fell ever so faintly.

Pietro began to cry, huge sobs coming from deep within him, his shoulders shaking uncontrollably. Stefano put his arm around Pietro's shoulders.

"It's okay, Pietro, they can't hurt us anymore," he said softly.

Pietro sobbed again, tears fell from his eyes onto Lucia's face. "I cry because I am so happy Signorina Lucia is still alive," he managed to say through his bloody lips.

Stefano heard a noise by the door. He looked up and saw a double-barreled shotgun poke out from behind the door. He prayed silently that it was not more thugs coming to join up with the other ones.

A face appeared from behind the door and Stefano relaxed when he saw it was Luigi. He held the shotgun very tightly, scanning the garage from wall to wall; his face showed terrible concern when he saw Stefano and Pietro kneeling over Lucia, Pietro still sobbing loudly. "Lucia! My Lucia!" cried Luigi. He ran towards them, stepping over the two dead thugs. "Is she dead? Is my precious little Lucia dead?" He looked at Stefano and Pietro, then he looked down at Lucia.

"Luigi, she is alive, she is going to be all right. She is unconscious because she was tied up and the rope around her neck cut off her air, but she is breathing now, I promise you," said Stefano. "Sheba and Pietro saved us from these vicious bastards. Sheba attacked two of them, and when the third one tried to kill me with a crowbar, Pietro came to and shot him."

Luigi looked around at the three dead thugs and saw Sheba, her fur and jowls all covered in blood. He lifted both arms and called to her to come to him. Sheba got up and came towards him. Luigi put his arms around the wolf's neck and hugged her to him, ignoring the fresh blood, which soaked his clothes. The wolf responded by licking his ear and purring like a cat. Luigi let go of Sheba and gave Pietro a hug, kissing him once on each side of his battered face.

"Grazie, Pietro, Grazie tanto," said Luigi.

"It was nothing," said Pietro. "Signore Stefano and Sheba saved Signorina Lucia's life and my life, too."

Luigi turned to Stefano and hugged him also, then turned his attention to his daughter. "How could anyone want to hurt my little Lucia?" He lifted her head and cradled her against him, kissing her softly on the forehead.

The wail of the sirens got louder outside, then abruptly stopped. The garage door was pulled wide open and six policemen in bulletproof face masks carrying bulletproof shields appeared, each one carrying a machine pistol. One of them shouted for the criminals to come out with their hands in the air.

Luigi shouted back, "Come in! The thugs are dead! We need an ambulance!" Two policeman advanced warily into the garage, back to back, nearly tripping over the first thug sprawled against the door. The other four waited nervously, in case it was a trick. The two policemen inside spotted Luigi and the little group and came over; looking around carefully, their eyes taking in the carnage, their minds shocked in disbelief.

Sheba growled a warning and the policemen halted, obviously scared by the sight of the wolf's jowls covered in blood. One asked Luigi if he should shoot the wolf. "No," said Luigi, "the wolf saved the life of my daughter. It did what it was trained to do; attack on command, trained by your police dog handler in Maranello."

The policeman lowered his machine pistol and checked the three men to make sure they were dead. It was an easy task, as one had a large hole in his back, the other two had only partial faces, their bloody skulls exposed from the wolf's tremendously strong fangs. The policemen checked under and inside the Testarossa. Finally satisfied, they called to the others outside that all was clear. The ambulance team, a man and a young woman dressed in dark blue tunics with a red cross on each sleeve, entered the garage carrying a chrome stretcher. The young woman took one look at the second thug's devoured face and promptly fainted. Two of the policemen carried her outside and tried to revive her. Another ambulance crew arrived and started to examine Lucia. Then they lifted her onto a stretcher and hurriedly carried her out to the ambulance, where one took note of her blood pressure and pulse and another placed an oxygen mask over her face to help her breathe.

Luigi stood up. "Come, Stefano and Pietro, you must go in the ambulance to the hospital." He took their arms as if to help them. Pietro stood shakily to his feet, his face was in a terrible state and he had obviously lost a lot of blood. Two more ambulance attendants came in and helped him out of the garage.

Stefano stood up and Sheba came forward and licked his hand. The pain in Stefano's side came in waves, and when he tried to walk, the pain in his groin reminded him what had happened. He took one step, leaning heavily on Luigi, and all of a sudden, the pain came faster and faster. He tried to keep walking, but his legs wouldn't move. He fell to the ground and lost consciousness. Luigi tried to break his fall, but was unable to react in time, and Stefano smashed his head against the concrete floor. Luigi cursed himself, realizing that he should not have let Stefano walk. He called to the ambulance attendants who came back, fetched a stretcher and put Stefano on it with great care.

One of the attendants felt the bulge in Stefano's waistband when they tried to straighten his leg, he withdrew the cocked revolver very carefully and gave it to one of the policeman, who uncocked it, opened the chamber and took out the five bullets. Satisfied it was now empty, he put it in a plastic bag.

"It's my revolver. I gave it to him when he came for the wolf. He never had a chance to use it," said Luigi. The policeman gave Luigi the gun.

The ambulance attendants loaded Stefano into the ambulance. Luigi put the gun in his pocket, and looked inside the ambulance. Lucia lay on a stretcher on one side. Pietro lay on the other side. The ambulance attendants pushed Stefano's stretcher into the middle and prepared to close the doors.

"Wait for a second, please," said Luigi. He went back into the garage where Sheba was standing, with policemen all around, making notes of the positions of the dead men. A large flesh wound on Sheba's back, where the second thug had hit her with the Luger, was evident.

"Well, Sheba, you did your duty, you are one corraagioso lupo," he said. "A very brave wolf indeed. Come, Sheba!" he called. Sheba followed him out of the garage. Chef Mazetti was on the edge of the crowd that had gathered. "Signore Mazetti, please take care of Sheba. Call the vet and ask him to tend to the nasty wound on her back. I am off to the hospital with Lucia."

"Si, Signore Luigi, I will look after her." The Chef called Sheba, who looked first at Luigi, then at the Chef. Luigi nodded and said, "Go Sheba!" The big wolf turned and followed Chef Mazetti through the crowd towards the hotel. The crowd parted to let them through, murmuring their thoughts, wondering what had happened in the garage.

Luigi went to the ambulance crew and asked to go with them. They opened the back door and Luigi sat next to Lucia. Holding her hand, he started to cry. While one of the ambulance attendants tended to Pietro and Stefano, the other started the engine and turned the ambulance around to point to the road, then drove slowly through the crowd that had gathered. Once clear, he turned on the siren, accelerated and started the trip towards Maranello hospital, ten miles away.

The ambulance siren wailed as the three patients lay on their stretchers, unaware of the speed at which they traveled. They were all unconscious. Pietro had been given a shot of morphine to ease his pain and had passed out.

5: HOSPITALS CAN BE PEACEFUL PLACES

Stefano was dreaming he was in a cage full of gorillas; they each took turns picking him up and throwing him against the bars. He would slide down the bars and crumple into a heap, his body sore in every place. Then the next gorilla, even larger than the first, would pick him up and throw him against the bars again. The gorillas stood in a line, each waiting their turn. When each one threw him, it would slink back to the end of the line to do it again. The dream had gone on and on, each time his body nerves screamed in pain, but no one came to help him. He was alone in the cage, with no way out.

He woke from the dream, still not sure if it had been real. He opened his eyes slowly, afraid that he would see the gorillas leering at him. He looked around, no gorillas, then he turned his head slightly and saw something out of focus looming over him. He cringed and tried to move his body away from the figure.

A voice came out of the silence. He thought he knew the voice, but could not connect it to a person. The voice was soothing, telling him everything was all right. Stefano blinked his eyes and tried hard to focus, but the looming image remained fuzzy, unclear, its voice fading, then sometimes clear, repeating the words in the soothing tone. Stefano tried to sit up, but could not; someone was pressing on his shoulders, softly urging him not to move. Stefano drifted into unconsciousness again and the gorillas returned to throw him against the bars.

When Stefano awoke again, this time he could see the image clearer. It was Lucia, and she spoke his name softly. He tried to smile up at her, to say he loved her, but even though he opened his mouth and said the words, no sound came out. He looked at Lucia and again spoke the words, "I love you." This time he heard his voice, very faintly. His vision became clearer until he could see Lucia smiling, her face angelic. "Ciao, Stefano, Come Sta?" she said.

"Bene Grazie," he replied.

"Tiamo, Stefano," said Lucia.

Stefano dug deep in his memory and suddenly remembered what 'Tiamo' meant. "I love you, too," he replied.

Lucia took hold of his hand and gently squeezed it. He felt better; the gorillas were gone, banished for eternity. He tried to sit up, and this time, his body moved as commanded. He looked around and realized he was in a hospital ward, blue curtains surrounded his cubicle. Lucia leaned forward and brushed her lips against his. Stefano strained to kiss her back, but she was gone and he was falling, falling from a great height into a deep void.

Many hours later, he awoke for the third time. This time, he felt better, more normal. His vision was clear and the pain in his side was less evident He looked for Lucia and there she was, still holding his hand. She bent forward to kiss him and this time he lifted both his arms and hugged her to him. They stayed like that for a long time, neither of them speaking. The nurse came in with the doctor who seemed very happy. Maybe they are lovers, Stefano thought.

The doctor said, "Signore Stefano, you are a very lucky man."

"I know," said Stefano, hugging Lucia closer to him.

"You are on the road to recovery. For a while there, I thought we had lost you. That bump on your head gave you a concussion and you went into a coma."

Stefano was startled. "A coma! How long was I in a coma?"

"Two days, Signore," said the doctor.

Stefano could not believe his ears. "Two days!" he said aloud.

Lucia spoke, "I was very worried about you, I prayed and prayed and it worked." She smiled. "God is good to us, Stefano."

"How are you, Lucia?" asked Stefano.

"I'm fine, I have wiped the whole incident out of my mind. I am over it now," replied Lucia, still smiling, happy to see Stefano recovered.

"Thank God!" said Stefano. "Now I must get up, we must go on our holiday. Will you still come with me, Lucia?"

"On one condition," said Lucia very solemnly.

"Name it," said Stefano. "Anything, my love, anything you want."

"That we get married as soon as you are fully recovered," said Lucia.

Stefano cried aloud, "Yes! Yes! My love, I am fully recovered now that you have said that you will marry me!" He grinned and jokingly flexed his arm muscles and tried to get out of the hospital bed. His legs did not move and he groaned. "What is wrong with my legs? They don't move when I tell them too."

"I think you need a few more days in bed before you try to walk," said the doctor. "You have three cracked ribs, one of which is pushed hard against your spinal cord, causing severe bruising and inflammation. The x-ray shows your spinal cord is intact, but the swelling is causing pressure on the spine and preventing you from moving your legs. In a few days, I think it will subside, but you must stay in bed and rest to allow it to heal."

Stefano remembered the kick to his side, the excruciating pain, the shotgun blast and Pietro's face. "Pietro? How is Pietro? Where is he?" asked Stefano, watching the doctor's face carefully, not wanting to hear bad news.

"I am okay, Signore Stefano!" a voice said from behind the curtain. The nurse pulled the curtain back so Stefano could see Pietro lying in the bed next to him, his face swollen with blue and yellow bruises and one eyelid puffed up to an enormous size, contorting his features.

"Pietro, my friend, how are you feeling?" asked Stefano.

"Pretty good, considering," replied Pietro, his words slightly slurred as his lips were, like his eyelid, puffed up and swollen. "They thought they had killed me, but they were wrong, Signore. I lay on the floor for a long time unable to move, just listening, but I knew I had to help you, so finally, I said to myself, "Come on Pietro, get up and help Signorina Lucia and Signore Stefano."

"You certainly helped us, Pietro, you saved our lives. That madman with the crowbar would have killed us all," said Stefano. "Grazie, Pietro!"

Lucia reached over and took Pietro's hand, "Grazie tanto, Pietro, you are a very brave young man." Pietro smiled and squeezed Lucia's hand very gently. "Thank you, Signorina. To see you sitting there alive is all the thanks I need."

"All right, gentlemen, now you must have your medicine, and rest. Tomorrow I will look in on you again. Until then, Nurse Bianca will look after you...rest well." The doctor turned and left with the nurse.

"I will stay with you, Stefano, I don't want to leave," said Lucia.

Stefano looked closely at Lucia. The rings under her eyes showed she had not slept much in the past two days.

"Lucia, my darling, you must go home now and get some sleep and come back tomorrow. I will dream of you until then," said Stefano.

Lucia shook her head, but Stefano pleaded with her to have a taxi drive her home, and sleep until she no longer felt tired. "I love you deeply, Lucia, do this for me, please."

Lucia nodded, "All right, but I'll come back as soon as I wake up, agreed?"

"Agreed," said Stefano. Lucia leaned over and kissed him tenderly on the lips. "Then we get married for sure!" said Stefano.

Lucia smiled. "Okay, I go now. Ciao, Stefano, Ciao, Pietro!"

Stefano watched Lucia leave, his heart beating very fast as he thought how lucky he was to have found her. She turned at the door and blew him a kiss, then disappeared. Stefano, sad now that she was gone, lay back on his pillow, reliving the image of Lucia blowing him a kiss.

The nurse came back and gave Stefano and Pietro each a tiny cup of medicine to sip; they finished the medicine and promptly fell into a deep sleep. Stefano dreamt of Lucia, and Pietro dreamt of driving the Testarossa. Stefano and Pietro rested in the hospital for the next two days. In their waking moments they got to know each other very well, talking about all the subjects under the sun. They talked about Pietro's childhood. Pietro told Stefano about his "Mama and Poppa" as he called them, and his five sisters, whom he loved more than anything in the world. Three of them were married now with young children who doted on Pietro.

Pietro told about the little house he'd been born in, with its tiny rooms and the noise of six children growing up together; how they were very religious and went to church every morning at six, rain or shine; how he had been an altar boy serving mass since the age of seven, and how his sisters would make fun of him in his cassock, chiding him for once falling asleep with the whole congregation watching.

Pietro told of his life on the mountain, tending his father's sheep and goats; how he would feed the newborn lambs with milk from a baby bottle in the Springtime, when the ewes got tired of feeding the lambs with their milk. He told Stefano about the Christmas Nativity scenes he had acted in, once as Joseph, and once as one of the three wise men. Both times he had forgotten his lines, causing the audience of parents and children to roar with laughter. Stefano asked him if he had a girlfriend, and when Pietro became instantly silent and sad, Stefano wished he had never asked.

Later that day, Pietro told Stefano why he had become sad.

When he was growing up, in school he always sat next to a little fair haired girl named Serenella, and they became very good friends, always laughing and joking. When Pietro became older, his feelings changed and he began to feel physically drawn towards Serenella, wanting to hug her. Many nights he dreamt of kissing her on the lips. One summer day on the mountain, they were lying in thick grass looking up at the blue sky talking nonsense as usual, when Pietro summoned all of his courage and told Serenella of his feelings.

Serenella told Pietro that she also had warm feelings about him.

They spent the next two hours kissing and cuddling, each swearing to the other that one day, when they were grown up and school was behind them, they would marry and have a little farm of their own. After that day, they became inseparable. Every chance they got they spent kissing and cuddling and generally having fun. Pietro told Stefano how everyone in his village knew that he and Serenella were sweethearts, and when school was finished and they turned sixteen, friends asked them when they were getting married. Pietro would say, "Soon," and Serenella would say, "Maybe tomorrow," jokingly, but half serious.

Pietro got on well with Serenella's parents, spending as much time in their house as he did in his own. He took a job with the local butcher, and Serenella worked in a little dress shop, learning to make dresses. They saved their meager incomes until they had enough to rent a cottage on the outskirts of the village. They knew they could not live together unless they were married, or the priest would never allow them in the church again. So Pietro planned to go to Serenella's parents and ask for her hand in marriage. He remembered that day very well. He awoke in the morning and told his mother and father what he was going to do that day. They had known it would come to that sometime and knowing how much the couple loved and respected each other, they had nothing to say but good wishes.

Pietro dressed in his best clothes, his shoes shined and his hair combed, and off he went to Serenella's house. On arrival, the house was quieter than normal, and even as Pietro knocked softly on the front door, he sensed something was wrong. Serenella's mother answered the door, her eyes red from crying. When Pietro asked her what was the matter, she told him how the night before Serenella had told her that she felt really tired and had gone to bed early. The next morning, she and Serenella's father had risen, washed and dressed to get ready to go to Mass. She had tapped on Serenella's door, wondering why she was not up eating breakfast and making jokes like she usually did. No answer came from Serenella. The mother, very concerned now, went in and found Serenella perspiring heavily, her breath coming unevenly, her face, normally a rosy complexion, was now dull and lusterless. The mother tried to talk to Serenella to find out what was wrong, but Serenella could not answer. Her temperature was high and her eyes were glazed and sunken. The mother sent her husband for the doctor who came immediately. When he saw Serenella, he, too, became concerned. By then her lips were blue. He asked Serenella's father to call an ambulance. While they waited for the ambulance, the doctor took Serenella's pulse and temperature, and the results shook him to the core. He told the parents that he suspected that her heart was not working properly. He did not know what could have caused such a fast illness to overtake Serenella, as she had never been a sickly child. Only the day before he had seen her in the street and said, "Good-day," remarking to himself how full of life she looked. The ambulance came and took

Serenella and the doctor to the hospital. Her father, out of his mind with worry, went with them, leaving his wife to look after the younger children.

"They have been gone three hours now and I am afraid, Pietro," said Serenella's mother. Pietro told Stefano how he had run to the railway station and took a taxi to the hospital. How he ran into the emergency department and saw all the activity happening behind the green curtains with nurses running back and forth. He knew instinctively that Serenella was there. He pulled the curtains aside. Serenella was lying deathly pale on the bed. The nurses and doctors told him to wait outside, but Pietro ignored them and went to the side of the bed, calling Serenella's name. She murmured something, opened her eyes and murmured again. Pietro bent over to hear what she was saying. She opened her eyes and whispered, "Pietro, you look so handsome, all dressed up. Let's get married today."

Pietro kissed her blue lips softly, then kneeled beside the bed. "Yes, Serenella, we will get married as soon as you are better."

Serenella smiled at him, then shuddering, she reached for him with her arms and hugged him tight. Pietro thought she was going to be all right; that maybe she would suddenly say, "What am I doing here, Pietro? Take me to our little white cottage and tell me again how much you love me." But instead of that happening, her arms fell back and the tiny glimmer of life left her eyes and she was gone.

With tears rolling down his bruised cheeks, Pietro told Stefano the final piece, how the nurses and doctors had tried to console him and how the priest had arrived to give Serenella the last rites.

Stefano grieved for Pietro's pain, imagining the terrible sorrow Pietro must have felt, losing his childhood sweetheart on the day he was to ask her father for permission to marry her.

Stefano called the nurse, who came and tried to comfort Pietro, thinking he was upset because of his pain, but her attempts caused Pietro to sob even more and the nurse became worried and called the doctor. He came in and prescribed a powerful sleeping tablet that knocked Pietro out within a few minutes.

Stefano lay in his bed, thinking how Pietro had overcome his pain in the garage, grabbed the shotgun from under the Testarossa, and saved all three of them. He continued to think about what might have happened, and as he drifted off to sleep, the last thought he had was that somehow he must repay Pietro for saving Lucia's life. He was sure the crazy thug would have killed them both, if Pietro hadn't shot him first.

The next morning Stefano awoke to find Lucia sitting next to his bed, smiling at him as he opened his eyes. He sat up and kissed her and held her tightly to him, overjoyed to see her, praying that nothing would happen to her, like the terrible tragedy that had happened to Pietro and Serenella.

"Good morning, my love," said Stefano, "Did you get any sleep?"

"I slept well, but I missed you very, very much and I decided to come and see you first thing this morning. How are you feeling?" she asked.

"A lot better," said Stefano. "Today I will try and do some walking and once I can do that we will go and get married and I will look after you and hug you every morning just like this, yes?"

"Yes, my sweetheart, as soon as you are well, I am ready," said Lucia.

Stefano looked across at Pietro who was still sleeping soundly from the pill he had taken the previous night. Stefano told Lucia what had happened to Pietro's love and Lucia burst into tears and cried, hugging Stefano to her as he comforted her.

When Lucia felt better, she told Stefano how she had met Pietro six years ago when he had come to the hotel with his little suitcase, looking for a job. All he had said was that he was from a mountain village, that he was honest and needed a job, and that he would work hard in whatever position they could give him.

Lucia had taken pity on him and fetched her father to interview Pietro with a view to giving him a job. Pietro had told them he had worked for a while for the butcher in his village, but now he wanted to do something different, to work in a hotel and learn the business.

Luigi sensed that Pietro was of good character and hired him to be a bellboy with a small salary. His room and meals were provided by the hotel. Pietro worked hard for six years and had just been recently promoted to be in charge of the bellboys and the valet parking. He had never discussed his village or his past with any of the staff, always changing the subject, if it ever came into the conversation.

"One thing he did say to me after he had worked for about three months at the hotel..." whispered Lucia, checking to see that Pietro was still asleep. "He told me how he came to Maranello and saw the Ferrari factory, with all the young men rushing around in blue overalls, and the bright red cars glistening in the sunshine, all ready for customer pickup or delivery. He went to the personnel office and asked for a job.

However he had chosen a bad day and was told to come back the next week, but he never did. He came straight to the hotel and my father hired him. Then he became interested in valet parking, but he had no driving license. My father said, if he got his license and drove very carefully, he could join the valet team. He passed the driving test with a perfect score and he joined the team. He has done it ever since. He loves to drive, but he doesn't have his own car. I guess he couldn't afford it? I don't know."

Stefano and Lucia looked across at Pietro who lay sleeping peacefully.

"He is a good boy, Lucia. We owe him our lives. It's such a sad story about his love," said Stefano.

Lucia hugged Stefano. "We must think only of the future, not the past. It was too terrible. I don't ever want to think about it again." Stefano silently agreed. He must guard Lucia, so that she would never again be in such a traumatic situation. The two hugged and kissed until the nurse came with food for Stefano, then Lucia left, promising to return bright and early the following morning.

The next morning Stefano felt a lot better; the bruises and swelling on his body were healing. The doctor came and checked him over, pleased with the progress. "Very good," he said, after examining Stefano's front. "Now turn over on your side. Ah! Much better! Today you should be able to try and stand up, and see if you can walk."

The nurse brought a wheelchair and crutches, and Stefano felt confident as he could now feel his legs, which moved on command, at least in the bed. The nurse helped him to sit up and showed him how she wanted him to use the crutches. "One under each shoulder to take your weight, then when I say lift, I want you to push yourself gently and slowly against the crutches and try to stand up. I will help you."

Stefano prepared himself, then on the nurse's count of three, he pushed himself against the floor and hoisted himself up in the air, his body weight resting on his shoulders. The tight elastic bandage wrapped around his ribs felt uncomfortable, but otherwise he felt quite strong. He put out his right leg and transferred some of his weight onto it and pressed down, easing the weight off of his shoulders. Pietro, who was in a more cheerful mood today, watched carefully from the other bed and applauded Stefano's efforts. "Good Stefano, now the left leg!" urged Pietro.

Stefano grinned and swung his left leg out, transferring his weight onto it. The leg took the weight and Stefano's confidence increased. He lifted his right leg again and moved it forward. The pain in his side increased as he put the weight on the right leg, but he tried to ignore it. He took three more paces and the nurse told him to turn around slowly and head back towards the bed. Stefano did as he was bid and made it back to the bed, breathing heavily, his side on fire.

"Very good, Signore, this afternoon we try again, a little further next time. It looks like you may be able to walk without crutches in three or four days, when all of the swelling has gone down."

Stefano leaned back against the bed, slipped off the crutches, and transferred himself to a sitting position on the bed. "At least I am not permanently crippled. It hurt, but I can do it." He was pleased because the night before, he had dreamed that maybe he would never walk again. Now he was immensely relieved and thanked the nurse profusely for helping him.

"It's my job, Signore, just my job," said the nurse, as she took the crutches from him and leaned them against the wall.

Stefano lifted his legs onto the bed and pulled the sheet over himself, happy to snuggle down in the warm bed and dream about Lucia.

The nurse turned to Pietro. "Your turn, Signore, we need to take some more x-rays, now that your bruises have started to heal."

Pietro pulled back his sheets and slid onto the wheelchair, which the nurse held steady for him. Once settled, she put a blanket over his knees and pushed him down the hall to the x-ray room.

"Good luck, Pietro!" called Stefano. Pietro put his hand up in the air with his fingers crossed and gave a short wave. Stefano closed his eyes and fell asleep. He awoke about half an hour later, when he heard Pietro returning. He looked across at Pietro and saw he had a sling on his left arm, but at least no plaster cast.

"Just some damage to my elbow where the bastards stomped on me, no broken bones though, just swollen cartilage, thank God! The rest of me is bruised, big lumps but no major damage." Pietro grinned, his swollen lips looking more normal today. The rest of his face and especially his puffed up eyelid still looked grotesque, but much better than it had looked two days ago.

"Signore Gapucci, you have two visitors to see you. May I fetch them now?" asked the nurse.

"Si, Signora, please ask them to come," said Stefano. The nurse hurried off and a minute later Stefano saw Luigi, the father of his bride-to-be, and Enzo Ferrari, coming down the hospital aisle. Both men were impeccably dressed in tailored suits, Enzo in black and Luigi in a camel colored twill.

"Buon Giorno, Luigi, Buon Giorno, Signore Ferrari," said Stefano.

"Please, call me Enzo, no Signore Ferrari. You are my son-in-law, you know," said Enzo with a twinkle in his eye.

"No, Enzo, I haven't forgotten, good to see you, and you also, Luigi! Allow me to introduce Pietro, the brave man who saved our lives."

Enzo bowed. "My pleasure, Pietro, you are a hero in Maranello. If there is ever anything I can do for you, please let me know."

Pietro was pleased and surprised to hear the great Enzo Ferrari call him by his name. "Signore Ferrari, it is indeed a great honor to meet you, I have read many books and articles about you and your great cars, and I love all of them. But never did I dream that I would one day meet you in person. Oh such an honor!"

Enzo shrugged and replied, "I am happy you also love the Prancing Horse. Maybe you will marry one, too, like our friend Stefano."

"I would if I could, Signore. Maybe I find a cheap one, if such a Ferrari exists, then I would give it all my love and devotion," said Pietro.

Enzo laughed, pleased to hear such compliments about his cars.

"How are you both?" asked Luigi. "I was so worried about you that night."

"We are both getting better, Luigi. Pietro's bruises are on the mend and my ribs are only cracked, not broken, and I managed to walk just now with the aid of crutches. And, in a few days, I won't need them, the doctor says," said Stefano.

"Good, very good," said Luigi.

Enzo nodded. "That is good news, I am so glad you were not hurt any more than you were. Those were vicious thugs — the police chief told me they came from Milan —a gang of villains looking to steal whatever they could. He thinks they may have been at the wedding in the square, saw the Testarossa and the gold, found out where you were staying, and went there to steal both the car and the gold. The police chief also told me that they had all been in prison before, for vicious assault, rape and burglary. Two of them were being sought by the police for the murder of a garage attendant last month, not far from here. You were all very lucky, God was on your side."

"I just came here to find out how you both were, and to thank you both for saving my little Lucia's life. I can never repay you enough, never forget that!" said Luigi sincerely.

"I speak for both of us when we say we were repaid enough that she was not hurt too badly, and that most of all, she is alive and well," said Pietro.

"My words, exactly," said Stefano. "Also, I love her deeply and want to marry her with your permission, Luigi."

Luigi straightened, looking very solemn. "You have my permission, Stefano, Lucia truly loves you, also. She tells me all the time how happy she is when she is with you, so how could I refuse her happiness? I know in my heart, you will look after her."

"Grazie Tanto! Luigi, Grazie!" said Stefano. "I would consider it an honor and a privilege if you, Enzo and Pietro would attend our wedding as soon as we can leave the hospital. I know Lucia wants to marry in the church, perhaps you could ask the priest that married me to the Redhead, if he will marry me to Lucia, Luigi?"

"I will ask him Stefano. Hopefully, he will have no problem. Even though I believe he was very sincere when he married you the first time, I think he will still allow you to marry Lucia even though you are already married in the eyes of God to your Testarossa," said Luigi.

"Now we must go. We wish you both a speedy recovery," said Enzo. "Luigi and I are going to my house to drink cappuccino and talk about old times."

"Arrivederci, Signore Ferrari, Arrivederci, Luigi."

"Enzo, gentlemen, Enzo…no Signore Ferrari," Enzo reminded them. He bowed and turned to leave.

Luigi said, "Thank you again, both of you, for saving my Lucia!"

"Oh, Luigi, how is Sheba?" called Stefano, "For she was our savior as well as Pietro."

"She is well, a bit of a cut on her back, but she does not seem to notice it too much, although she rips the bandage off as soon as we put it on," said Luigi.

"That is good news. Give her a steak for me, Luigi," said Stefano.

"I will, I promise. Arrivederci, gentlemen." Luigi followed Enzo down the hall.

"A great man, Enzo," said Pietro. "It was thrilling to meet him."

"Yes, indeed, a man of few words, but a genius in producing the world's most beautiful, thoroughbred cars," said Stefano.

Lucia came to visit just before lunch with a surprise. The nurse was upset at first, when Lucia brought the huge silver wolf into the ward. She put her hands up in horror at the sight and rattled off in staccato Italian, muttering about hygiene and fleas and the possibility of dog poo dirtying her shining floors. Lucia quieted her down, explaining how Sheba was tame, house-trained and a heroine as well. The nurse relented and allowed them to stay. "Just for a little while only, mind! If the sister comes on the ward and sees that wolf, I will lose my job for sure." Lucia assured her that such a thing would never happen, and the placated nurse went off to her office.

Stefano and Pietro made a great fuss over Sheba who loved the attention, playfully snapping at them as they played with her from their beds. The nurse brought lunch on a trolley and Lucia shared some of Stefano's salad and ate all of his dessert, at which he jokingly protested. Stefano told Lucia that his legs felt much better and that he thought he would be walking on his own, with a cane in, a few days.

Lucia was pleased. She had worried that Stefano's back had been damaged by the beating, but had not said anything on her previous visits. Pietro fed the last of his lunch to Sheba, piece by piece off his fork, and she gobbled it down without even chewing, then curled up on the floor and went to sleep.

Stefano told Lucia how Luigi and Enzo had visited just before she arrived, and that he had asked Luigi for Lucia's hand in marriage and Luigi had said yes.

Lucia's eyes sparkled and she started to talk about the wedding and what she would wear.

"Then we can leave for Rome, like we planned," said Stefano.

"Oh, Stefano, I am so looking forward to it again. Please get better quickly, then we can get married and leave," said Lucia.

Pietro was silent, knowing that this conversation was private to Lucia and Stefano and that he should not really be listening, but he had no choice.

Lucia noticed Pietro's quietness and turned to him. "Pietro, would you like to come with us on our trip?" she asked.

Pietro started to protest. "No! It is your honeymoon, you don't want me around."

Stefano said, "No, Pietro, I think it would be good for you, although how we could fit you into the Redhead, I am not sure."

"Pietro can drive my Alfa if he wants and Sheba could travel with him!" said Lucia.

"Now that sounds like a great idea!" said Stefano. "What do you say to that, Pietro?"

Pietro was overjoyed with the idea, but he still had misgivings about intruding into their honeymoon and voiced his opinions.

Lucia and Stefano wouldn't take no for an answer. They would talk to Luigi about giving Pietro time off to come with them, they were sure he would agree it was a grand idea. "We will drive the cars together, eat at the same cafes along the way and see Rome all three together, with Sheba along for fun and also to protect Lucia," said Stefano, looking at Pietro to get his approval.

Pietro looked at Lucia and then at Stefano. They nodded and he saw they were sincere. He lay back in his bed and stared at the ceiling. One minute passed and he said nothing. After another minute had passed, he sat up again, "If you really would like me to come and you are sure it will be no trouble, then I would be really and truly happy to come with you, and I will take extra care of Signorina Lucia's Alfa Romeo Spider Veloce!"

"On one condition," said Lucia looking very solemn.

Pietro looked at her, "Whatever you say, Signorina."

"Just call us Lucia and Stefano, no Signore or Signorina. You are our friend and we are your friends for life."

Emotion welled up inside him, and Pietro felt unbelievably happy. He started to cry. He gulped and said, "Thank you, Lucia and Stefano, I am proud to be your friend."

"That's settled then," said Stefano. "Now all we need to do is to get better and get going." Lucia smiled and got up to leave. Sheba jumped, ran around and gave a low howl, causing the nurse to come back and start shushing her, although she had only howled the once.

Lucia gave Stefano a juicy kiss, said her good-byes and left with Sheba on the leash.

Pietro grinned at Stefano. "Oh Signore! I am so happy!"

Stefano, stern-faced, said, "Pietro, you can't come if you keep calling me Signore."

Pietro grinned again. "Sorry, I forget!"

The two young men laughed together and Stefano told Pietro of the route he had planned with Lucia, and that he might even drive for Enzo in the 24-hour Le Mans Grand Prix, if he was well enough. At hearing this, Pietro whooped for joy. The nurse came back and scolded them both like children. They were both solemn while she ranted and raved, but they also saw she was not really serious, so when she had finished, they laughed aloud and the nurse, seeing she had made no impression on them whatsoever, threw her hands in the air and smiled. What could she say to these two naughty men? She decided to forgive them, because she knew that laughter was a good sign that both their minds and their bodies were recovering from their traumatic ordeal.

The nurse asked Stefano and Pietro if they would like to sit on the verandah in the sunshine. They didn't need to be asked twice. Pietro helped Stefano into the wheelchair and pushed it behind the nurse, who had tried to get Pietro to use a wheelchair also. But he had assured her that his legs were strong with only some bad bruising on the knees and shins where the thugs had kicked him to the floor with their heavy boots, before kicking him in the head once he was down. At hearing this terrible tale, she had shuddered and given in and now, with Pietro pushing Stefano, the nurse showed them to the verandah at the end of the hall.

The double doors were open and quite a few patients sat in the sturdy white plastic chairs, taking in the view and the sunshine. Some of them had visitors who had brought small children with them to see a relative or friend in the hospital. The verandah was a cleverly designed, large wooden deck about 80 feet by100 feet, shaded in part by silver birch trees that had been left in place when the deck was built around them.

Pietro set the brake on Stefano's wheelchair, found himself an empty chair and pulled it up next to Stefano. He settled in the chair and felt the warm sun on his face. "Oh, this is good, Stefano, this is the best!" He leaned his head back and enjoyed the sun's warmth.

Stefano was practicing lifting each leg slowly, about four inches from the step of the wheelchair. Then he would put that leg down and repeat the process with the other leg, the way the nurse had explained to him earlier. The two young men sat there, Stefano doing his exercises, and Pietro, his eyes closed, taking in the sunshine. Sounds of the children playing were tranquil, no violence was present, and Stefano and Pietro relaxed, letting the sun play its healing warmth on their battered faces.

The nurse, Bianca, had taken a liking to Stefano and Pietro and bought them out a small tray with two cups of cappuccino, which she set down on the table.

"Thank you Signora. Just what we needed," said Stefano.

She smiled and left them to their sojourn in the sun. They drank their cappuccino and sat silently for a long time until the other patients and visitors had left, and the sun started to slide down over the distant mountains. The deepening shadows of the birch trees indicated that dusk would come soon. The nurse came out and told then to come in before the evening air turned cold. Pietro rose and stretched, then helped Stefano get the wheelchair brake off and back they went, into the hospital. This time Stefano refused to be pushed, wanting to wheel himself. Pietro agreed and they went through the double doors and back down the long corridor to their ward.

Nurse Bianca was waiting for them and had put crisp, clean white sheets on their beds. She asked Stefano to try walking with the crutches again before getting into bed. Pietro held the wheelchair steady while the nurse helped Stefano position the crutches. Stefano boldly gripped the crutches tight and swung himself off of the wheelchair into a standing position, nearly overbalancing. But once standing up, he ignored the pain in his side and took five or six steps without any problem. He stopped, gritted his teeth and eased first the left crutch, then the right crutch to a slanting position, so that all of his weight was on his legs and the crutches were just being used for balance.

The nurse said, "No, Signore, it is too early to try and walk without the crutches. You may experience tremendous pain and your spine may react and you will fall down."

Stefano was adamant. "Please, Signora, I will try just a few steps."

Nurse Bianca was unhappy and motioned Pietro to stand on Stefano's left while she stood on his right, to be prepared to catch him if he fell. Stefano summoned all of his energy, and putting out his right foot, moved it forward and transferred his weight to it. Then he did the same with the left foot. The searing pain hurt like hell in his side, but, having taken one full step, he was determined to take two more. He breathed in deeply and took three full steps, right, left, right and stopped. The pain had not gotten any worse and he felt confident, so shuffling his feet, he slowly turned around and took five steps back to the bed. Turning ever so slowly and using the crutches, he eased himself down until he was sitting on the bed.

The nurse and Pietro were smiling. The nurse shook her head and said, "You crazy man, Signore, that is quite enough for today. You did well, but now you must rest, or you really will damage your spine."

She was stern, but Stefano could see she was pleased at his progress. She took the crutches from him and helped lift his legs onto the bed. She pulled the sheet up around him and said, "Now you sleep until suppertime. You too, Signore Pietro." She turned to cover Pietro who had got into his own bed. They thanked nurse Bianca for letting them enjoy the sunshine and she bustled off, happy, but muttering to herself about heroic young men who did not do as they are told.

"I think she believes she is our mother," said Stefano to Pietro.

Pietro nodded. "She is a good woman, Stefano. She takes care of us; we are very lucky." They lay back on their crisp pillowcases and closed their eyes, not really sleeping, just day-dreaming. Stefano dreamed of Lucia while Pietro dreamed of his lost Serenella.

That evening about 7:30, Stefano had another visitor. He had been thinking about Lucia, when in walked the young girl, Anna Capello from the agency. "Buona Sera, Signore Gapucci," she said.

Stefano sat up in his bed surprised to see her. "Buona Sera, Signorina Capello, it is good to see you."

"I came by to see if you were recovering successfully. I read in the newspaper of your terrible ordeal and wanted to say goodbye before I return to Rome tomorrow."

"That is very kind of you, Signorina. I am feeling much better now, thanks to this hospital and the doctors and nurses who have been so kind. But my friend here, Pietro, he is the one I owe my life to. Without him I would be at the funeral parlor." Stefano turned towards Pietro, but Pietro was fast asleep.

"Pietro," called Stefano. "Wake up, there is someone I want you to meet...wake up now." Pietro grunted and turned over.

"Please don't wake him on my account," said Anna. "He obviously needs the rest."

Pietro heard Anna's voice in his sleep, woke up and opened his eyes. For one moment he thought he was seeing Serenella, as Anna had the same fair hair and complexion. Pietro blinked and looked again.

This time he realized it was not Serenella. How could I think that? he thought. Serenella is in heaven and I am in hospital.

"Pietro, permit me to introduce you to Signorina Anna Capello; she is the young lady who arranged the wedding to my beautiful Redhead."

"Pleased to meet you, Signorina. 1 apologize for staring just then, but I thought you were someone else for a moment, please excuse me," said Pietro, flustered.

"No problem, Pietro, nice to meet you." Anna grimaced as she caught sight of Pietro's right eyelid and the terrible bruises on his face. "Oh my God! What did they do to your face? Those terrible people!" she said, approaching Pietro's bed and looking down at his battered face.

"It is nothing, Signorina. Hopefully soon, my eyelid will go back to normal and I won't look so much like a monster."

"You poor man," said Anna, 'they must have hurt you terribly."

Anna's voice was full of real concern; she had obviously never seen anyone so beaten up before.

"Please, Signorina, it really is nothing. I will soon be better, I hope," said Pietro.

"Such wicked men, I am glad they are dead. Doing such terrible damage to you like that is unforgivable!"

Pietro was unsure how to respond. "You are very kind, Signorina, to have concern for me, but poor Stefano suffered even more. He can barely walk on crutches!"

Anna turned to Stefano. "Is this true? Can you not walk? Oh! Dear God! What sort of beasts were these men?"

164

"Anna, please don't worry about us, we will recover. It looks and sounds worse than what it is, we are all three — Lucia, Pietro and myself — very, very lucky it didn't end up much worse. We are getting over it and soon as we get out of the hospital, Lucia and I are getting married. Then the three of us are taking off for a holiday to Rome, then to Naples, Genoa, Switzerland and France.

Anna was speechless. She stood next to Stefano's bed, her eyebrows raised, taking in what Stefano had just told her.

"That's fantastic! I am very happy for you, Stefano. It was only a few days ago that you married your Redhead, as you call her, and now you marry Lucia. Oh! That is great news. Where are you getting married?"

"Lucia's father, Luigi, is arranging it this time. In a church I am sure!"

Then Stefano had a thought. "Why don't you stay here one or two more days and come to the wedding? Then you can travel to Rome with us, Pietro won't mind the company, I am sure. What do you say, Anna?"

Stefano turned to Pietro before Anna could answer. "How about it, Pietro? That won't be a problem will it? Sheba can sit in the back of the Alfa and Anna can sit in the front seat with you."

Pietro nodded. "Certainly, it is okay with me, if Anna would like to come with me in the Alfa." Pietro was a little hesitant, as he felt somehow he was betraying his Serenella, but he hoped she would understand he was doing a favor for his new found friends.

"Well, I was going by Autobus tomorrow, but I would like to come to your wedding, Stefano, and I would be happy to travel to Rome in the Alfa with Pietro. It will be fun. Is Sheba the wolf they wrote about in the newspaper?" Anna asked.

Stefano laughed. "Sheba is a real wolf, but you will love her when you see her and she will love you, I am sure."

"Great! I will call ahead to Rome and tell them I will return two days later than planned. 1 have to tell my boss or he will worry that something has happened to me."

Anna was thrilled. She smiled at Pietro, who was a little embarrassed, but shyly smiled in return. Anna went and sat on Pietro's bed and looked down at him. Her body up close, in the blue dress, reminded Pietro of Serenella. Anna even had the same alluring fresh smell as Serenella and the way she smiled was very similar. Pietro was confused; maybe she really was Serenella come back to life.

"You must get better soon, Pietro, or I will have to drive and that could be dangerous," she joked.

"I will, Signorina, I promise."

Anna laughed. "Forget the Signorina, I am Anna and you are Pietro." She put out her hand and Pietro took it in his and squeezed it gently. Her hand was soft and the nails were pink like Serenella's used to be.

He held onto Anna's hand, again thinking about Serenella, forgetting where he was, remembering the days when he would take Serenella's hand and they would go for long walks in the mountains.

Pietro gulped. I must not keep comparing all the girls I meet to Serenella, or I will go crazy, he thought sadly. His mind came back to the present and he realized he was still holding Anna's hand.

"Mi Scusi, Signorina, I am very pleased to meet you," he said.

"And I am very pleased to meet you, Pietro, I am sure we will be good friends." Pietro released her hand with reluctance. It had felt good to hold her hand, and he would have liked to hold it longer, but he knew it would seem odd.

Anna got up. "I must go. I will call Lucia and find out the time and the place of the wedding and see you both there. Arrivederci, Stefano! Arrivederci, Pietro!" As she spoke she smiled at Pietro and he found himself blushing.

"Arrivederci, Anna," he said, then added, "please take care."

"Ciao! Anna," said Stefano. "See you in church!"

Anna left and Stefano turned to Pietro. "Hey, Pietro, now we can have more fun with four of us off to Rome!"

Pietro nodded. I hope so, he thought, I hope Serenella will not mind. Inwardly, Pietro was concerned. Maybe he should have said no about driving Anna to Rome, but he didn't want to go back on his word. Besides, Anna was very pleasant, and she probably had a husband or a lover back in Rome, so she wouldn't be interested in Pietro anyway. He lay back on his pillow remembering how Anna had reminded him so much of Serenella. He closed his eyes and hoped his face would get better soon, so he wouldn't look quite so weird the next time he met Anna.

Stefano and Pietro slept soundly that night. Stefano dreamt of Lucia driving the Redhead, its engine howling and running at tremendous speed on a winding mountain road. Lucia drove very fast into the turns, changing the gears down at just the optimum moment, the powerful 12-cylinder engine revving to 7,000 rpm as it decelerated, the huge tyres gripping the road until it seemed impossible to not spin out.

Then, just as she came out of the turn, Lucia floored the accelerator and Stefano felt a huge hand pushing from behind as the Redhead shot like a bullet into the straight at over 120 mph until the next turn came up. Then Lucia decelerated again and repeated the process, her hands on the steering wheel, manipulating the wide car with such confidence it thrilled Stefano to the core.

Pietro dreamt of Serenella lying next to him on the hillside; he hugged her to him and kissed her neck, her smell driving him wild, wanting to rip off all her clothes and cuddle her naked body in the long green grass. He turned his head, and over Serenella's shoulder, he saw Anna beckoning to him. But he didn't want to leave Serenella, and the image of Anna faded into a blue sky dotted with little white puffy clouds, billowing in the gentle breeze.

Morning came and Stefano rolled over, alert and not sleepy any longer. He felt better this morning; the pain in his side was much less than yesterday. The ward was quiet and dawn was approaching. As he looked out of the window on the other side of the ward he could just make out the image of the trees. Even as he watched, the tree images became clearer and clearer as the sun started to appear in the sky, to turn the dark into light.

Stefano looked across at Pietro and studied his features. Why, he couldn't be more than 21 or 22, thought Stefano. Quite a baby face, now that the lumps have receded, although his eyelid and lips are still swollen. Stefano imagined the terrible grief that the boy had lived through when his sweetheart had died.

He thought about the night of terror in the garage and how Pietro had sat against the wall, his fingers gripping the smoking shotgun, his eyes glazed and seemingly unseeing. If he hadn't had the strength and courage to pull that trigger, I would be food for worms, in a wooden box under six feet of soil by now, thought Stefano. And God only knows what might have happened to Lucia! He wondered how he could repay Pietro. He thought and thought and then an idea came to him, like a light bulb switched on deep inside his brain. Of course! It would be easy, he would talk to Luigi and get his opinion. Luigi would know if it were a good idea or not.

Stefano felt relieved that he had thought of a way of repaying this young man who had lost his love. Deciding to try and get up and watch the sunrise from the verandah, he pushed the bedclothes back and swung first one leg, then the other, to the floor. With his toes he found the hospital slippers and slipped his feet into them. Very slowly and carefully, he put his weight onto his legs and lifted his body from the bed until he was standing erect. Then he reached out for the crutches leaning against the wall and put them in place under his armpits. He took a few steps to see how bad the pain in his side would get, but miraculously, today he felt only a little pain, nothing like the knife-like pain he had felt yesterday. He slowly made his way down the corridor towards the verandah.

Everyone else was still fast asleep. It must be around 5:30, he thought. He reached the double doors and turned the key in the lock to open them. Stefano made his way slowly out onto the verandah. He spied a chair and shuffled towards it. Reaching the chair safely, he managed to slide into it without hurting his underarms with the crutches. He lay the crutches down on the floor, leaned back in the chair, and gazed up at the sky.

On one side of the sky he could see stars twinkling high above him, against the inky black void of space. On the other side, the first rays of sunshine were peeping over the top of the mountains. Here the sky was turning a brilliant blue, laced with orange light from the sun. He sat silently in the chair, watching the light from the sun increase as more rays came flowing across millions of miles, to warm the earth, and provide light that gives both warmth and life to all plants and living creatures. He sat and watched the miracle of sunrise and enjoyed being alive. He mentally thanked God and Pietro, for being able to enjoy it, and Lucia for being his love.

About an hour had gone by when Stefano heard the click of the door opening and looked around to see the doctor approaching.

"Buon Giorno, Signore," said the doctor, "How are you feeling today?"

"Good, thank you, I feel very well. Hardly any pain, only some when I walk with the crutches, but that is getting less; at least, much less than yesterday," replied Stefano.

The doctor had a cup of coffee with him and offered it to Stefano. "I will go and get another for myself and then we can chat if you like."

"Thank you, doctor, the coffee is most welcome," said Stefano. The doctor went off and soon came back with another cup of coffee. He pulled up a chair and sat down beside Stefano.

"Every morning at this time I come out here to see this beautiful view and drink my coffee. It makes the rest of the day so much easier to deal with; it is so pleasant here."

Stefano told the doctor how he planned to get married the next day. The doctor smiled. "I am sure then that you would like to leave the hospital today?"

"If you think I have recovered enough, I would like that very much," said Stefano.

"Well, I will examine you later this morning, and if there are no major problems, I don't see why you can't leave after lunch, if you feel up to it," said the doctor.

"That would make me very, very happy, doctor. Much as I like your hospital and your nurses, I would like to prepare a little bit for my wedding."

"Maybe a walking stick would be easier for you than the crutches. If you feel strong enough, we can try that at the same time as your examination."

"What about my friend, Pietro? Is he well enough to leave today, also?"

"Maybe…I will let you know for sure after I have examined you both. That will be around 11 o'clock, as I have to first operate on a patient this morning."

Stefano felt relieved it was not he who was going to be operated on. He sat back and drank the cup of delicious coffee, pleased that he had met up with the doctor.

After a few minutes, Nurse Bianca came out and joined them. She sat at the same table, bidding good morning to Stefano and the doctor. She seemed very quiet and made no attempt at conversation, not her normal commandeering self, just gazing at the view.

Stefano had the feeling that the nurse and the doctor were more than close work associates, so he decided to go back to the ward and leave the two to their privacy. He was a bit stiff when he started to get up on the crutches, but the nurse and doctor noticed, and they both helped him to get started. Once on his feet with the crutches supporting him, Stefano felt in control again and headed for the door.

The doctor walked ahead and opened it for him and they both bid him a pleasant, "Arrivederci." Stefano thanked them and turned to watch them walk back to the table. He saw the nurse slip her hand into the doctor's. They sat close together, talking away, obviously in love. Stefano smiled, noting the glow on Nurse Bianca's face as she looked at the doctor.

He went back to the ward and saw that Pietro was still sleeping, so he took his wallet from the night table drawer and went back down the hallway to little lounge where there was a pay phone. Stefano dialed the hotel. At the sound of the pip, pip, pip, he inserted a 100 lire coin.

The hotel front desk clerk said, "Hotel Bella Montagna, how may I help you?"

Stefano said, "La Signorina Lucia, per piacere."

"Attenda," said the clerk. A few seconds went by and Lucia came on the phone, "Pronto, chi parla?" asked Lucia.

"Hello Lucia darling, it's me, Stefano!"

"Hello Stefano, I just woke up and was thinking about you. How are you feeling?" said Lucia in a sleepy voice.

"Full of love for you, my sweetheart…I miss you and wanted to call and say hello," said Stefano.

"I miss you too, my love. When can you leave the hospital? Is it today?"

"I just spoke to the doctor; he thinks it should be around midday today. He says he must examine me first, but that is just a formality."

"Oh Fantastico! Tonight I will be your nurse, I will look after you," said Lucia. 'Then we can get married tomorrow as we planned. The church is all booked and the priest has agreed to marry us. I am so thrilled, I can't wait, my love."

"Marvelous," sighed Stefano. "I can't wait to kiss the bride! Lucia, listen now, I have an idea, but I may need help from your father and Enzo to pull it off." Stefano told Lucia of his idea to repay Pietro and Lucia laughed.

"That is a great idea! Pietro will be thrilled. I will talk to father and he will sort out the details with Enzo. You are a good, unselfish man, Stefano, and I love you even more for thinking of Pietro."

"Good," said Stefano. "I will call you later after the doctor has examined us, and let you know the verdict. Then you can come and pick me up in the Redhead if you like."

"Yes, Stefano, I can't wait, call me soon."

"Can you bring some clothes for me from my closet and some for Pietro, too?"

"Yes, darling, just call me as soon as you can. I love you," said Lucia. She blew kisses into the phone and hung up.

Stefano put the phone back in its cradle and smiled to himself. He was overjoyed to hear Lucia say she loved him. He wanted to yell aloud, but he restrained himself, remembering that most of the patients were still asleep.

Stefano sat down on the sofa in the lounge and wondered what Luigi and Enzo would think about his plan for Pietro.

Back at the hotel, Lucia went straight to her father's room and knocked on the door.

"Chi è?" said Luigi.

"Lucia, Papa."

"Avanti, Lucia," said Luigi.

Lucia went in and saw that her father was already dressed in a dark blue suit with tails and a vivid red bow tie.

"How do you like it, Lucia? I thought it would be good to wear to your wedding tomorrow?"

"You look very handsome, Papa, I only wish Mama could be there tomorrow also," said Lucia wistfully.

"I know my child, I do, too, but God has taken her to heaven and I am sure she will be looking proudly down at you tomorrow in the church."

Lucia recovered herself. "Father, Stefano called from the hospital just now, he has a beautiful idea to repay Pietro for his courage and suffering. Stefano feels it is all his fault that the horrible thing happened and he wants to make it up to Pietro." Lucia explained Stefano's idea to Luigi.

He nodded. "It is good, Pietro will be very surprised. I, too, have thought about Pietro and I have decided I will also give him a little present, but now I will call Enzo and meet with him to discuss how we can make this idea of Stefano's happen. Off you go, my girl, get dressed and I will see you later." Luigi kissed Lucia on the forehead. "Never forget, even though you marry Stefano tomorrow, you are still my little girl and I love you very, very much."

"I know, Papa, and I love you, too, ever so much."

Luigi called Enzo and explained what Lucia had told him of Stefano's idea. Enzo laughed and thought it a great idea. "Maybe I modify it a little. Listen, Luigi, give me an hour to set it up and I will come to your hotel in two hours time and we can talk about it over a cup of Cappuccino, What do you say?"

Luigi agreed, "Ciao, Enzo!"

"Ciao, Luigi, see you soon!"

Eleven o'clock came and went and Stefano became anxious that maybe the doctor would not be able to make his rounds today due to some emergency. He talked to Nurse Bianca who assured him the doctor would arrive within the next hour and that it was rare for him to be more than a half an hour behind schedule, as he was really efficient in planning his day. Stefano lay in his bed waiting, occasionally chatting to Pietro who was also anxious to hear the doctor's decision for him and Stefano.

Around 12 o'clock, the doctor walked in very calmly, surrounded by three junior doctors who were still in the studying phase of their profession, spending most of their waking hours in the emergency room downstairs, and gaining knowledge on the vast subject of medicine. The daily round, accompanying the head doctor, was a welcome escape from the trauma of the emergency room for these interns.

Doctor Firenzo came up to Pietro's bed and scanned his medical chart, then passed it to one of the interns, a tall academic young man dressed in a white coat that was a little short in the arms. The doctor asked for the intern's opinion on the status of the patient. The intern hastily read the chart and replied in very fast Italian that the blood pressure, temperature and physical state of the patient appeared to have stabilized and improved significantly from that time three days ago when he was brought in. Also, no fractures were present. The intern recommended that an external examination be held at once, together with a physical movement test of all limbs, and if nothing was observed to be out of order, that a patch be applied to cover the left eye which was still swollen, and then the patient could be discharged. Having said all this, the intern returned the chart to the head doctor and awaited his comments.

The head doctor was impressed. "A good solid analysis from such a brief look at the chart. Let's proceed with the examination." He selected another intern who was standing quietly, nearly asleep on her feet. She had been awake for almost 24 hours downstairs in the emergency room, with only two catnaps of 20 minutes apiece to keep her going. She was very thin and looked pale and undernourished, but she snapped awake and rattled off four or five questions to Pietro.

"Have you had any new pains? Any vomiting? Any loose bowel movements? Any strange giddy feelings? Any headaches?"

Pietro replied, "No" to all her questions, so the intern requested he get out of bed and remove his gown for examination.

Pietro did as she bid and stood by the side of the bed while each of the four interns examined him from head to foot, looking carefully at the now yellow bruises on his body, listening to his heart and lungs through a stethoscope, and peering into his ears and eyes with different devices. The young intern put her hand under Pietro's scrotum and asked him to cough, which he did obligingly, she then asked him to put on his robe and walk away from them in a straight line, one foot directly in front of the other. Again, Pietro did as he was bid and performed flawlessly. Lastly, the intern asked him to walk back normally and stop in front of them. He did this and when he stopped, she asked him to put out his left hand and touch his nose with his index finger and then do the same with his right hand. Pietro completed these tests and the intern made a few notes on her writing pad and passed the pad to the doctor.

The head doctor, again impressed, nodded. "Good, Signorina Petrelli, now let us confer in private for a few moments and we will announce our decision, whether or not we can discharge the young Signore." The head doctor and the interns filed off to the nearby nurse's office to discuss Pietro's status.

Meanwhile, Stefano had carefully observed the thorough examination they had made of Pietro and was seriously concerned that he could only do half of what Pietro had done, due to the injury to his back. But he was determined to be discharged, so he told himself to relax, be cheerful and do his damnedest to convince them that he, too, was fit enough to leave the hospital.

The doctor and interns came back, and with a smile, Doctor Firenzo announced his verdict. "Signore Pietro, I am pleased to say that we consider you well enough to be discharged, providing you limit your exertions to the minimum for at least a week and that you change the dressing on your eye once a day. Do you agree to this?"

Pietro grinned and agreed, then, smiling, he thanked the doctor and each intern separately and also gave Nurse Bianca a kiss on both cheeks. "Grazie, Signora Bianca for taking such good care of me."

Nurse Bianca flushed red, then gave Pietro two eye patches, one black and the other white, plus a small package of cream and a bandage. "You can wear white with your black suit and black with your white suit, Signore. It was a pleasure to look after you, but you cannot leave until after lunch, which is in half an hour!"

Pietro smiled, sat on the bed and looked across at Stefano. "Well, friend, now it is your turn. Good luck!"

Doctor Firenzo repeated the same process for Stefano as was done for Pietro. He asked one of the interns to analyze Stefano's chart and make an assessment. This time the intern was a short young man with long, unkempt hair that seemed to grow sideways from his head, presenting a very unusual appearance. The intern took the chart and read the information on it, then looked at Stefano.

"Blood pressure normal, no fever, still a considerable amount of pain in the spinal area and the groin, three cracked ribs which are causing inflammation around the spinal area, but no infection. The concussion appears to have improved, no headaches, no blurred vision, unable to walk without the aid of crutches." The intern recommended an examination of Stefano. No mention of discharge was made.

Next the intern asked Stefano to remove all of his clothes and lie back on the bed. Stefano did as requested, straining a bit when trying to remove his pajamas, but succeeding eventually. He lay still on the bed while the intern prodded him and asked if it hurt when he did so. Stefano winced a few times, but responded that it did not hurt.

After removing the bandage around Stefano's ribs, the intern worked his way down and prodded one of the cracked ribs, causing Stefano to clench his teeth with the pain. Each rib was given the same treatment and Stefano was surprised at the pain. He was asked to spread his legs and when the intern pushed down gently on his groin, Stefano nearly passed out with pain, barely managing to stifle a scream.

Stefano's legs, except for one kneecap, seemed intact; bruised but not painful. The intern asked him to turn over and lie on his stomach. With some difficulty, Stefano did so, but the effort was considerable.

The head doctor told the intern to please stand aside so that he could examine the inflammation around Stefano's spine. The skin was red and swollen over an inch higher than normal, for about six inches down his back. The doctor gently felt the inflamed area.

"There seems to be only local bruising...no tendons are involved. This should go down within a few more days. One moment, please, Signore, while I confer with my staff. Please put your clothes on and wait here."

Again the three interns went into the nurse's office. They were there for over ten minutes and Stefano came to the sad conclusion that they were not going to allow him to leave yet. Finally, the doctor and interns returned.

"I'm sorry, Signore, but the prognosis is that you must stay at least three more days in the hospital until both the spinal inflammation and the tendon inflammation around your groin area have improved," the doctor advised.

Stefano was visibly upset. He explained to the doctor that he was getting married the following morning, and leaving Maranello for Rome immediately after the wedding. He told them he was sure he would be all right, as Lucia and Pietro would be with him and he would make every attempt to rest his back whenever possible.

"Very well, Signore, we understand. I can let you leave on the condition that you visit my colleague in Rome when you arrive, and if he thinks the inflammation is improving, then he will allow you to continue on your honeymoon. But if the swelling increases, and the pain of course, then you must stay in his clinic until you recover. Is that agreed?"

"Certainly, Doctor. Thank you very much for all you have done for me. I am very grateful," Stefano said.

The doctor proceeded to replace the bandage carefully around Stefano's ribs. "One thing that may help — as I suggested this morning — you may wish to try two walking sticks rather than the crutches, as the weight of your upper body on the crutches is actually not good for the particular injury you have." He turned to the nurse. "Nurse Bianca, please fetch two walking sticks and let the Signore try them."

Nurse Bianca went off and soon returned with two strong looking wooden walking sticks with curved hand rests and black rubber tips on the ends. Stefano took the walking sticks, thanked the nurse, and with one in each hand, pressed down on them and lifted himself to his feet. He was a bit shaky at first, but once he felt he had control of his balance, was able to walk a few steps with less pain than with the crutches.

"These are much better than the crutches, Doctor," Stefano said with a weak smile on his face.

"Good," the doctor replied. "You may then leave at the same time as your friend, but if the pain increases please call me. I will think about what I can give you to relieve it. Right now, I would prefer not to give you any painkillers, as you may get overconfident and do some serious damage without realizing it. The pain is there to remind you to take it very easy over the next few days."

"Grazie, Doctor."

"Enjoy your wedding and enjoy your life with your future bride," said the doctor. He shook hands with Stefano and Pietro and continued on his rounds. The three interns solemnly followed him up the aisle of the ward to the next patient.

Stefano and Pietro hugged each other.

"It is a grand moment, Pietro. I shall go and call Lucia and tell her to pick us up as soon as she can." Stefano went off down the corridor on his new walking sticks, happy to give Lucia good news. He had been pleasantly surprised that the doctor had allowed him to leave. That's what getting married does for you! thought Stefano.

He telephoned Lucia and she was ecstatic. "I can't wait to see you, Stefano my love. Please be careful now until I come and get you. By the way, Enzo and my father are locked away in father's office. I shall tell them the good news and we will come and pick you up in about an hour. Love you! Love you!" cried Lucia.

"I love you, too, Lucia, with all my heart. Drive carefully!"

"I will, my love. See you soon," Lucia said, and hung up the phone.

Stefano and Pietro were having lunch, while eagerly awaiting the arrival of Lucia. Pietro was concerned that if she turned up in the Testarossa, he might have to take a taxi, and his wallet was back at the hotel, but he didn't say anything to Stefano. Stefano munched on his salad and chatted to Pietro about his plans for the trip; that he would call the hotels he had booked earlier, explain why he never made it on the previous dates and rebook the same hotels for two rooms as before: one for Stefano and Lucia, and one for Pietro.

Pietro listened and smiled, inwardly thinking about the financing. He didn't have a lot of money to spend on fancy hotels. Maybe I could get an advance from Luigi, he thought, I need to find out from Stefano how much I will need for two to four weeks' vacation. He imagined that it would be too much money and far more than he could raise. Pietro decided to wait till that evening and ask Stefano then, rather than now. The last thing he wanted was for Stefano to offer him a loan, which would take him a long, long time to repay!

While Pietro was thinking about this serious problem, Stefano carried on about what great fun it would be to travel together. Pietro nodded and smiled, but felt embarrassed. Maybe he should ask Stefano now. He summoned his courage and started to interrupt Stefano when Lucia walked in, accompanied by Enzo and Luigi. Pietro groaned; the moment was lost. He must find out tonight, when Stefano was on his own.

Lucia gave Stefano a hug and a long kiss on the lips, then gave Pietro a hug and a kiss on both cheeks. She opened a paper bag she was carrying and spread the clothing on the beds: a blue short-sleeved shirt, blue trousers, blue socks and casual shoes for Stefano; and a red shirt, black trousers, black socks and shoes for Pietro. Out of her pocket she pulled two pairs of white underpants.

"I don't know which is which, but I guess they'll fit." She blushed.

Stefano and Pietro gave out loud whoops and went off to dress behind a curtain, saying friendly hello's to Luigi and Enzo who stood smiling, not saying anything, just watching the two young men acting like children at a party.

When Stefano and Pietro stepped out from behind the curtain, both looked resplendent in their colorful clothes. Pietro had on his black eye patch, which made him look a bit like a pirate, but it suited him and he was happy to cover his still swollen eyelid.

Stefano leaned on his walking sticks and smiled at Lucia. "Shall we depart?" he asked.

"Have you got everything now?" Lucia asked. "Was there anything in the drawers or cupboards?" Stefano shook his head and Pietro did the same. "Let's go then," Lucia said, and the five of them went down the corridor.

"We must say one more goodbye to Nurse Bianca," said Stefano. They found her in her little office, working on some patient charts.

Stefano stepped in the doorway and knocked politely. Nurse Bianca looked up. Seeing Stefano all dressed up, she exclaimed, "Oh, Signore, you are so handsome in your street clothes!" She looked past Stefano to see Pietro. "And you, too, Signore, you look marvelous with that black patch, and so handsome."

"Nurse Bianca, we would like to say thank you again for all you have done for us and for all the work we have caused you in the past four days," Stefano said. Nurse Bianca stood up and Stefano slowly moved forward on his walking sticks, put all his weight on one stick, propped the other one against the desk and gave Nurse Bianca an awkward hug. The nurse squeezed him back.

"Look after your lovely fiancée and yourself, Signore. Not too much walking now." She shook her finger at him, a twinkle in her eye. Stefano thanked her again and moved out of the way so that Pietro could give Nurse Bianca a final hug.

"You, Signore, you are so young...stay out of trouble!" she said. Pietro started to protest that he always tried to stay out of trouble, but stopped in mid-sentence when he realized she was just teasing him. "You two have been my best patients in a long time. I will miss you. Now, off you go!" She shooed them out of her office and watched them all walk down the corridor; Stefano going quite fast considering the pain she knew he still felt.

Stefano and Pietro turned and waved as they reached the end of the corridor. Nurse Bianca waved back, then went into her office, shut the door and started to cry. "I hate good-byes," she said aloud.

After a while she composed herself, pulled out a white linen handkerchief, blew her nose, checked her makeup in a little mirror on the wall and went back to working on her charts.

6: THE MONDIAL

The group of five reached the main exit and Luigi held the door open for Lucia, and for Stefano to get through with his two walking sticks. The sun shone warmly and the sudden transition from hospital lighting to bright sunshine caused Stefano and Pietro to blink and adjust their eyes.

"Oh, what joy to be back in the world again," said Pietro. "We are very lucky, my friend." He slapped Stefano playfully on the back and grinned.

Stefano asked Lucia where they were parked. Lucia pointed to the car park beyond some small bushes. Stefano looked and smiled. He could see his beautiful redhead glistening in the sun, its exotic design even more stunning than he remembered.

As they walked across to the car park, Lucia put her arm around Stefano and he stopped and kissed her on the cheek. "My love," he said, softly whispering in her ear. He sniffed the delicate scent of perfume and couldn't resist one more kiss. They walked on to where the Testarossa sat: its fiery red paint and sleek low profile making it look as if it were already in motion — running at 180 mph — even though it was standing still.

Next to the Redhead, Luigi's car was parked, looking sedate and so different in body shape, but still it was easy to see it was a well kept car, fitting for a man of Luigi's stature. Pietro was more interested in the car next to Luigi's. It was bright red, the same brilliant red of the Testarossa, but this was a convertible, with the softest fawn leather hood cover sitting atop the rear.

"Bella! Bella!" shouted Pietro, "a Mondial Quattrovalve Cabriolet…beautiful!" He walked around the car taking in its exquisite design with the large air vents just behind the doors. "This car is positively gorgeous! I have always loved the Testarossa with its twelve cylinders, but always in my mind I think of the Mondial as the ultimate convertible…at least in my mind. Can I sit in it for a second? Is it yours, Enzo?"

"For a short time, yes, Pietro, it is mine. Please sit in it. I love to see such pleasure from one so young who can appreciate such a car."

Pietro opened the door, climbed into the car and sat in awe. The seats surround me like a leather glove, such a design, such a car! he thought. He put his hands on the steering wheel with its embossed black and yellow insignia of the prancing horse. "Vrooo-om!" he shouted. He looked up at Enzo, who was smiling down at him. "Oh, excuse me, Signore! I got carried away!" He started to get out of the car, but Enzo put both hands up in the air to restrain him.

"No, Pietro, stay in the car, it suits you…one so young and full of life!" Pietro sat still. Enzo took a set of keys from his pocket and passed them to Pietro, who looked long at the keys and asked, "Would you like me drive the great Enzo Ferrari?" There was great emotion in his voice.

"No, Pietro, we want you to drive yourself. Luigi, Stefano and I collaborated to repay you for your bravery the other night. We want to repay you for many reasons; one, because Luigi can hold and hug his only daughter today; two, because you certainly saved Stefano from either death or severe disfigurement and disability. And finally, on a more minor note, you saved the reputation of Ferrari by not allowing those thugs to gain notorious publicity and escape with the car, which would have sent tremors of concern to all Ferrari owners that the same might happen to them!

"Take the keys and enjoy your very own Ferrari. Use it, enjoy it, and don't feel embarrassed at accepting it. It comes with sincere respect from Stefano, Luigi, myself and, of course, Signorina Lucia!"

Pietro was astounded, his heart pounded in his chest, his brain comprehending what Enzo had just said. "No, Signore, No. I cannot accept. I only did what had to be done in the circumstances. Anyone in the same situation would have done what I did. There was no choice. I certainly don't deserve such a gift, and although my heart says yes, my head says no."

"Pietro, you suffered a lot of hurt also. Please accept this gift as our repayment. Please!" said Stefano.

Pietro looked from Stefano to Enzo, his mind in a whirl. The thought of owning his own Mondial excited him to the core of his soul. He sat still and thought about what Enzo and Stefano had just said to him. Here was a poor farmer's son who was being offered the gift of a lifetime, his dream come true. Even then, he thought about the high costs, the insurance, the services, the petrol and the holiday costs. Also the hotel rooms and food. His mind swayed first to say yes; then to be honest, and say no. In his position at the hotel he could just afford a good bicycle, some clothes and his precious collection of books on Ferrari. He decided to be honest, as was his nature.

"I would love to accept this beautiful piece of machinery…this important piece of Italian history, but I am but a working man, still in the job of Head Bellboy and Head of Valet Parking. I will have many years to save before I could pay for the insurance and service, and to be quite honest, Stefano, I could not come with you on holiday with this car or Lucia's beautiful Alfa, as I have very little money. I was going to tell you tonight, but the time must be now."

Pietro hung his head. There, it is done, he thought. Now I must get out of this perfect car and travel back with Luigi to the real world, the hotel and my job, which I love and know how to do.

Pietro again went to open the door of the Mondial, but this time Luigi stepped forward and put his hands on the door preventing Pietro's exit.

"My Boy, we thought of that already. I had decided two days ago to promote you to Assistant Manager of the hotel to replace Lucia."

Pietro gulped and a tear rolled down his cheek. What a kind gentleman Luigi is, he thought. Pietro began to thank him, but Enzo interrupted.

"In the glovebox are four documents; one is full insurance in your name for as long as you live, covered by the Ferrari Factory's insurance, all legal and signed by our insurance agent. The second one is a certificate of title showing myself as the original owner, transferring the title of ownership to you. Third, there is a special service certificate made out in your name and signed by me, for you to bring the car to any Ferrari service location for all service and repair for as long as you live.

It says all service repair costs are to be charged to the Ferrari Factory at no cost to you."

Pietro heard what Enzo had said, but could not reply. Such a warm day, his head was spinning.

Enzo continued: "I will leave Stefano and Lucia to tell you what is the fourth document."

Stefano looked at Lucia. "Come on, Lucia, it was your idea…tell Pietro." He winked at Lucia who smiled, her beautiful white teeth showing so well against her soft red lips.

"Pietro, the fourth document is an envelope containing a Maranello Bank passbook with quite a large amount of Italian lire deposited; more than enough for you to pay for this holiday, the petrol, the hotel rooms, your food and new clothes…and enough for you to buy a small house whenever the time comes and still leave a lot left over. Please think of it as a gift from Stefano and myself. It's the very least we can do, and you deserve every penny of it. You are a decent, brave young man with a long, happy life ahead of you. Even without the car and the money, people speak highly of you and they like you. The staff and guests and tradesmen like you, so don't change because of the money, just carry on being the same young Pietro that everybody knows and loves."

After such a long speech, Lucia stepped forward, nudged her father politely out of the way, moved closer to Pietro, put her arms around him and kissed him on both cheeks. Then she held him as he sobbed, the tears running down both cheeks now.

He tried to speak but his emotion was too deep and words failed him. He slowly and carefully opened the door of the Mondial and got out, careful not to bump into Lucia who had stepped back a little. Pietro stood in the sunshine; a young man who had just been given his ultimate dream.

"I am so full of joy. My little Serenella would be happy, too, I know!" Pietro hugged Lucia tightly. "Grazie, Signora Lucia, Grazie tanto!" He turned to Luigi. "Grazie, Signor Luigi, you are too, too kind. I will do my best for you as Assistant Manager, I promise." He put out his hand and shook Luigi's hand very firmly, then he turned to Enzo. "Signor Enzo, you have made me the happiest man in all of the world. I cannot thank you enough. I will love the Mondial as much as I loved my little Serenella. I am most proud that you have owned this car also, that it is not just a Ferrari Mondial Quattrovalve, but it was Signor Enzo Ferrari's own Mondial Quattrovalve. Such an honor for me, such an honor!"

He shook hands with Enzo who had finally managed to get Pietro to take the keys. Pietro looked at the keys and at the leather tag with the insignia of the prancing horse embossed in black and yellow. Pietro looked again at the Mondial, still unable to believe he could be so lucky. Finally, he went across to Stefano, looked him deeply in the eyes, trying to see into Stefano's soul.

"Thank you, my friend," he said softly. "I know all of this was your idea. Thank you from the bottom of my heart!" Pietro put both arms around Stefano and hugged him. Stefano groaned aloud and Pietro released him quickly. "Sorry, my friend, I forgot your ribs, oh stupid me!" He hugged Stefano again, only gently this time, and solemnly kissed Stefano first on one cheek then on the other. With tears still in his eyes, Pietro stepped back so he could see the three men and Lucia. "I will always remember this moment."

"Enough now, Pietro! Get in and try it out, see if it fits you. Drive it well, enjoy it!" said Luigi.

Pietro opened the door and got into the Mondial. He put the key in the ignition, turned it. The starter motor whirred and the eight-cylinder engine caught instantly. The exhaust note was crisp and exciting. Pietro sat quietly looking at the gauges, checking oil pressure, water temperature and petrol. He revved the engine gently and the resulting sounds coming from behind were music to his ears.

The others stood silently, enjoying the look of pleasure on Pietro's face.

"Enzo, would you like to come with me?" shouted Pietro. "I will show you how well I drive your beautiful machinna!"

Enzo shrugged his shoulders. He knew that if he said no, Pietro would be sad. Why not let the boy show me his driving skills? he thought. He nodded to Pietro and walked around to the passenger side, opened the door and got in. "See you in church tomorrow!" he called to Lucia. "Ciao!"

Pietro pressed the clutch and eased the gear lever into first gear. He waved to the little group, let the clutch up and pressed down on the accelerator, at the same time releasing the hand brake. The Mondial took off very fast and Pietro tooted the horn, changed into second gear and accelerated towards the road out of the car park.

Enzo sat silently, his dark-lens sunglasses perched on his nose, smiling at Pietro's exuberance. He settled back in his seat and put on his seatbelt.

The red convertible was soon out of sight, but Stefano listened as Pietro entered the road and accelerated, the engine singing, its two hundred fifty horses in a burst of power.

Luigi breathed a sigh. "What an emotional young man. For a minute I thought he would burst his heart, he was so happy. Oh, to be so young again!"

"Papa!" Lucia admonished her father. "You are young at heart also. You are the best father in the universe and I love you so much!"

Luigi got into his car and rolled down the window. "See you back at the hotel. Drive carefully." He started his car and drove sedately away towards the road.

Lucia and Stefano waved until he was out of sight.

Stefano, balancing again on one walking stick, hugged Lucia to him and kissed her passionately on the lips. Lucia moaned. They went to the Testarossa.

"Well Stefano, who will drive? You or me?"

"You had better drive, Lucia. I will just sit and enjoy looking at you and give you a kiss now and then, if that's okay."

Lucia smiled and went around to the passenger door, opening it wide so Stefano could get in. Stefano grasped the roof sill and swung himself onto the seat. His walking sticks fell to the ground. Lucia picked them up and put them behind the front seat.

"All tucked in?" she asked, as she closed the door, then went around to the driver's side and got in. Her short blue skirt rose up revealing shapely knees and a considerable amount of thigh.

Stefano's eyes feasted on the sight. He leaned back and said, "I am going to enjoy this, Lucia. You have such gorgeous legs!"

Lucia shook her head, laughing, and leaned across and kissed Stefano, who kissed her back ferociously. They kissed for a long moment, enjoying it so. Finally, Lucia broke off, put the key in the ignition and started the Redhead's engine. The roar from the flat twelve reminded Stefano just how much he had missed that sound during his four days in the hospital. He sat with his head back, drinking in the sound, occasionally looking at Lucia, his next bride-to-be.

Lucia pressed the clutch and moved the chrome shift lever into first gear. She revved the engine, let up the clutch, and with a beautiful growl the Redhead rushed forward. Lucia turned the wheel towards the road, simultaneously changing up to second gear. She paused briefly on the entrance to the road, then still in second, gunned the Redhead, accelerating swiftly. The long, low car streaked down the road.

Stefano watched Lucia as she drove. She handled the huge car as if it were a part of her. She kept the speed to just above the posted limit, but each time she got the chance, she opened it up and the vast power unit obeyed her every command with intricate precision. Stefano experienced the same feeling that he had felt when Lucia drove on the racetrack. She was a rare breed of person who was totally at ease driving powerful cars; no hint of indecision as she changed from second to third, then back down to second again. As they came up on a slow moving car, Lucia checked her mirrors, pulled out and accelerated past, and was back in her own lane within two seconds. This was some young lady!

Lucia caught Stefano watching her and smiled, accelerating all the while until they caught up with the next slow car. Then off she went again, and passed this car in two seconds as well. She was obviously enjoying herself, and Stefano, watching her, was also enjoying the ultimate drive in the gorgeous, red Testarossa.

Within fifteen minutes they were on the winding road leading up to the hotel. Lucia knew every inch of the road by heart. She threw the huge Redhead into the turns and at the precise moment, down-changed to a lower gear and floored the accelerator, causing the Redhead to effortlessly charge out of the corner on to the next straight, the engine howling and singing like an unleashed symphony orchestra at full blast.

At one point there was a straight section for over 150 yards and Lucia roared up the hill at over eighty miles an hour, the trees and bushes flying past. She prepared for the next sharp turn by braking slightly, then with a deft hand and foot movement, she changed down to second gear and blasted into the turn, the trees and bushes only a millimeter away from the gleaming red paintwork. Stefano watched her driving, her skill ever increasing as she became more and more confident. Never a hint of danger; she was prepared for anything to occur on that road. If a herd of cows were around the next bend, she would have known exactly how to brake without skidding, change down rapidly through the gears, and stop, well before the first cow.

They came in view of the hotel and Lucia slowed to a crawl to avoid scaring the living daylights out of any of the guests that might be taking a stroll on the path that led to the forest. She drove the Redhead around the back of the hotel, where Stefano saw there were additional garages. He was glad they weren't going to park in the same garage as before. Too many bad memories would have returned.

Lucia stopped the car in front of a large garage, put the gear lever in neutral, set the hand brake and turned off the engine. The silence was strange after the howling of the twelve-cylinder engine. "Voila!" said Lucia.

"You drive like the Romans drove the chariots in the olden days, with flair and agility. I think you must be practicing for Le Mans," said Stefano with a smile, leaning over to kiss Lucia softly on her lips. "You smell gorgeous, I could eat you all up!"

Lucia laughed and got out of the Redhead and went to open the big garage doors. She swung the doors wide and got back into the Testarossa. Starting the engine, she drove the car inside.

"I think this one is better. Now your bride can sleep peacefully."

Stefano noticed that this garage had an inside door leading directly into the hotel. Stefano helped Lucia close the big doors as best he could, but his walking sticks got in the way so he had to leave Lucia to do the final honors. She lifted a wooden block and slid it into position so that neither door could be opened from the outside. Taking her keys, she unlocked the inside door. They entered the hotel and Lucia locked the door from the other side.

They were in the same wing where Lucia had her apartment. She unlocked her door and stepped inside. Stefano followed in silence, remembering the time they had spent together the last time they were here, lying in the dark, holding each other and kissing all the while. He took Lucia in his arms, dropping his walking sticks and, unmindful of the pain in his side and back, hugged her to him. He had never known such an incredulous feeling of happiness.

Lucia clung to him and they found each other's necks, faces, lips and eyes, kissing each place tenderly. Lucia, filled with passion, could not believe the tremendous fire racing through her as she clung to Stefano.

Although their love was not yet consummated, the two lovers felt as one, living for the moment with no other thoughts in their heads but the magnificent pulse felt each time they kissed, flesh against flesh.

Meanwhile, another love was being consummated to the fullest. Pietro was driving his new love, another Bella Macchina. The beautiful 3.2 litre Quattrovalve Mondial Cabriolet zoomed down the road that led to the town center of Maranello. Pietro was in love with the machinery; each change of gear made his body convulse. He occasionally changed down, just to hear the V-8 engine sing and to feel the immense power of the 32 valve 260 horsepower just waiting to be driven to its limit.

Enzo watched carefully, just as Stefano had been doing on another road in another direction. Enzo noted how Pietro drove, his immaculate gear changes, his fluid steering motion…and such confidence emanated from him! Enzo saw all this and smiled. He saw the devotion in the way Pietro drove, how he was fully aware of other traffic, but gave it no heed, staying well back until a chance to overtake came up. Then with a double declutch down-change and a firm press on the accelerator, the Mondial would surge past the car in front and, only when it was well clear, pull back into the right lane of the narrow road.

The Mondial was rock steady, the engine singing, and Pietro sat in his seat looking proud and incredibly relaxed. Enzo was so pleased that the young man drove with fire, yet did it with such confidence and safety. Here was a young man with potential. Enzo's mind whirled with ideas on how he could win many Grand Prix with this young man driving his beautiful red racing cars.

Pietro came up to the Ferrari Factory and prepared to turn into the main gate, but Enzo asked him to turn left into the racing track gate. Pietro did as requested and pulled up by the Racing Department Building, expecting Enzo to thank him for the ride and get out.

But instead, Enzo asked, "Pietro, how would you like to take a spin around the Ferrari track?"

Pietro did not need to be asked twice. He nodded furiously and put the Mondial into first gear, let up the clutch and headed in the direction Enzo pointed. When the Mondial entered the slipway to the track, Pietro looked around to see if it was clear, saw that it was and floored the accelerator, causing the Mondial to tear forward onto the main track. Pietro changed swiftly to second gear, accelerated to 6000 rpm, then changed up to third gear. The Bosch fuel injection system, combined with the Multiplex ignition system, flawlessly ignited the petrol, and the Mondial surged forward with tremendous gusto. The wind was more noticeable now, but the raked windscreen still gave good protection with little buffeting. The Mondial reached 95 mph effortlessly and at 6500 rpm Pietro changed up to fourth gear. The red convertible, its engine singing in the background, sped forward like a bullet to reach 120 mph. Pietro watched the rev counter climb to 6500 rpm again and changed into fifth gear at 135 mph. The revs dropped to 5500, but the car continued to gain speed. Coming up to the first bend, Pietro saw 150 mph on the speedometer. He braked gently, steered into the bend, and rapidly changed down from fifth to fourth, then fourth to third, causing the engine to do the braking, and took the first corner at

100 mph. Pietro judged the next corner to be a tighter bend and let the engine brake further to 85 mph. As he exited the bend, he gave a burst on the accelerator to power the car onto the next straight, accelerating back up to 100 mph. Round the bends he went, taking a beautiful line each time, taking the car to its absolute limits of adhesion, the huge 240/55 VR390 Michelin tires squealing occasionally, but holding their line impeccably.

Enzo watched Pietro and a warm glow came over him as he saw the brilliance of this young man, making confident judgments on a complex circuit. The Mondial screamed around the last bend before the main straight and Pietro, still in third gear, accelerated back up to over 100 mph. The engine revolutions increased to 6,800 rpm and Pietro executed a fantastically fast change up to fourth, the engine not even hesitating as the power was increased again and the eight cylinder 3185 cc engine performed incredibly, reaching 130 mph within a few seconds.

Pietro grinned and felt at one with this remarkable, beautiful machine. At 7,000 rpm he reached the peak 260 horsepower and changed up to fifth gear with a distinct click as the gear lever entered the slot. The Mondial was now traveling at 160 mph, the steering wheel steady as a rock with no tremors or shudders. Pietro held 160 mph until he saw the lower bend come into sight: allowed the revs to drop, braked gently until the speed slowed to 120 mph, at which point he double declutched and clicked the gear lever into fourth. The engine began to brake, the car slowed again to 100 mph, and Pietro changed down again to third gear and steered into the bend. This time, he only gave a short burst on the accelerator to come out of the bend. Once clear, Pietro allowed the Mondial to slow again, then drifted into the next bend at 80 mph, round this one, revs dropping, slight acceleration, to exit from the bend. Then slowing again, Pietro changed deftly down to second gear and exited back onto the slipway at 60 mph. Coming up to the Racing Department Building, he braked gently and the Mondial rolled to a stop. Pietro took it out of gear and the engine idled perfectly, as if eager to get going and do it all over again.

"Mama Mia!" shouted Pietro. "That was an unbelievable, incredible delight." He turned to Enzo who sat quietly, smiling. "Signor Enzo, you are the true father of automotive brilliance. What a car! What a car!" Pietro felt as if he had been drinking very strong liquor, he was so elated. "La Bella Macchina! What more can any man or woman ever want but to drive this beautiful machine, this red-blooded beauty full of pulsating energy." Pietro sat back and relaxed. He had run out of comments.

Enzo just sat there and smiled. After a few moments he asked Pietro, "Where did you learn to drive like that, Pietro? A skill such as yours does not come from parking customers' cars at the hotel. Surely, you must have been driving fast at some time or another to learn how to take those tight bends at such a speed and in the right gear. Even my best race drivers take those track bends a little slower. Tell me how you learned. I am very interested."

Pietro looked across at Enzo. He still could not believe that he was sitting next to this great man whom he respected so much, who had given him his very own Ferrari.

"Enzo, I will tell you how I learned to drive your great cars so fast!" Pietro cleared his throat, which was suddenly dry and itchy. "Six years ago, my fiancée Serenella died of a weak heart on the day I was to ask her father for her hand in marriage. I was overwrought with shock and disbelief. Every day I would go to her grave and talk to her, willing her to come back to me, even just for a short while. But she did not come back and I watched the flowers that I had planted on her grave growing. Day after day I would spend many hours at her graveside, whispering to her how much I loved her and how I would always love her. But then the flowers would die and I would plant new ones, and my tears watered the soil and the new ones bloomed until they too died.

"The priest of the village, who was very old and kind, would talk to me every day as I was leaving the cemetery. He tried to explain that it was God's will that Serenella should die and that now she was in heaven and watching over me, one of God's angels. Every day I argued with him that if God had loved her, he would have let her marry me and we would have lived in our little cottage and loved each other and had lots of little Serenellas. For that, too, was her dream, to make lots of babies and have a large family.

"After many, many days and weeks passed, I resigned myself to the fact that she truly was gone forever and I decided to end my own life and join her. One day I bought a shotgun from a friend and took it to the cemetery in a sack. I knelt by Serenella's grave and took out the shotgun, but before I could point it at myself, the old priest appeared and told me that if I did such a deed I would be banished to Hell, and never would I go to Heaven, never would I see my Serenella again in this life or the next. The priest took the shotgun from my hands and I could not prevent him. His strength was ten times mine, as if he were powered by the Holy Ghost. He took the shotgun and twisted the barrel with his bare hands until it was unusable. I could not believe my eyes, but took it as a sign from God that I should not do it.

"Then the old priest shouted at me, telling me to go into the world, to leave the village and not return until ten years had passed when I would be more mature and the pain of losing Serenella would have gone. The priest said, 'Go now in the eyes of God and seek peace elsewhere in the world.' I rose to my feet, said my last good-byes to Serenella and left the village, stopping only for a small case of clothes and photographs of Serenella.

"I walked out of the village, not knowing where I was going, my mind still full of the sight of the priest banishing me from the village. All night and all the next day I walked along the road, not hearing or seeing anything. A farmer I knew stopped his car and asked me where I was going, but I didn't answer and he must have thought me very distraught, because he tried to force me into his car to take me back to the village to the doctor. I wrestled with him, broke free and ran down the road, and the farmer drove off. I was worried he would send the police or someone from the insane hospital to get me. I walked until it became very dark and started to rain, then sought shelter under a tree by the side of the road. But I slipped on the wet grass and rolled down an embankment and into a small river. The force of the fall caused my case to open and everything fell into the water. I screamed and shouted, trying to find my photographs of Serenella in the pitch black of the night, but found nothing, not even the case.

"I crawled back up the embankment and lay under the tree, shivering and shaking, and eventually I fell asleep, exhausted with walking for two days and having eaten nothing. In the morning I awoke and the sun was shining. I crawled out from under the tree into a patch of sunlight and felt the warmth of the sun drying me out. I lay there for many hours in a semi-awake state. Towards afternoon, I suddenly remembered the case and rushed down the embankment to find it. There it was, floating in the river, caught by a branch of a small tree. I fished it out and searched for the photographs, but all I ever found was a few items of clothing further downstream.

"I took all my clothes off and waded into the river, hoping to glimpse the photographs, but I never found them. They were gone…lost forever. I finally gave up in despair and tried to drown myself, but the river wouldn't let me; each time I went under the current would force me to the surface further and further downstream. I stopped attempting to drown and slowly made my way back to where my clothes were. They were warm and dry and as I put them on, I felt better, somehow relieved. I put the few clothes that I had found that morning into the case and set off again on the road.

"A short time passed before a car stopped and offered me a lift. This time I accepted. My good Samaritan was a nun on her way to Maranello. She talked of Maranello and how she loved the town and the people. All the way she talked and talked, telling me about God and the Virgin Mary and how she had become a nun to serve God for the rest of her life. We stopped at a little roadside inn where she bought us bread and water. I remember being ravenous, eating with both hands, stuffing large pieces of bread into my mouth and swallowing them whole, I was so hungry. The nun asked me what I would do when I got to Maranello. When I said I didn't know, she told me I must find work, for work is the gift from God; to earn a few lire so that we can live to pray to the Lord for giving us life.

"I nodded and she started to clean me up like a mother with her baby. Taking the cloth napkin that the warm bread had been in and tipping water from the carafe onto it, she proceeded to clean the mud off my face, all the time telling me how happy I would be when I could work and then say my prayers at night. She never asked why the mud was on my face, just cleaned it off and then said, "Now we must go!"

We took off again in her little Fiat 500, which was very old and rusty. She told me how she loved to drive it, although I noticed that she would sometimes forget to push the clutch when she changed gears and the poor little car would grind loudly until she suddenly remembered the clutch. Then she would change gear and violently let the clutch up, and the little car would bounce down the road until she decided it was time for the next gear change.

"As we came into Maranello, she told me there were two places she thought might give me a job. One was your Ferrari Factory, Signor Enzo, and the other was the hotel on the hill above the town. I said I would try the factory first and she agreed. She took me there, dropped me off, said a prayer and went off to her convent somewhere outside of the town.

"I went in and asked the gate man, "Who do I see to get a job?" He pointed out the little office to the side of the main building. I went there and asked, but the manager said he had no work today, but to come back next week. I asked him how to get to the hotel and he gave me directions, so I set off in the general direction of the hotel.

I walked and walked, finally finding the hotel at the top of the long winding, uphill road. Quite exhausted, I went in and asked if there was any work I could do. Luckily, Signorina Lucia was there and asked her father to give me a job. I expect she felt sorry for me as I was in a pretty disheveled state, to say the least. Luigi gave me a job as a bellboy on a month's trial basis and I was shown to a little room which I was to share with another bellboy named Vincenzo, given a clean shirt and uniform, told to bathe myself and appear for work afterwards. So I washed myself, put on my clean shirt and began my work at the Bella Montagna Hotel for Signore Luigi.

I learned the job of being a bellboy and worked from seven in the morning to seven in the evening six days a week. When it wasn't busy, I would stand outside the hotel and chat with the valet parking attendants and watch them skillfully park the customers' cars. The art of driving began to fascinate me and I asked Signore Luigi if I also, could learn to drive and split my time between being a bellboy and a valet parking attendant, so that I could park customers' cars, and pick customers up from Maranello in the hotel shuttle bus.

Signore Luigi asked the valet parking attendants to teach me to drive the hotel shuttle bus on the backroads behind the hotel. They took to the task with great enthusiasm and soon I was sitting in the shuttle bus at every opportunity, with them teaching me how to use the clutch and gears and how to steer around corners and use the rearview mirrors.

Learning to drive the bus was a great honor for me and I took the lessons very seriously, at the same time enjoying every minute of it. Then the day finally came when Signore Luigi said I was ready to go into Maranello and take my driving test. I was at first very nervous when the government tester got into the bus and asked me to pull away and take the first turn left, but once I started moving, my confidence returned, and determined to show that I was competent, I drove the bus along the test route without making any mistakes. When the tester told me I had passed the test, I was overjoyed for the first time in many years.

At every opportunity I would drive the bus to pick up or drop off customers from the train station. One Friday evening, I was about to return to the hotel from Maranello after dropping off some customers in town, when I saw a new car rental agency had opened up and was advertising special rates on Ferrari rentals. I went in and asked their prices and nearly fell over when they told me how much a twenty-four hour rental would cost. I calculated it would cost me about one month's wages. Embarrassed, I turned to leave when the rental agency owner, who was very friendly, asked me why I wanted to rent a Ferrari. I told him it would just be for fun to drive a fast car for a few hours in the mountains, not really to have a destination in mind. He worked out a deal so that if I rented a well-used Ferrari 308 GT4, it would only cost me two weeks wages.

"I took his card, wrote all the costs down and went back to the hotel to think about it. I didn't think for long, I had saved most of my wages for the last six months and decided I wanted to drive a Ferrari at any cost. That long night I remember well. I didn't sleep a wink, just lay on my bed in the darkness dreaming about how it would be to drive a real Ferrari 308 GT4."

7: THE DRIVING LESSON.

"The following morning was my day off, so I telephoned the rental agency owner as soon as he opened, to reserve a Ferrari 308 GT4 for that Saturday afternoon and evening.

"I got a lift into Maranello that afternoon and went straight to the rental agency, filled in a few forms, paid in advance, and was given the keys to an old Ferrari 308 GT4, shiny red nonetheless, with a V-8 engine. I sat in the 308 and studied the dashboard and the gear shift pattern for about five minutes, then read the handbook for another ten minutes.

"Finally, I summoned up the courage to take it for a drive. I put the key in the ignition, made sure the gear lever was in neutral, and started the engine which fired up immediately with a throaty growl. I pushed down on the clutch and put the gear lever carefully into first gear, pushed down on the accelerator and took off out into the traffic, not knowing where I was heading. Changed into second gear and accelerated gently, impressed with the power of the engine and loving the seating position, looking out onto the slow slung fiery red hood. To me, it felt just as I had imagined it, like sitting in a racing car. I eased my way through traffic until I was out of town and on a narrow country lane, then pressed the accelerator. That beautiful Ferrari engine surged forward faster and faster. I watched the revs climb to about 5000 rpm. I changed into third gear and the 308 GT4 shot forward.

"My heart pumped furiously, unsure how to cope with such power, after driving only customer cars slowly in the car park, and the occasional run to Maranello in the little shuttle bus. I buzzed along in third gear, gradually getting the feel of the car and gathering more and more confidence as the miles clicked by. Rounding the bends, I would change down carefully to second gear, then accelerate out of the bends and get back into third,   holding around 65 mph until reaching the next bend. Then I would brake gently, hit the clutch and change down into second gear and negotiate the bend at, to me, the fast speed of 45 mph. I drove and drove, enjoying driving this magnificent car, which had immaculate road-holding manners.

I drove until the sun started to set and then came upon a little garage which had one petrol pump. I pulled in and stopped by the pump, turned off the engine, set the hand brake, and got out. I walked around the 308, admiring the style of the body work, found the petrol tank cover, opened it, and taking the petrol nozzle from the pump, put it in and started to fill the tank.

Out of the garage came a little old man in greasy blue overalls, wiping his hands with a clean rag. "Buon Giorno, Come sta?" he said in a friendly tone.

"Buon Giorno, bene grazie, ei lei?" I replied.

"Bene, Bene," says the little old man. "For one so young, very expensive car though."

"I rented it for a few hours, just to see what it is like to drive a real Ferrari," I said.

"How you like it? Fast eh ?" said the old man with a smile.

"Very fast," I replied. "I am still learning how to drive it. I have to drive it a little slow until I get used to it."

"A car like this, it does not like to be driven slowly. It is built to drive very, very fast. I know, I used to drive for the great Enzo many years ago…a few wins, a few losses, but mainly wins. Enzo builds only beautiful, powerful cars," said the old man.

"I would like to check the oil and water, can you help?" I asked.

"No problem, Signore, it is a pleasure for me and it is good that you remember to check oil and water. Not many people do these days, they just drive in, fill up with petrol and zoom away forgetting that oil and water to a car is like blood to a human being…too little and everything stops." He pulled on the bonnet and engine compartment latches from inside the car and they opened in unison. He examined the water level, gave a grunt of satisfaction and turned his attention to the engine.

"Ah, there is an engine, Signore, what a beast, so full of power. It's a Rocchi designed 90 degree V-8 with 2927 cubic centimetres and double overhead camshafts on each bank of cylinders, compression ratio of 8.8 to with four Weber twin choke carburetors that in good tune produce 255 horsepower at 6600 rpm!"

I was amazed. I had no idea of any of those details, but I knew the old man knew what he was talking about. Such knowledge, I thought, Here is a man that really knows something about Ferrari engines.

The old man found the oil dipstick, pulled it out, wiped it off with his rag, put it back in and gently pulled it out again. He looked at it for a few seconds and smelled the end where the oil was.

"Looks good," he said, "Up to the mark and still a good golden color, which means it has been changed recently. Thank God, someone knows to care for great engines. Smells good too, no petrol smell…if it smells too much of petrol, then that is not a good sign. Also, if it is thick black it means it is old oil and needs changing, or if it is grey then it usually means there is water in the oil, not good and needs fixing. But this, this is good."

He put the dipstick back and took the breather cap off and shook it to see if there was any water from condensation. "Looks good, no water here either." He put the breather cap back. "How is the oil pressure?" he asked. "It should read between 25 and 50 percent of the gauge, idling at 850 rpm, the closer to 50 percent the better."

"I will be honest, I didn't really look at it. I haven't been driving very long, only a few weeks and only a hotel shuttle bus, but now I will pay attention and keep an eye on everything you have showed me," I said.

"Good. Three more things to check, but only when the engine is cold. Take off the radiator cap and check to see if the water is clean or dirty and oily looking. If so it needs attention, but don't try that when its hot or you will get boiling water in your face, capische?" said the old man.

"Capische, Signore ! Grazie!" I replied.

"Also feel the water hoses when hot or cold; if they feel soft and mushy then they need to be replaced. At the same time look carefully at the fan belts, any cracking or visual deterioration means they must be replaced immediately!"

"Grazie, Signore, I have learned many things today. I will keep a notebook from now on and write all your advice into it, so I do not forget."

"Come and have some Cappuccino. I just made some, good and hot, like your engine!" He laughed.

We closed up the bonnet and engine compartment cover, pulled out the petrol nozzle as the tank was now full, put the petrol cap back on, and just to be cautious, I locked both doors.

We went inside the little cottage, set aside from the main garage, to a small, comfy looking sitting room. The coffee pot on the wood stove was bubbling away and a strong coffee aroma filled the room. The little old man closed the door and gestured to me to sit on one of the large soft armchairs, covered in a bright flowery fabric.

"My wife, God rest her soul, loved bold colors as you can see." He smiled, then held out his hand. "Vittorio Brazzano, pleased to know you," he said warmly.

I shook his hand. "Pietro Franziini, a great pleasure to meet you Signore Brazzano."
Vittorio poured the strong coffee into delicate china cups, passed one to me and we sat there sipping it…glorious coffee, the best I have ever tasted."

At that point Enzo, who had been listening intently to Pietro said, "Vittorio Brazzano! I remember him well, he was a brilliant racing driver, with a lot of fire in his heart! You tell a good story, Pietro. Please continue, I am very interested to hear what happened next."

"Are you sure, Signore Enzo?" Pietro asked. Enzo nodded in reply.

"I asked Signore Brazzano what you were like and he got very excited as he explained his memories of you. 'Enzo was a man with a passion for racing; he loved to see his cars with the Cavallino Rampante insignia roar around the track, their engines screaming and howling as they tore into the bends, hurtling along, overtaking all the other cars, racing to see who would reach the coveted chequered flag first!' Vittorio sat on the edge of his chair, reliving his memories as a racing driver.

"The smell of gasoline and hot engines, the roar of the crowd and the speed, it was a very exciting time. Nothing can be better than racing with the finest team and the finest engines in the world, all because Enzo loved to race his cars!"

Vittorio continued, knowing that Pietro was a willing listener, knowing that this boy had never seen a real Grand Prix race with its tensions, and relief when you cross the line first, and the chequered flag is waved and you do a victory lap around the track and the crowd cheers to see the Prancing Horse, pride of Italy, leading in manufacturers' points over Mercedes, Porsche, Jaguar, Lola, Ford and Brabham.

"Yes my boy, it was the ultimate experience to drive into the pits and celebrate with huge magnum bottles of champagne, spraying the team and the crowd, such fun after a long hard race."

"How did you get into racing, Signore?" asked Pietro.

"I was lucky, I worked for Alfa Romeo, first in the engine construction department. One day the foreman asked our team if we would like to try our skill on the track, as the racing department was looking for new blood to drive their cars. I was about your age and excited as hell. I was first in line to drive around the track The head of the racing team stood there with his stop watch ready. I strapped myself into the car and took off with tires smoking and drove that track as fast as I could, accelerator to the floor all the way for two glorious laps. They waved me in and I saw them writing my name in a little book. I never found out what the time was, but I knew it was fast.

"Two days later, I was asked to join the team on a three month trial. I never looked back. I drove always my best, winning my first two races unbelievably. The cars were strong and fast and I learned to listen to the engine, so that I always knew how hard I could drive it without blowing it up. I did all my own service checks on the engine before every race, and that way I knew every strength and every weakness.

"After a few years with Alfa Romeo, the racing management team changed and I also felt it was time for a change. I called Enzo and asked him if I could drive his Testa Rossa. Enzo had seen me competing against his cars on the track. He never even hesitated, 'As soon as you want Vittorio, I look forward to it,' so off I went to drive for the Great Master.

"Those years were the best in my life. The Testa Rossa was the true symbol of the real racing car era, Its power was so tremendous that it took great courage to drive it flat out.

Enzo would always be there. 'Keep the revs in maximum in each gear before you change up or down and we will win all of the races,' Enzo would say to me, and I found it to be true. We won race after race and became manufacturers' champions year after year. Now, looking back on those days from here in my little house, I am sad sometimes that I cannot drive in the great Le Mans Grand Prix again. But it was a true honor to drive with Enzo Ferrari's racing stable and I am very proud of that."

Pietro looked around the room and saw small photos of the cars and the teams in the pits, the mechanics all cheering at the end of long days at the races, having spent hours tuning the engines, changing the tires, and refueling the big red, beautiful racing cars.

Pietro was excited. "Tell me, Vittorio, how can I learn to drive like you did, with courage and split second gear changes and taking corners at 100 mph?"

"Well, my boy," Vittorio said gently, "I could teach you all I know, but in the end you must be the driver. You must be aware of every other car on the track and your nerves must tingle and your hand-eye coordination must be flawless when you make decisions to change up or down...especially when you are roaring down the straight, neck and neck with a Porsche at 200 mph and the next bend is on you before you know it. You steel yourself to keep applying the power until, at the very last instant, you have to change down and brake at the same time. Otherwise you will hit the fence and the car will explode into 1000 pieces, you being one of them!

"Racing is a brave art and only the most skillful can win. You must be in top physical condition, because if you cramp up at 180 mph it's all over, so you must train your body to drive the car."

Then Vittorre added, "If you really want to learn to drive fast and safe, then I will teach you, but you have to want it more than anything else in the world. No drinking, no girls and no overeating."

Pietro said, "I'm all yours, Vittorio, teach me!"

Vittorio smiled. "All right. First, you must show me how you drive today. Then I will tell you how to improve your skill and how to drive racing cars."

They went out to the 308 GT4. Vittorio hung a CLOSED sign on the petrol pumps, and they climbed into the car with Pietro driving. They drove for a few miles up into the hills. The road was fairly deserted and Pietro put on a show of charging into the bends and accelerating out of them, using the gears and engine to brake, rather than stamping on the brake like he had done when he'd just learned how to drive, a short time ago.

Vittorio observed Pietro's driving for a while then asked him to pull over and stop. Pietro did so. The V-8 idled and Vittorio spoke, his words full of feeling. "The first two things you must learn are, one, when you change gear the car must never jolt, the passenger must never notice the pace of the car has changed, the gear change must be executed at exactly the right revolutions. That way, no matter how fast you are going, changing up or down, there is never any undue stress on the gearbox, the drive shaft, the back axle or the clutch. The car will remain strong and you will always have total control."

"How do I do that?" asked Pietro.

Vittorio took a box of matches from his pocket and placed it on end on the dashboard. "Now," he said, "if the match box falls because of a jerky gear change, you will know you have to improve."

"All right," said Pietro, "I understand."

"Good. Second, when you change down, I want you to double de-clutch."

"What is double de-clutch?" asked Pietro. "It sounds very difficult."

"No. Once you get the hang of it, it becomes second nature and you will do it with ease," Vittorio instructed. "Say you are in third gear at 80 mph and 5,000 rpm. If you want to change down, you press down the clutch with your left foot, put the gear lever in neutral and press the accelerator with your right foot until you hear and feel the engine and gear box are exactly in sync together. There are no precise rpm for every gear as every car has a little different gearing, but once you try it you will understand. Then the gear change will go like a hot knife through butter with no jerks and under complete control. Once you reach the right engine speed, you change down from third to second and then immediately lift your foot from the clutch. There will be no jerks and no stress on the gearbox or drive shaft, just pure power and total control. Now I want you to try it."

Pietro grinned and put the 308 GT4 into first gear, checked his mirror then smoothly accelerated, watching the matchbox as he rapidly gained speed and changed into second gear. The matchbox trembled slightly, but stayed standing. Pietro reached 5,000 rpm and changed up into third gear, and just as he let the clutch up and pressed on the accelerator, the matchbox fell backwards. Pietro grimaced and looked across at Vittorio who smiled.

"It takes time and practice. Changing up is usually easier to keep it standing. You will get the hang of it soon, I'm sure."

Pietro nodded and Vittorio stood the matchbox up again. Pietro now told himself he would drive so smoothly the matchbox would never fall over again. He learned with Vittorio's help to listen to the engine.

Twice more the matchbox fell over, but then as if by magic, Pietro mastered what Vittorio had taught him; to listen to the engine, change up just at the split second when the engine is singing at its most glorious, down with the clutch, gear lever up and over with a distant click as it engages, then up with the clutch. Then, just as the clutch engages, pile on the power by pressing the accelerator. The 308 GT4 knew it had found its master. It growled, its V-8 with the double overhead cams working away quickly raised the revs to 5,000 to 6,000, and the car flew down the road into the setting sun.

Pietro and Vittorio both knew the instant Pietro had mastered the fluid gear change. "Now, I want you to learn to double de-clutch as we go down this hill," said Vittorio.

Pietro, now in fourth, roared down the hill with the first bend coming up. He pushed down on the clutch, put the gear lever in neutral, revved the engine to 5,500 and swiftly moved back from neutral, across the gate and clicked into third. He let the clutch up smoothly and the car braked gently but evenly, the engine revs dropping, slowing the car into the bend. The matchbox stood grandly as it if were glued. Pietro breathed a sigh of relief.

"Wow! That was fun and it feels so fluid as if you don't need a clutch, if you get it just right."

Vittorio nodded, pleased with his young pupil. "Ah, you feel the difference already. Instead of forcing the synchromesh, the gears take all the force. The double de-clutch matches the engine speed to the transmission speed, and that's why it's a much smoother gear change with no stress on the gearbox, drive shaft, clutch or back axle!"

"I love it!" Pietro cried out. "Now I have learned it!" He tried again, his youthful dexterity enjoying the challenge of getting it just right until his confidence showed in the way that he changed gears. "Thank you, Vittorio, you are a great teacher. In one hour, I have learned many new things from you. Thank you, again!"

"My pleasure!" said Vittorio. "I have many more things I can teach you. It will take time and patience, but if you have the time, I have the patience."

Pietro was overjoyed. "I can only rent a car about once every three or four months because it is so expensive, but I can practice what you taught me today in the hotel shuttle, and every time I come to see you I will learn more, I promise."

"Sure," said Vittorio, pleased that the young man thought so highly of him. "Let's go back to my garage and I will write down some maneuvers you can practice."

Pietro turned the 308 GT4 around in a neat three-point turn on the narrow road, and they headed back to Vittorio's garage. On the way, Vittorio explained about the need to always warm up the car to its correct operating temperature before driving it hard.

"When you start a Ferrari from cold, you should let it idle around 1,000 rpm for about a minute, then rev it to 1,500 for about thirty seconds or so. Then you can drive it at 30 or 40 mph for three to four miles at around 3,000 rpm until the temperature gauge registers normal. Only then, when all the components, engine, transmission and back axle are warm, should you drive it hard. Never rev a cold engine unnecessarily. That places a tremendous amount of stress on the engine, as the fluids are not circulating freely when cold." Vittorio's explanation made sense to Pietro, and he stored the information in the back of his mind.

Pietro drove back fast, but with a new level of comprehension about the techniques of driving, that he had just learned from the very interesting champion race driver. Pietro loved the 308 GT4, the way the aluminum spoke steering wheel felt, nearly in the center of the car rather than off to the side. Especially, he liked the roar of the V-8 behind his head and the incredible view forward over the long bonnet, which dipped like a cheese wedge away from him, giving him the feeling that this was not just a road car but a true racing car. With the engine already singing at 5,000 rpm, Pietro accelerated to 6,500 rpm and the car screamed like a Banshee as it ate up the miles, curving neatly into the bends and accelerating swiftly out of them. The matchbox stood erect as he changed up and down, enjoying himself immensely.

"You tell a good story, Pietro," Enzo remarked. "I am impressed. Vittorio taught you well. Please continue, I want to hear more." As they sat in the Cabriolet, Pietro suddenly rebounded back into the present.

"I got so involved telling you about Vittorio, I forgot where I was for an instant in time. I was reliving that first night with Signore Vittorio. Are you sure you want me to continue, Signore Enzo?"

"Please," said Enzo. "Vittorio is a good friend of mine."

So Pietro told Enzo how, when they arrived back at the garage, they went in, and Vittorio made more of his delicious coffee.

"Come, Pietro, I will show you my garage. I think you will find it interesting." Vittorio led the way, holding his hot cup of coffee in one hand, his keys in the other. They went out the back door of the cottage along a little path to a large building that looked like a barn. It was set back behind a large tree, which is why Pietro had not noticed it before. Vittorio set down his coffee cup on a workbench by the door, selected a key and unlocked the large padlock. He took it off and clipped it back into the hasp to swing free. Then with another key, he opened the deadbolt on the main door.

Pietro sipped his hot coffee while watching Vittorio. He thought there must be some very expensive tools in there to require such hefty locks. Vittorio grasped the handle on the door and slid it sideways. The door made no sound, as it was well oiled on its runner. Vittorio stepped inside and felt for the light switch. A 'click' and the whole barn came ablaze in bright light.

Pietro looked through the doorway, and as his eyes adjusted to the light, he nearly spilled his coffee in surprise. The barn was not a barn after all. Pietro went through the door, his eyes taking in the wondrous scene before him.

Vittorio stood to one side and watched Pietro's reaction. He laughed. "Not what you expected? Ah! Pietro, this is my holy place, built over thirty years. Everything you see has something to do with racing. I collected all of this, brought it here and set it up. Now, when I'm feeling sad or a little old, I close the garage and come here to reminisce. What do you think? You like it?"

Pietro stood there, amazed, taking it all in. And there was a lot to take in. He was looking at what first appeared to be a huge factory floor, about 120 feet long and 80 feet wide. The floor was painted in dark blue, startling against the walls that soared twenty feet to the roof. Each wall was made up of multiple sheets of 10 x 10 feet square polished aluminum panels, glistening in the bright light that came from long neon tubes suspended from the roof in clusters. Along each wall were four feet high workbenches also made of aluminum, extending the length of the building. Along the walls behind the workbenches were tools in polished chrome, ranging from metric spanner sets to torque wrenches, piston extractors and electric grinding hand tools. Every tool imaginable hung on the walls. On four of the work benches were huge 12-cylinder Ferrari engines in varying states of assembly. The other workbenches contained huge hydraulic drills, metal presses and metal lathes. On the end wall benches were containers of engine parts from crankshafts to cylinder heads and pistons, all sparkling clean and shiny with oil.

Pietro smiled. "What a fantastic workshop, Vittorio. You spend your time in here building engines! Everything is so clean and orderly, I am overwhelmed. It is like a Ferrari factory, if I could imagine how one would look!"

"Yes, it's very clean. It helps that I keep the temperature at 18 degrees centigrade constantly, year round with air conditioning."

"What about the cars you bring in here? Are they yours or do you rebuild customer's cars?" Pietro asked.

"Neither, Pietro. Only one car comes in here. In fact it is already in here," said Vittorio.

"Where is the car, Vittorio? I don't see it. Is it all in pieces and you are building it?"

"No, Pietro, I will show you a real racing car. One you can drive right in here at 180 mph!"

Pietro was puzzled but watched as Vittorio unlocked one of the workbenches and took out what looked like a television remote control. He pressed a set of coded numbers into it and a door panel, on what looked like a fuse box on the wall next to him, slid up, exposing another keypad with two large handles, one painted red and the other blue. Vittorio lifted the blue handle and locked it into place. He then entered another set of coded numbers into the keypad.

A low rumbling sound came from the center of the blue floor. Pietro gasped in astonishment, as two 20 x 20 foot sections of the floor slid away from each other, exposing a 40-foot hole. The sliding stopped. Vittorio lifted the red handle and locked it into place. He then entered another set of codes into the keypad. A hissing sound came from hydraulic pumps under the floor.

Out of the cavernous hole in the floor rose a long red object surrounded by thick steel barriers, most of which were covered in light gray protective rubber. As the red object came into view, Pietro stood, astounded by what he was seeing.

The red object was a racing car, but this was no ordinary racing car. This one was coated in the brightest red paint you could ever imagine. It was so red that it reflected the light like red embers of the hottest fire imaginable. The whole 40-foot square section rose majestically, with the red racing car on top, like a king of beasts coming out of its lair. The hissing of hydraulic pumps stopped as the new section came level with the rest of the floor.

"Go take a look, Pietro," said Vittorio. "Please, the floor is safe, locked into place. You can trust it."

Pietro put down his coffee cup and walked slowly towards the magnificent red beast in the center of the floor.

His eyes took in the sculpted body, long, lean and low. In front of the long, beautiful bonnet was a large oval shaped grill whose task was clearly to draw in air and cool the radiator. In the center of the bonnet, about a foot from the front was the Ferrari insignia - a Black Prancing Horse on a background of Modena yellow. Pietro knew this insignia was known as the "Cavallino Rampante". About 2 feet from the insignia, a long air scoop protruded, situated directly over the engine compartment. The scoop had an opening in the front, designed to direct air into the carburetors.

On each side of the car, sculpted wheel arches rose like wings over the front and rear wheels. The headlights were set back inside the front wings. Each wire wheel was held in place with a single large knock-on nut, for quick changes during a race. A double set of exhaust pipes, one above, and one below, hung under each side of the car.

In front of the two-seater cockpit was a low windscreen. Behind the driver seat was a molded headrest that extended all the way back to the end of the car. The steering wheel was wood-rimmed with three spokes, and the "Cavallino Rampante" was prancing again in the center of the horn button. The gear lever sat proudly in its gate, and a chrome encased rearview mirror was mounted on the dashboard.

To Pietro, who had never seen a real racing car up close before, it was a most awe-inspiring sight. The huge long bonnet with its brilliant red paintwork fired Pietro's desire to race in a car such as this.

Vittorio came over and unlatched the chrome clips that held the engine compartment air scoop cover in place. He removed it so that Pietro could see the 12 upright throats of the six 38 mm twin Weber double-throated carburetors running between the bright red camshaft covers.

"This is a 1957 250 Testa Rossa with a 3 Litre V-12, outputting 300 bhp at 7,200 rpm. There are only four in the world today. This one I raced in Buenos Aires, the Targa Florio, Nurburgring and, Le Mans. This beautiful car beat Jaguar, Aston Martin and Porsche in all of the races, and finished first in every race. It was unbeatable! Brilliant engine design and fantastic handling are the only way to win races, and this car has both! Enzo gave me this one when we won the World Championship five years in a row."

"So that's what happened to that car!" said Enzo. "I always wondered what he did with it. What a character!" Enzo chuckled. "Please, finish your story, my boy, I find it ever more interesting." Pietro continued, pleased that Enzo was enjoying the story.

Vittorio explained how the tyres were resting on eight steel rollers which allowed him to drive it all speeds, causing the rollers to spin as the tyres gripped. He attached two long rubber tubes to the exhaust pipes. Each tube was about six inches in diameter, lined with aluminum coils for durability. He explained that these two long tubes allowed the exhaust fumes to be vented outside the barn.

Having done that, Vittorio motioned Pietro to get into the passenger seat, and he got into the driver's seat. Vittorio started the huge 12 cylinder engine, which fired instantly with the deepest growl you could possibly imagine. Vittorio sat with the engine idling at 1,000 rpm, warming up.

Pietro closed his eyes and listened to the sound, which even at 1,000 rpm, gave off its own splendid melody of camshaft chains and valve noise. A music that the more you listen to it, the more it excites you, thought Pietro.

Vittorio raised the revs to 1,500 and the sound changed and become more intensive, power just waiting to be unleashed. He pressed down the clutch and moved the gear lever into first gear with a decisive click, then released the clutch, revving the car up to 2,000 rpm. The wheels spun on the rollers. With a deft hand Vittorio shifted from first to second. Pietro was mesmerized by the speed of the change, unbelievably fast and smooth.

Now the car was warm and Vittorio increased the revs to 3,500, shifting to third just as fast as before. The speedometer was showing 80 mph and the music from the racing engine was intense, a powerful pulsing of an unleashed tiger. Vittorio pressed the accelerator again and the revs rose to 6,500 as he changed into fourth gear, the speedometer showing 140 mph.

The whole car was purring now. Vittorio piled on more fuel and the speedometer went to 160 mph as he changed into fifth gear. The sound of the engine bounced back off the aluminum walls of the barn, a crescendo of music like the 1812 Overture.

Pietro watched the revs climb again to 7,000 rpm and the speedometer steady at 200 mph. Vittorio held it steady for about a minute, then gently eased the speed back down to 160, 140, 120, 80, 60 and finally dropped to idle. He shifted to neutral and turned to grin at Pietro.

"Great fun, eh! You like it?" asked Vittorio.

Pietro nodded. "It is unbelievable, such an engine, such a sound!" Pietro shook his head in disbelief.

Vittorio shut the engine off and they sat there listening to the uncanny silence after such a concert of sound.

"Next time you come you can try it for yourself. It's a great way to learn speed shifting too. Anyway it keeps me happy, that's the main thing." Vittorio and Pietro got out of the racing car and Vittorio disconnected the extended exhaust vent tubes. Back at the control panel, Vittorio reversed the procedure and the great red car slowly slid down into its lair, the blue floor closing up tight behind it as if nothing had ever been there.

Vittorio locked up the barn and they went back to the cottage. He wrote in a little red binder some basic maneuvers for Pietro to practice and handed him the binder. "Just a few for now, and I will think up some more before you come again. Here is my phone number, give me a call a day or so before you come."

Pietro thanked Vittorio profusely and headed out to the 308 GT4. Vittorio waved goodbye as Pietro took off down the road.

"And that was it?" asked Enzo."

"I went back as often as I could afford to rent the 308 GT4 over the next six years, and every time I learned more and more from Vittorio. One of the most important skills he taught me was to control the car so that it would not get into a tailspin. He kept at me to push the car to its limits on the bends, but always to know the limit of adhesion, that split second when too much power coupled with a tight bend, can cause the rear end to break loose and go into a terrifying spin.

"A few times when we went out, it rained really hard and Vittorio had me purposely break the rear end loose so I would know the feeling and know what to watch for. After two spinouts in which we spun completely around twice, I knew what to expect and now I can take a bend to its absolute maximum without spinning out. Vittorio showed no fear, and that day he said, 'Now you know how to control a car properly.'

"I guess I was there about fifteen times altogether. Vittorio is a great race car driver, a great man and a great teacher!"

"Certainly, from the way you drive today, he taught you well. I must pay him a visit. It is a long time since I saw him last," said Enzo. He opened his door and turned to Pietro. "My boy, enjoy this car. I know you will…you have the true gift of a racing driver. Come to the Le Mans circuit with Stefano and Lucia. I want you to drive for me. I have four specially built cars that I know can win with the right drivers. Capische?"

Pietro nodded. "Thank you, Enzo, I will do my best."

Enzo nodded and got out of the Mondial. "Buona Fortuna. Arrivederci!"

"Arrivederci!" Pietro said with a big smile.

Enzo closed the door on the Mondial and then he was gone, disappearing into his Racing Department entrance.

Pietro took a deep breath. There went a true hero, the master behind all the beautiful Ferraris in the world; the cars that men and women alike, all over the world, loved to see and loved to drive. Even if you could never drive one, Pietro remembered his heart skipping a beat each time he saw a Ferrari go by. And now…now he had his own Ferrari, given to him by no less than Enzo Ferrari himself! What an honor! Pietro cried out in joy at the beautiful car that was now his.

He started the Mondial engine. The brief high-pitched whistle as the engine caught changed to a beautifully refined whine when the fuel injectors set the revs to idle, which excited him. He was completely overcome with the beauty of the car; the multi-colored dash panel showing the checks for fuel level, coolant temperature, oil pressure…all flowing with ravishing color even in daylight. He looked around at the tan seats molded in exquisite leather, designed for comfort as well as for holding you in place for fast driving.

Looking at the empty seat beside him, Pietro had a vision of Serenella sitting there. She was talking to him, saying something that he couldn't hear, her smile the same as ever. Pietro shook his head and the vision was gone, the seat empty with no trace of Serenella. Then he realized that he knew what she had said. "Pietro, enjoy yourself, love your car. Don't worry about me, I am happy for you." That's what I think she said, Pietro thought. Okay, Serenalla, I will take your advice and give all of my love to this beautiful car, and one day we will meet again in the next life.

He pressed down the clutch and put the polished steel gear lever into first gear, checked his mirrors and pulled away from the factory towards the road, his head still spinning from the vision he had just had. Slipping into second gear, he entered the main road, turning right toward the direction of the hotel. He pushed down on the accelerator and the glorious Mondial took up the challenge and roared away. The beautiful howl of the V-8 in his ears calmed Pietro, his head cleared and he felt reborn as he steered the Mondial Cabriolet along the road into the traffic.

8: PREPARING FOR THE TRIP

Back at the hotel, Stefano and Lucia were busy packing for the trip. Lucia packed only the bare minimum, and Stefano had so few clothes with him that they all fitted neatly into the custom made Testarossa luggage. After they had finished, Lucia called her father to ask him to collect her one hour before their 11 o'clock wedding tomorrow. Then she left a message for Pietro to meet Stefano in the lobby at ten the following morning, seeing as he was going to be Best Man.

Stefano heard Lucia leaving the message and suddenly realized he had not bought her a wedding ring. As soon as she got off the phone, he told her to get dressed. "We must buy you a wedding ring, and maybe it is too late…."

Lucia laughed and said, "Don't worry, Stefano. My father gave me my mother's wedding ring." She took a little black box out of a drawer, opened it and showed him an ornate ring with fine cut diamonds set in a heavy gold band. Lucia tried it on and showed Stefano. "See, it fits perfectly."

"It's a beautiful ring, mi amore, but are you sure you don't want me to buy you a new one?"

"No, Stefano, I will be honored to wear my mother's ring, and it would hurt Papa if I say no after I already said yes."

"Then wear the ring, my sweet. I, too, am proud that you wear your mother's ring."

The problem was solved and Stefano relaxed again. He took Lucia in his arms and kissed her hard. They took off all their clothes and got into Lucia's bed, cuddling up close to each other. Stefano had a terribly strong desire to make violent love to Lucia, but he restrained himself and made do with a warm cuddle. They talked for a little while until Lucia, sleepy and warm, drifted off to sleep.

Stefano lay awake with his love pressed against him. He was so content he could not believe how in love he was with this cuddly young lady. He kissed her hair gently, then he also closed his eyes and fell asleep.

Pietro decided to pay one last visit to Vittorio before taking off with Stefano and Lucia. He drove the now familiar route at high speed, using every ounce of power from the Mondial's magnificent engine. Enzo and Vittorio had both told him that to drive a Ferrari was to drive at maximum revolutions in each gear, in order to make the engine sing and perform what it knew best and what it was designed for.

Occasionally Pietro would spy a slower car ahead of him on the winding mountain road and he would plan ahead for the overtake. First, to make sure there was nothing coming in the opposite direction, then to approach in the gear suitable, to attain the most power possible, at the moment of overtaking. When he was 100 yards from the car ahead, he would toot his horn twice to let the slower driver know he was coming, then he would pull out and surge past. As soon as it was safe he would slide back into the right lane of the narrow winding road, task accomplished, the engine singing and growling like a mountain lion having accomplished its kill.

Soon Pietro came up to Vittorio's garage and, carefully double de-clutching, changed swiftly down through each gear until he eased gently off the road into Vittorio's forecourt. He rolled to a halt, put the gear lever in neutral, set the hand brake and turned off the engine.

Pietro got out of the Mondial and hurried into Vittorio's garage, the one that he used for customer repairs. Vittorio was lying on his back, working on an old Fiat 124 Spider.

"Buon Giorno, Vittorio! Comesta?" said Pietro. He was calm, but his voice betrayed him, the emotion of the day catching up with him.

Vittorio poked his head out from under the Fiat and promptly dropper his spanner, which fell to the concrete floor with a loud clang. "What has happened to you, Pietro? Have you been in an accident? Your face is all mashed up, and why are you wearing that black patch over your eye?" Vittorio rolled out from under the Fiat and stood up to take a closer look. "Ah, such wounds! Tell me, my boy, what happened? Come, I make coffee."

He led the way to his cottage, wiping grease from his hands with a blue rag. Vittorio opened the cottage door and bade Pietro inside. "Sit down and tell me what has happened. How come you didn't call me and tell me about it?"

Pietro sat down while Vittorio fussed with his coffeepot. "It's a long story, Vittorio, but first I have some good news. I met with Enzo Ferrari today and we drove around the racing track in Maranello. He was impressed with my driving skill and asked me to drive for him in the 24-hour Le Mans Grand Prix in three weeks time!"

Pietro's voice was so excited that Vittorio stared at him for a long moment. This boy, this young man, had seen the light. The fire in Pietro's one good eye told the tale. "Fantastico, Pietro, Molto fantastico, and you, of course, said yes?"

"Si, Vittorio, with all my heart and soul I said yes! After all you have taught me in the last six years, how could I possibly say no!" Pietro jumped up and hugged Vittorio, who nearly dropped the coffeepot in surprise.

"Sit down, sit down, and tell me your other news. Tell me about the Mondial Quattrovalve you are driving," said Vittorio.

"How did you know it was a Mondial, Vittorio?"

"Well, I have eyes and saw it sitting on my forecourt when we came here for coffee. But I knew long before I saw it. I listened to you changing gears and double de-clutching, coming down the road, and I said to myself 'Here comes my pupil, Pietro. Only he knows to drive like that, because I taught him.' Also, I know what a 32-valve V-8 Ferrari is supposed to sound like and this one you have is very well tuned by the sound of it. Almost as if I had tuned it myself. Certainly whoever tuned it last knew exactly what they were doing, that's for sure!"

Pietro nodded. "It is a beautiful car to drive, it revs freely and everything about it brings me only a great feeling of happiness. Just to know that it was Enzo's personal car for the last year is enough for me. I shall keep it and treasure it forever."

"Now, tell me why Enzo gave you this great automobile that you love so much. Tell me what happened to your face. Why are your lips all split and swollen, and why are you wearing that patch over your eye?" Vittorio asked.

Pietro took off the patch and Vittorio stared at the nasty, swollen and bruised eyelid that hung weirdly over Pietro's eye. He examined the lumps and cuts and heavy bruising on Pietro's face and neck. Vittorio whistled softly. "Oh, Pietro, did you fight a tiger or a bear? What manner of beast did this to you?"

So Pietro related his sad tale of the night he was to sleep with Stefano's Testarossa, and how late that night the three thugs had come into the garage to find him polishing the Testarossa. How they beat him when he refused to tell them where the keys to the car were. How they kicked him after smashing him to the ground, and how he had passed out after a sickening kick to his head. How he had awakened lying in a pool of his own blood and vomit and stripped of his clothes which they had taken off to search for the keys. Finally, how he had reached for his shotgun while one of the thugs was kicking at Stefano, and how he had shivered in terror seeing Lucia tied to the wall, her face bruised and swollen and her body exposed.

"I had no choice, Vittorio, they were madmen. While the wolf was dealing with two of them, I raised my gun and blew the other one to hell." As Pietro remembered that terrible night, he shivered again uncontrollably. "After I left the hospital today, I found out that Stefano, Luigi and Enzo had all joined together to give me Enzo's very own Mondial as a reward for saving Lucia and Stefano's lives from that third maniac. So, here I am, come to see my good friend Vittorio! What do you think? Do I deserve such a reward? At first I said no, but they wouldn't listen."

"You poor boy, Pietro, what a terrible nightmare. You have suffered enough and I am glad you said 'yes' to the reward. You deserve it and you are a true hero, so don't worry. Now you must get fit again if you want to drive in the Le Mans Grand Prix in three weeks time!"

"Yes," Pietro said, "I need to get my arm back into shape and get rid of this damn patch. Fortunately, the doctor at the hospital said, amazingly there were no fractures, just massive bruising, and in a couple of weeks I should be back to normal."

"You need to go to a physiotherapist for the arm. They will advise you of the best exercises to heal it without causing further damage," said Vittorio.

"Tell me more about the Le Mans circuit, Vittorio. I want to forget what happened that night and concentrate on winning the Le Mans for Enzo, to repay him for giving me his Mondial."

Vittorio got up, went over to a small cupboard set in the wall and took out a heavy roll of paper. He unrolled the paper across a small side table, humming to himself as he sorted through the detailed maps of racing circuits from all around the world. "Ah ha!" Vittorio exclaimed. "Here is a good map of the Le Mans circuit." He put one of the maps aside, rolled the rest neatly, and put them back in the cupboard. He spread the map out on the carpet in front of the sofa, sat down on one end and beckoned Pietro to sit next to him so they could study it.

Vittorio told Pietro all he could remember about the 11-mile long circuit. "Here…" He pointed to the little checkered flag marked on the map, "…is the start and finish point. From there you drive up to the Dunlop Bridge, then immediately after you hit the Esses, a series of fast

234

bends you can take at 100 mph, but not more. Then you bear right on a curve around Tertre Rouge. This curve you can do at 140 mph, maybe a little more." Vittorio took a pen and marked the speeds on the map. "Then you enter the Mulsanne Straight, which runs for nearly four miles. It is here that you can drive flat out at over 200 mph, if you have the power. I think Enzo has a couple of prototypes that will do 250 mph. So here is your chance to get in the lead.

Vittorio traced the path with his finger and Pietro leaned in for a closer look.

"Then, as you come to the end of the straight, which will take you about one minute at 240 mph, you bear right again around the Mulsanne Corner, which you can take at about 90 mph. Then speed up immediately to 170 mph until you get to Indianapolis Corner, which you must take in third gear at between 75 and 95 mph. This leads into Anane Corner, which you can accelerate out of at top speed for about a mile. Then comes Porsche Curves at around 90 mph, into the White House bends at 100 mph, change down to third and negotiate Ford Corner. There you will hit a straight for about a mile and a half, where you can go flat out. Finally, slow for the last curve before the checkered flag where you started!

"So there, my boy, is your challenge. Do as many practice laps as they allow to get used to the circuit. Be careful if it rains and go early into the pits to get a change of tires and fill up with petrol. The weight of the fuel and the heavy tread tires will stop you from spinning out. Any questions?" Vittorio leaned back and looked at Pietro, waiting for him to reply.

Pietro thought for a moment before answering. "Vittorio, I have many, many questions, but I think you have taught me so much over the past five years that you have already answered all the questions that I have today. One thing I do know, is that I am somewhat afraid. Is that normal?"

Vittorio laughed loud and long. "Pietro, don't be concerned about being afraid. To drive in the Le Mans takes a tremendous amount of courage. It is like the bullfight in Spain. The matador, skillful as he is and must be, trembles before he enters the bullring, wondering how fast the bull will be today, how close will the razor sharp horns come to his chest. Oh, yes! The Le Mans can be compared to facing the largest, fastest fighting bull in the whole wide world. When you drive in the Le Mans, you drive on your nerves, but the secret to winning is nerves of steel and utmost concentration. Know exactly where all the other cars on the track in your vicinity are positioned. Outthink them, outsmart them and drive as fast in every gear as you possibly can. Beware of the slower cars in front of you; always find a gap well in advance so you can pass them as fast as possible, as they may also be preparing to overtake an even slower car and may pull out right in front of you, only they may be going much slower than you. And remember if, God forbid, a crash occurs ahead of you, just slow down and drive around it. Whatever you do, don't stare at it for more than a second, and then only to find a clear path around it. Keep your concentration in that moment entirely on driving your car, because if you stare at a crash or a plume of smoke and fire for too long, you will lose your concentration. You might not be able to get it back fast enough to negotiate the next bend, or to avoid hitting someone in front of you who thinks it's good to slow down when a crash occurs, forgetting that there may be ten cars right behind with nowhere to go.

"You are right to be afraid, it is normal. I was always afraid before a race, before every race. But never show your fear to anyone else. Walk with your head up and your back straight. Then, when it is time to race, put on your helmet and your scarf, get into the car, and drive as skillfully as you can. And always drive to win, even if you know you are only third or even sixth. The strangest things happen in racing and you can win, not only because you drive faster than anyone else can, but also because your car may be stronger than theirs or use less fuel. There are many reasons to always drive to win. With that thought in mind and your skill at driving, I know you can win. Enzo will give you his best car I'm sure, and you will drive in the Le Mans. Once you are driving, all fear will disappear and your adrenaline will flow, and you will concentrate on winning the race!"

Pietro smiled at Vittorio. "I feel better already. I will drive to win for you and for Enzo, and for my beautiful Serenella, God rest her soul."

Vittorio went to the same cupboard as before and pulled out a neatly folded scarf woven of the finest silk. Its colors were green, white and red, with the cavallino rampante embroidered in black, on a background of Modena yellow, just like the insignia on all of Enzo's racing cars.

"Here, Pietro, wear this when you drive in the Le Mans. I hope it brings you luck. I wore it in every race for many years. It's getting a bit old, but the silk is still soft and the colors are bright."

"Grazie Tanto, Vittorio, I will wear it with pride and it will help me remember all that you have taught me," said Pietro. He put the scarf around his neck.

Vittorio held out his hand. "Buona Fortuna, Pietro!"

Pietro shook Vittorio's hand and replied, "Grazie, Vittorio."

Vittorio opened the door and they walked out to the garage forecourt where Pietro's shining red Mondial Cabriolet sat waiting for him. Vittorio looked it over.

"Bella Macchina," he said quietly. Pietro got into the Mondial and started the engine, which whistled briefly then settled down to a perfect idle. Vittorio looked down at Pietro and smiled. "Drive well, my friend, and enjoy the Le Mans. I will think of you there, driving against the world's best racing cars and the world's best drivers. Arrivederci!"

Pietro pushed down the clutch and selected first gear. After easing off the hand brake he raised his hand in a brief salute. "Arrivederci, Vittorio." He let the clutch up and drove off. Reaching the road, he turned again to see the silhouette of Vittorio standing against the setting sun. Vittorio waved. Pietro gave two blasts on his horn, then drove out onto the road, gathering tremendous speed as he changed to second gear, then third, each time revving the V-8 engine to the maximum, the Mondial growling in its enjoyment of the open road.

Vittorio stood unmoving until Pietro was out of sight. Then he turned and went indoors, thinking back to his racing days long ago when he, too, was to drive in the Le Mans Grand Prix for the first time.

Pietro sped down the road into the fast approaching dusk. The tail ends of the scarf billowed in the wind. The Mondial carved its way through the air, its engine singing as Pietro accelerated in fourth gear to

6,000 rpm, heading towards the hotel he had called home for the last six years. The visit with Vittorio had renewed his courage, as he knew it would. He was both relaxed and totally concentrated as he drove. He practiced taking the mountain road turns the way Vittorio had taught him, getting the maximum amount of power from the Mondial by perfectly timing the gear changes, and hugging the inner corners, reducing the distance required to round the bends. In a twenty-four hour race such as the Le Mans, this might make the difference between winning and losing.

Darkness fell and Pietro switched on his powerful driving lights and concentrated his sight far ahead of the car, on the very perimeter of the headlight beams, just as Vittorio had taught him.

Stefano and Lucia slept peacefully, snuggled up against each other. Their world was peaceful tonight, but tomorrow would be hectic with the wedding. Occasionally Stefano groaned when his ribs reminded his brain of the trauma they had suffered, and Lucia unconsciously hugged him a little closer. Her warmth and smell told his brain to ignore the pain and enjoy her nearness, so he never woke in pain, but drifted into a deep warm slumber.

Pietro drove up to the hotel as quietly as he could. He parked the Mondial in a spare garage. Turning off the engine, he got out of the car, closed the door quietly and blew a kiss to his beautiful new love. He locked up the garage and went to his room to sleep and dream about the Mondial, the Le Mans and the challenge ahead of him.

9: THE WEDDING DAY

The new day dawned and the sun burst upon the day in a blaze of sunshine. A shaft of sunlight entered Lucia's bedroom and shone through the open curtains onto Lucia and Stefano.

Lucia woke up and stretched her magnificent body under the bedclothes. She turned her head and smiled when she saw the tousled head of Stefano, still sleeping soundly, his arm draped around her. She gently removed Stefano's arm and sat up, her black curly hair contrasting with her white shoulders and breasts.

Sliding out of the bed, she found her dressing gown, hanging on the back of the bathroom door. Putting it on, she searched for her slippers, and found them under the bed where Sheba had taken them. The wolf had a liking for sleeping with Lucia's slippers.

Lucia made herself a cup of coffee and took it out on to the balcony to watch the glorious sunrise.

Two hummingbirds hovered in front of a hanging basket of flowers. Their wings beat amazingly fast as they sucked nectar through their long, pointed beaks. Lucia watched, fascinated by the speed of their beating wings, which could be seen only as a blur. In an instant, they were gone, and Lucia resumed drinking her tasty hot coffee.

A loud howl caused Lucia to hurry to the front door and let Sheba in. The wolf sensed Lucia was not alone and found Stefano still sleeping under the blankets. She stuck her muzzle under the covers and with a carefree shrug, tossed them over her shoulder and onto the floor. Lucia laughed as Stefano awoke, rubbing his eyes. Sheba went into her lunging mode and gave out a loud growl. But, instead of biting Stefano, she came up to him and put her wet nose against his cheek.

"Oh, Sheba!" Lucia cried. "You gave Stefano a kiss! Good girl! For that you get a biscuit." She opened a small cupboard door, took out a box of dog biscuits, and gave one to Sheba. The wolf took it in her teeth and marched out to the balcony, lay down on her stomach and happily devoured the treat.

"Coffee, Stefano?" Lucia asked.

Stefano nodded. "Yes, please, my love. Coffee is just what I need." He looked down at himself. "Oops! No clothes on! I had better get dressed in case you have some human visitors."

Lucia set about making Stefano's coffee and called to him that he could take a shower if he liked.

"No thanks, Lucia, I will just drink the coffee then go shower and change in my own room. Today is a big day for us both!" He laughed, and seeing him laugh, made Lucia very happy.

"You know, by Italian tradition, you should not see the bride on her wedding day, until we meet at the church. But I think tradition and the Lord will forgive us. What do you say?"

"I hope a big policeman doesn't come to lock me up for seeing you," replied Stefano, chuckling. "I would tell the judge, 'I love my little Lucia so much I had to see her. Please forgive me and I will pay you a handsome fine'."

Lucia shook her head and laughed again. "Do you want your coffee in bed, my love?" she asked.

"No, no!" replied Stefano. "Let's drink it on the balcony." So they took their coffee to the balcony and sat together on the chaise lounge. Stefano leaned over and gave Lucia a very wet kiss.

"Buon Giorno, Signorina!"

"Buon Giorno, Signore!"

They laughed then leaned back, drinking their coffee in the warm sunshine. "I think I am in heaven, just to sit here with you on this balcony, drinking my coffee and enjoying the sunshine. What more could anyone ask?" Stefano sat back and looked up at the sky. "Even the weather is perfect, such a deep blue sky!" He set down his half-empty cup of coffee and turned to look at Lucia. "You are such a beautiful sight, I need to cuddle you again." He put his arms around Lucia and held her tight.

Lucia smiled, enjoying his embrace. "Come on, Stefano, you must go to your room to shower and change." She looked at her watch. "Oh, my goodness! I have to do my face and hair yet, Stefano. If you don't let me go I will be late for the wedding!" She kissed him on the nose. "Late for our wedding…."

Stefano chuckled. "If we are both late together, then it's like not being late at all," he said with a grin.

"The priest will know. If we are late, he will say 'they are not coming' and go on to the next wedding, and then we won't be able to marry today and you won't be able to love me like you said last night," said Lucia, waiting for Stefano's reaction.

"In that case I must leave. We must be on time, for I could not spend one more night dreaming about making love to you. I would die of unfulfilled passion…I was this close last night." Stefano put his index filter and thumb one millimeter apart. He sat up and gave Lucia one last kiss then got to his feet. "Arrivederci, my sweet one. See you in church at…what time?"

"Eleven o'clock, and it is already eight thirty. Shoo, now, Stefano!" Lucia blew him a kiss and he went off to his own room. As he passed Sheba, she sat up and let out a little growl, then lay back down again.

"Bye, Sheba, guard your mistress well," said Stefano, carefully stepping over the wolf's body. He opened the door and went down the hall to find the stairs to his own apartment. He whistled the tune softly, "Here comes the bride…."

Luigi had been up since six-thirty. He had double-checked that all of Lucia's aunts and uncles would each have their own limousine to take them to the church. He had called the florists to send huge flower bouquets to the church door, and now he was sitting in his favorite armchair in his study, thinking about his little girl Lucia getting married.

He thought back to the happy days when Lucia's mother was still alive, when every day was a pleasure to wake up and find his great love moving around in the bedroom preparing herself for the day ahead, combing her hair and putting on her face, as she called it.

Luigi sighed and wished she could have been there today to see her daughter get married in the little Maranello church. At least Stefano is not a crook, thought Luigi. He seems a decent young man who is genuinely in love with Lucia. And she loves him, too. So that is good.

Luigi got up from the chair and went to look out the window. The weather was fine, a beautiful day for a wedding. He went to his stereo and selected an old 78 rpm record by Beniamino Gigli, the famous Italian tenor. "La Donna e Mobile…" The tenor's voice was powerful, yet gracious. Luigi listened as the tenor, together with the orchestra and chorus of Teatro Alla Scala, Milan, performed his favorite aria. He sat down again and with eyes closed listened as Beniamino's voice soared to the rooftops. Ah, what a maestro! thought Luigi, as he hummed along with Beniamino, waiting for that vibrant part…so beautiful….

The record ended and Luigi still sat there. The next time I hear that song, my little girl will be married, he thought. Ah, well, she has to live her own life. Thank God she is alive and full of life, at least I can be thankful to God and Pietro for that!

Luigi rose from the armchair and went to the door to do some last minute work at the front desk before going off to the wedding of his little girl.

Stefano showered and shaved, put on his best blue shirt. Instead of a tie, he put on a dark blue silk cravat, navy blue wool trousers, blue socks and his best Alfani slipon shoes with no laces. He gave his hair a quick brush, checked himself in the full-length mirror and went to leave the suite. Halfway to the door he suddenly remembered that the ring was in his other jacket pocket along with his wallet. He retrieved them both from the jacket in the wardrobe and carefully stowed the ring in his hip pocket and his wallet in his inside pocket.

He looked at his watch. Only 9:30! Ah, plenty of time to take the Testarossa for a spin! Off he went down the stairs, taking them two at a time in his happiness.

Pietro, a typical young man, slept late and it wasn't until 9:15 that he awoke. Rubbing his eyes and stretching his arms, he glanced at the clock on the bedside table. Wow! It's late! Am I supposed to work today? With his mind misty and groggy from his deep sleep, he decided that maybe today was a day off… He lay back down again and felt something hard under his back. He rolled over and pulled out his eye patch from under the sheet. Suddenly it dawned on him. Today was Stefano and Lucia's wedding!

He jumped out of bed and ran for the shower. He caught a glimpse of his face in the bathroom mirror and groaned. His face was still black and blue, and his eyelid looked worse than yesterday. The swollen lump of skin hung dauntingly over his eye. He shuddered. What can I do about it? Nothing for now.

Pietro showered quickly and shaved at the sink. Running into the bedroom, he grabbed a shirt and tie from a hanger in his wardrobe and hastily put them on. He took out his best navy blue suit and literally jumped into the trousers, found some dark blue socks stuffed in his Sunday shoes, and put them on.

Again, he glanced in the mirror. His eyelid looked terrible, red, raw and still hanging down! He searched the bed for his white eye patch, eventually found it and put it on. Certainly it was a great improvement, making him look nearly normal except for the yellow and blue bruising on his cheeks. At least the swelling on his lips had started to go down, so he no longer looked quite like a prizefighter. He squirted hair oil from a bottle onto his hands and passed his hands through his thick black hair, rubbing the oil well into the scalp like he had always done and as his father had done before him.

Pietro rinsed his hands under the bathroom tap and ran a comb through his hair, combing it straight back in the Italian tradition. He put on his suit jacket, checked himself once more in the mirror, grabbed his keys and wallet from the bedside table, and ran out of the room towards the garage.

He opened the door to the garage where the beautiful red Mondial sat quietly, waiting for him. It gleamed like fire and the tan leather looked so soft and opulent. "Mama Mia!" Pietro shouted. "Mama Mia!"

Lucia looked at the wedding dress hanging on the hanger clipped over the cornice above the wardrobe. The dress was white, made entirely of lace in many layers. It was over thirty years old, her mother's wedding dress. Lucia's mother had given it to her the week before she died. Lucia thought back to that day when she went to visit her mother in hospital and saw the large flat box by the side of her mother's bed.

She remembered distinctly the smile on her mother's face as she asked Lucia to open the flat box. Her mother loved to give things. All her life she was gifted with the joy of giving and never thought about receiving. Always a happy person, she glowed with affection. Lucia remembered the aura of her mother, such a happy, caring person. Even when things went wrong, she would always look on the bright side, saying, "Every cloud has a silver lining," a motto she truly believed in.

Lucia looked again at the dress and tears clouded her beautiful brown eyes. "Oh, Mama! I wish you were here today to see me in your dress," Lucia whispered.

Then she remembered her mother's words as she gave her the dress. "Wear this dress on your wedding day, my child. Wear it for me, and whatever happens between now and then, enjoy your life, your youth and your beauty. Only one thing I will ask, marry only a man who you truly love and who truly loves you, then you will always be happy together. Tell me you will wear the dress on your wedding day?"

"Oh, Mama," Lucia had said, "it is a beautiful dress! I will wear it with honor on my wedding day and you will be proud of me, Mama!"

"I won't be at your wedding, dear Lucia…except through my dress. The cancer will have taken me by then, but I will be watching you from above…"

Lucia wiped her eyes and looked again at the dress. She took it off the hanger and put it on. It fit almost perfectly.

She reached for her lace veil and set it on her head. The exquisitely embroidered lace hung over her shoulders to her waist, and a thick layer of the finest Italian lace hung over her face. Lucia pulled the veil to one side and pinned it in place. I don't need to cover my face; I want Stefano to see how happy I am! she thought. Finding her white gloves and shoes, she slipped them on and looked in the mirror. "Thank you, Mama!" she said.

A knock came on the door. "May I come in, Lucia?"

"Of course, Father, I am just this second ready…such good timing." She laughed.

Luigi came in, resplendent in a black dress suit complete with tails and a grey top hat.

"Oh, Papa! You look magnificent!"

Luigi smiled. "No, my child, you are the one who looks magnificent. You are as beautiful as your mother was the day she wore that dress. You look lovely!"

"Is it time to go yet, Papa?" asked Lucia.

"It is ten thirty. It takes about twenty minutes to drive there, so we just have time for a quick drink, if you would like one?"

Lucia nodded. Luigi pulled out a silver flask from his breast pocket, unscrewed the little cup on the top and poured a small amount, then handed the cup to Lucia. She took it and sipped it. "To your health, Papa!"

She drained the tiny cup and handed it back to her father who filled it again, and raising the little silver cup, said, "To my darling daughter on her wedding day. Salut!" He drained the cup in one go and screwed the cap back onto the flask then put it back into his breast pocket. "In case I get thirsty!" he said, laughing. "Come, my child, your carriage is waiting."

Luigi and Lucia walked through the hotel foyer arm-in-arm. Those few hotel personnel who were unable to attend the wedding ceremony cheered and shouted "Bravo!" as Luigi and Lucia went past.

Alberto, who was to be their chauffeur once again, bid them a hearty "Buon Giorno, Signorina é Signore," and escorted them to his Cadillac. He saw them in and closed the door then hurried around to the driver side, got in and started the engine. The Cadillac glided down the drive towards the road to Maranello. Luigi sat back, relaxed and patted his beautiful daughter's hand.

Alberto drove slowly down the hill to Maranello. He smiled as he looked in his rearview mirror and saw how beautiful Lucia looked.

Stefano Gapucci is a lucky man, thought Alberto, to marry such a gorgeous woman. Mama mia!

Pietro drove his brilliant red Mondial Cabriolet fast down to the little church in Maranello. He reflected on this incredible change in his life. Here he was driving his very own Ferrari, going to his first ever wedding, to see his dear friend Stefano marry his love, Lucia. Pietro was so excited he drove extremely fast in his joyous mood and suddenly, checking his speedometer, saw he was driving double the legal speed limit. He grimaced and slowed to a more legal speed, the V-8 singing in his ears and the wind whipping through his hair.

He thought of the upcoming vacation; the trip to Rome, Naples, Genoa, Switzerland, and then to Le Mans, where he would drive for Enzo, his great hero. The little church appeared and Pietro slowed again, searching for a parking spot. Seeing none near the church, he decided to park between two large limousines neatly parked nearby. He pulled off the road onto the grass verge, turned off the engine and set the hand brake. He got out of the Mondial, locked the doors and walked swiftly to the church entrance, hoping he would not be late for the wedding.

Stefano had taken the Testarossa for his last spin as a bachelor. He turned away from Maranello at the bottom of the hill and set off for a drive in the mountains. Like Pietro, he drove fast, but with caution. I don't want to have an accident on my wedding day! he thought. He slowed on the turns and accelerated out of each bend only if the road was totally clear. Thoroughly enjoying himself, he guided the wide Testarossa around hairpin after hairpin until he was running along the top of a high mountain. He checked his watch. Ten fifteen. Oh! Oh! Best to turn around and head for the church. Can't keep Lucia waiting; I love her so much!

He made a neat U-turn and zigzagged back down the mountain, dreaming of his beautiful bride-to-be, Lucia. "Oh, my true love!" he shouted over the sound of the growling Redhead's engine.

Stefano made it to the church about two minutes before eleven. He parked the Redhead near Pietro's Mondial on the grass verge. He got out and checked his watch. Amazed at the time, he hurried to the church where Pietro was waiting for him just inside the door.

"Is Lucia here already?" he asked, out of breath and limping badly, as his back and leg were reminding him to slow down.

"'No," replied Pietro, laughing. "You have plenty of time. Where are your walking sticks?"

Stefano grinned. "I was in such a hurry I left them in the car. I must be getting better!"

"You forgot because you are so much in love I think," said Pietro. "Would you like me to get them for you, Stefano?"

"No, thank you. I will try and make do without them. To hell with the pain, I don't want Lucia and her family to think she is marrying a cripple, do I?"

"It's your decision, Stefano. As long as you don't faint before the 'I Do' part."

Stefano looked closely at Pietro. "You still look like a walking wounded soldier with your magnificent patch. How are you feeling?"

"Pretty good, today. I'm looking forward to your wedding. This is my first!" Pietro replied.

They stood together on the steps of the small church. A slight breeze blew gently through their hair. Small clouds scudded across the sky, but the sun shone through, throwing its warmth on the little town of Maranello.

Stefano noticed the limo as it entered the drive. He grabbed Pietro's arm and turned around. "Here she comes, Pietro, yahoo!" he shouted. "Let's go in before she sees us." The two young men went into the church and walked slowly down the aisle, Stefano trying not to limp by leaning on Pietro's shoulder.

Alberto turned the corner and pulled into the driveway of the church and stopped the limousine gently in front of the main door. He got out of the car and hurried around to open the rear door so that Lucia and Luigi could alight in style. As they entered the church, Luigi held Lucia's arm and looked solemnly around. The organist began playing the Wedding March.

The church was full to the brim and all eyes were on Lucia and Luigi as they came down the aisle towards the waiting priest who was beaming at them. They stopped in front of the altar and the wedding music slowly faded. The priest beckoned to Stefano and Pietro who were standing in the front pew.

Luigi turned to Lucia and smiled. "Well, my lovely daughter, it's time for me to give you to Stefano. Buona Fortuna and God go with you. Remember, I will always be there for you if you need me!"

"Grazie, Poppa, grazie." Lucia squeezed her father's hand. "I love you, Poppa, I will always love you and always be your daughter."

Luigi stepped back a few paces and Stefano came to stand on Lucia's right side. Pietro approached and stood at Stefano's side.

The priest began the wedding ceremony; first reciting in Latin of the Grace of God and blessing the couple and the congregation. Then he proceeded to ask the questions:

"Do you, Stefano Gapucci, take Lucia Constanetti for your lawful wedded wife in the sight of God, to have and to hold in sickness and in health till death do you part?"

Stefano replied, "I do."

"Do you, Lucia Constanetti take Stefano Gapucci for your lawful wedded husband in the sight of God, to have and to hold in sickness and in health till death do you part?"

Lucia replied, "I do."

The priest looked out at the congregation and asked, "If there is anyone among you that knows of any reason why Stefano Gapucci and Lucia Constanetti should not be joined together in Holy Matrimony, then speak now or forever hold thy peace!"

The church was silent; no one spoke. The priest put his hands together, then made the sign of the cross over Stefano and Lucia. "In Nomine Patris, et Filii, et Spiritus Sancti.Amen" The priest turned to Pietro. "The ring, please."

Pietro, having only moments earlier received Lucia's mother's ring from Stefano while waiting for Lucia, dug into his pocket and found the ring. He handed it to the priest who gave it to Stefano. Stefano slipped the ring onto Lucia's finger.

The priest chanted in Latin for some moments, eyes closed. Then he opened his eyes and looked at Stefano and Lucia. "In the sight of God, I now pronounce you Husband and Wife! You may kiss the bride."

Stefano grasped Lucia gently by the shoulders and the couple kissed with passion.

The organist played loudly and all the people in the church stood and clapped. As the wedding guests shouted and whistled, the few babies present who had been so quiet during the ceremony, burst into tears and cried because the sudden commotion came as a surprise.

Stefano was still kissing Lucia, even as the priest was saying, "God bless you, my children. God go with you in peace." They finally and reluctantly stopped kissing, and turned to walk back down the aisle, their faces happy and Lucia blushing, as most brides do. With the organist bellowing out grand music, the newlyweds walked to the front of the church. At every pew, people congratulated and cheered them on.

About half way to the door, Stefano could not resist stopping and kissing his beloved Lucia. He turned to her, grasped her in his arms and kissed her deeply and lovingly. His emotion flowed through to Lucia and she kissed him back just as passionately. The people in the church cheered, "Bravo! Bravo!"

Stefano stepped back from Lucia and gazed into her eyes. "I will love you forever, my darling, come what may!" Lucia embraced him. She was so overcome by emotion the tears started to roll down her cheeks. "Don't cry, my sweetheart," Stefano said.

"I am crying because I am so happy, Stefano. This is a wonderful day. You are my true love and I feel it deep in my heart." Stefano gazed into her eyes and kissed her. The crowd in the church loved it. They whistled and cheered, happy to see a couple so much in love.

Outside, the sun shone in all its glory. Luigi had hired two photographers to capture the moment, and what a moment it was! The couple stood on the church steps while the photographers took photos from every angle, capturing the refreshing happiness emanating from Lucia and Stefano.

Enzo, Luigi, Pietro and the priest came out, and Lucia had them stand next to her and Stefano, two on either side for a great photograph. The aunts and uncles were next to line up, all dressed in their colorful finery. Then the photographers had the whole congregation line up in rows, and took wide-angle lens shots so that everyone would be in the picture.

At last, all the picture taking was completed and it was time for Lucia and Stefano to leave for the hotel and the reception. Pietro borrowed Stefano's keys and drove the Redhead in front of the church steps.

Stefano opened the passenger door for his bride and tucked her dress in, which was billowing out of the door in the light breeze. He closed the door, went around to the driver side and got into the car. Someone in the family had remembered to tie some old boots and cans to the back, and as Stefano drove off, he and Lucia waved, and the tin cans clattered on the roadway. Stefano gave a double blast on the Redhead's horn and accelerated off towards the hotel.

And then they were gone. The crowd, still in a happy mood, stayed and talked with each other about how beautiful the bride looked and how passionate the kissing was. The limousines rolled up to take Lucia's family to the reception. Soon all was quiet and just Luigi, Enzo and Pietro were standing on the steps.

"Bellissimo! A beautiful bride and a beautiful wedding," Enzo boomed.

"Come, Enzo and Pietro, let's drink a little champagne back at the hotel," said Luigi.

Enzo said, "Can you give me a lift, Luigi? I have no car today"

Pietro looked at Enzo and Enzo laughed. Then Luigi laughed and finally Pietro laughed.

Alberto opened the limousine's door for Luigi and Enzo, and whisked them away to the hotel. Pietro sat down on the steps, and with a sudden memory of Serenella his lost love, he burst into tears and sobbed for her to console him. The priest came out of the church and hurried to comfort Pietro who looked so forlorn.

"What is it, my son? What is troubling you?" asked the priest.

Through his tears, Pietro told of his beautiful Serenella and how they were to be engaged to be married, and how she had died in the hospital. The priest patted Pietro's shoulder and told him how everything in life has a purpose and that Serenella had gone to the angels and even now was watching over Pietro, guarding him from evil.

Pietro went back into the church with the priest and they each lit a holy candle for Serenella, then said a prayer for her soul. Pietro thanked the priest for consoling him and left the church, his mind relieved by the priest's kind words.

He got into his Mondial and drove slowly to the hotel, wondering what it would have been like to have married his sweetheart in the church today, as Stefano had married Lucia. Oh, well, he thought sadly, I will never know. But I will always love my little Serenella, God rest her beautiful soul. He drove into the hotel driveway, parked around the back, and walked into the wedding reception.

A five-piece violin and accordion orchestra was playing at the back of the dining room. The music was pure Italian, full of passion and fire and fitting for the occasion. Most of the people from the church were already there; some sitting at the tables, drinking and eating, while many couples were letting their hair down and dancing to the fiery music.

Little children chased each other around the dance floor, making lots of noise and thoroughly enjoying themselves.

Lucia and Stefano were sitting at the large table near the band, surrounded by the aunts and uncles who were lavishing affection on the happy couple. Next to Lucia and Stefano sat Luigi and Enzo, and next to them sat Anna, the pretty young girl from the agency. She saw Pietro enter the room and stood up to catch his attention, pointing to an empty chair that had been saved for him. Pietro straightened his shoulders, took a deep breath, and made his way across the room carefully, avoiding treading on some small children rolling on the floor.

"Pietro! How nice to see you!" said Anna. "Sorry I missed you at the wedding. It was so lovely, such happiness. How are your wounds?"

"Better, thank you, Anna. Just my eye is still very ugly, so I must wear this patch," Pietro replied. He suddenly remembered that Anna would be coming with him to Rome today. How could he have forgotten? Everything had moved so fast in the last few days, what with the hospital and the Mondial and the request from Enzo for him to drive in the Le Mans. That must be it! Soon he would be back to normal, he hoped.

"Are you all ready to leave for Rome, Anna?" asked Pietro.

"Whenever you say, Pietro. I brought my one case to the hotel so I am ready to go. I'm very much looking forward to it; much better than going alone on the bus."

"Good," said Pietro, "we will leave when Lucia and Stefano are ready. Would you like a drink while we wait?"

"I'll have a white wine, please," Anna said.

Pietro found a bottle of white wine on the table and a clean wineglass. He poured a glass for Anna and handed it to her.

"Grazie, Pietro," she said. Pietro spotted some lemonade in a jug and poured himself a glass.

"Salut," he said as he clinked his glass with Anna's.

She smiled and sipped her wine. "Delicious!" she said, gazing at Pietro.

Pietro had a strange feeling when Anna smiled at him. Her smile was so much like Serenella's smile, he thought. He sipped his lemonade, leaned back in his chair and looked around the room. He felt a little embarrassed with his patch and battered face, but no one seemed to be bothered by it, so he started to relax.

Luigi clinked his wineglass with a silver spoon to gain the attention of the guests. The reverberating sound of the crystal stilled the conversations, and the orchestra leader raised his index finger to his lips to shush the exuberant members of his quintet. Almost immediately the room became silent, all eyes looked towards Luigi in expectation.

"My dear friends and relatives. Thank you for coming today. I would like to propose a toast to the happy couple!" Luigi raised his glass. "Let us drink to Lucia and Stefano, may their life together be a happy and joyful one and may they present me with lots of grandchildren to bounce on my knee and compensate me for losing my daughter to this lucky young man." Luigi paused, smiled broadly, raised his glass higher and said, simply, "Salut to Lucia and Stefano, Buona Fortuna!"

"Buona Fortuna!" cried the guests, raising their glasses in honor of the couple. Everyone sipped whatever he or she was drinking, from the old aunties to the young children, eager to mimic this grand man, Luigi. "And now I would like one dance with my daughter, then I will turn her over to her new husband!" said Luigi. He drained his wineglass and turned to Lucia, offering his hand.

Lucia stood up and moved forward to her father, grasped his hand and followed him onto the dance floor, as the guests who had been dancing melted quietly to the sidelines. The orchestra struck up "La Donna e Mobile" and Lucia and Luigi danced together to the melody. Luigi wondered how the musicians had known it was his favorite tune. Strange, he thought, but forgot about the amazing coincidence and danced with his beautiful daughter. He gazed at her while dancing. How radiant she looks, he thought, just like her mother. His mind took him back to his own wedding day when he had danced with his bride thirty years or more ago, to the very same tune. And she, as Lucia today, had worn the same wedding dress and had looked so radiant! So happy, so full of life!

The music came to an end and Luigi bowed and smiled at Lucia. "Thank you, my daughter, you have made an old man happy!" He beckoned to Stefano. "Come, Stefano, your turn now to dance with your new bride. Look after her well."

Lucia squeezed her father's hand and leaned forward to give him a quick kiss on the forehead. "Grazie, Papa, you, too, have made me so happy on my wedding day."

Stefano stepped forward, took Lucia's hand in his and started to dance with her. The orchestra struck up the classic Italian wedding aria, and Lucia and Stefano glided around the dance floor, gazing at each other with deep passion.

After they had circled the dance floor three times, the guests also started to dance, as was the custom, and soon the dance floor was crowded with exuberant couples, as well as little boys dancing with little girls. Sounds of the accordion and violins bounced off the high ceilings, causing the dancers to move faster and faster.

Enzo danced with one of Lucia's aunts, and Luigi danced with a young lady. Only Pietro and Anna were left sitting,. Pietro summoned up his courage. "Would you like to dance, Anna?" She nodded enthusiastically. Pietro led Anna to the dance floor. She turned to him. He took her left hand in his and put his other hand on her waist. He was nervous, not having danced since the old days with Serenella, in their little village.

Once they started to dance, Pietro began to enjoy it. The sounds of the violins and accordion, and the musky scent of perfume that Ann was wearing made Pietro feel free and easy, without troubles or pain.

He danced with Anna, just as in days gone by he had danced with Serenella.

The dancing went on, everyone having fun to the great sounds of the quintet. Pietro was enjoying a slow waltz with Anna when Stefano tapped him on the shoulder.

"We are going up to change and get our luggage, then take off. Are you nearly ready to go?" asked Stefano.

"Anna is all packed and ready, but I have a few things to do," replied Pietro.

"Okay, we will meet you in the lobby in half an hour," said Stefano.

"Fine!" said Pietro. "See you then."

Lucia and Stefano made their way through the dancers and went off to Lucia's room. Pietro asked Anna if she would like to wait for him here, or if she would like to come to his room while he finished packing.

"I'll come with you, Pietro," she said. "All this dancing has exhausted me. I need to sit down for a little while."

Pietro took Anna's hand and led her off the dance floor. Her hand felt good. Pietro hazily remembered years ago when he and Serenella would walk in the woods holding hands without a care in the world. His throat tightened as memories of Serenella and their good times drifted through his mind. He found himself gasping for air and had to stop and lean against the wall for a moment.

"What's the matter, Pietro? Are you not feeling well?" asked Anna.

Pietro pulled himself together and took a deep breath. "It's nothing, Anna, I'll be all right in a moment. It's just the excitement I guess. I am feeling better already!" He took another deep breath and started off again, still a little giddy.

"Should you see a doctor, Pietro? Maybe you left the hospital too early?" said Anna.

"No. Honestly, Anna, I feel much better now, I promise."

"Very well, but promise me if you feel ill again, we will go straight to a doctor," said Anna, still with a note of concern in her voice.

"I promise. Let's go and pack my things. Once we are in the car in the fresh air, I'm sure I will feel better," said Pietro.
Pietro unlocked the door to his room and they went inside.

Anna took a glass from the sink, filled it with water and handed it to Pietro. "Drink this, it will help."

Pietro drained the glass of water and did feel better. "Thank you, Anna. Please have a seat." he gestured to a chair by the window. "I will pack and then we will pick up Sheba, and wait outside for Lucia and Stefano."

Anna sat and watched as Pietro took his small suitcase from under the bed, opened it and placed his shirts, trousers and jackets into it.

"Oh, Pietro, let me do that. Everything will be so crumpled if you pack like that! You sit down and I will pack."

Pietro looked at how he had stuffed everything into the small case. She was right, of course, he never had been much good at packing. He sat down and watched as Anna neatly and efficiently folded his clothes and packed them in the case, amazed at how easily she did it.

Anna closed the case and looked at Pietro with a smile. "All done. Anything else to go? Are you going to take your toothbrush?" She went into the bathroom and gathered up Pietro's things. "Do you have a bag for these?" she asked.

"In the cupboard behind the door is a red bag, Anna," Pietro called.

Anna found the bag and put Pietro's razor, toothbrush and toothpaste into it. She appeared in the doorway. "Can you check your drawers and cupboards to see if there is anything else you will need, Pietro?"

Pietro got up and rummaged through his closets and drawers. "That's it, Anna, everything I need is in that little case."

"You can buy new clothes in Rome. They have great shops there. I will take you to a few I know, and if you will permit me, I will pick out some comfortable, colorful clothes and shoes for your trip."

"That will be nice, Anna, thank you."

"Shall we go?"

Pietro looked around the room. "This has been my home for six years. It will be interesting to travel, but I will miss my little home here," he said.

"If you like it so much, you must return and live your life here, Pietro," said Anna.

Pietro lifted the suitcase and opened the door. As Anna went out, Pietro turned and said a silent goodbye to his little room. They walked together to the lobby and Anna retrieved her case from the concierge.

Luigi came out of the dining room. "Ah, Pietro, you are leaving?"

"Si, Luigi, we wait for Lucia and Stefano outside."

Luigi shook hands with him. "Drive carefully, my boy, and enjoy your holiday." To Anna he said, "Look after him, Anna. He is still frail. See that he gets some rest from time to time." Anna smiled and said she would.

"Oh, oh!" said Pietro. "We nearly forgot Sheba!" He put down his case and went off to find the wolf, calling to Anna and Luigi that he would be back in a moment. He hurried down to the Chef's apartment and knocked on the door.

The Chef's wife, Isabella, opened the door. "Ah, Pietro! You come for Sheba. She is all ready to go. Here is a bag of dog food she likes. Be sure and buy the same brand when you have finished this one."

"I will," said Pietro, lifting up the large green bag of dry dog food.

The two children came into the hallway with Sheba, who was now on a long leash with a heavy chain around her neck. They each gave Sheba a hug. Then the little one gave the leash end to Pietro solemnly. "Look after our Sheba, Signore Pietro, we love her very much."

"I promise, my little ones. See you in a few weeks!"

Isabella gave Pietro a hug. "Take care of yourself, Pietro, we love you too!"

"Grazie, Isabella, you also take care. I love you very much. You have always been good to me."

Isabella stepped back, little tears forming in her eyes. "Go now and enjoy yourself. I will come out in a minute when I have composed myself, and wave goodbye."

Pietro called to Sheba to come and they went down the hallway. Sheba turned at the end of the hallway and let out a howl as if to say goodbye, then went with Pietro towards the lobby.

Pietro introduced Anna to Sheba, who wagged her tail and leaned against Anna. "Oh Sheba, you are a sweetheart", said Anna happily. "I wasn't sure how you would take to me, but I can see we are going to get on fine."

They went through the double doors held open by a pair of excited bellboys. "Buona Fortuna in Le Mans, Pietro!" they shouted.

"Grazie! Grazie! See you soon," said Pietro. He put the bag of dog food down next to the two suitcases that the bellboys had brought out. "Wait here, Anna, I will get the car." He gave Anna Sheba's leash and went off to the back of the hotel.

There, waiting for him in the sunlight, was his gorgeous Mondial Cabriolet. Pietro stopped and admired its beautifully sleek lines with the roof down. Such a car, and it is mine. Unbelievable! thought Pietro. He opened the door, got in, started the engine and drove around to the front of the hotel.

Anna saw him coming and cried out in amazement. "Pietro! What a beautiful car! I thought you were going to borrow Lucia's little Alfa! Did you steal this one?"

"It's a long story, Anna, I will tell you when we get on the road." Pietro opened the boot and put the suitcases and the dog food inside. "Lucky we don't have any more luggage. Except for the space in the front, the boot is full," said Pietro. He took Sheba's lead from Anna, opened the driver's door, pulled the seat back forward, and told Sheba to jump in the back. Sheba needed no second bidding, jumped in, and sat, her huge head held high.

At that moment the Chef's two children came running up. "Hey, Pietro! Don't forget Sheba's water and food bowls!" One child carried the two bowls, the other held a gallon jug of water.

"Grazie!" said Pietro. "It would have been difficult without these." He squeezed the bowls and the water into the boot and shut it carefully.

Anna was admiring the Mondial, oohing and aahing, stroking the leather seats and the fleece of the folded top. "So soft and luxurious…oh, Pietro, I am going to enjoy the drive to Rome in your car. It's stunning! I love it!"

Pietro was pleased Anna expressed her emotions so openly. He, too, loved the Mondial, not just as a car but as a true work of art. Not only was it a sculptured goddess, but it had a beating heart that no other sculpture in the world could match.

The commotion in the hotel lobby rose to a higher pitch as Lucia and Stefano came through the double doors, covered in colorful confetti. The guests streamed out, saying their good-byes and good wishes to the happy couple.

Aroused by the sound of so many strange people, Sheba let out a loud, piercing howl, which caused many a guest, to look nervously at the huge silver wolf, sitting in the back seat of the Mondial.

Enzo was there also, and borrowed Stefano's keys to fetch the Testarossa from the parking area behind the hotel. Within a minute he was back, parking the beautiful Redhead next to Pietro's Mondial. The crowd grew silent, taking in the tremendous beauty of the two red Ferraris glistening in the sunshine.

Enzo got out and handed the keys to Stefano. Luigi came down the steps with Lucia who was now dressed in blue corduroy slacks and matching waistcoat over a white silk blouse.

Luigi gave her a hug, then shook hands with Stefano. "Buon Viaggio, my children, drive carefully. Have fun, look after yourselves and come back safely," he said.

The guests flocked forward and threw more confetti until Lucia and Stefano were covered in tiny flakes.

"Are you ready, Pietro?" called Stefano over the din.

Pietro smiled and nodded. "Si, Stefano, let's go. What route do we take?"

"We drive about fifty miles then stop at a little town in the mountains. I will give you a signal with my hand about one mile before we turn off. Anna knows the place, she helped Lucia plan the route, so you should be okay. If you need to stop, flash your lights and I will pull over."

Stefano finished packing the luggage and closed the front bonnet and the boot. He opened the door for Lucia, waited for her to get in, then bent down and gave her a long kiss on the lips. The crowd cheered with enthusiasm.

Pietro pulled the front seat into position and Anna got in. Then, on the spur of the moment, he leaned over and gave her a peck on the cheek. The guests howled and cheered. Pietro reddened, overcome with embarrassment. He smiled, waved to the guests and said good-bye. Quickly moving to the driver side, he got into the Mondial and started the engine to conceal his embarrassment from Anna, who was pleasantly surprised at his kiss on her cheek.

Stefano got into the Redhead, closed the huge door and started the massive Flat-12 engine, which roared into life, all but muffling the V-8 sounds of the Mondial. Stefano pressed the clutch, put the gear lever into first and pulled away, He tooted his horn and waved. Lucia turned and waved also. The crowd cheered as the tin cans rattled behind the Redhead. Pietro followed Stefano out onto the road, waving and tooting his horn twice for luck.

Sheba gave a loud howl in response to the horns and then they were gone, onto the road, down the hill towards Maranello. The crowd watched the two beautiful cars until they were out of sight. Then Luigi requested that they all come in and dance and eat until the food was gone and the orchestra too tired to play anymore. Everyone went inside, eager to keep the happy party going.

10: THE JOURNEY

Stefano drove the Redhead at moderate speed down the hill then turned off at the bottom to head South towards Rome, taking the route he had planned with Lucia. He kept a close eye on the rearview mirror from time to time, checking that all was well with Pietro who followed about a hundred yards behind.

The Two Ferraris sped through the Italian countryside, the scenery exhilarating with little traffic on the back roads. An occasional Fiat would appear ahead then disappear as a speck in the rearview mirrors as the two overtook with incredible ease. The sun shone as they took the ring road around Modena, heading ever South towards Rome.

Stefano turned off on the narrow road towards Zocca, into more splendid mountain scenery. Sheba, unperturbed by the motion of the Mondial, sat happily in the back seat, enjoying the fresh mountain air and occasionally letting out a loud howl whenever she spotted a dog or a cat along the road.

Soon they entered the little town of Zocca and Stefano parked in the town center next to a bistro, beside a small river flowing through the town. As soon as Pietro stopped, Sheba leaped out onto the grass to relieve herself. Pietro took her water bowl out of the boot and filled it with water. While Sheba lapped thirstily, Stefano found an empty table with four chairs and they sat down as the waiter came to take their orders.

"What shall it be, girls?" asked Stefano. "Would you like wine or lemonade?" They decided on lemonade and a large slice of pizza with ham and pineapple topping. After taking their order, the waiter went back in to get their drinks. Sheba sat back on her haunches and watched carefully, as a group of children appeared as if from nowhere, and came closer and closer to the two magnificent red Ferraris, each child commenting on which they preferred; the convertible Mondial or the wide Testarossa.

"How fast do they go, Signore?" asked one brave little boy.

"Very fast, very fast indeed!" replied Stefano, grinning.

"Which one is faster?" asked a little girl who had a massive mop of curly hair.

"Guess," said Pietro.

The little girl conferred with her friends. She giggled with embarrassment then pointed to the Mondial. "This one is fastest because it has no roof?"

"Close," said Pietro. "You are a clever girl. When the Mondial is going fast, it feels faster than the Testarossa because the wind blows through your hair, so, personally, I think it is the faster car."

"No way," said Stefano. "The Testarossa will eat the Mondial!" The two young men started a lively discussion with the children as to which car was more powerful. Neither Stefano nor Pietro would back down on whose car was more powerful, so they decided to switch cars for the next leg of the drive to Rome.

Stefano got out the map. "Here is Lucca. It's just a few miles from Zocca. To prove which car is faster on a normal road, we can see who arrives in Lucca town center first. What do you say, Pietro?"

"Well, I thought we were going to make a slow, back-road trip to Rome, but if the ladies agree then I am game," said Pietro.

Lucia and Anna were concerned. "You are both still recuperating. Maybe it is too much for you. If you drive too fast and make a mistake, it will not be so much fun," said Lucia.

"I agree," said Anna, "let's just take it slowly, the way we have up to now, and enjoy the drive, not race to Lucca."

Stefano and Pietro pondered on the wisdom of their young ladies. "Maybe they are right. I have a new idea," said Stefano. "How about we leave the racing till we get to Le Mans, then we can truly race on a real track?"

Pietro agreed and the two shook hands. "Until Le Mans! We don't race each other, just have fun," Pietro said.

They finished their lemonade and pizza, said goodbye to the children and took off for Lucca. The children waved and the two Ferraris vanished into the mountains, leaving the beautiful sleepy town of Zocca to its peace and tranquility.

Even though they weren't really racing, Stefano and Pietro still had some fun when the road was clear of other traffic. Pietro would shift down to third gear, toot his horn once to warn Stefano, then floor the accelerator, and the Mondial would rocket past the Testarossa. Stefano would wait until the next clear stretch then, with a phenomenal burst of speed from the Redhead's Flat-12, effortlessly pass Pietro, giving a double toot on his horn.

The two girls just leaned back in their leather seats and occasionally waved to each other from time to time. When Pietro accelerated, Sheba would let out her piercing howl, sitting still and straight in the back seat, enjoying the wind and the sound of the V-8 engine.

The mountains turned into foothills as they descended towards Lucca. They went through the town of Lucca, on to Vecchiano and then to Pisa, where Stefano got lost, and more by accident than by design, arrived at the base of the famous Leaning Tower.

They parked and went to gaze at one of the most unusual sights in the world. The whole tower leaned at a precarious angle, looking as if it was about to fall at any moment. But, as one of the guides was telling a group of tourists, it had stood like this for many centuries, and probably would do so for many more.

After Anna took photographs of their group, they found a café and drank Cappuccino and ate tasty doughnuts. Stefano took a nap on a bench while Lucia, Anna and Pietro took Sheba for a walk. The huge wolf caused many a wary tourist to walk carefully around them rather than risk walking next to Sheba.

Stefano was still sleeping when they returned, and everyone laughed when Sheba went up to Stefano and began to lick his face with her very long, raspy tongue. Stefano awoke. Sheba looked at his nose and sat watching him, her face right up close to Stefano's. Stefano rubbed his eyes and grinned at the wolf as the others laughed.

They walked back to the parking lot to find a throng of locals and tourists admiring the two Ferraris. One young man was busy explaining to the crowd that both cars were designed by Pinninfarina and how one was powered by a Flat-12 Boxer type engine and the other by a 3.2 litre V-8. "Both are capable of over 150 miles per hour," he said confidently.

Seeing Lucia with the wolf on a leash, the crowd instantly split down the middle, and Stefano, Pietro and Anna followed this little path to where Lucia bade Sheba jump into the Mondial's back seat. With a tremendous lunge, Sheba shot over the side of the car, landing neatly in the back seat, where she sat licking her lips.

The crowd loved it even more as Pietro and Stefano started their engines and Sheba gave out one of her blood-curdling wolf howls. The two cars pulled away and Stefano found the coastal road to Livorno.

Coming over the top of a hill, they saw before them nothing but blue sea - a beautiful view. They drove along the winding coast road, enjoying the fresh sea air. The sun started its descent as they motored lazily through Livorno with its glorious houses set on the side of a hill overlooking the sea.

Soon they came to Castagneto Carducci, and Lucia got out the address of the place they were to stay. They drove around the small town looking for the street. Finally Stefano gave up and asked a little old lady on a bicycle for directions. She told them how to find the street, then took off on her old bicycle, the front of which had a little basket filled with vegetables and flowers.

They turned down a leafy lane that led towards the seashore. The lane was narrow for the width of the Redhead, and Stefano edged along carefully, trying to avoid branches that stuck out from the bramble bushes that formed the walls of the lane.

They rounded a bend and came upon a little white house, nestled close to the seashore, its dark red tiled roof faded from the sea spray. The house was surrounded by white painted stone walls covered with flowering bushes.

The front of the house had a porch with a stone balustrade running along the entire width. Across the balustrade grew the same wild, colorful flowers that grew on the outside walls. Along the drive, large carved stone containers were placed here and there, overflowing with colorful flowers. Stefano and Pietro turned off their engines.

"This must be the house, I'll go and ask," said Lucia, who had reconfirmed their booking a few days earlier. She got out of the Redhead and went up the steps to the pretty porch. Just as she was about to knock, the door opened and a small, jovial looking lady wearing a flowery dress and an apron, came out onto the porch.

"Buona sera, Signora," Lucia said with a smile. "You must be Signora Lambardi?"

"Si, Signorina, I am, and you must be Signorina Constanetti?"

"Si, but now I am Signora Gappuci. Stefano and I were married today. Please, call me Lucia."

"Ah, congratulations! My name is Bella. Please call me Bella." The lady was warm and friendly and laughed when she saw the big silver wolf, Sheba. Lucia relaxed. She had forgotten to mention the wolf and was glad that Bella was not angry.

Bella fussed around as Stefano and Pietro carried the suitcases in from the cars. "Oh dear!" she exclaimed on seeing Pietro's bruised face with the eye patch and Stefano's rather bruised features. Stefano was walking stiffly to conceal his limp as his back and legs were stiff from driving. "Have you two been in an accident? Are you all right?" she asked.

"Si, Signora, a little accident on the road, but we are better now. Thank you for asking."

Sheba ran past Lucia into the house and found the kitchen. She went in and sat on her haunches, her head up and panting slightly, as she watched Bella come into the room.

"You beautiful animal, are you thirsty?" asked Bella. "Come, I give you some water to drink." Bella took a large white bowl from the cupboard, filled it with water and put it in front of Sheba, who immediately began to lap it up with her huge tongue.

Lucia followed Sheba into the kitchen and saw the wolf lapping at the bowl. "Oh, dear, she will make a mess on your floor when she is finished. She always drips about a gallon of water all over the place. I'll take her outside and let her finish her drink in the garden."

"No, Signora, let her be. It is no matter if the floor gets a little wet. It is tile and it will dry. Besides, I like animals." Bella looked closely at Sheba. "She is a wolf, yes?" she asked.

"A very tame wolf, Signora, and house trained. She doesn't do any business or pee indoors. She always sits by the door and lets out one long howl when she needs to go out. Are you sure it's okay for her to be indoors?"

"Of course, my dear, I used to have a dog; a black Labrador called Bessie, but she went to the doggie heaven some years ago and I never did get another one to replace her. I was sad for a long time."

Lucia looked at Bella and saw the old lady was near to tears, but she perked up when Sheba finished drinking and looked up at her as if to thank her for the water.

"Come, Lucia, I show you and your husband the house and you can choose which rooms you would like, as there is no one else staying here tonight. Just me and my husband, Umberto. We live in the little cottage in the back. I do the cooking and Umberto looks after the house and garden.

Bella and Lucia went out onto the porch to find Anna, Stefano and Pietro admiring the sea view. "Such a gorgeous view!" said Anna.

"Yes, it is," replied Bella. "I have lived in this house since the day I first married Umberto, over forty years ago. I always looked out to see to see his fishing boat come home in the evenings, and I would wave and he would wave back, and then I would start the dinner knowing he was safe. Now is he retired and we live on the little income from renting the house by the week or by the day to nice people like yourselves."

Bella was a very Italian-looking lady. Her thick hair, once black but now grey, tied up in a net bun; her face tanned from the wind and the sun. She was a well-preserved, happy person, obviously content in her little guest house covered with flowers. "Come, I will show you around the house," she said with a smile.

They followed her through the house; first she showed them the kitchen, which was light and spacious. "If you get hungry and I am not around, please, look in the refrigerator for cold food and here in the pantry for bread, biscuits and wine. But tonight I will cook you my special spaghetti with meat sauce. I hope you will like it!"

Bella led them into the large main living room, which again was very light with many windows and two huge floral sofas with matching armchairs that looked very comfortable. She showed them two bedrooms at the back of the house; one at each corner and each with its own bathroom. Then they went back to a small dining alcove set in front of a picture window facing the sea.

Upstairs were two more bedrooms, again each with its own bathroom. "Please, Signora and Signorina, choose whichever rooms you like." She looked at the little clock on the mantle over the fireplace. "It is now six o'clock. Is dinner at eight too early for you?" Bella looked at Lucia and Anna.

"It is fine, Bella, thank you. We love your house and we will be very careful with it, I assure you. Grazie tanto!"

Bella smiled. "You're very welcome, Lucia." She disappeared into the kitchen and the clanging of pots and pans announced that Bella was preparing dinner.

"Let's unpack then take Sheba for a walk on the beach," said Stefano.

They jokingly took a vote on who would sleep where, and Stefano and Lucia decided on taking the bedroom upstairs on the left. Anna would take the one on the right and Pietro would sleep downstairs with Sheba for company. That settled, they took the suitcases to their rooms to put on T-shirts and shorts for the walk on the beach.

They put Sheba on her leash and took off for the beach, finding a little trail that led down through the trees and straight to the seashore. Sheba howled at the seagulls and the small waves, as she had never seen the sea before. She ran in at the shoreline and dipped her snout into the blue-green water. The salty taste surprised her and she came out immediately, shaking her great wolf's head in dismay, trying to get rid of the salty water that had gone up her nose. She looked so surprised it was comical and the four burst out laughing, which confused Sheba even more.

They walked up the sandy beach towards the headland where a lighthouse perched high on a hill. The sun was setting as they chatted about the day…how well the wedding had gone and how beautiful the scenery was. Golden rays appeared as the sun slid down into the sea like a magical golden orb. Stefano held Lucia close as they walked, and occasionally stopped to give her a big kiss.

Pietro and Anna played with Sheba, letting her off the leash as hardly anyone else was around, and throwing sticks for her to fetch. At first she was interested, but after discovering she was supposed to bring the sticks back each time, she got bored and set off to chase the seagulls that were sitting on the sand in groups. She succeeded in causing many gulls to fly up into the air in protest, but fortunately never caught one.

They walked for a mile on the golden sands in the warm evening air, and then turned around and headed slowly back to the little villa. They made their way up to the house with Sheba in the lead, bounding around still full of energy even after the long walk.

Inside they were met by a beaming Bella, who ushered them into the dining alcove. "Please sit, you're just in time for the sunset. It's always best seen from this window. I love to watch it." She had laid the large round table for four, and Stefano sat close to Lucia still holding her hand, while Pietro and Lucia sat opposite watching the sunset.

Bella poured wine for them and Pietro and Anna toasted the newly married couple. The table was lit by two large candles, which flickered occasionally in the draft from the open window. Bella brought in her special, large plates of spaghetti covered in a dark meat sauce made of beef, mincemeat and onions and mixed with secret savory herbs that she had developed over the years in her back garden. They tucked into the hot food and salad, which was enhanced by Bella's own special dressing.

The last rays of the setting sun lit up the room and finally sank into the sea on the other side of the world. Bella appeared with a chocolate cheesecake. More wine was poured and soon the four were sitting back in their chairs, calling compliments to Bella on her splendid feast as she cleared the dishes away.

"You are splendid, Bella. Such tasty food and the cheesecake was delicious!" said Stefano with a smile.

"Just a little something, I'm glad you enjoyed it. Now I bring coffee, not so strong but very tasty!" When it came, they were surprised by its delicious flavor.

"Bella, tell me how do you make coffee taste like this?" asked Anna.

"Ah, my dear, I buy fresh beans every week and mince them into powder, put in one tablespoon per cup and add hot milk and a spoonful of Demerera sugar. Is good, yes?"

"Very good, Bella, excellent! You run a beautiful guest house. You must have many return visitors I would think," said Pietro.

"Yes, most of my guests come once or twice a year for a long weekend because it is so peaceful here," said Bella proudly. Stefano thanked her and excused himself from the table to go out on the porch. Pietro followed and the two girls sat chatting about women's things.

The two young men sat in the wooden swing on the porch feeling relaxed and contented. "So, Pietro, what did you think of the Mondial today?" Stefano asked. "Did it run well?"

Pietro leaned back in the swing. "It is a faultless car; it goes wherever you point it, it has vast reserves of power, and what I like most are the wide sweeping curves that it eats up. The seats are comfortable and the instrument panel is good. The clutch and the gear lever feel like a part of me, so now I can change up or down in a split second, and rarely do I need to use the brakes as the engine does all the braking for me. What about the Testarossa, Stefano, is it all you ever dreamed of?"

"Even more than I dreamed," said Stefano. "The engine is like a rocket motor, with unbelievable power and yet still graceful. All day long the engine sings to me; sometimes growling like a bear, sometimes shrieking like a banshee; mostly it sounds like an orchestra played with its valve gear and camshaft in concert with the beat of the twelve cylinders. Such cars come only once in a lifetime. We must enjoy them and let them go as fast as possible without being dangerous drivers."

The two young men sat in silence, content to look at the two red demons parked in front of them, shimmering in the moonlight.

Bella came out and wished them good night and they thanked her again for the good food. Pietro smacked his belly lightly. "Such spaghetti sauce I have never tasted before. Bellissimo!" he said.

Bella smiled. "Grazie, Signore, Buona Notte!" She turned and left quietly to go to her own little house where Umberto was probably snoring in his chair after a day's work in his garden.

Lucia came out with Anna and they both leaned against the little stone wall, laughing at Stefano and Pietro. "You are a pair of lazy bones," said Anna with a smile.

"I'm so full I can't get up," said Stefano. "You two will have to help me." Lucia and Anna each grabbed an arm and pulled Stefano to his feet.

"Sleepy bye time, "Stefano, we have more to drive tomorrow and then we will be in beautiful Roma!" said Lucia.

"Okay, off we go to bed. Goodnight, Anna, goodnight, Pietro. See you in the morning!"

"Not too early," said Pietro. "I feel so lazy on holiday, I might just sleep in again."

"Sleep in as long as you like," said Stefano, taking Lucia's hand and going indoors and upstairs to their room.

"Come, Anna, sit on the swing. It is so comfortable. Would you like a nightcap? I think there was a drop of white wine left."

"Just a little bit, Pietro. Then I am off to bed. All this food and fresh air makes me so sleepy!"

Pietro went into the kitchen and found the half-empty bottle of Chablis. He filled two wineglasses, took them out on the porch, and gave one to Anna. "A toast, to Anna's pretty smile," said Pietro. He lifted his glass and drank the clear liquid. "Ah, so good!" he murmured.

"To Pietro for his bravery!" said Anna as she sipped the wine.

Sheba stirred and rolled over on her side. "Sheba wants a belly rub." Pietro leaned over and stroked Sheba's chest and belly ever so gently. Sheba purred like a kitten, enjoying the affection.

Anna sat next to Pietro on the swing and watched him stroking Sheba in the pale moonlight. "Tomorrow I show you Rome, Pietro. It is such a magnificent old city. I love it so much!"

"I look forward to that, Anna," Pietro replied.

"Now I must go to bed. Buona notte, Pietro, sleep well."

"Buona notte, Anna, sweet dreams." Pietro stood up, took Anna's hand in his and kissed the back of it. "To tomorrow and what it may bring!"

Anna stood up and kissed Pietro's cheek. "You are a strange man, Pietro, but I like you a lot. Good night."

Anna went in and Pietro stood leaning on the little stone wall thinking about Anna. Such a sweet girl, he thought. Very much like my Serenella in some ways and so different in other ways. He was tempted to go after her, to kiss her soft lips, but the moment passed and he did not move. Too much wine, he thought. Too much wine, but a nice idea.

He walked down to the cars and checked that the Testarossa was locked. Then he lifted the cloth roof on the Mondial and closed it, locking the doors as well. Bella had said the night mist was sometimes very wet, so it was probably worthwhile. Going inside with Sheba, he made his way to his room, undressed and lay on the bed. Sheba stretched out on the floor and went to sleep. Soon sleepiness overtook Pietro also and he switched out the light and slept.

Upstairs, Stefano and Lucia lay in bed, enjoying their long-awaited privacy. Caressing each other and exchanging fiery, passionate kisses, they made love deep into the night.

Later they lay together, still entwined, their hearts beating at twice the normal rate. Lucia kissed Stefano's cheek and he kissed her lips in return. They drew apart a little and smiled at each other.

The moonlight shone through the window as the two lovers fell asleep. Outside on the beach, the tide began to ebb, while on the other side of the world, on another beach, the tide began to turn and the sea inched deeper across the sand, flooding inlets and waterways in its ever-recurring sequence caused by the pull of the moon.

11: THE ROAD TO ROMA

Anna awoke to sunshine streaming in through her window. She got up, showered quickly, dressed and went down to the kitchen to make coffee. Sheba was already up, padding to the stairs to meet Anna. The big wolf wagged her tail then ran to the porch door and scratched it lightly. Anna opened the door and let Sheba out, keeping an eye on her to make sure she didn't take off down the road. But Sheba did a little pee and came straight back in. She followed Anna to the kitchen where she curled up in a sunny spot by the table.

Anna found some instant coffee and put the kettle full of water on the gas to boil. Pietro awoke when he heard the sound of the kettle whistling in the kitchen. He got up, showered and dressed, and went into the kitchen.

Anna sat sipping her coffee, her fair hair resting on her shoulders. Pietro stood quietly in the doorway, as visions of Serenella sitting in the same position came floating back to him. Anna's profile was similar to Serenella's, and for an instant, Pietro nearly called Serenella's name, but corrected himself at the last second.

"Buon Giorno, Anna!"

Anna turned, "Buon Giorno, Pietro. You are up early. I thought you were going to sleep in. Would you like some coffee?"

"Yes, please." Pietro sat down at the table.

"Shall we take Sheba for a walk after you drink your coffee?' asked Anna.

"Good idea. No sign of Lucia or Stefano yet then?"

"No, it's only seven o'clock. I think they are still sleeping," Anna replied, handing Pietro a hot cup of coffee.

"Grazie, Anna." Pietro drank his coffee, and then they took Sheba for a walk on the beach, this time in the opposite direction, towards the harbor where the fishing boats were leaving for deeper waters many miles offshore to trawl for the day's catch.

"I love boat harbors!" said Pietro. "They are always such calm and peaceful places. I always wanted to be a fisherman and have my own fishing boat, but where I grew up there were only mountains, rivers and sheep, so I became a shepherd. Now I work in a hotel. Life is so strange!"

"You could always leave your job at the hotel, live here and work on a fishing trawler until you found out if you like the life," said Anna. "You have no ties yet and you are young; if you really want to do something, then you must try it at least."

"It was only a dream, because when I was very young my father took me to a fishing port to do some business. We stayed two days and nights on a trawler in a little cabin. It was a great adventure for me and I spent all day on deck watching the waves lap against the side of the boat and fishing for crab with mussels for bait. I was seven years old and it was great fun. That was the only time I was even on a real boat, but I remember it as if it were yesterday. That's when it got inside my head that one day I might become a fisherman."

"And now you get to drive in the Le Mans Grand Prix. You must be very excited," said Anna.

"I am excited, you're right, but I also want to win for Enzo and I worry that I am not good enough. But I will do everything in my power to win."

"You drive well, Pietro. Yesterday I watched you. You drive smoothly and with great confidence. I'm sure you will do well, don't worry," said Anna.

"I must get fit before I can drive my best. As soon as my eyelid heals, I will take up running. Every morning I plan to run at least a mile, and every evening another mile. That will get me fit for Le Mans," said Pietro.

"Let me see your eyelid, Pietro. I remember seeing it in the hospital, maybe I can tell you if it is better."

Pietro slid the patch up and Anna gazed at his eyelid. "It's definitely healing, it is only bruised, I think, and it looks much better now. In a couple of days it will be just like the other one." She looked again at Pietro's face. "You have beautiful big brown eyes."

Pietro didn't know what to say to her compliment. Instead he gazed at her. "You are very beautiful, Anna. Your eyes are blue like the sky and you have a pretty nose." He wanted to tell Anna that she looked like his lost love Serenella, but he knew somehow that this was not the time. "Your hair is fair like ripe corn," Pietro said with a smile. "You know, if you stood in a cornfield no one could ever see you."

"Thank you, Pietro, I like your compliments. You always say such nice things to me. It's a long time since I met such a gentleman," Anna said, laughing.

They sat for awhile longer on the bollards watching the last of the blue and white fishing boats chug out to sea, and then started to walk back to the house to see if Bella was going to cook breakfast. The fresh morning air had given them good appetites.

As they made their way back to the house, Sheba saw a cat ahead and took off after it with a ferocious howl, but the cat was faster than Sheba and leapt up into a tree then turned and spat at Sheba from its safe perch.

"Come on, Sheba, leave the poor cat alone," called Pietro. "Anna, let's run back to the house."

"I'm game!" said Anna as she speeded up, racing ahead of Pietro who was having a hard time catching up. Sheba, distracted by their running, left the cat and chased after the couple. Out of breath, they ran up to the house and made it to the porch door at the same time.

"After you, Signorina," said Pietro. "You can win this time!"

They went into the kitchen and Bella asked them what they would like for breakfast.

"Eggs and bacon, please," said Pietro.

"Same for me!" said Anna. "I'm hungry. That was fun!" She gave Pietro a kiss on the cheek. "Thank you, Pietro."

Pietro liked being kissed on the cheek by this fair-haired beauty. "Any time, Anna. My pleasure!" he said with a smile.

Stefano and Lucia had also woken at dawn, but instead of getting up like Anna and Pietro they lounged in bed and enjoyed each other's company, cuddling, kissing and exploring each other. They made slow, unhurried love once again, reveling in the pleasure they both felt. Afterwards they lay in silence, enjoying the cozy warmth of their two bodies. They dozed off again and awoke to see the sun much higher in the sky.

"Whoa! It must be late!" said Lucia. "Pietro and Anna must be waiting, poor people."

"They won't mind," said Stefano. "They know that this is our honeymoon." He gave Lucia a soft kiss and she kissed him back with fervor.

"Come on, Stefano, today we go to Roma. Let's get up and have breakfast!" They showered together, laughing and splashing like a couple of children.

When they were dressed they hurried down to the kitchen. "What's the time?" asked Stefano.

"Ten fifteen," said Anna. "Did you sleep well?"

"The bed was magnificent, soft and warm, and my old husband was even warmer," said Lucia to Anna with a wink.

Anna smiled. "You are very lucky, Lucia, to have such a handsome husband. And how he loves you! I see it in his eyes all the time."

Stefano and Lucia ate a quick breakfast, then the four packed the cars ready for Roma. Stefano and Pietro argued over who was to pay the bill and Pietro won, so he paid Bella in Lire from his wallet.

"Grazie, Bella, Your house is ever so beautiful, we will never forget it, and we will come back again one day, I promise."

"Buon Viaggio," said Bella. "Drive safely and enjoy Roma."

Sheba jumped into the Mondial's back seat and the four waved goodbye to Bella who stood on the porch waving back to them. Then they were off! Following the coastal road to the grand city of Rome.

The two red Ferraris sped along the winding road which ran through picturesque villages by the Tyrrhenian Sea. They stopped briefly in Piombino to look across to the Island of Elba. Then off again to Montalto Di Castro, through Civitavecchi to Santa Marinella, where they stopped to let Sheba have a stretch. The four travelers drank Cappuccino and ate pastries at a little bistro set right on the edge of the water, the waves breaking gently at their feet. Sheba howled in fury when the occasional wave sprayed her with sea water.

Passersby stopped to admire the two magnificent red cars and comment on their sculptured lines, discussing the differences in design among themselves. Every Italian knows all the Ferrari models as well as they know their own family members. To see two such cars in one day made them feel proud that Italy is the home of the most beautiful cars in the world. Each person, young and old, felt a tremor of pleasure to see such powerful Italian elegance parked in their sunny little town.

12: ROMA.

On the final leg of their trip to Rome, they took the Autostrada, driving in the fast lane at 130 mph whenever possible, the engines singing at high revs as Stefano and Pietro piled on the massive power which seemed to leave all other cars standing still. The City of Rome became visible ahead and they took the route towards the center, with Pietro's Mondial leading down the Via Veneto to the Piazza Barberini. Following Anna's directions they turned onto the Via Quattro Fontaine and pulled up outside the Hotel Anglo Americano, an eloquent older style hotel which, despite its name, is frequented more by native Italians than English or American tourists.

They left Sheba sitting proudly in the back seat of Mondial and went to check in. The concierge was friendly. "My name is Omero. If there is anything you need, I am at your service day or night. Stefano explained that they needed a garage for the cars and Omero showed them how to get there. "You drive up to the first left, turn and take the first left again, and there you will see the garages at the rear of the hotel. Here are the keys to a double garage, numero ten," he said with a smile.

Lucia asked if having Sheba in the room would be a problem. "No, Signora, no problem. If you need someone to look in on her while you are out, I can arrange it."

"Grazie Omero," said Lucia.

"You are very welcome, Signora. Enjoy your stay with us. Your rooms are 402 and 404 on the fourth floor."

The four went out to the cars, found their way to garage number ten and parked inside the garage, side by side.
Luckily, there was a door to the hotel inside the garage, so they didn't have to walk all the way to the front entrance again. They unloaded their luggage, and went into the hotel with Sheba secured on a leash, in case she saw a cat.

The Anglo Americano Hotel was decorated in typical Italian style with marble floors, polished walnut walls and comfortable sofas surrounded by many vases of flowers. Lucia and Anna chatted to each other about the pretty décor as Stefano and Pietro carried their luggage to the lift.

"Fourth floor, here we come," said Stefano. The lift ran smoothly and in a few moments they were there. Stefano found room 402 and next to it 404. He opened the door to 402 and he and Lucia went inside. He popped his head back out the door and said, "Give us a knock when you have settled in, then we can go for a walk if you like."

Pietro opened the door to 404 and he and Anna went inside with Sheba.

"Oh dear, Pietro, there is only one room! I cannot stay here alone with you. I must go to my apartment for the night," she said softly.

"Don't be silly, Anna, there are two beds. Please stay. I promise I will be a good boy," he said with a touch of humor in his voice.

Anna looked at Pietro, who sat down on the bed nearest the door. "If you really want me to then I will stay, Pietro," she said, "but we sleep in separate beds. Okay?"

"Of course, Anna. I want you to stay. You can sleep in that bed next to me and we can hold hands if you want." Pietro was teasing her. Little did she know he really wanted to hold her hand, but his repressed fears of letting Serenella down held him back.

The decision made, Anna and Pietro took Sheba and went to the door of 402 and knocked. "Hey, young married couple, open up. We want to go for a walk, would you like to come with us?" yelled Pietro.

"You two go. We are going to stay and have a nap. Give us a knock when you go for dinner," Stefano called back.

"Okay, Ciao! See you around seven for dinner. Sleep well!" Pietro winked at Anna. "I think our friends are very much in love. They want to spend time alone. That is good, it means that they are having fun and that is most important in keeping the flame of love alive."

"I didn't know you had studied psychology, Pietro," said Anna.

"I didn't, Anna, but I think I know how they feel, that's all. Come, let's go for that walk."

So off they went, down to the foyer to ask Omero for directions to the Spanish Steps where Anna wanted to take Pietro. Omero led them outside. "Follow this road up the hill and you will come to the Spanish Steps," he said. "Enjoy your walk. Arrivederci!"

They thanked him and set off with Sheba. The sun was still shining and all was well with the world. They looked in the shop windows at the different displays with no desire to buy anything, but having fun anyway.

Pietro relaxed, and when they crossed the wide plaza, he took Anna's hand to guide her around a motor scooter that was riding right toward them. Her hand felt good in his and he decided to keep on holding it even after they had crossed the plaza and were walking slowly up the little hill. Sheba was behaving herself for once and took no notice of the traffic or the other pedestrians.

Soon they came to the top of the hill and there in front of them was a beautiful view over the City of Rome. To their left stood the massive dome of Saint Peters, along with the beautiful buildings that make up the Vatican. Further in the distance, the Coliseum rose majestically. Behind them, was the Spanish Church with its splendid tower, and right in front of them were the Spanish Steps, over 300 feet wide and centuries old. Tourists and locals alike were sitting on the steps. Couples embraced and children sat on their mothers' laps.

Anna and Pietro made their way down the steps to the middle, sat down and looked around. People from every nation imaginable were enjoying the famous steps. They got Sheba to sit and spent a half hour enjoying the scenery and watching the many different races of people who came to visit Rome.

When Sheba became restless it was time to go. They walked on down the steps and into the fashionable shopping district, with its displays of shoes, dresses, coats and jewelry from the best designers in Italy.

Anna saw a green dress she fell in love with. Pietro went in and bought it for her.

"A present for you, Anna, it will go well with your fair hair. You must wear it tonight," said Pietro with a bow. He handed her the bag containing the dress.

"Oh, Pietro, that is wonderful of you! Thank you." Anna kissed him hard on the cheek in her exuberance. Pietro moved his head and brushed his lips against hers. They tasted so sweet he was overcome. Flustered, they broke apart, each knowing that something special had occurred. They walked on in silence, holding hands and smiling occasionally at each other.

Back at the hotel, they decided to take a nap before dinner. Anna lay down on her bed, closed her eyes and drifted off to sleep. Pietro lay on the other bed, but sleep did not come. Instead he thought how pleasant Anna's lips had tasted, so soft, warm and sweet. He felt immensely happy and looked across at the sleeping Anna, her eyes closed, a tiny hint of a smile on her pretty face. Her long, shapely legs looked delicious to Pietro.

Pietro woke Anna about ten to seven. She stretched and opened her eyes like a soft cat. She smiled at Pietro and he smiled back.

"Time to wake Lucia and Stefano. I will go and knock on their door." Pietro got up, went out on the landing and gave two knocks on room 402. "Ten to seven. See you in ten minutes for dinner?" he called.

"Okay, Pietro, we'll be ready," called Lucia.

A few minutes later Stefano and Lucia came to Pietro and Anna's room and the four went off to find somewhere to eat. Omero suggested Ristorante Tiberius, a short walk from the hotel.

It was busy at the restaurant, but their luck was in and they got a table by the window. Musicians playing old Italian melodies, together with dim lighting and candles on the tables, made the atmosphere romantic. The wine was poured and they tucked into their food with great gusto.

After more wine, the couples became relaxed and the music tempted them to dance. Pietro asked Anna to dance, and the two drifted around the floor to a fine old waltz. Pietro held Anna close to him and smelled her perfume. At one point, Anna's cheek came very close to Pietro's and he couldn't resist giving her a brief kiss.

Stefano and Lucia, also dancing, noticed Pietro's amorous behavior and smiled at each other as if to say, Ah ha! Here is a couple who are falling in love. But they said nothing when the music stopped and it was time to sit down at the table again.

"I have an idea for tomorrow," said Anna. "The best way to see Roma is to take a tour. That way you have a guide who knows everything about the places. I think you will enjoy it and find it interesting. What do you think?"

"I'm game," said Lucia. "How about it, Stefano?"

"Fine by me…whatever you like, my darling," replied Stefano.

"Pietro, will you come?" Anna asked.

"Yes, Anna, that will be fun. But how do we book it?"

"Omero will book it for us. I saw a brochure on the wall in the hotel that mentioned two tours; a half day or a full day with a bus and a guide. I have never been on a tour, so it will be interesting for me also, even though I've lived in Rome for many years," Anna replied.

They paid the dinner bill and walked slowly back to the hotel. Both couples were holding hands, for now Pietro was a little more confident and the wine and dancing had made him feel very romantic.

At the hotel, Anna spoke to Omero who booked them on the half-day tour leaving at eight thirty in the morning.

They went up in the lift. Stefano and Lucia went to their room after agreeing to meet for breakfast at seven thirty. Anna and Pietro took Sheba out for a late night walk, then returned to their room.

Anna brushed her beautiful hair and cleaned off her makeup. By the time she had finished, Pietro was sound asleep in his own bed dreaming of dancing with Anna. Anna pulled up his covers then went to bed herself. She lay in the dark thinking about Pietro and how he was such a gentleman. She knew he was attracted to her, and she to him. Remembering his soft kiss on her cheek while they were dancing slowly to the waltz, she wondered what it would be like when Pietro, Stefano and Lucia were gone in a few days, and she was saddened by the thought.

Oh, well, I will live for the moment…one day at a time, she told herself before curling up and falling asleep.

The morning dawned. Pietro took Sheba out for a quick walk, fed her in the room, made sure she had plenty of water in her dish, then went downstairs and joined the others for breakfast. The city tour bus arrived at the hotel, and they hopped aboard.

The tour guide's name was Aldo. A dapper little man, dressed in the best Italian tradition with a pink shirt and tie, plaid jacket, light green trousers with knife-like creases, ivory colored socks and highly polished black shoes.

The tour went to the most scenic places in Rome. Along the Via Veneto to the Quirinal Palace, residence of the Italian President, located on Quirinal Hill, the tallest of the seven hills of Rome. Then to the Trevi Fontaine, the most beautiful fountain in the world with its magnificent marble statues of people and horses. After that, to the Pantheon, which housed the tombs of Italian kings and queens. Next stop was Piazza Navone, with Bernini's most famous fountain of the Four Rivers, where they gazed at the wide river Tiber from one of the bridges. From there they went to St. Peter's Square and the Basilica, where they marveled at Michelangelo's masterpieces.

Aldo spoke many languages. He split the tour group up into Italian, English and French. At each stop he would tell about the location in each language, with eloquent and flowery descriptions. Always smiling, Aldo told stories of the history of Rome, adding his own humorous tales which made the tourists laugh.

They returned to the hotel on the bus and said their good-byes to Aldo who was scheduled to guide the tour to more Roman wonders in the afternoon. They explained to him, that they would have loved to continue the tour, but were hoping to have the doctor check Stefano and Pietro in the afternoon.

The two couples found a little open-air restaurant and had a light lunch with some wine. They talked about the marvels they had seen and the humor of Aldo, whom everyone had liked tremendously. After lunch they took a taxi to the doctor where Stefano and Pietro were to get a checkup, as requested by their doctor at the Maranello hospital.

Lucky for them, the doctor, a large pleasant man by the name of Giamo Bellazi, had a free hour and his nurse ushered them into a comfortable waiting room. A few moments later, Stefano was called and he disappeared through the thick curtains that covered the double doors to the doctor's surgery.

Stefano stripped down and the doctor examined him, prodding and pressing various parts of Stefano's anatomy while asking questions about how it had happened and where it hurt most and whether, on the whole, Stefano felt better or worse since leaving Maranello.

"Definitely much, much better," said Stefano. "In Maranello only a few days ago, I could hardly walk without two canes, but since my wedding and the trip with my dear wife and our two friends, the pain in my ribs has nearly gone and so has the pain in my legs. In fact I am surprised, myself, how such a vast change could occur in such a short time!"

The doctor tapped his forehead. "The mind is a great healer," he said. "I think the joy of getting married and your relaxing holiday has a great deal to do with your recovery. If you were under personal or financial stress your recovery would possibly have taken much longer, but you appear to be mending very well. You still have massive bruising by the ribs, but it is definitely healing, so other than putting a new elastic bandage on for support, I recommend you continue your holiday with your bride and friends. But no stress or extra strain for a week or so at least!"

"Can I start exercising after next week, Doctor?" Stefano asked. "I had the honor of being asked to drive in the Le Mans Grand Prix in two and a half weeks, and I need to start running and exercising to be really fit if I am to really drive my best. What do you think?"

"To be truthful, I would say next week is too early, but if you are determined then I suggest you start out slow jogging and then work up to running. Don't immediately start running at top speed, your muscle tissue in certain places may react violently. So just go easy and don't attempt more than you feel comfortable with. That's all I can say." The doctor held out his hand. "Good luck in Le Mans. I will watch it on television to see how you do. The nurse will put a new bandage on your ribs."

Stefano shook hands and thanked the doctor for his time and sound advice.

"Please ask your friend Pietro to come through", said the doctor.

Pietro came in and shook hands with the doctor who asked him to remove his shirt and pants for the examination.

The doctor shone a bright light into Pietro's eye to see if there was any damage; first the left eye, then the right eye. "You were very lucky, Signore, your eyes are clear with no visible damage. Only the eyelid and surrounding area sustained injury, and that seems to be healing. But it will take time. A week or so and the eyelid should be nearly back to normal. I will give you some ointment that will speed up the process. Just apply a light smear on the swollen areas once at night and once again in the morning. Also, I will give you some very thin gauze that you can wear under the patch. You need only use it for the coming week and then you can leave the patch off and let nature heal the final stage."

He examined Pietro's neck, back and legs, which were still badly bruised, but the bruises were now fading to a pale yellow color. "That is a good color, Signore, it means they are healing and there is no long-lasting damage. Do you have any problems that I should know about? Any dizziness, fainting, loss of vision or violent headaches?"

Pietro told the doctor that the only real problems he'd had were on the one occasion when he had nearly passed out after dancing at the restaurant a few days before. Also how sometimes his consciousness seemed to drift back into the past and how he kept seeing Serenella when he was looking at Anna.

"If you have another reoccurrence of nearly passing out, you must get to a hospital immediately for a checkup. To happen once may be understandable to a degree, given the severe blows you suffered to the head. But if it recurs, it indicates all is not well and you may require a CAT scan to determine if there is cartilage damage in your head or neck. Don't worry about it for now, but if it happens again go to the nearest hospital."

The doctor admitted he was puzzled over the "drifting back into the past" events. "This sounds more psychological than physical, although in rare cases, extreme physical pain can trigger psychological problems to surface. But I would suspect that somehow the person you see when you look at the other is due to some quirk of fate; some mannerism or body language is visible to you because both persons exhibited the same mannerism or body language. Are the two persons related?"

Pietro shook his head. "Not that I know of, doctor."

"Well, all I can suggest is to see if the problem persists after the rest of your body has healed. If so, then come and see me and I will recommend you have a session with one of my colleagues who is a specialist in that area of medicine."

"Very well, doctor. Thank you for your time and advice. So, otherwise, you think I will heal soon and have no physical after effects?"

"You are young, Signore, and the spirit of youth is a marvelous healer." The doctor shook hands with Pietro. "Buona fortuna," he said.

"Grazie, Dottore. Arrivederci!"

Pietro dressed and went out to the waiting room where Anna, Lucia and Stefano were waiting to hear what the doctor had said.

"Well, Pietro, don't keep us in suspense. What did the doctor say?" asked Anna looking concerned.

"Everything seems to be healing. In one more week I can take off the patch, all the rest of me is on the mend." Pietro turned to Stefano. "How about you, Stefano?"

"Everything is healing with me, too, Pietro. We are very lucky! Let's go and celebrate our good fortune. Let's find another restaurant with music and dancing. Oh, it's great to be alive!" Stefano kissed Lucia softly and gave Anna a hug.

The four did a lively jig in the waiting room. The nurse looked in at all the commotion. She saw them all smiling and said, "I am glad you are all so happy. The doctor must have given you good news!"

They hailed a taxi in the street and went to the hotel, where Omero greeted them with a friendly smile. Back in room 402, Sheba was excited to see them and obviously anxious to go out and relieve herself.

"Let's take Sheba and walk to the Coliseum," suggested Pietro.

"Good idea!" said Anna. "It will be fun, and we can go to the restaurant later." She put on Sheba's leash and they all set off to the Coliseum, with Anna explaining how to get there.

"Very simple, we turn left out of the hotel, walk up the hill past the fountains set in the wall and turn right; carry on as far as it goes and we will come to the Coliseum."

So off they went along the narrow pavement, with Sheba sniffing at every opportunity, thoroughly enjoying herself and ignoring all the mopeds and Fiats dashing along the road just a few feet away.

The walk from the Anglo Americano Hotel to the Coliseum was not far and they were pleased to see the towering spectacle at the end of the road. Crossing a busy street, they walked along the pretty gardens that led up to the entrance, past tables with people selling postcards, souvenirs and cold drinks.

They gazed in awe at the soaring Coliseum, its superb architecture still standing after two thousand years, and silently looked down at what was left of the arena; marveling at the lower tunnels where once gladiators had braved ferocious lions, where once great Caesars decided whether they lived or died.

"What a magnificent piece of Italian history," Lucia said. "I have often read about it, but it is everything and more than I expected." She was overcome by the sheer size of the vast structure.

They sat on a stone wall, each thinking about the things that had happened here centuries before; each conjuring up their own visions of a massive crowd, of Roman soldiers guarding Caesar as he was entertained by the poor slaves and the mighty gladiators, fighting with swords and nets for their very lives.

They bought ice cream cones from a street van and strolled slowly back towards the hotel. Arriving back about five thirty, they decided to take a nap before going to a restaurant.

Anna dozed off and Pietro sat on the other bed stroking Sheba, who was lying on the floor at his feet, sound asleep. Her massive front paws were together as if in prayer and her back legs were straight in the position she always took when sleeping.

Pietro looked across at Anna. She looked so soft and warm, he wanted to lie next to her, but was afraid he might wake her. He sat quietly, thinking about their trip and where it would end.

Anna awoke and saw Pietro looking somewhat forlorn, sitting on his bed and stroking the sleeping wolf. She moved over to the far side of her bed and, hearing the bed creak, Pietro looked up at her. Anna held her arms out, wordlessly beckoning him to come to her. Pietro got up from his bed and walked the short distance to Anna's bed. He sat on the edge and they gazed into each other's eyes.

Anna clasped his shoulders and gently pulled him down next to her. Pietro stretched out alongside Anna. Feeling her warmth made him relax as she cuddled him to her. They lay together, each enjoying the warmth of the other, as the sun's golden rays illuminated the room.

For a long time, which seemed to go on forever, neither of them spoke; they just lay together without movement. The last rays of the sun disappeared and the room grew darker.

There was a light knocking at the door and they heard Stefano's voice. "We're about ready to go out to a restaurant and eat, then maybe dance a little. Do you want to join us?"

Pietro whispered to Anna, "Would you like to stay here instead?"

Anna whispered back, "Si, Pietro." She kissed him lovingly on the lips.

Pietro called out. "You go with Lucia, Stefano. Anna and I are staying in tonight."

Stefano replied that he would see them in the morning, then went back to his room to take Lucia to dinner. He was a little surprised by Pietro's refusal of the dinner invitation, but when he told Lucia, she smiled.

"I know it! They have fallen in love! Oh, I am so happy for them!" She squeezed Stefano's hand. "Come, we will go and dance awhile, then we will come back and you can make love to me all night if you wish."

Stefano laughed. "Ah, that sounds good! Let's hurry so we will be back all the sooner." They went out hand in hand, two happy lovers very much in love.

13: ANOTHER WEDDING

The morning dawned and Stefano and Lucia awoke to a knock on their door.

Coming," said Stefano as he pulled on his trousers, then opened the door.

Pietro and Anna stood in the hall. Anna was blushing. "Tell them, Pietro," she said.

"Tell us what?" Stefano asked, looking closely at Pietro and Anna who looked as if they shared a secret.

"We are off to get married!" Pietro gushed. "Will you be my best man, Stefano? And Lucia our Maid of Honor?"

"Surely, with pleasure! Lucia, come quickly! There are two crazy people here who want to get married, right away!" shouted Stefano.

Lucia came to the door and Stefano repeated what Pietro had said. On hearing, she embraced first Anna, then Pietro. "This is wonderful news. When do you want to get married?"

"Right now, this very minute! I've already called the priest in the little church down the road. He has agreed to marry us at nine o'clock."

Stefano looked at his watch. "It's eight forty-five already, we had better hurry. Come, Lucia, let's dress quickly. Come in and wait five minutes while we get ready. Oh, fantastico! This will be two honeymoons together!"

Stefano and Lucia rushed around the room, searching for clothes to put on.

"Will we do?" Lucia asked, grabbing Stefano's arm and circling around for inspection.

"Fine!" said Pietro. "Let's go now."

Pietro and Anna were married in the little church just a short walk from the hotel. They borrowed Lucia's wedding ring for the ceremony, and when the priest said the words, "You may kiss the bride", Pietro kissed Anna with great passion.

The two young couples walked back to the hotel. When they arrived, Omero greeted them and asked how they were doing. When he found out about the wedding that had just occurred, he snapped his fingers and had his staff set up a white linen-covered table in the little dining room. The chef made up some delicacies while Omero poured champagne for his guests.

"On the house, Signore and Signorina, a toast to the bride and groom. Salute!" Omero enjoyed himself immensely, clucking and sighing over the happy couple and pouring out his congratulations. Pietro and Anna smiled a lot but said little. Most of the time Anna sat on Pietro's knee and gave him big wet kisses, which he gratefully acknowledged by kissing her passionately in return.

Having eaten smoked salmon and drunk champagne to their fill, Anna and Pietro announced they had some plans for the morning and would meet Stefano and Lucia back at the hotel in the afternoon. They thanked Omero, who bowed graciously in response. They went upstairs to fetch Sheba before setting off to Anna's apartment to collect a few things and to call on her work to ask for a longer vacation.

As soon as Pietro put the Mondial's top down, Sheba jumped in the back seat, happy to be out of the hotel room. Pietro drove into the crazy Roman traffic, following Anna's directions to her apartment. They soon arrived and Pietro told Sheba to stay while he and Anna went inside the building. Pietro stole a look back to check that Sheba was going to stay, and judging by the contented smile on her jowls, he decided she was going to do as he asked.

They went up to the third floor in a very old lift that sat in the middle of the floor and was really no more than a black metal cage suspended by thick cables.

Anna unlocked the apartment door and Pietro stood amazed at the large, sumptuously appointed room. Massive floor to ceiling windows covered one wall, allowing the full morning's sunlight to fall on the solid marble floor set in large black and white tiles. Elegantly styled wooden tables and chairs were interspersed between the supple white leather sofas on either side of the room. Lying in the center of the seating area, was a huge Flokati white wool rug that looked soft enough to sleep on. Large colorful paintings of the Amalfi coast decorated the walls.

Anna led Pietro through the main room into her bedroom, the walls were painted a soft pastel pink but what caught his eye was the largest four poster bed he had ever seen. The mahogany frame stood high off the wooden planked floor. An intricately woven white lace canopy arched across the top of the bed and a white silk duvet cover with tiny pink flowers enveloped the thick goosedown comforter.

Pietro placed his hand on it and pushed down slightly. His hand disappeared into the softness. He looked at Anna and laughed. "So soft! Your apartment is like a palace. I didn't know you were rich, Anna!"

"I only bought the paintings, the rug and the duvet to brighten the place and make it comfortable. The rest was already here. My Great Aunt Francesca left it to me in her will. She was a grand old lady, she passed away at ninety-two last year."

"I'm sorry," said Pietro.

"Don't be. She lived a good life and was spiritually ready when the time came. She always told me she had lived life to the fullest with many husbands and many lovers, too. No, she just fell asleep one night and never awoke. The doctor told me she was smiling when they found her in her bed."

"Do you mind, Pietro? Will my money make any difference to our love, my sweet?"

Pietro shook his head. "I love you for you and not for any property or money you may or may not have. If you have property and money, then that is good also!"

Anna laughed as Pietro threw himself on top of the bed. "I have to try it, it looks so comfortable," he said. "Come, Anna, you, too." He held out his hand to help her up.

Anna kicked off her shoes and jumped up next to Pietro. They spent the next fifteen minutes kissing and cuddling, until Pietro suddenly remembered Sheba. He got off the bed and looked out the window.

"Oh, no!" he exclaimed.

Anna opened one of the side windows and they looked down to the street. Sheba had her head lifted to the sky, emitting a loud wolf howl that Pietro and Anna could now hear through the open window. A small group of teenagers had gathered around the fiery red Mondial, and Sheba was warning them to keep their distance. But the teenagers seemed to be taunting her.

"I must go down, Anna. Collect your things that you wish to take and I will wait for you in the car." Pietro blew Anna a kiss as he rushed out the door.

Anna closed the window, took a small suitcase from a cupboard and started to look through her wardrobe, deciding what to take with her.

Pietro took the stairs, racing down them and arriving on the street within thirty seconds. He took in the scene. One young boy was howling like Sheba, deliberately taunting the huge wolf.

Pietro pushed his way through the crowd, which was rapidly growing larger, and stood between the car and the boy.

"Signore, is this your car?" called the boy.

"Yes it is. Don't taunt the wolf anymore. The last time she got annoyed, she ripped out the throat of that person. Fortunately he was a would-be murderer or the police would have put Sheba down."

The boy's face went white and he backed away then melted into the crowd and was gone, darting down an alleyway. The rest of the boys started to drift off, not wanting to see the wolf in action.

Anna came down with a small case packed to the brim. Pietro laughed on seeing it. "I don't know how we are going to fit that one in with all the rest of the stuff you have at the hotel, but we can try." He put the case in front with the spare tire and managed to close the front bonnet by squeezing down on the case.

Anna got in the Mondial and shrugged her shoulders, smiling. "That was the least I could bring if we are going to be away three weeks."

Pietro laughed again and got in and started up the Mondial's V-8. The engine fired immediately with a great burst of sound. Pietro pushed the clutch down, put the gear lever into first, checked his mirror and shot into the flow of traffic, neatly finding a space and accelerating away.

"Where to now, Sweetheart?" he asked.

"Go left at the next light. Straight down till you see a huge marble statue of Romulus and Remus with the wolves, then left again. The office where I work is on the right."

Pietro sped along the Via Veneto, spotted the statue and made a left turn. Anna showed him how to get to her office from there. They pulled up outside a vast old building that had frightening looking gargoyles along the roofline and beside each window.

"Come on, Pietro, come in with me and meet my friends. I want to show you off. I'm so proud of my Pietro!" said Anna.

They left Sheba to sit proudly in the back seat, watching the world go by.

Inside was a large open-plan office complex filled with people on the phone or dashing around with what looked like large leather-bound photo albums clasped to their bodies.

Pietro had never seen such commotion. "What do all these people do?" he asked.

"This is an advertising agency. The people design ads for large corporations. Some of the ads are in magazines and some go on television…anything to sell the products," said Anna.

"Is that what you do, Anna?" asked Pietro. "Do you design ads, too?"

"No, Pietro, I work in Customer Relations, finding out what the customer wants or likes. Then I talk to the designers and together we create an idea for an ad. They design it and I take it to the customer to see what they think."

Pietro was impressed. The business was obviously making money, with elegant desks and chairs in chrome and leather dotted around the room. The walls were covered in huge paintings in vivid colors depicting all manner of subjects from chocolate to cars and flowers, silk stockings and cameras.

"No Ferraris," said Pietro.

"Ah, but yes. Come with me," said Anna, leading Pietro to the far wall and turning the corner. Pietro looked up and gasped. On the wall were full size original oil paintings of Ferraris; Testarossas, GT 40s, 328s, and off to one side, his Mondial Cabriolet.

"Mama mia! It is even more beautiful when I see it here. What a car!" he said in awe.

"We do all the advertising for Ferrari here in Rome. That's why when Stefano was looking for a company to arrange his wedding to the Testarossa, he asked Enzo who could do it best. Enzo immediately recommended us and I got the job."

"Ah, now I see why you were in Maranello," said Pietro.

"I usually work out of this office, but now I will work wherever we live, Pietro, if they let me. Otherwise I will try and find a similar agency in Maranello, if that's where you want to live," said Anna.

"Well, I do have a new position as Assistant Manager at the Hotel, and I would like to live there if you would like to live there with me, as my wife."

"Let's go and see my boss and ask him," said Anna. She squeezed Pietro's hand and kissed his cheek. "I do want to live in Maranello with you at the hotel. Come on." She pulled on his hand and he followed her across the huge room to a large desk behind which sat a gray-haired man with pince nez spectacles on the end of his nose. He was studying a photograph intensely, but looked up as they approached.

He beamed a smile at Anna and stood up to greet her. "Anna, my dear, good to see you. How was Maranello…and who is this young man? Is this your boyfriend?" The older man held out his hand. "I'm Constantino…" Pietro shook his hand and looked across at Anna.

"Constantino, meet my husband, Pietro. We just got married this morning, and I need two favors from you. First, I need four weeks off for my honeymoon. Pietro and I are going to Le Mans where he has been asked by Enzo Ferrari to drive in the race. Second, when we return I will be living with Pietro in the Bella Montagna hotel in Maranello where Pietro is the Assistant Manager. I can work on the Ferrari account from Maranello instead of Rome if you will agree…" Anna paused to get Constantino's reaction.

He was visibly surprised, but he recovered himself immediately. "My dear, congratulations, and to you, Pietro. You are a very fortunate young man. He turned to Anna. "Please, Anna, take the four weeks, more if you want. Only promise me you will come back and work for me in Rome, Maranello or anywhere in the world. I know wherever you are you will keep our customers happy with your sound business sense and your fantastic way of making the customers feel confident that they are in safe hands with our company. This calls for a celebration!"

Constantino opened a cupboard in his desk and took out some champagne glasses. From another cupboard containing a cooler, he withdrew a large bottle of champagne. With practiced ease, he ripped off the foil and opened the wire holding the cork in place, pointing the bottle away from his visitors. The loud POP caused many people in the office to look over to see Constantino pouring champagne. Within moments a small crowd of Anna's colleagues had surrounded them and Constantino shared the news about Anna's marriage, while taking out another champagne bottle and more glasses.

"A toast to Anna and Pietro, newlyweds. Salut!" he said, at them. Anna's colleagues toasted Anna and wished her and Pietro good luck in their new life together.

The newlyweds sipped at the champagne, and after exchanging a few words with her friends, Anna told Constantino they had to leave, as their friends were waiting to drive to Naples with them. Constantino bade them good luck and Buon Viaggio again. The couple managed to escape as more office colleagues came over to have champagne.

Pietro was glad to get out of there. He liked people, but was not used to such a commotion and said to Anna on the way out, "Nice people, but very noisy, also very friendly. They all adore you there, you should be very proud."

"Nonsense, Pietro, it is just a job. I only want to be with you now, and forget all about work for the next month," said Anna, smiling. "Let's hurry and go get Lucia and Stefano then start our honeymoon properly."

Pietro agreed. He gave Anna a resounding kiss on the lips. They leapt into the Mondial and Pietro drove fast back to the hotel.

They found Stefano and Lucia drinking cappuccino in the café at the hotel. "Are you ready to leave?" asked Pietro.

"Whenever you are, my friends," Stefano replied.

"Then let's go," said Pietro. They went to the front desk and Stefano and Pietro settled their bills with Omero, who was sorry to see them go.

"Come back again one day, Signora and Signore. Ah, one more thing…" he produced two tiny boxes and gave one to Anna and one to Lucia. They looked at the boxes in surprise. "Please, open, just a little gift from me for two such beautiful young ladies on their honeymoons. It is not every day that the Anglo Americano Hotel has two such gorgeous brides staying at the same time!"

Lucia and Anna opened the boxes. In each was a tiny silver brooch shaped like the Coliseum. They thanked Omero profusely.

"A little memento from a sentimental old man. Buon Viaggio. Arrivederci!" Omero added with sincerity.

The four shook hands with Omero and went out to the garage. Pietro suddenly remembered that Anna's luggage was still in the hotel room. He went back in to get the key to room 402 from Omero.

"No problem, Signore. I will have the bellboy fetch them. He is very fast. You go to your car and your luggage it comes in five minutes!" Pietro thanked Omero once again. He was about to leave for the garage when Omero spoke. "Signore, I think you have chosen a beautiful and special young lady as your bride. Enjoy your life."

Pietro nodded and said, "I think so, too, Omero. Anna is like a breath of fresh air come into my life and I know we will be happy forever. Arrivederci!"

"Ciao!" said Omero.

Pietro went out to the garage. He and Stefano backed the two Ferraris into the narrow street and let their engines warm up to their normal running temperature. A few minutes later, the bellboy brought Anna's other suitcase and Pietro's small folding suit bag.

"Grazie," said Pietro and tipped the bellboy.

"Grazie tanto, Signore!" said the bellboy who then stood in wonderment, taking in the beauty of the two bright red Ferraris. "Ah, so beautiful cars. You are very fortunate, Signore. One day I will save enough to buy such a car."

Pietro smiled, thinking back to a few weeks ago when he was a bellboy and loved to wonder how it would be to own such a car.

Sheba jumped into the back of the Mondial. Lucia and Anna hugged each other then Lucia got into the Testarossa and Anna into the Mondial.

"See you on the road to Naples, Stefano. I will follow you to the main road if you can find it," said Pietro with a grin.

"If you can keep up with me," said Stefano with a laugh.

The two young men got into their cars and took off down the road with a burst of power. The bellboy leaned up against the garage doors, wishing he could have gone with them. One day, one day, he thought. Then he closed the garage doors and went back into the hotel to tell Omero and his friends of the beautiful ladies, the extraordinarily beautiful Ferraris and the big silver wolf sitting in the back of the Mondial. The effect of seeing the two Ferraris made him tremble with excitement and he ran into the hotel to tell his tale.

14: PARIS.

The honeymooning couples sped out of Rome and headed South for Naples. The weather was magnificent, with sunshine all the way and just a breath of wind from the sea to prevent Pietro, Anna and Sheba from cooking in the open Mondial Cabriolet.

They stayed that night on the outskirts of Naples in the little seaside village of Portici. Their inn had a gorgeous view of the Bay of Naples. The next morning they drove onto the ferry bound for Genoa and relaxed on deck and in their cabins while the ferry made its long haul up the coast, stopping at little ports along the way. The scenery was beautiful and for two days and two nights the young couples basked in the sunshine, drank wine, ate good food, and made love passionately.

They arrived in Genoa early in the morning of the third day and drove off the ferry, heading for Milano. Driving through the city they made their way up to Lugano and stayed the night in a cottage on the shores of Lake Como. On a campfire they cooked Italian sausage and onions until the skins burst, then put them into long loaves of bread and munched on them while sipping Piniot Grigio in the moonlight.

The next day they drove to Domodossola, where they drove the two Ferraris onto a train that took them through the Simplon Tunnel under high mountains to Brig in Switzerland. From there they drove to Sion and stayed the night at the home of an old friend of Stefano's. The next morning they gasped at the silent beauty of the mountains soaring into the sky.

After breakfast, they thanked their host and hit the road again, first heading Southwest to Martigny, then North to Montreaux. They picnicked on the banks of Lake Geneva at Evian, and went Southwest again to the grand city of Geneva.

Here they parked their cars and strolled around the beautiful city, with Sheba on a leash enjoying herself immensely. Driving South into France they took the back roads to Lyon, where they found a small quiet inn on the outskirts of the city and away from the traffic, overlooking the River Saone.

Pietro and Stefano borrowed fishing rods from the inn and spent the afternoon fishing, while Lucia and Anna sat and chatted about the good things that had happened in the last few days. The four had become close friends during their trip together, and each day was more fun than the last.

Anna and Lucia went back to the inn to buy a bottle of good wine and borrow some glasses. Sheba romped along beside them, sniffing the unfamiliar smells of the French countryside.

Meanwhile, Stefano and Pietro, their fishing lines baited and lying in the current of the river, sat and discussed the two Ferraris. They were both surprised by the number of people that flocked around the cars when they stopped in towns or little villages. Both young and old men would gather around, literally expressing open devotion to the proud symbols of Ferrari's brilliant engineering and Pininfarina's magnificent sculpted body styles.

Pietro and Stefano were also surprised by how few Ferraris they had seen on the trip so far. To see two at the same time roaring into a village must be a spectacular treat, when most people only see one Ferrari a year.

The two young men realized how fortunate they were, and many times tried to rationalize why they were so lucky. Beautiful, loving wives, good friends, fantastic weather, and driving two of the most magnificent cars in the world! They exchanged deep feelings about how the powerful engines stirred their excitement and adrenaline when they drove the beautiful red machines.

Occasionally, Pietro would state his opinion that driving the open top Mondial V-8 was much more fun than Stefano's Testarossa. But Stefano refused to admit to any such thing, pointing out the design differences and the sheer power difference between the Mondial's V-8 and the Testarossa's flat opposed 12 cylinder design, regardless that it was not a convertible.

The girls returned with the wine and they all sat around, quietly sipping wine and waiting for the fish to bite. But as dusk came, the four gave up and went back to the inn, joking about not being very good fishermen.

The evening was spent playing cards and discussing the upcoming Le Mans 24 hour race. Pietro and Stefano, not just a little nervous and excited, were concerned that they must get a lot of exercise before the race, lest they get cramps during the long hours driving at high speeds. Bedtime came and Stefano and Lucia curled up in their comfortable bed and made love until the early morning. In the adjoining room, Pietro cuddled Anna and stroked her hair while she slept, after a passionate bout of frenzied lovemaking.

The next day they decided to drive the 210 mile hop direct to Paris in one day, using the wide French autoroutes where they could let the Ferrari engines off the leash and cruise at over 100 mph when traffic allowed. They drove fast, first North to Dijon, then Northwest to Auxerre and finally through Fontainebleau and on into the city of Paris. Stefano led them to his house on a small street near the Champs Elysse, where they drove the cars into his large backyard. After parking their cars in Stefano's garage, they went into his house, exclaiming at the exquisite architecture, high ceilings and comfortable furniture. The house gave off a warm, comfortable atmosphere and the four sank into the soft sofas while Sheba curled up on the thick wool rug that covered the floor.

They relaxed in Stefano's house for two days, sleeping late and reading all manner of books and magazines, dining on fresh bread and cheese washed down with French white wines. On the third day, Stefano took them on a tour of the city, up to the top of the Eiffel Tower, then to the Louvre, where they marveled at the world's most famous paintings. They spent the afternoon with Sheba in the park. Who knew that a wolf could play ball?

That evening they dressed up and went to Maxine's Restaurant in the Latin Quarter. There they dined and danced and listened to Maxine singing her French blues songs with such emotion that, after each song, the audience stood up and roared for more. Maxine wore a long blue silk dress that showed off her curvaceous body and accented her way of swaying erotically when she sang.

The evening ended with Stefano and Lucia and Pietro and Anna dancing to a slow waltz. The two young men held their brides very close and amorously stole kisses at every opportunity. They took a taxi back to Stefano's and collapsed into their beds, sleeping through till ten the next morning.

Over breakfast they agreed it was time to start getting into shape if they really were to drive in the Le Mans Grand Prix. They went for a slow jog in the park across the road, with Sheba on a long leash leading the way. They stopped for an ice cream and coffee at a small café, then turned around and jogged back home again. Stefano was sore after the run, but in good spirits, as it had been fun to exercise in the beautiful park in the center of Paris.

Stefano made a telephone call to Enzo in Maranello to find out if the Ferrari Racing Team was in Le Mans yet, for the race was now only a little over one week away.

"Yes," said Enzo, "they arrived yesterday. I recommend you drive down there the day after tomorrow. I will tell them to expect you and they will arrange for a trailer for you to sleep in." Enzo gave Stefano the telephone number of the Ferrari Pit Office and told him to call when they got to the city of Le Mans, and get instructions on how to find the Ferrari team.

"I will be there in three days time," said Enzo. "Then you can start practicing to drive my F40's. Ciao!"

"Ciao," said Stefano. He hung up and told the others of Enzo's plan. "Today is Monday. If we leave on Wednesday at 9 in the morning, we should be there by midday. I looked at the map and it's about 130 miles to Le Mans from Paris. When we get close I will find a phone and call the Ferrari Pit Office to find out how to drive into the circuit. Enzo told me there is a special entrance for competitors."

With two days to go, the girls decided to go shopping. Pietro and Stefano decided to change the oil and filters on the two Ferraris, as Stefano had a full set of tools and jacks; all they needed to buy was oil and the special Ferrari oil filters.

"I know where the Ferrari showroom and parts department is, as I spent many an hour gazing at those beautiful red cars months before leaving for Maranello to buy my own. Let's take my Redhead, as I would like to surprise the manager there. He was always trying to sell me a Ferrari, but I told him I was going to order one from the factory and collect it myself. I'm sure he never believed me, but now I think he will!"

They went to the garage and started up Stefano's Testarossa. Stefano opened the engine compartment cover and they watched the flat 12 cylinder idling as it warmed up. "A precious work of art," sighed Stefano in sincere adoration. "It is so beautiful, every time I see it I can hardly believe it is really my car! I love Lucia madly, but I am still in love with my gorgeous Redhead also!"

"No more than I love my Mondial Quattrovalve Cabriolet. I love Anna and the Mondial equally and no man can love more passionately than I," avowed Pietro with passion, determined to prove to Stefano that he loved the Mondial even more than Stefano could ever love his Testarossa.

The engine now warm, they jumped in and sped off to the Ferrari showroom where Stefano indeed surprised the manager, who watched him drive up and park outside the main entrance to the showroom. He came out to admire the Testarossa and recognized Stefano at once.

"Ah, M'sieur, you bought your Testarossa just as you said you would. Did you drive her from Maranello?" he asked.

Stefano nodded and told him of the wedding in the Maranello square and the manager was thrilled and excited. "M'sieur, you are one eccentric person, but your taste is exquisite. Such a car! I am so glad you achieved your dream. I will tell all my customers of your wedding, it is a fantastic tale. I will set up a wedding ceremony as a temptation for my customers — perhaps a marriage under the Arch De Triomphe with all the traffic stopped for the occasion would equal your marriage in Maranello. Maybe I will sell more cars that way. Who knows?"

Stefano and Pietro laughed. "Maybe," said Stefano. "Good luck in your endeavour, but tell me, M'sieur, I want to change my oil and filter. What sort of oil is recommended? May I speak to your head mechanic?"

"Of course, M'sieur, right this way." The manager led them through the showroom and out to the rear of the premises where a gleaming service facility had been built to service only Ferraris. The manager found a tall Italian looking mechanic, with thick black wavy hair, wearing blue Ferrari overalls and introduced him to Stefano and Pietro, explaining their question about the oil.

The head Ferrari mechanic's name was Giulio. He listened to the question about the oil and gave his reply. "I would prefer we change the oil and filter here, M'sieur, you may have many tools in your own garage, but we can do it here very fast and efficiently at minimum cost while you wait. We can also check all of the other fluids and seals, and ensure the torque settings are correct. You have the ultimate decision, but this is my recommendation."

Stefano and Pietro discussed Giulio's recommendations and decided to accept. Maybe it was better to have an experienced mechanic check and change the oil and filter, at least for the first time.

"I accept your offer, but we also need to do the same on my friend's Mondial and we would have to go and fetch it from my garage. Can you do that today as well?" Stefano asked.

Giulio said he could do both cars in less than 2 hours, and loan Stefano a car to go pick up the Mondial while he started work on Stefano's Testarossa.

"You may borrow my own car, M'sieur. You will find it interesting to drive compared to your Testarossa," said Giulio. He led them outside to where a bright red Ferrari 328 GTSI was parked. He handed Stefano the keys in exchange for Stefano's keys. "You may have to warm her up before driving, but you will find her quite different to drive than your Testarossa. I have tuned her a little." Giulio smiled. "See you in a while."

Stefano and Pietro got into the 328 and Stefano started the engine, which gave off a lively roar before settling down to idle at 1,000 rpm. They admired the interior of the car while waiting for the engine to warm up. When the engine was warm, Stefano pressed the clutch, selected first gear, released the hand brake and eased the 328 out into the traffic, accelerating gently to merge into the flow.

Stefano saw a gap in the next lane and pushed on the accelerator. The 328 roared in the direction Stefano steered it and the torque was phenomenal. Stefano quickly changed into second gear and accelerated again. The 328 literally shot forward like a bullet, and Stefano had to adjust his driving technique to match the torque curve on the 328. They headed down the Champs Elysse at high speed, Stefano now in third gear, accelerating past other traffic as if it were stopped.

"I think he tuned it, all right," said Stefano, "I don't think this is a standard 328 at all." They turned into Stefano's street and he stopped the 328, put it into neutral, and with the hand brake on, opened the engine compartment lid. They both whistled. Inside the engine compartment were two huge turbo fans that had obviously contributed to the extra torque that Stefano had experienced.

"Certainly non-standard, but very impressive!" said Pietro. "Same engine as mine but with turbos added. I still prefer my Mondial." Pietro went with Stefano to open the garage. Pietro reversed his Mondial out until it was level with the 328 and let it idle. He opened his engine compartment and they compared the two engines. Except for the blowers, the engines were very similar.

Stefano closed the garage door and the engine compartment lid on the 328. Pietro closed his lid and they drove back to the Ferrari service area.

Giulio stopped working on Stefano's Testarossa when he saw them drive in and came out to greet them. "You like my little modification, M'sieur?" he asked with a grin.

"Well, it certainly has a great deal of torque, more than I expected," admitted Stefano.

"It should do, M'sieur, the turbos are the same ones as used in the F40."

Stefano said it was fun to drive. "Nearly as fun as my Testarossa, but not quite."

"Ah, M'sieur, you are a true Ferrari owner. No car is as good or as fast as one's own. I know the feeling." Giulio went back to work on the Testarossa and with the help of his assistant, declared the car all done within half an hour. He rolled the Testarossa out of the service area and drove Pietro's Mondial in.

Pietro and Stefano watched as Giulio deftly changed the oil and filter and checked all the belt torques and fluid levels. Another twenty minutes went by and he was finished. He wrote out the bill and presented it to Stefano who looked at it and raised his eyebrows in surprise.

"This bill is for zero franks. Surely you have made an error, Giulio?"

"No, Signore Stefano," said Giulio with a grin. "I read in a Ferrari factory bulletin that both of you gentlemen are driving in the Le Mans for Enzo. As this is my most favorite race in the world, how could I even think of charging you?"

"Grazie tanto, Giulio" said Stefano.

"Prego, Signore Stefano" Giulio put out his hand and shook first Stefano's, then Pietro's hand. "Buona Fortuna in the Le Mans. I will be in the pits to cheer you on!"

Stefano and Pietro drove their cars back to Stefano's house, made some strong coffee and discussed the oil change.

"I agree with Giulio. It was far more efficient for him to change the oil and filter and check the belts and fluids than if we had done them here. I think we would still be working on your Testarossa now, with mine left to do late tonight. And he was right about the tools and the importance of torquing the parts to the correct specifications. I would hate to see oil coming out of my engine!" said Pietro.

"You are quite right, Pietro. We may drive well, but we are not Ferrari mechanics, even though we like to think we know enough," said Stefano.

The girls came back from the shops and showed off their purchases.

"Oh, no…," said Stefano, laughing. "Where can we put all the new clothes? Certainly there is no more room in the Testarossa!"

Lucia and Anna had both bought large wide-brimmed hats to wear at Le Mans.

"I thought you were going to drive, Lucia," said Stefano. "Are you going to drive in that big hat?"

"No, but when I am not driving I can wear the hat with my dress and shoes and sit with Anna and watch the race," said Lucia quite seriously.

"I am not sure you will have the energy to change between drives," said Pietro. "If you drive at 180 mph for two hour stretches, with two hours in between, you will be recouping your energy in the periods when you're not driving."

"We will see," said Lucia. "Maybe I will, maybe I won't. Only time will tell, but I will take my new clothes anyway, just in case."

"We are going to have to drive some practice laps before Enzo makes his final decision anyway," said Stefano. "If all goes well, then we will drive in the race, but the practice laps are timed and the results decide who will actually get behind the wheel. Let's hope we all get to race."

"Not me!" said Anna. "I will just sit and watch. I will be so nervous, it's such a long race!"

The four chatted further about the Le Mans circuit and Pietro got out the drawings he had received from Vittorio and showed them all the twists, bends and straights. Evening came to a close and they went to bed, with thoughts about what had seemed like a dream only a week and a half ago, but was now becoming serious reality. They had plenty to think about between now and two days' time when they would be in the Le Mans Ferrari pit area.

The next day they went jogging with Sheba in the park. The day dragged slightly after that, as the four anticipated leaving the quiet solitude and peace of Stefano's house for the noisy pit area of Le Mans. They knew instinctively that it would be incredibly different than anything they had ever experienced before.

The light jogging was taking effect. Both Pietro and Stefano were feeling fitter and more limber. Stefano was not sore any more, as his muscles became more flexible and his ribcage and back no longer hurt. Pietro, too, was feeling really good. His eyelid swelling had receded significantly, and today he took off the patch and felt more human.

"Whoever heard of a racing driver with an eye patch, anyway!" he said.

Anna was happy to see him remove the patch and she kissed both of his eyes tenderly. Pietro couldn't resist making the most of the event. He picked her up and carried her to their bedroom, where he closed the door and made mad, passionate love for the rest of the afternoon. They hadn't a care in the world as they caressed each other and mouthed sweet nothings in each other's ears.

Stefano and Lucia stayed up for awhile, kissing and cuddling on the sofa. Then they, too, went up to bed and continued their amorous cuddling until they fell asleep holding each other.

Morning dawned and they all rose early. By eight they were showered and dressed and sat down to coffee and croissants covered with butter. Stefano and Pietro checked the maps for the route to Le Mans. The girls packed their clothes. Stefano and Pietro just took basic jeans and T-shirts, as little as possible. Neither had any racing overalls so they hoped Enzo's team would have spares for both of them and for Lucia.

They took Sheba out for a quick jog in the park, packed the cars, locked up the house and finally, they were off.

Next stop, the Le Mans Grand Prix circuit.

15: WELCOME TO LE MANS.

Taking the Southwest route out of Paris, they passed by the
magnificent Palace of Versailles, and traveled on to the town of
Maintenon joining the autoroute to Le Mans just South of Chartres. The
road was remarkably free of traffic, and Stefano and Pietro sped along at
a cracking 100 mph, the two Ferrari engines purring and growling like
unleashed tigers out on a romp.

A dark blue Porsche Carrera came up behind them, beeping its
horn and flashing its lights, the driver obviously looking for a race.
Stefano and Pietro let the Porsche overtake; accelerating briskly until it
was a small spot in the distance. Stefano pulled alongside Pietro and
pointed in the direction of the Porsche. Pietro understood, bipped his
horn and accelerated to 130 mph, catching up to the Porsche very
quickly and overtaking it. Stefano was right behind and the two red
Ferraris accelerated again up to 150 mph and left the Porsche standing.

In their mirrors they could see the Porsche trying to catch them,
but it gave up when the two Ferraris again accelerated to 160 mph. At
that speed, the Porsche driver lost his nerve, and quickly faded from
view, obviously embarrassed by the awesome power of the two Ferrari
engines.

The sun shone and the two red beasts sped along the autoroute,
back to their 100 mph cruising speed, effortlessly eating up the miles as
they closed in on Le Mans. One hour later they joined the crawl of

trucks and cars going towards the racetrack. Stefano pulled into a garage, followed by Pietro. They stopped by a phone booth.

Stefano called the Ferrari pit telephone number, explained who he was and asked for directions to the competitor's entrance to the Le Mans circuit. He listened carefully, thanked the Ferrari mechanic, and told him that he and Pietro should be there soon.
He explained the route to Pietro, who decided to just follow Stefano.

They followed the directions and found the first security gate marked "Competitors Only." The security guard checked their id and waved them through, having already been briefed by the Ferrari team that Stefano and Pietro were on their way. They drove down the private road towards the circuit and the huge stands which could hold over 100,000 people, came into sight. Their hearts beat faster as the immense size of the stands became apparent. Coming closer they began to hear the roar of highly tuned, powerful engines practicing on the track.

They entered the competitor's area through another security gate, and this time the guard called the Ferrari pit crew to request clearance for Stefano and Pietro. When clearance was given, the guard gave them each a pass marked "Ferrari Team No 21 and 22" and asked them to put the passes in the windscreen so if they wanted to go in or out in the future, no telephone calls would be necessary.

Stefano and Pietro thanked the guard and drove through the open gate making their way into the competitors' parking and workshop area. They passed by the Porsche and Mercedes area, then saw the dazzling cars of Enzo Ferrari. The Prancing Horse decal marked his territory; on all the cars, on the huge trailer doors and on the four flags that fluttered way above their heads. They found spaces to park, cut their engines and got out of the cars. Sheba howled loudly at the intense noise of high-powered racing cars zooming by on the track.

Stefano led the way and the others followed as he headed towards the track, thinking correctly that the pit office must be fairly close to the track. The Ferrari area was buzzing with activity. Mechanics in traditional Ferrari blue overalls with the Prancing Horse decal on the front, were coming and going between large workshops, carrying race car parts and wheeling huge tires.

Coming to an open door marked "Ferrari Office" they entered. The office was vast with a large window directly overlooking the main pit area. Along the walls were large maps of the track, and lists of race car parts showing quantity available and storage bin locations. The office had desks against the walls and chairs grouped around each desk. Three teams were pouring over diagrams of racecars, all talking at once and very loudly. Everyone in the room sounded confident as they discussed various strategies to win the coveted Manufacturer's Championship. This award demanded they not only had to win their group classification, but also had to have at least half of their entries complete the entire 24-hour race.

One of the men looked up as the four approached his team. "Ah, Signore and Signora, you must be Stefano and Pietro with your beautiful wives Lucia and Anna," said the man with a beaming smile. "I am Giovanni, master mechanic. Enzo called ahead and told me to expect you about now!" He held out his hand and shook hands with each of the four. Seeing Sheba, he knelt down and patted her flank very gently, whispering to her something about wolves. Sheba warily accepted the patting, and as Giovanni whispered to her, she became visibly calmer and even seemed to be listening to whatever he was saying.

Giovanni stood up. "Such a beautiful wolf! What is her name?"

"Sheba," said Lucia. "You seem to get on well with her."

"I have two German Shepherds that I love even more than I love Ferrari engines, so I have had lots of practice giving affection to dogs. I thought maybe this wolf speaks the same language and it seems like she does." He patted Sheba again, calling her by name now, and Sheba listened to him, her ears fully erect.

"Welcome to Le Mans, my friends. Welcome to Ferrari territory."

Giovanni called to the other teams and one by one they stopped talking and turned towards him. "My friends, come and meet our new friends and drivers."

The mechanics crowded around and shook hands with the four newcomers. Laughing and joking, they were a happy group of young men. Some commented on how beautiful the drivers were getting these days, looking long at Lucia and Anna.

"If you are ready, I would like to brief you on what I know about the coming race so you will know what you are up against." Giovanni chuckled. "Don't worry if you get nervous…all drivers get nervous when they hear about the competition. Come, I will find a quiet office where we can go over some of the details."

They followed Giovanni to a large trailer parked outside, went in and Giovanni bade them sit on the comfortable built-in sofas lined along the walls. He sat in a leather swivel chair bolted to the floor, leaned back in a relaxed manner and began his briefing.

"This year 85 cars applied for an entry to race. The committee chose 65 cars and 8 reserves. Of the 65 cars, 25 were invited to Le Mans with no pre-qualification required, and 40 have to pre-qualify. The two major classes are GT1 and GT2.

GT1 contenders must weigh at least 1,000 KG, and their horsepower must be less than 851 bhp. For manufacturers such as Ferrari, we have to produce at least 15 cars to be eligible.

GT2 cars have to weigh at least 1150 KG, and their horsepower must be less than 450 bhp. The manufacturers have to produce at least 1,000 cars to be eligible."

The four listened carefully to all this new information.

"The car Ferrari will race in the GT1 class is the F40 LM; a new prototype. The name LM is short for Le Mans. They have 760 horsepower with twin turbos that can power the F40 up to 229 mph on the Mulsanne Straight."

Stefano looked at Lucia and winked. Lucia was nervous and Stefano squeezed her hand to give her courage.

Giovanni continued in his very relaxed manner: "We are entering six F40 LM cars with 12 drivers. Our main competition will come from McLarens, Corvettes, Porsches, Jaguars and Williams Renaults. There may be other specialist cars entered privately that will offer stiff competition also, but we are confident we have the strongest, fastest, and best engineered cars in the world, so we will win I am sure!"

Giovanni paused. "Any questions?" he asked with a smile. He looked from Lucia to Stefano to Pietro, to the frightened look on Anna's face. "Oh, my dear," he said to Anna, "it is a very safe race. These days all drivers are fast, but very careful not to cause or get into an accident. In days gone by it was more dangerous, but the high caliber of the machines and drivers lessens the possibilities of an accident. So please don't worry your pretty little head."

"Tell us about the F40," said Pietro.

"Everything you can," added Stefano.

"Okay, I tell you," said Giovanni, still smiling. "The F40 engine is a V-8 of an all alloy construction, 2.9 liters in capacity, twin turbochargers producing on a production car 478 bhp. On our car, highly tuned, it produces 760 bhp. The car has two Weber-Marelli integral injections systems, each feeding a bank of four cylinders and a five speed gearbox fitted with an oil cooler. The clutch is a Borg and Beck dry double plate, hydraulically activated. The suspension is all independent with double wishbones coil springs and Koni shock absorbers. Steering is rack and pinion, brakes are hydraulic without servos and with independent circuits front and rear. The brake disks are 12.9 inch ventilated and drilled cast iron and aluminum. The tires are Pirelli P Zero, 245/40 ZR17s on the front and 335/35 ZR17s on the rear. The chassis is tubular steel cell with carbon fiber/Kevlar weave.

"The stunning bodywork design is by Pininfarina of Turin. Length is 171.6 inches, width is 77.6 inches, wheelbase is 96.5 inches and height 44.3 inches. It weighs 1100 KG or 2425 pounds. Maximum speed on the production F40 is in excess of 201.3 mph, which is 324 kph. Zero to 100 kph or zero to 62.1 mph takes 4.1 seconds. Zero to 200 kph or 124.3 mph takes 11 seconds, and zero to 241 kph or 150 mph takes less than 18 seconds.

"The LM cars you will be driving, named especially for Le Mans, have nearly 300 bhp more than the production models, so you will be going much faster…around 3.1 seconds for zero to 100 kph or 62.1 mph, with a top speed around 229 mph. The drag coefficient is 9.34. The increase to 760 bhp is made by using larger turbochargers and intercoolers with hotter camshafts and a modified Webber-Marelli electronic engine management system. The power curve torque develops 760 bhp at 7,500 rpm. Compression ratio is 7.7 to 1 with four valves per cylinder actuated by two overhead camshafts on each bank."

Giovanni paused; then said, "That, my friends, is all I know about the F40 LM, so let's go and look at one. You can get your first taste at driving it later this afternoon, after we fit you up with overalls and helmets. Then, this evening, we can talk about racing techniques."

The four sat there full of admiration for this master mechanic who knew his machines intimately.

Giovanni led them out to the pit area, where, like a stunning piece of art, sat an F40 LM, a low red beast with an aggressive and intimidating shape that exuded tremendous power even while standing still. The great width of the bonnet dominated the appearance. Waist high, the car was awe inspiring, just waiting to get on the track….

"Come close," said Giovanni. "I show you the car." He opened and swung back the entire rear engine compartment tail section and secured the strong rod latch. The huge turbochargers and inlet manifolds were stunning to look at. Such a brilliant piece of engineering, thought Stefano, overwhelmed by the design. Giovanni went over the racing car, explaining every detail in his methodical engineer's manner. He got in, ensured that the gear lever was in neutral, turned the ignition key 180 degrees, then pressed the rubber starter button just below and to the left of the ignition key. The F40 V-8 burst into life with a low growl.

"I love it!" Anna said. "Such a pure bred racing car. Even I would love to drive it just once, but not in the race…just on the track to feel all that power."

Pietro grinned. "Ah ha! Anna is becoming a real Ferrari convert. If Giovanni agrees that if one of us wins the race here at Le Mans, you will get to drive the victory lap. Is that allowed, Giovanni?"

Giovanni smiled. "If we win then we will all drive a victory lap. Yes, Pietro, I agree, that will be a prize for Anna, who has to sit patiently and watch you guys and lady," he nodded to Lucia, "racing around this track for 24 hours. I don't think Enzo will mind. He so wants to win this race and especially in an F40 LM." Giovanni leaned into the F40 and turned the ignition key off and withdrew it. "Come, let's get some Cappuccino and we can discuss some racing techniques before you drive one of these beauties."

They walked to the cafeteria situated at the end of the pit area, went into the lounge area and sat down in comfortable chairs while Giovanni ordered Cappuccinos for everybody and water for Sheba. He then came and sat down.

"Have any of you raced before?" he asked, looking from one to the other.

"I have raced in Formula 3", said Stefano.

"I have been taught by Signore Vittorio Brazzano for the last six years," said Pietro.

"Tell me briefly what you learned," said Giovanni.

Pietro told of the trips to Signore Brazzano's garage every three months, and how he had been taught everything that the old racing driver had been able to remember, how they had driven fast on the winding mountain roads with every movement monitored and advised on by Signore Brazzano.

"It sounds like you were taught well, Pietro," said Giovanni. "How do we get all that knowledge into Lucia and Stefano's heads in the next few days?" The five discussed ways of doing that, but it all came down to practice laps and more practice laps, and in between, brief lectures on how to keep the racing cars on the road while taking the turns as fast as possible.

"I suggest we have Antonio in one car with Stefano and Roberto in another car with Lucia. They are both seasoned Le Mans drivers and will race in their own cars with Francesco and Lorenzo as their co-drivers in the race. Let's go get your helmets and racing overalls and see if they will agree to teach you what they know in a very short time," said Giovanni.

He rose to his feet. "If Enzo thinks you are both good drivers, then I, too, have confidence in you."

16: PRACTICE LAPS ON THE TRACK AT LE MANS.

They went back to the Ferrari pit area and Giovanni had an assistant fit them out with helmets and Ferrari overalls. Anna, too, received her very own set and she was pleased, parading around, making strange "vroom, vroom" noises at which they all laughed.

Back in the pit area, Giovanni introduced them to Roberto and Lorenzo, two solemn looking young men who readily agreed to go out with Lucia and Stefano and give them as much advice as possible. Giovanni requested his mechanics roll three F40's out of one of the locked garages.

"Lucia, you take the number six car, Stefano number eight, and Pietro can take number twelve. I will ride with him," said Giovanni. They climbed into the cars and buckled up, put on their helmets and started the engines.

Lucia, under the watchful eye of Lorenzo, sat waiting for the F40 engine to warm up, then pushed the heavy clutch to the floor, eased the gear lever into first, released the hand brake and took off in the direction Lorenzo pointed, towards the Le Mans track. She entered the pit area, checked for a clear track, eased the clutch up and pressed the accelerator down. The F40 #6 took off like a bullet, Lucia changing swiftly to second gear as she approached 60 mph. Steady as a rock and not afraid to gun the F40, she was very soon doing 110 mph down the wide track, coming to the first bend leading up to the Dunlop Bridge.

"Keep the speed to about 110 mph for this lap, Lucia," Lorenzo advised. "Then you can increase it on the next lap, once you get the feel of the track." Lucia nodded and roared into the bend then, as she rounded the curve, accelerated out of it in a perfect line.

Lucia felt the tremendous power of the F40 as she accelerated into The Esses, a series of S bends that demanded a level head to deftly steer through them, having the correct gear selected in order to leave one bend and immediately enter the next bend in the opposite direction. Lorenzo watched Lucia and was impressed with her confidence in handling such a fast racing car. He knew she was enjoying it, as well as showing skills that few racing car drivers ever attain. A natural! A bloody natural! Enzo, you old dog, you may well have a winner here, if she can handle a racetrack full of cars for twenty-four hours, thought Lorenzo.

Lucia accelerated fast out of the last S bend, and increasing revs, she brought the bright red F40 up to 100 mph. Within ten seconds she reached the Tertre Rouge, a sharp right-hand bend. She changed down deftly and maintained again a perfect line around the bend. She saw a long straight coming up and gunned the F40 up to 6000 rpm and held it at 110 mph as she zoomed down the Mulsanne Straight. She saw the first Chicane coming up and changed down again to third gear, skillfully entering the first right-hand curve, which abruptly turned into a left-hand curve. She gripped the steering wheel lightly and steered the F40 out of the Chicane and back onto the Mulsanne Straight. Accelerating briskly, she was soon back up at 110 mph in fifth gear, the engine purring at 4000 rpm.

Lucia checked her rearview mirror and saw that Pietro and Stefano were about 100 yards behind her in their F40's, with no intention of overtaking. She took the second Chicane with the same skill as the first, powering out of the curve at 90 mph and speeding down to the Mulsanne Corner, at which she slowed to 75 mph, changed down and charged around the right-hand bend, testing the limits of adhesion of the F40, which stuck to the road as it if was glued. Lucia increased speed out of the bend and revved back up to 110 mph, changing up to fifth gear.

The three F40's sped around the near empty track into the Indianapolis Corner, then the Armace Corner, up to Porsche Curves, a quick set of turns at White House Curve leading to the Acute Ford Corner bend, then back to the Straight leading to the start area of the pits.

As they passed the pits, Lorenzo, now comfortable that Lucia could handle the F40 as well as he could, told her to go as fast as she wished on the second lap and then pull in for a debriefing. Lucia punched the accelerator and the F40's 760 horsepower responded instantly, causing her to be pushed right back into the seat with the speed at 150 mph before she had realized it. At the higher speed she had to work harder on maneuvering the corners, but she handled them with the same skill as she had done at the lower speeds on the first lap.

Reaching the Mulsanne Straight again from the Tertre Rouge Corner, she came out of the corner in third at 7000 rpm, the car traveling like a speeding bullet. She changed up to fourth at 145 mph and increased the revs again in the higher gear to reach 165 mph, at which point she changed up to fifth and pressed the accelerator again.

The F40 engine responded incredibly and the turbochargers howled as Lucia's speed increased to 190 then 195 mph. Seeing the first Chicane coming up, she slowed, changed down and took the Chicane at well over 110 mph, maintaining a perfect line through the right and left curves and coming out of it at 130 mph. She accelerated again and the F40 speed built up to 200...205...210 mph, and then the second Chicane came up and Lucia slowed gently, using the brakes a little until she was ready to change down from fifth to fourth to third and enter the Chicane at 130 mph.

Lorenzo was impressed! He visibly shook his head in surprise at Lucia's confident skill. The rest of the lap went at the same flat-out pace, and Lorenzo doubted if Stefano, Pietro or even himself could have overtaken Lucia. She pulled into the pits in second gear, drove up to the Ferrari area and pulled the car to a stop.

Lucia and Lorenzo climbed out of the F40 and removed their helmets as Stefano and Pietro came roaring up to the Ferrari area, parking right behind Lucia's F40. They got out and approached Lucia. Stefano gave her a hug and a big kiss on the lips.

"Wow!" he said, "What a girl! Do you know how fast you were going on the Mulsanne Straight, my sweetheart?"

Lucia shook her head. "I was watching the rev counter, but I didn't note the speed. I was concentrating too hard," she said.

"Well, 205 mph was on my dial, and you were still pulling away from me!" yelled Stefano.

Lorenzo smiled. "Lucia is a natural racing driver. She hugs the lines in the corners and always she is in the right gear for every bend. It's quite amazing...incredible driving!"

"Let's go back to the trailer and talk about the two laps," Giovanni said. "What did you think while driving? How did you feel?" Back in the trailer Giovanni asked each of them to relate their experience. "It is important," he said, "to find out how you really and truly felt out there, because on the day of the race you need to feel supremely confident and at ease, even though you may be nervous in anticipation. Now this may sound mixed up, but in motor racing it happens.

"Let's start with Pietro telling us about his experience, then Lucia, Stefano and even Anna. Although Anna didn't drive, she can tell us how she felt watching you on the track," said Giovanni.

Pietro began. "What can I say? The car is a monster...so utterly powerful it tears up the track like a jet fighter plane. At first, I was tense, but halfway through the first lap I felt totally in control. That's because the car is so well balanced and hugs the ground. Then when you accelerate it lets loose instantaneously, a huge push in the back when the turbochargers wind up. It's a very, very fast car, but precise and accurate even at 200 mph. I need more practice, but I have supreme confidence that with this car we can win Le Mans." Pietro leaned back and relaxed. He had said his piece.

"What about you, Lucia?" said Giovanni.

"The F40 is like a fleeting leopard. It growls with hunger, then when you ask it to accelerate it flies like the wind, ever faster, howling like a crazed wolf! I loved it! I want more. It is the third love of my life after Stefano and Sheba."

Giovanni laughed. "You are a very gifted young lady, Lucia. How about you, Stefano? Tell us what you felt."

Stefano grinned. "Four great things have happened in my life in the last month. I met and married Lucia, who I love with all my heart and soul. We met great friends, Anna and Pietro, who Lucia and I love like brother and sister. I married my second love, my Redhead Testarossa, and finally, I just drove in a racing car that can only be described as a beast from hell! The power curve is incredible. It drives like 760 race horses; my heart is still pounding. It was second to Lucia in giving me the thrill of my life. Enzo has a definite winner. Nothing can possibly beat the F40 at Le Mans. I am totally confident that we will win the race. No power on earth can match the magic of Enzo Ferrari."

"I trembled when I saw my love and my friends driving so fast," said Anna. "But I will have patience to sit in the pits all night when the race is on, and I feel that you will all do well. Sheba, good Sheba kept me company while you drove, so I am happy that you drove so well and enjoyed it, too. I must say the F40's are so splendid to look at, so wicked and so powerful. I'm looking forward to driving the winners' lap, whoever wins!" Anna hugged Sheba and Sheba responded, giving Anna a big wet lick on her cheek.

"Well, you all seem very confident," said Giovanni. "So let's move on to the next lessons. First, I want all three of you to go out and do one lap at whatever speed you feel comfortable with. Then on the second lap I would like Stefano and Pietro to drive side by side and practice what it feels like to have another car inches away from your car. Then, halfway around the second lap, Lucia should change places with Pietro and drive side by side with Stefano. What you will find is that, on some of the abrupt corners only one car will fit on the bend, so the other must give way. Pietro, you give way to Stefano twice then Stefano will give way to Pietro twice, and the same with Lucia and Stefano.

"Keep the speed below 150 mph for these laps until you feel comfortable, then tomorrow you can take the speed higher. The main thing is to get used to having other cars on the track. Tomorrow you can practice overtaking techniques and learning pit signs. Remember your car numbers: Stefano is #8, Lucia #6 and Pietro #12. The pit signs are used to bring you in to refuel and change tires, and you must come in when your number is shown."

They discussed the side-by-side plan until they felt confident that they knew what to do, then left the trailer, went back to the pit area and got into their cars. This time there were no co-drivers, so all three were a little nervous. They started the F40's, waited for them to warm up, and after checking their mirrors, accelerated away out of the pit area, onto the track.

Anna sat and waited in the pit area with Sheba on the leash. Anna didn't feel she had to drive, although wistfully she wished she could have taken part. But she knew her limits and was content to sit and watch the other three, as they sped past her on their practice laps.

The side-by side-laps went perfectly with no mishaps and soon the three F40's came rolling back into the pit area.

Giovanni came up to them and said, "That's it for today. I would like you to think about what you did, what you have learned and how you can improve your techniques. Tomorrow we will start early. You can eat breakfast at seven in the cafeteria and I'll meet you here at eight."

"Where do we sleep?" asked Lucia.

"Good point, Lucia. I'll show you to your trailers." Giovanni led them past the planning trailer, to an area where two large trailers were parked. "Lucia and Stefano take this one, Anna and Pietro will use that one." He pointed to the trailers as he spoke. "They are identical and very luxurious. The cafeteria is open twenty-four hours a day, and if you need me for anything, please call me at the pit office. Each trailer has a telephone." Giovanni gave them keys to the trailers and made sure they got inside okay, then waved goodbye and went off back to his pit office.

Stefano and Lucia went inside and looked around. "Wow! What luxury!" exclaimed Stefano, admiring the soft sofas and pastel covering on the walls.

"It's just like an apartment!" said Lucia. They had a large living area with tables and chairs, an electric cook top, microwave and refrigerator. In the back they found a large double bed with covers matching the curtains. There were reading lamps and books in English, French and Italian in a little bookcase and also a small clock radio.

The refrigerator was stocked with deli foods such as sliced ham and turkey, lettuce, tomatoes and mayonnaise, as well as milk, soft drinks and wine. In a cupboard were fresh bread and biscuits.

"They really thought of everything," said Lucia. "Let's go visit Pietro and Anna." They went out and knocked on the door of the other trailer. Anna opened the door and welcomed them in.

"Isn't it wonderful?" Anna said. "I had visions of some tiny garage we would have to live in for three days, but this is the Ritz; cozy and sumptuous."

"Even Sheba likes it. She is curled up under the table," said Pietro.

"I'll make coffee and sandwiches," Anna said.

"Sounds like a very good idea," Lucia replied.

"I'll go and put the top up on the Mondial," Pietro said on his way out the door. "I'll be back for some hot coffee in five minutes."

"Take Sheba with you, she needs go out before we go to bed," said Anna. Sheba understood. She got up and stretched, then followed Pietro out the door.

The wolf and Pietro walked slowly to where the Mondial and the Redhead were parked. Pietro turned the corner and set eyes on his Mondial. "Hello, you gorgeous beauty," he said laughingly. "I hope you didn't mind me driving your sister the F40 today." He put the top up with ease and looked lovingly at his car. "Buona Notte, my love, and to you, too, wild Redhead." He blew them each a kiss then walked back to the trailer where he and Sheba went inside to the cozy smell of hot coffee.

"Ah, this is the life!" Pietro kissed Anna on her neck as she was preparing sandwiches and patted her round behind.

"No, no, Pietro, we have company. Be good now, please!" said Anna.

Stefano and Lucia laughed. "Looks like you are in for a passionate night, Anna," said Lucia.

Anna smiled. "Every night is passionate. We love each other very, very much."

The four sat and drank coffee and ate Anna's delicious ham, lettuce and tomato sandwiches. They talked about the magnificent F40's, the incredible power of the machine and the marvelous sound at

7000 rpm when the valves and camshafts sang in harmony with the growl of the exhausts.

The evening wore on and they decided to have an early night in order to be fresh for the morning practice laps. Stefano and Lucia bade Pietro and Anna goodnight and slipped away to their own trailer where they snuggled down into the large, comfortable bed, falling asleep in each other's arms.

Pietro and Anna went to bed and held each other tight. They talked into the night about their plans. Anna wanted children; a boy and a girl. Pietro kissed her. "As many as you like, my darling," he said. "First, I want to win Le Mans for you and for Enzo."

Anna was secretly scared of the race to come. She had heard about how some of the Le Mans races had wrought terrible tragedy on the drivers and even the spectators when a race car hit another then careened off the wall and exploded into a million pieces. She pushed the thought to the back of her mind and hugged Pietro close to her. What will be, will be, she thought. I will never speak of my fears to Pietro. He will never know that I am afraid for him. He loves to drive so much! They fell asleep, cuddled up close.

Morning came and at 6:30 a.m. Stefano knocked on their trailer door. "Pietro! Anna!" he called. "See you for breakfast in half an hour."

Pietro sat up in bed and looked down at his still sleeping Anna. He kissed her forehead, got up and went to have a shower to wake himself up. Anna awoke to the sound of Pietro singing in the shower and Sheba licking her face. She crawled out of bed and gave Sheba a biscuit from the cupboard. She yawned and stretched, then called to Pietro.

"Any room for me, Pietro?" Pietro opened the shower cubicle door and Anna went in. The two hugged each other under the jet of freezing cold water. "Oh…Pietro, you crazy man. I thought it would be a least warm!" She shivered but stayed there clasped in his arms. Pietro began to sing an old Italian song and Anna joined in. The two giggled and laughed in their exquisite happiness.

Anna came out, found a towel and dried herself down then found a pair of jeans and a T-shirt and sandals. She dressed quickly and threw the towel to Pietro when he came out. "You crazy man, taking a cold shower! Next time we have a warm one for me," she said.

Pietro dried himself quickly and came over to give Anna a big kiss. "Anything you say, my sweet," he grinned. "Anything!" He dressed and combed his black hair. Anna put on a little mascara and combed her hair into a bun at the back.

"Come on, let's go for breakfast. I'm starving!" she said. They took Sheba with them and knocked on Stefano and Lucia's trailer door. The two came out and they all walked down to the cafeteria. Inside, Giovanni spotted them and beckoned them to come to his table, where several Ferrari mechanics were sitting.

They all got up and Lucia as Anna approached. "Buon giorno!" "Buon giorno!" They pulled up another table next to Giovanni to make room for the foursome to join them. The couples sat down and Stefano ordered coffee with croissants for them.

"You sleep well?" asked Giovanni.

"Very well, thank you. The trailers are very comfortable," said Pietro. Stefano nodded agreement.

"Good. Today is a special day. First, Enzo will arrive around noon. He called me this morning from Rome Airport. Second, look over there and you will see some of our newly arrived competition." They looked around a group of men in yellow overalls. "Our friends and enemies, the Team Porsche! The track will become much more crowded today as more and more teams arrive to practice. But Porsche is our mortal enemy. We must beat them this year. We must kick the dust in their faces!"

Pietro and Stefano looked at Giovanni. He was deadly serious. "No problem," said Pietro. "We will win, because we have the best cars and the best team in the world!"

The Ferrari mechanics reacted to his statement, toasting Pietro with their coffee cups held high and yelling, "Viva Italia! Viva Ferrari! Viva Cavallino!" Sheba, surprised by the noise, got up on her haunches and let out a magnificent howl. This caused the Ferrari team to yell even louder in boisterous enthusiasm. "Our mascot, the silver wolf! She howls like the Ferrari engine!" they yelled.

The Porsche team members, hearing the commotion, looked across at the Ferrari team, then turned back to their discussions, whispering among themselves. Obviously they too, knew that Ferrari was their major competition.

Giovanni reviewed the plan for the day, with practice laps for the first two hours, followed by two hours of lecture on pit stops, rules and procedures, yellow warning flags and lights to warn of accidents, and a discussion of techniques. Then more practice laps until they were fully knowledgeable and comfortable with the whole track and the cars.

Giovanni drained his coffee cup and stood up. "Well, my friends, see you in half an hour at the pit office. The cars will be warmed up and ready for you at 8 a.m. precisely." Giovanni left with most of the Ferrari mechanics. The waiter brought the foursome coffee and croissants. They hungrily attacked the breakfast, spreading butter on the warm croissants and sipping their delicious hot coffee.

After breakfast they went back to the trailers to get their overalls and helmets. Anna decided to take Sheba for a long walk around the inside perimeter of the track.

"Okay, we will watch out for you and flash our lights, my love," said Pietro, kissing her softly on the lips.

"Take care. I'll see you around eleven or twelve o'clock and we can have lunch," said Anna. "Come, Sheba, walkies!" Sheba, ever willing, let out a howl of happiness and took off with Anna holding her on a long leash. The others grabbed their overalls and helmets from inside the trailers, put the overalls on and went off to the Ferrari pit area.

The day went smoothly for the drivers, with Lucia, Stefano and Pietro becoming ever more familiar with the circuit, which was very busy with cars of all shapes and sizes roaring around the track. The three drove close together in formation, flashing their lights once to warn the slower cars in preparation for overtaking, then roaring past in a crescendo of fury. The F40's sped ahead, their awesome power way ahead of the competition.

Enzo arrived about 12:30 with an entourage of Ferrari marketing folks from all over the world, all waiting to see the F40's in action. Enzo locked himself up in an office with Giovanni for over an hour as Giovanni briefed him on the condition of the cars, the team and the progress of Stefano, Pietro and Lucia. Enzo came out of the office smiling broadly, his arm wrapped around Giovanni's shoulders. He was pleased with what he had heard, now he wanted to see for himself.

Giovanni told the pit boss to flag Lucia, Stefano and Pietro to bring them in. They had been practicing since 12:30, following lunch with Anna. Lucia was the first to see the pit sign signaling them to come in after this lap. A Porsche tore past her as she slowed to check the sign. The driver of the Porsche put two fingers up, mocking Lucia. Lucia noted the Porsche's number 28 in her mind and pressed the accelerator to the floor. The F40 responded with tremendous ferocity, rocketing after the Porsche. Lucia gradually approached the Porsche, but the driver zigzagged across the lanes, refusing to let her pass.

She knew that the Tetra Rouge Corner was coming up, so she changed down to third gear and held the position just behind and to the left of the Porsche. The bend came up and the Porsche steered into it, maintaining its line. Lucia waited until the Porsche was right in the middle of the curve, then put her foot flat on the accelerator, swung right and positioned herself to overtake while the Porsche was still steering around the curve, unable to zigzag. The F40 responded to her request with a tremendous series of barks as the turbos forced the fuel into the engine. The revs rose to 7500 rpm and in third gear she flew past the Porsche who had no way of stopping her or catching up with her; he was just too slow.

Lucia entered the Mulsanne Straight changed up to fourth gear at 160 mph with the revs climbing until she was at 7000 revs and 180 mph. She changed deftly to fifth gear and the Porsche became a diminishing speck in her rearview mirror. She put her right hand out of the window and lifted two fingers. Soon the Porsche was no longer visible and only Pietro and Stefano could be seen in her rearview mirror.

She slowed and cruised the rest of the lap then pulled in neatly to the pit entrance area, slowed to the restricted speed and pulled up right in front of the Ferrari area. She turned off the engine and climbed out of the F40. Instantly, four Ferrari mechanics were all over it, checking suspension, wheels and engine for anything loose or overly hot from stress.

Lucia took off her helmet and her thick black hair released, flowed around her face. She looked up to see Enzo Ferrari standing there, dressed in his immaculate black suit as usual. He came forward smiling. "Lucia, my dear, the Ferrari colors have never looked better than with you wearing them! How do you like the F40?" He kissed her first on one cheek and then on the other.

"It has the power of one thousand dragons, Enzo. I love to drive it; it is so exhilarating, so incredibly fast, it feels like a part of me. When I ask it to accelerate, it responds as fast as my brain can tell my foot to press the accelerator! Also, it is much faster than those old Porsches." Lucia motioned toward the Porsche pit area.

Stefano and Pietro came rolling in, braked and jumped out of their cars, taking their helmets off and walking towards Lucia and Enzo.

"Lucia!" said Stefano, "You were absolutely marvelous the way you feinted and took that Porsche right in the middle of the curve!"

"What is this?" said Enzo, laughing. "The race is not until the day after tomorrow and already you are showing your rear end to the Porsches. Good girl! Good girl, that is the sort of spirit I love!" Enzo shook hands with Stefano and Pietro. "Congratulations, Pietro, on your marriage. I want to meet your beautiful wife. Where is she?"

"Anna will be coming by around three o'clock when we have a break. I will introduce you then and I'm sure you will love her, too, Enzo. She is such a wonderful girl and we love each other dearly."

"I look forward to it, Pietro," Enzo said. "I hear from Giovanni that you enjoy driving the F40 and that you drive like a professional. He has great confidence in you, Lucia, and Stefano, and he congratulated me on asking you to drive the Le Mans."

"The F40 is so well engineered and so powerful that we can win this race for you, I am sure, Enzo," Pietro replied.

"It would be nice, Pietro, to win again at Le Mans. It has been many years since the Cavallino Rampante crossed the finish line first at Le Mans. Too many years!" said Enzo. "But this year I think you bring me luck. We will see, my young friend."

Giovanni came to talk to the three young drivers. "Take a half hour break while the mechanics check out your cars. We also have slight aerodynamic modifications we want to try out before tomorrow's officially timed laps, to decide which position you each will start in. Also, you need to drive tonight from ten to midnight to get a taste of driving the circuit at night, so I suggest you drive this afternoon until five, then take some time off and return at nine."

They nodded and went off to the cafeteria to drink more coffee. They would need it to keep awake through the long day. At least the coffee was the best they had ever tasted.

They practiced relentlessly until five o'clock, then climbed out of the cars feeling quite exhausted due to the tremendous amount of concentration required to negotiate the circuit at top speed while dodging the slower cars. As they walked slowly back to their trailers they agreed to take a nap, then have dinner, meeting again at nine that evening.

Pietro fell asleep on the sofa, his head cradled in Anna's lap, while Sheba stretched out on the floor. Anna could feel the tension in Pietro; the intense schedule was starting to get to him she knew. He muttered in his sleep something about "wheels, must turn the wheels," then drifted off to sleep again.

At nine, they went back to the pit area. Darkness was falling as Pietro, Stefano and Lucia climbed into the warmed-up cars. The mechanics showed them the switches for controlling high and low beam, to make sure they knew their location. Giovanni came by and wished them Buon Viaggio. "Take it easy at first until your eyes get adjusted to the dark, then give it all you've got and we will time the laps to see how the darkness effects you."

Lucia took off first, hurtling away down the road, joining the track at about 100 mph and merging in with other team cars that were also testing their night driving skills. She wound the F40 up to about 130 mph and held it there while she negotiated the first lap.

Even though the F40's halogen headlights were superb, the difference between driving in bright daylight and driving at night was a taxing challenge. Lucia's concentration level was high, and as she adjusted to the circuit, she began to travel faster and faster. The F40 trembled as she increased the revs in each gear. The music of the camshafts and valve gear sang in her ears, and after a few laps she felt totally in control of this beast of a car, roaring and snarling around the track at speeds of 190 mph with plenty of power in reserve. Driving in the dark, lap after lap, she felt remote from the world, battling her skill against the twisting bends and running flat out on the Mulsanne Straight, reaching 7000 rpm in fifth gear, the adrenaline rising as she changed down for the Chicanes, which she hurtled through in a perfect line, occasionally having to change lanes to pass slower cars.

Pietro and Stefano kept close behind Lucia in their previously agreed upon formation. It was all they could do in just keeping up with the skillful Lucia. The two hours passed quickly and it seemed too soon when the lighted sign called them in on the next lap. All the cars behaved magnificently, their robust design and incredible aerodynamics keeping them glued to the track, while the world's most powerful 2.9 liter engines gave their all with incredible ease, revving to the red line in each gear, speeding past the slower opposition time after time.

They pulled into the pits and walked back to their trailers, with the vision of the track, and the sound of the valve gear still vivid. They played cards for an hour in Stefano and Lucia's trailer, until one by one the three drivers fell asleep where they sat. Anna lifted their legs onto the sofa and put pillows behind their heads and went off to sleep on Stefano and Lucia's bed. Thank God, only three more days and it will be over, she thought. Please, God, keep them safe!

The following day at 11 a.m. they were officially lap-timed by the organizers of the Le Mans Grand Prix. Not surprisingly, Lucia broke the track record to get the pole position, Stefano came next one tenth of a second behind Lucia to get a place in the second row, and Pietro was a whole one half second slower, which put him in seventh place in the fourth row. Enzo was delighted with the times and applauded the three drivers with a look of sheer happiness on his face.

The whole Ferrari team crammed into the pit office where Giovanni gave them official time results and assigned drivers to four cars, with two cars in reserve. "Lucia, you will drive in number six alternating with Lorenzo. In the race you will drive two hours then Lorenzo for two hours and then Lucia again for two hours and so on. If you or Lorenzo burn out, then the other will drive three hours so the burnt-out one can recover. Four hours is the maximum any one driver can drive in one go.

"Pietro, you drive number twelve alternating with Antonio, two hours each. Stefano, you'll drive number eight alternating with Roberto. Giuseppe and Enrico will drive number fourteen." Giovanni unrolled a large diagram of the starting grids showing where each F40 would be at the start. Each car would be diagonally parked against the inside wall of the track, nose pointing out.

"All drivers must be in their cars by ten minutes to four tomorrow, Saturday afternoon. Keep your eyes on the clock. At one minute to four, watch the two banks of starting lights. When the lights go green, start your engines and go as fast as you can for the next twenty-four hours, until the race finishes at four on Sunday afternoon.

"First car over the finish line with the most completed laps is the winner. Starting drivers are Lucia, Stefano, Pietro and Giuseppe. Any questions?" asked Giovanni.

"What is the plan between now and four tomorrow afternoon?" asked Lucia.

"Well," said Giovanni, " I would like you to spend the next two hours practicing pit stops for refueling and tire changes to get the time down to where it is physically impossible to do it any faster. It's good to practice today so that any problems with fuel pumps and tire swaps get resolved now, rather than during the race.

"Tomorrow we start at nine and practice till noon, at which time the track is cleared of cars and the officials ensure there is no debris left on it. From noon to four o'clock is nerve time; time to rest and relax for the race or whatever you want to do. The mechanics will make a last check on all cars after pit stop training. After that it's in the hands of the gods."

The team went out to the pit area and started up the F40's, burning away down the pit lane onto the track to do two laps each, then come in for refueling, tire swaps and driver change. Only a small amount of fuel was added each time to allow the procedure to be executed many times over the two hour period.

The Ferrari team members were such professionals, they worked together in rigid precision at each pit stop of the four cars. One mechanic on each trolley jack, one at each wheel and two ready with the fuel pump. Finally one mechanic would race around the car checking suspension, steering and engine mountings and then checking with each driver if any abnormalities had been noticed during the two laps.

At the end of two hours, the team was perfect; their timing superb. But they were also exhausted and Giovanni had them take a two hour break before doing the final checks on all the cars to see if any part needed replacing. When racing at 200 mph for hours on end, a tremendous amount of stress is placed on every component.

That evening when they went back to the trailers, Stefano, Lucia and Pietro could do nothing but talk about the upcoming race tomorrow. For the first time ever, there was a strange aura of tension in their moods. The tension of driving at high speeds for hours on end had reached some nerves buried deep in their bodies. Anna felt it immediately, and she was determined to overcome it. She saw that if they didn't unwind, the tension would still be there tomorrow, so she sat on the sofa to think and stroked Sheba while she tried to come up with a way to get them to unwind. She thought back to the nights when they had fun and it came to her instantly. Why not?

"Lucia, where is that fancy outfit you brought with you? You know, the one with the wide brimmed hat?" asked Anna.

"Somewhere in the cupboard," replied Lucia distantly, not looking at Anna, as if she never really heard the question. Anna went to Lucia's cupboard in the bedroom and found the clothes Lucia had raved about back in Paris.

"Here, Lucia, you have five minutes to get ready. Come on, off with those overalls and on with your nice clothes," said Anna, draping the beautiful clothes and the hat across the sofa.

"Don't be silly, Anna, why would I want to put those on? We have to practice again tomorrow morning and I'm too tired to change my clothes just to go to the cafeteria," said Lucia.

"We are not going to the cafeteria. I am going to drive us all into Le Mans, find a restaurant with a dance floor, where we can have a good meal, drink some good wine and do some dancing. Come on, all of you, get out of those overalls and let's go. It will be good for us all to have some fun together again." Anna said this in a stern, commanding voice.

Stefano and Pietro looked up at Anna, thinking about what she had suggested. Anna could almost hear their exhausted minds thinking about her idea.

"Five minutes! Come on, let's do it!" she said. "Dancing is good for the soul."

The other three looked at Anna then looked at each other. Lucia got up. "Okay, Anna, you win, it's a good idea." She went into the bedroom and changed into her new clothes. By the time she came back, Stefano was busy changing. Pietro and Anna had gone to their own trailer.

17: DANCING & SMILING ARE GOOD FOR THE SOUL.

Ten minutes later they all piled into Pietro's Mondial and Anna drove them into Le Mans to find a restaurant. The town was packed with tourists and cars, with hundreds of people in the streets and in the bars and bistros. Anna drove through the town center then took a small side road leading out of town. They crossed a little bridge and came upon a little restaurant with chairs and tables outside. It looked fairly crowded, but the tourists didn't seem to have found it yet.

Anna pulled into the only remaining parking spot, turned off the engine and set the hand brake. The June evening air was warm and sultry. Music floated out through the restaurant windows; a good sign Anna thought.

Inside the restaurant, there were about twenty tables and a small dance floor. A few couples were dancing a fast tango. The band was lively, with a bass, guitar, drums, piano and a solitary female trumpet player. The Maitre d' welcomed them and found a table by the window. They sat down, ordered wine and looked at the menu. Stefano and Pietro chose steaks cooked rare, while Lucia and Anna selected the House salad.

They sipped their wine and watched the customers, mainly locals by the look of them, enjoying a Friday night out. Stefano asked

Lucia for a dance and they whirled around the little dance floor to the tune of a Samba played exquisitely by the young lady trumpeter.

Anna watched Stefano and Lucia laughing and having fun. She winked at Pietro who caught the wink, smiled and motioned Anna to the dance floor. They danced, slowly at first, then the trumpeter broke into a ragtime melody full of fire. Pietro swung Anna around and then caught her coming the other way and they began to come alive. Pietro's tension was visibly leaving him at every twist and turn to the beating music.

More and more customers got up to dance until the little dance floor was crowded. Everyone was having a great time; throwing off their cares and letting themselves go, dancing to the fabulous music. The band ended their melody and took a break to get drinks from the bar.

Stefano and Pietro escorted their girls to their table where the food had just arrived. "Good timing on the band's part," said Stefano. The excellent food was washed down with good French wine.

Stefano and Pietro mopped up the rich sauce left on their plates with chunks of French bread, drank a little wine, then leaned back in their chairs and watched the band start to play again. This time they played a classical blues melody in Louisiana style, full of solos, first by the drummer using brushes, followed by the bass player plucking his strings to create a deep rumbling sound that made the whole room resonate. Soon the customers' feet were beating the floor to the rhythm. The trumpeter gave out a soul-searching blast on her trumpet and the whole band joined in until the restaurant was filled with the plaintive sound of the blues. The band played and the customers clapped and danced. Even the waiters were moving in time to the marvelous music.

The music changed to a waltz and Pietro and Anna took to the dance floor again, followed swiftly by Stefano and Lucia. The two couples danced slowly, cheek to cheek, occasionally exchanging kisses and ear nibbles. The evening wore on and the tempo of the band changed again to an old Edith Piaf number, with the trumpeter playing the part of the famous singer, with high notes alternating with incredibly low notes, just like the way Edith sang. It was an exhilarating evening with great music and lively uninhibited customers

The four danced until they were too hot to dance anymore. They returned to their table, paid the bill and set off for the car, passing by the band and thanking them for a great evening. The young lady trumpeter smiled broadly, as she waved goodbye to them.

Anna, having drunk the least wine, drove again, and they took off in the Mondial Cabriolet with the top down, cruising back through the center of Le Mans, which was crowded with many people in a festive mood.

Anna drove them back to the track road and roared down the final stretch toward the pit area, the Mondial's V-8 engine singing a song of passion and power. They arrived at the parking area where Anna slid the Mondial in next to the Testarossa.

Pietro got out and put the hood up, patted the Mondial and said, "Goodnight, sweetheart," to his beautiful red car. Stefano murmured some affectionate endearments to his Redhead, and they all trudged slowly back to their trailers, arms around each other, singing the blues and jazz songs they had heard that night.

"See you at eight. Sleep well!" said Stefano. "It was a nice evening. Thanks, Anna, for the really good idea. You took all our tension away."

Anna smiled and said goodnight. They went into the trailers, took off their evening clothes and climbed into bed, the delicious boom of the band playing boogie still in their heads.

18: UNGENTLEMANLY CONDUCT ON A RACE TRACK.

The next morning at eight, they were up and off to the cafeteria for a light breakfast of coffee and croissants. The whole Ferrari team was there as well as many teams they had not seen before. Private entrants, the Mercedes team, Jaguar and Porsche were all there, and the cafeteria hummed as the teams discussed the upcoming race.

During the morning practice, Lucia sat in the brilliant red F40 with the clutch down and first gear selected. Giovanni gave the thumbs up go signal they had previously agreed upon, Lucia hit the starter button and the F40's V-8 burst into life. She pressed the accelerator hard and let the clutch up. The F40 leapt forward with tremendous power, the rear tires spun and smoked as the rubber began to grip. 40, 50, 60 mph came up in under four seconds. Three seconds later in third gear she joined the main track at 100 mph. The V-8 screamed at the 7000 rpm red line as Lucia kept her foot on the accelerator. 140 mph came up and she changed up to fourth, the turbochargers propelling the F40 like a rocket into the first bend. Lucia eased off and changed down to third to take the curve. Her adrenaline pumping, Lucia tightened the line and the F40 was a half inch from the wall. She came out of the bend with 7000 rpm back on the rev counter and the G-force pushed her hard back into the seat. She came to the Mulsanne straight and punched the accelerator, valves singing as the car reached 180 mph. Lucia held that speed, wanting to save the car for the race.

But even as she thought of backing off, the yellow Porsche #28 came up right beside her. She looked across and saw the grinning sneer of the driver, as he looked her right in the eye. He accelerated past her up to 200 mph and Lucia decided to let him go. She would save the car for the real race. She caught up with him in the first Chicane. He obviously wasn't as daring through the bends. Lucia overtook him with ease, using all her skill to roar round the curve on his inside again. The Porsche driver raised his fist in anger and Lucia could see his fist raised in her rear view mirror.

On the straight, he again roared up next to her, putting his car within inches of Lucia's. She slowed and let him pass. Then he drove right in front of her, zigzagging again across the track. But Lucia ignored him and took the rest of the lap at much lower speed than normal, controlling her urge to just blast past the stupid Porsche.

She came into the pits and turned off the engine then sat there for a minute, promising herself that she would beat that Porsche in the race if it was the last thing she did on earth.

Pietro and Stefano had seen the Porsche zigzagging in front of Lucia. Joining her in the cafeteria for coffee, Pietro saw some of the Porsche drivers sitting together in their usual spot. He walked up to them and in an angry tone asked who was driving #28.

A tall, fair-haired driver stood up and said, "Who wants to know?"

"Me, that's who," shouted Pietro. "Why you zigzag like that; you want to cause an accident and kill my best friend?"

"Ah, you Ferrari drivers, you are all the same…a lot of talk and no action."

Pietro walked over to the driver of #28, looked him in the eye then punched him on the nose. The man fell backwards, crashing into a table. The other Porsche drivers grabbed hold of Pietro who was ready to go after the guy again.

Lucia and Stefano came to Pietro's rescue. "Let him go, you pigs," said Lucia. "We're here to race, not to fight. But tell your friend that drives #28, if he acts dangerously on the circuit in the real race, he must suffer the consequences." Lucia's voice was low and commanding. "I said let him go, or do I report you to the race officials?"

They let Pietro go and he shook them off, then turned towards Lucia and Stefano. The #28 driver lunged at Pietro's back, but he was too slow. Stefano hit him in the stomach with all his might and the driver fell to the ground. This time he didn't get up, but lay there cursing and groaning.

Lucia ordered coffee and the three sat in their usual seats, determined to ignore the infuriated Porsche drivers who were calling insults to the Ferrari team. In a cool controlled voice, Lucia said, "Let them insult us now, but we will show them our dust in the race."

Pietro and Stefano smiled at her. Pietro shook his head in wonderment. "Lucia, you are a rare young lady; you drive like a tornado and you issue commands like a general. I think those Porsche drivers are actually scared of you! Stefano, you have one hell of a wife, you know that?"

"I know, Pietro," said Stefano. "That's why I adore her so much. She is such a forceful person once she gets angry."

Anna came into the cafeteria with Sheba and sat down at the table. She sensed something was wrong and asked Pietro what was the matter. Pietro told her of the stupidity of the Porsche driver on the track and said that he had just given the driver a piece of his mind.

"A sore nose is more like it," said Stefano with a grin.

The Porsche drivers came over to the table and one of them started to threaten Pietro and Stefano. Sheba reared up on her hind legs, put her paws on the speaker's shoulders and let out a tremendous howl, her jaws open wide exposing her wolf fangs. The driver backed off, reaching for Sheba's paws, but she moved with him, keeping her paws on his shoulders, her fangs an inch from his face. The Porsche driver stopped and stood frozen.

"Tell this damn wolf to get out of my face!" he shouted. Sheba snarled and snapped her teeth together as if warning the man to be quiet.

"Apologize for your team, and I will call her off," said Lucia. "Quickly, or she will bite you for threatening us and your nose will be her lunch!"

The Porsche driver apologized in a very nervous, faint voice. Lucia called to Sheba to come and the wolf dropped to a sitting position but still on guard. The Porsche team left quickly and Anna breathed a sigh of relief.

"Sheba, you are such a brave wolf. I must get you a biscuit," she said, going to the counter to order one. The young man at the counter selected a large wholemeal biscuit and gave it to Anna.

"No charge," he said. "That is one very ferocious guard dog, or is it a real wolf?"

"Thank you," said Anna. "Yes, Sheba is a real wolf from the mountains of Northern Italy, from the same part of the country where they build Ferraris." The young man was astonished to see a tame wolf as a pet, yet still so ferocious.

Anna gave the biscuit to Sheba who gulped it down in two seconds and looked up for more. Anna gave her a pat on the head. "All gone, Sheba. Never mind, it will soon be dinner time and then I will feed you. Good girl!"

"Well," said Stefano, "one more hour of practice and they close the track till 4 p.m. We all know what happens then. I suppose we should get back to the pits. I'll inform Giovanni of our little conflict with the illustrious Porsche team. Hopefully, he'll agree with our point of view."

They left the cafeteria and walked back to the pit area. Press and television crews were everywhere now, photographing the cars, the drivers, the mechanics and anything that moved. One TV interviewer approached Stefano boldly and put a microphone in front of him. He asked if Stefano thought Ferrari would win this year. Stefano smiled and said he certainly thought the F40 was a winner. "The most powerful, most superbly designed race car ever to compete in Le Mans," he added.

After Stefano reported the track and cafeteria incidents to Giovanni, he was pleased to see that Giovanni was totally on their side. "I'll talk to the Porsche team Manager to tell him to put a stop to any zigzagging of a dangerous manner. Normally, zigzagging to prevent overtaking is frowned upon but allowed. In this case it was done in anger, and that is not allowed," said Giovanni.

Stefano, Lucia and Pietro climbed into their racing machines for the last set of practice laps before the race. The mechanics asked them to note any abnormality in steering, gearbox, suspension and engine performance however small, as this would be their last chance to make any corrections or major replacements before race time. The F40's roared away to the track, each driver striving to stress their car to its limits prior to the long 24-hour race, which was soon to start.

Anna had found a spot on the grass by Tetre Rouge Corner that she liked. She sat on a small mound and watched the Ferraris come out of the turn and accelerate away down the Mulsanne Straight. The sound of the engines at maximum rpm's was deafening but exhilarating. She saw Pietro leading Lucia and Stefano and waved. Pietro's hand went up to acknowledge her and then in an instant he was gone, streaking down the straight at 180 mph, Lucia and Stefano right on his tail.

Anna stroked Sheba who was lying next to her, her head resting on her huge paws, no doubt trying to understand where all the noise was coming from and why Anna was so contented to watch these metal objects screaming past every two seconds.

At noon, Anna walked back to the Ferrari pit area. As she walked with Sheba, she saw masses of people beside the track, laying out their blankets and getting ready to watch the race. The good vantage points were already taken by families with children, deck chairs, and picnic baskets. Some had brought their dogs and even their cats on leashes. The area was buzzing with activity as new people constantly arrived.

The guard on the pit area recognized Anna and let her through, but he had his work cut out to turn away hundreds of sightseers who wanted to see the racing cars close up. Anna saw that Stefano, Lucia and Pietro were in the Ferrari pit office, together with the other drivers and the mechanics. Giovanni and Enzo were giving a last minute briefing. She sat on a chair outside and waited.

After awhile the meeting broke up and Pietro came out, saw Anna and bent down to give her a big wet kiss. "How are you feeling, Pietro?" she asked with a smile.

"My stomach is full of butterflies, but other than that I am ready, my love. And the cars are ready too; all in perfect condition and ready for their grueling task! Let's go to the trailer," Pietro said. "We don't have to be back until 3:30, so I want to be alone with you until then. I want to hold you tight and look into your eyes and tell you how much I care for you."

Lucia and Stefano came out and Pietro told them he was going to the trailer with Anna and would see them at the pit area at 3:30 precisely. They walked back to their trailers together and Stefano said, "See you at 3:30 then."

Pietro and Anna lay on the big double bed and talked about the coming race. "You know, when I am driving today, I will think of you all the time, my sweet one," said Pietro, nuzzling Anna's soft neck. "You smell so good, like fresh flowers on a windy hillside."

"You just be careful out there, Pietro," said Anna solemnly. "You must watch out for the unexpected. I love you too, too much to lose you; I would die of a broken heart."

"Let's not talk about the race anymore now. Let's talk about after the race. Where are we going to go? Shall we drive straight back to Maranello, or shall we go with Stefano and Lucia to Nice on the coast?" Pietro was stroking Anna's back.

"Let's see after the race," said Anna. "I would like to go to Nice for a few days, then we could drive back along the coast, cross the border to Italy and then drive home." They talked and planned, changed their minds, disagreed a little, then made up, kissing and cuddling. They took their clothes off and went under the sheet, playing like children in a tent. Anna giggled as Pietro tickled her. He wouldn't stop so she grabbed him and tried to hold his arms down. In the ensuing scuffle they fell out of the bed onto the floor. Pietro pulled Anna on top of him and they lay there on the floor, not speaking, just enjoying the moment of peace as the clock ticked the seconds away.

Stefano and Lucia were in bed making love. The days of fast driving had given them a new height of excitement that they had never experienced before. Afterwards, Lucia turned onto her side and Stefano curled up against her spine. The listened and both noticed the quiet outside. No revving of engines, no whooshing sounds coming from cars roaring around the track, a peaceful world, so different from the last three days of intense practice. Neither moved until the little travel clock on the table said 3:15.

"Come on, Stefano, time to go!" Lucia jumped out of bed and started to put her underwear and overalls on.

Stefano groaned. "Come back to bed, I miss your warm body. Don't leave me, Lucia."

"No, sweetheart, we must go now. Otherwise we won't make it by 3:30," said Lucia. There was a knock on the door and the sound of Pietro's voice calling them. "Coming, coming," said Lucia, grabbing her helmet. "Come Stefano, we must go!"

Stefano finished putting his overalls on, took his helmet and followed Lucia out of the trailer, shutting the door behind him.

Anna turned to the other three. "Hey, you guys, I want to hug each one of you and wish you luck and a safe drive." She went to Lucia, hugged her tightly and kissed her on the cheek. Then she did the same to Stefano, who kissed her back. She turned to Pietro. "Drive well, my love, good luck and be safe. I love you much."

Pietro gave Anna warm hug and a big kiss. "See you in a couple of hours," he said. Anna was nearly crying, so Pietro hugged her again. "Sheba, take care of Anna for me." Sheba howled in response.

Anna started to leave, then turned and said, "I'll go back to Tetre Rouge if there is still any room." She waved and blew Pietro a kiss then turned and took off with Sheba.

The others went to the Ferrari pit, just making it by 3:30. Giovanni was waiting for them. "Okay, your cars are now on the track, so at 3:45 walk out to the cars and get ready for take off at 4 o'clock. Giuseppe will be driving the fourth car, #14."

Enzo came over, smiled and told them how proud he was that they were driving the Ferrari F40's in the great race. "I would love to drive today, but I am too old. Fifty years ago perhaps, but not today." He laughed. "My reactions are a little slow to say the least. So, God go with you. Buon Viaggio." He turned and went back to stand next to Giovanni, tall and straight. He looked happy and Lucia, Stefano, Pietro and Giuseppe knew then that this race was very important to Enzo. The culmination of all his great designs, the F40 would make his dream come true. If only they could win for this great man!

The next ten minutes went slowly, but time never stands completely still and at 3:45 precisely, the Ferrari team headed for the track. Lucia and Stefano hugged each other and patted Pietro and Giuseppe on the backs. They wished each other luck and got into their cars.

19: LADIES AND GENTLEMEN START YOUR ENGINES.

The stands were completely full. All the spectators were cheering the drivers as they got into their cars. The Ferrari fans were especially loud. The racetrack clock's hands moved to 3:55 and the huge starting lights powered on to show brilliant red lights.

Lucia, in pole position, sat calmly in the F40, her hand ready to hit the start button, gear lever locked in first, clutch down. Pietro and Stefano, further back, checked their watches and set their cars also in first with clutch down ready for the off.

The loudspeaker boomed as the announcer intoned, "One minute, drivers. One minute to start." He repeated it in French and the stands grew silent as they all knew the most prestigious, demanding race was due to start in seconds.

Lucia watched the light, even as it changed to yellow. She hit the starter button and, as the light turned green, the F40 burst into life. She floored the accelerator, let the clutch up and the F40 screamed down the track with seventy other cars on her tail.

The sound of seventy Grand Prix racing cars all running at high revs at the same time was incredible. The cacophony of sounds reverberated off the walls of the stands and could be heard clearly in the town of Le Mans. The old men who hadn't gone to the circuit felt renewed vigor in their lives as the noise of the engines reminded them of the early races at Le Mans when they were young. Back then they also went to the track with their friends and their sweethearts to watch the fury of man and machine battling each other for 24 straight hours.

20:   THE 24 HOURS OF LE MANS.

The spectators in the stands loved the noise, whooping and
cheering as the seventy racing cars sped down the track, each car
looking for gaps to overtake, to get to the front and take the lead. The 24
heures des Le Mans had begun!

Lucia kept the revs as high as she dared in each gear before
changing up to the next, and the F40 snarled and howled, surging ahead
and keeping well out in front of the pack, which was bunched up in a
dangerously close line, each driver trying ferociously to find a gap to
pass the one in front, to show that their car was the best, to lead, to win.

Pietro had had a few terrifying moments at the start as he floored
the throttle when the flag dropped and the light changed to green. The
power of his forward thrust propelled him forward so fast, he was
immediately forced to brake to avoid hitting a low slung Jaguar that had
difficulties in the initial acceleration take off. Pietro jabbed at the brakes
and eased off the accelerator, the nose of his F40 only inches from the
Jaguar. Three other cars caught Pietro up, one on each side and one right
on his tail, their lights flashing, trying to overtake. The Jaguar suddenly
burst into life and began to accelerate, having cleared the problem.
Pietro hung right behind it, looking for a gap to pass, but the Porsche
next to him had the same idea and accelerated past Pietro and the

Jaguar, its engine screaming at maximum revs. The five cars entered the first corner that lead up to Dunlop Bridge. The track was two lane, but all five cars were trying to overtake each other with only room for two cars. Pietro saw a tiny gap appear, maybe just enough to get through. He changed down to second gear and floored the throttle. The revs went up to 7,000 then 7500 and the F40 howled into the gap, Pietro anxiously estimating how many inches on either side were left in the gap. The Porsche, the Jaguar and Pietro all entered the curve at the same time, tires screaming at the limits of adhesion. The Jaguar and Porsche changed down and gave Pietro his chance. He was nearly at peak revs, dangerously close to blowing the engine past the red line. He surged ahead, the twin turbochargers whistling and the camshaft and valves emitting a fantastic symphony. He came through the gap and steadily increased his lead, changing up to third in a split second. The F40 was now 10 yards, 20 yards, 30 yards ahead, the revs built up again and Pietro screamed over the Dunlop Bridge at 150 mph, the Jaguar and Porsche falling off behind.

Pietro had been holding his breath for the past 20 seconds. He took a huge gulp of air in and changed up to fourth at 160 mph. His F40 came up on the car now in front of him, a white McLaren. Pietro pressed the accelerator and the F40 soared past the McLaren. Pietro was now behind Stefano, who was battling it out with another yellow Porsche. Pietro tucked in behind Stefano's F40 as the Porsche raced neck and neck with Stefano through the Esses and onto Tetre Rouge. The three cars changed down from fourth to third to second to negotiate the sharp right-hand curve. Stefano gunned the F40 out of the turn, the revs crept up from 6000 to 7000 and the powerful F40 engine outran the

Porsche and entered the Mulsanne Straight. Pietro, in the slipstream of Stefano's car, passed the Porsche with ease and changed up to third to keep up with the speed of Stefano.

Stefano saw another white McLaren ahead and there in the far distance was Lucia. He was determined to catch up to her; he had already overtaken two of the cars in front of him and felt unsurpassed confidence in the F40 engine. He pushed his right foot down and the F40's revs went up to 7000. Stefano changed up to fourth and his speed went up to 175 mph. Another change up and he was running at 205 mph, gaining slowly on the McLaren. Pietro tucked in behind Stefano, kept the same speed but required fewer rpm's because all the drag was forced on Stefano.

At 215 mph in fifth gear, Stefano came up alongside the McLaren, the first Chicane came up and the three cars went into them, revs screaming, engines howling as they changed rapidly down from fifth to fourth to third to second. Speed dropped to 90 mph and Stefano used all his skill to steer through the Chicane and position himself to out accelerate the white McLaren. But this time the McLaren was faster out of the corner, increasing distance from Stefano until it was 100 yards in front, maintaining its distance and increasing its speed back up to 200 mph on the Mulsanne Straight again.

Stefano cursed as he realized he had been out-maneuvered in the last curve, not keeping his revs to the maximum between each gear. Pietro also noticed that Stefano had muffed the last bend, but decided to stick behind him until he could see a clear opportunity to overtake his good friend and take the McLaren at the same time. The rest of the first lap went incredibly fast as they negotiated Mulsanne Corner,

Indianapolis Curve and Armage Bend before coming up to the stands again, which they roared through at 175 mph, curving right and left before entering the approach to Dunlop Bridge.

The very excited announcer reported the current top five after the first lap: "Ferrari #6, Lucia Gappuci; McLaren #21, Jimmy Blue; Ferrari #8, Stefano Gappuci, Ferrari #12, Pietro Venini, and Porsche #28, Einhard Getchner."

The spectators cheered loudly as they heard that Ferrari was leading, even though many of them were French and supported the Williams Renault team as well as Team Peugeot in the GT2 class. Like almost all racing fans, they acknowledged Enzo Ferrari's cars to be the fastest and finest road and racing cars in the world. The mystique, power and allure of Enzo's cars were inbred in every little boy from the tiny scale models that he played with as a child to the real road going classic cars that Enzo produced year after year at his factory in Maranello.

Stefano was determined to take the McLaren on the next lap and pushed the accelerator down hard in fourth gear. The revs rose to a crescendo at 7700 rpm and the F40 thundered up the approach to the Dunlop Bridge, over the top at 190 mph, the rev counter precariously close to the red line, the engine screaming change up, change up! Stefano changed up to fifth and the F40 careened forward, the revs dropping to 5000. Stefano again floored the throttle and soon was doing 200 mph. The Esses came quickly and he was forced to change down to fourth gear at 7500 rpm, then another change to third had the F40 at 7800 rpm. Slowing now, Stefano took a direct line through the sharp curves trying to lose as little momentum as possible.

Pietro had been unprepared for Stefano's takeoff and now lagged four or five hundred yards behind, surprised at the ferociousness of Stefano's driving, so early in the race. Stefano kept the revs as high as he dared, screaming out of the Esses at 150 mph, changing up to fourth he raised the speed to 175 mph. Taking the right-hand curve into the Tetre Rouge Corner with tremendous velocity, the F40 flew like a bird. Stefano thought at one point that he had over-judged the distance and would never make the tight right hander. He braked hard and shifted the gear lever from fifth to third, causing the F40 to scream at 8000 rpm. He was just in time; the car slowed into the curve and Stefano was able to gun it right on the neck on the curve. He swung the steering wheel to the right and missed the opposite metal fence by half an inch.

Stefano was sweating. Calm down! Calm down, he told himself. You have two hours left to catch that McLaren! His mind told him what he should do, but the spirit in him told him the opposite and he accelerated to maximum revs again, entering the Mulsanne Straight. He could see the white McLaren ahead and he felt better. Changing up to fourth, he let the F40 build up speed to 195 mph and 7700 rpm before changing to fifth. The F40 shot forward like a bullet and reached 210, then 215. Still Stefano kept his right foot hard down on the accelerator. At 220 mph the F40 came up to the McLaren and Stefano passed it on the left with a flash of his lights to tell the McLaren driver of his intention. The F40 pulled ahead…10 yards, 20 yards, then 30 yards with the speedometer showing 230 mph.

Before he could believe it, the first Chicane was coming up and Stefano was determined to try and take them in fourth gear at over 160 mph if possible. He left it to the last second to change down and steered to the middle of the curve, keeping the revs high, the engine pushing the F40 around the first bend, the tires squealing dramatically as the G force tried to unglue it from the road. Stefano exited the first turn and accelerated magnificently out of the corner into the next curve. Again the F40 tires reached their limits of adhesion and the F40 threatened to charge into the metal fence. Stefano braked slightly, pushed down on the accelerator and actually took the corner on two wheels, coming out of the Chicane and back on the Mulsanne Straight. He was perspiring heavily, but now he was happy.

He was fast approaching Lucia, who had eased up on the last bend, thinking she didn't need to go so fast any more for awhile as she had such a clear lead. She looked in her rearview mirror and saw Stefano catching up. She was of a mind to accelerate away, but she resisted the urge and let him catch her. The two F40's roared splendidly down the Mulsanne Straight at 215 mph, side by side. Stefano looked across at Lucia and gave her a thumbs up. She ventured a quick look and blew him a kiss. Stefano smiled and started to relax.

They went into the second Chicane together and expertly swung left, then right, changing down to fourth, then to third, accelerating away out of the curve and back together on the final stretch of the Mulsanne Straight. Back up to 210 mph with no cars in the rear view mirror, they cruised the rest of the lap together with Ferrari fans cheering wildly as the two vivid red racing cars came past the stands neck and neck. The announcer's voice showed his astonishment at the feat of the two F40's.

The third and fourth laps passed and they were still way ahead of the rest of the cars. The F40 turbochargers bellowing away, the valve gear singing at high rpms. The spectators by the side of the track were on their feet, enraptured at the sight of the two red Ferraris leading the field. Anna watched Lucia and Stefano go by, knowing their number by heart, and watched as the white McLaren went by, with Pietro right on its tail looking for an opportunity to pass it and get up there with his friends.

Halfway around the fifth lap, the whole race changed for Lucia and Stefano. Lucia saw it first; a gray Porsche 911 tucked in on the right, going about 170 mph ahead of her on the Mulsanne Straight. She flashed her lights and overtook it with Stefano following, both doing about 200 mph. They increased the revs and roared towards the first Chicane. Even as Lucia entered it, she knew she would have to slow right down as two more 911's were side by side, battling each other. Lucia hit her brakes and changed down to third gear, flashing her lights to let the two Porsches know she wanted to pass. At last the blue Porsche 911 pulled ahead of the silver one and now it was time for Lucia to pass, but precious seconds had been lost, and even as she screamed past the two Porsches, she saw in her mirror the white McLaren right behind Stefano, with Pietro right behind it.

Lucia pushed down on the accelerator, waited till the revs increased to 7000, then changed up to fourth gear. With 190 mph on the speedometer she entered the Mulsanne Straight. More revs and soon she was rocketing down the Straight at 220 mph, passing more and more slower cars. Entering the second Chicane she was suddenly behind an Aston Martin. She flashed her lights, changed down and overtook the Aston Martin on the inside, the F40's tires squealing trying to maintain adhesion.

Now the Le Mans became a tremendous test of skill; how to go as fast as possible and still avoid hitting the slower cars that kept appearing. Time after time Lucia was forced to slow down, sometimes to second gear, and each time the McLaren immediately came up behind her and Stefano. Pietro knew that he could outrun the McLaren, but each time he was ready, a slower car would appear in front of the McLaren and Pietro's chance was gone as there was only room for two cars side by side at the same time.

Another factor entered the race. The big Jaguar and the Porsche #28 were now on his tail, all trying to find a point where they could overtake. Pietro decided he would take the McLaren on the next lap at the Mulsanne Straight, even if he had to go beyond maximum revs. He waited for his opportunity, and at Tetre Rouge Corner he changed down to third gear and stayed within six feet of the white McLaren. His chance came, a minute gap appeared and Pietro stood on the accelerator pedal. The F40 responded beautifully and Pietro slid past the McLaren at 180 mph, revs close to 8000. He changed up to fourth and the F40 leapt forward until he was well clear, only to run right up against two more Porsche 911's side by side. Pietro flashed continuously, but the two Porsche's were evenly matched and their 190-mph top speed kept Pietro in check, unable to overtake. He followed the Porsches down to the first Chicane, and as the Porsches slowed, the lane opened up as they took a single lane instead of two. Pietro changed down to third and went by them like a bat out of hell with the McLaren right on his tail.

Now the F40's were running first, second and third and the world watching on television and listening on the radio was cheering and shouting, "Viva La Ferrari!" As the three cars passed the stands on the eighth lap, Enzo beamed.

"Ah, it is so good to see Ferraris leading Le Mans. This is where they excel. La Bella Macchina!" The Ferrari mechanics shouted with joy to see their cavallinos in the lead.

After twenty-five laps the Ferrari sign went up to call them in for fuel. The four Ferraris came in, one lap between each. The mechanics refueled in under eight seconds and each roared back out on the track again, a little slower now as they had just added 125 liters of fuel to their weight.

At the end of the first two hours, they were called in again, this time for driver changes. Lucia came in first, jumped out fast and gave the thumbs up sign to Lorenzo, who got straight into the F40 and buckled his four point seatbelt. When Giovanni banged on his roof as the pre-arranged signal that all was clear and ready to go, Lorenzo took off at tremendous speed to join the main track, the F40 engine screaming, tires spinning as they fought to get to grips with the tarmac.

Lucia waited patiently for Stefano, Pietro and Giuseppe to come in and swap drivers. When all cars were back on the track, they went off with Anna and Sheba to the cafeteria. They sat at their usual table, the drivers slowly regaining their equilibrium as the forces at work at 200 mph do strange things to the mind.

The off shift of Ferrari mechanics sat with them, laughing, joking and celebrating the lead positions they were in. At least two of the mechanics had formed crushes on Anna and Lucia and they kept asking them if they would like more coffee, a cappuccino perhaps or a small sandwich? Stefano and Pietro noticed this but decided not to spoil the occasion. Nevertheless they sat closer to their wives to show the young mechanics who was who.

Enzo came into the cafeteria, accompanied by a dapper little old man dressed in a three piece suit with a broad brimmed hat. Pietro looked up as Enzo and his companion approached. At first glance from a distance, he knew there was something familiar about the man in the suit. As the man came closer, Pietro recognized the odd walk of his old friend and he leapt up and shouted, "Signore Brazzano! Signore Brazzano! You have come to Le Mans!"

Enzo and the dapper little man came to the table and Enzo introduced him. "Signore Vittorio Brazzano, my very old friend who won the Le Mans in a Ferrari Testa Rossa in 1958."

Pietro excitedly explained to everyone at the table, "This is the man, this great racing champion, who took the time and trouble to teach me to drive a racing car."

Vittorio shook hands with everyone and sat down at the table next to Pietro and Enzo. "It seems I taught you good," laughed Vittorio. "You are doing well out there, very well. I congratulate you."

"Grazie!" said Pietro. "I remember everything you taught me all of the time and it works, it really works. Oh, I am so happy to see you. Please meet my beloved wife, Anna."

Vittorio took Anna's hand in his and kissed it softly, bowing graciously even though sitting. "Pietro is a very lucky young man to have such a beautiful young lady for his wife," he said. Anna smiled and thanked him for the compliment.

Pietro asked Vittorio to explain how he was in Le Mans today. "You never told me you were coming!"

So Vittorio told them how Enzo had driven out to his garage and they had talked about Pietro…and how Enzo had said quite simply, "You must be there, Vittorio, you must! I will send a Ferrari limousine to your house the day before the race. The chauffeur will have your plane tickets and drive you to the airport for your flight to Le Mans. And, of course, we'll fly you back after we celebrate winning Le Mans!"

Vittorio told them how confident Enzo was that they would do well in the race. "He is much softer now than he was in the old days. Then he would say, 'Vittorio, go out and win the race.' I couldn't let him down, so I did win the race. Lucky for me," he added with a smile.

Pietro introduced Lucia and Stefano again. "My very best friends in the whole wide world. I owe them, Enzo and Luigi all my good fortune."

"No, Pietro, that is not entirely true. You saved our lives. If you had not done what you did that horrible night, I think we would not be alive and sitting here. So you don't owe us anything!" said Stefano.

"Well, maybe so," said Pietro, "but I am so glad we are together. I cannot tell you how much it means to me…."

Enzo could see that Pietro was close to tears, so he tactfully changed the subject. "Tell us, Pietro, how is it to drive the F40?" he asked.

Pietro looked at Anna and smiled. "Here is my very true love, Anna, who I love more dearly than anything else in the world. But when I am driving the F40, the feeling is indescribable, such a fast machine, so eager to accelerate; the valves and camshafts actually make music, with the turbochargers and exhaust sounding like the bass and drums.

When I am in second gear coming out of a corner and I push on the accelerator it is as though I'm strapped into a rocket heading for the moon. The power is always there in every gear. Like a bullet it flies through the air, so balanced, so perfect. There can never be an equivalent racing car in the world. I'm sure, Enzo, that you have created the perfect machine."

"Bravo! Bravo!" cheered Vittorio. "There speaks a true Ferrari racing driver who loves his car nearly as much as he loves his beautiful wife. Enzo, what more can you ask?"

Enzo laughed. "I remember thirty years ago, sitting in a cafeteria with you here in Le Mans, and you kept on and on about the Testa Rossa. 'Such a car!' you would say. 'La Bella Macchina,' you would say." Enzo looked around at the Ferrari team. "Would you like me to tell you what Vittorio did each and every time it was his turn to race in the Testa Rossa?"

Everyone nodded their head and waited eagerly to hear what Enzo was going to say.

"Do you mind if I tell them, Vittorio?" asked Enzo.

"Why should I mind? I was in love and I still am, so tell if you wish. I am not one to be embarrassed," said Vittorio.

"Vittorio had a scarf made of the finest silk in colors of green, white and red, with the Cavallino Rampante embroidered on it with a background of Modena yellow, just like the insignia on all Ferrari racing cars. He would take the scarf off, polish the Ferrari emblem on the bonnet of the Testa Rossa. Then, when he was happy that it was shining the way he wanted it, he would lean down and kiss the emblem just like he was kissing his sweetheart!"

"Ah, Signore Brazzano!" They all sighed around the table. "You are a true lover of Ferrari racing cars."

Vittorio chuckled at the memory. "Fancy you remembering that, you old dog!" he said affectionately.

"How could I ever forget? You did it at least a dozen times in just that one race. There I was thinking, the seconds are ticking by, Vittorio, get in the car and drive. But, no, you would perform your little ceremony then tie the scarf around your neck, check in the mirror that it was in just the right position. Then and only then would you get into that car and race, while I was nearly having a nervous breakdown!"

Pietro unzipped his overalls and removed a silk scarf from around his neck. It was green white and red; the Cavallino Rampante embroidered on it. He handed it to Enzo who was astonished… "The same scarf?" The scarf Vittorio wore for years and years?" Enzo was unable to conceal his surprise.

"The very same, Signore…given to me by one Signore Vittorio Brazzano to bring me luck in this race," said Pietro.

Enzo shook his head in amazement. "That scarf is a real piece of Ferrari history. I never thought I would see it again." He gave the scarf back to Pietro, who put it around his neck then zipped up his overalls.

"So that's why you wear that scarf every day, Pietro. You never told me the story behind it, and there I was thinking you were catching a cold and needed it to keep you warm! Silly me!" said Anna, smiling broadly.

Pietro leaned over and kissed her cheek. "I was going to tell you after the race, but now you know why I am wearing it…just for good luck and to remind me of everything Signore Vittorio taught me."

The whole team laughed, and then the mechanics took off to go back to the pit area, wishing the drivers, "Buon Viaggio! Buona Fortuna!" as they left.

Stefano looked at his watch. "We have only thirty minutes before we drive again. That went really fast! Anyone like more coffee?" They all declined and decided to walk back to the pit area and see how their teammates were doing.

Giovanni gave them a quick update in the pit office. He was happy.

Lorenzo in F40 #6 was leading, followed by Porsche #28, then McLaren #32. Roberto in F40 #8 was next, followed by Antonio in F40 #12, then another Mclaren#16, a Jaguar #18 and then Enrico in F40 #14. Quite a few of the private entries had fallen out of the race due to engine, suspension and gearbox problems. No crashes had occurred, but lots of near misses on some of the corners had been observed.

Giovanni was a little concerned about Enrico's #14, as Enrico had to slow down on some of the corners due to some imbalance that he felt going in, but that disappeared coming out of the corners. The mechanics had checked the car out on the last fuel stop, but couldn't find the reason, so they let Enrico go and were now discussing the possible cause in the pit office.

The clock marched on and the mechanics came out of the pit office. "We think the problem is caused by one of the rear engine mounts being cracked or loose, so we will change both mounts at the next driver change," said Beniamino, the head mechanic. "That would be a logical reason for why it only occurs when power is reduced going into a bend, as the front engine mountings take the load coming out of the bend."

"Good decision, Beniamino, have the parts and tools ready," said Giovanni. "We will call Enrico in first, after the next lap."

The sign went up to call F40 #14 in, and one lap later Enrico rolled to a stop and jumped out. Immediately, the engine cover was lifted back to expose the beautiful F40 V-8. The announcer reported that Ferrari #14 was in trouble in the pits and soon enough a race commentator came to ask Giovanni what the problem was. Giovanni explained briefly what they thought was wrong and what they were doing to fix it.

As he spoke, one of the mechanics lifted out an engine mount that was cracked in half. "Voila!" he said as his colleague was already fitting new mounts to each side, just in case the other side had also weakened. Giuseppe got into the car, buckled himself in and was ready to go. The other mechanics filled up the fuel tank, and as they finished, the engine mount mechanic yelled "Ready!" and closed down the engine compartment. Giovanni gave Giuseppe the thumbs up signal and banged on the roof with the flat of his hand. Giuseppe started the engine and took off very, very fast to do his two-hour stint and try to recapture some of the five minutes that had been lost in time.

The other three F40's were called in, drivers swapped over, together with a quick refuel, and all three made it out in less than ten seconds.

Lucia, Stefano, Pietro and Giuseppe were now all back on the track, doing their utmost to regain their positions and get to the front again. The battle for the first four places was ferocious, with the Ferraris all screaming around the track, taking the engines to maximum revolutions in each gear before changing up and doing it all over again.

Enzo, Giovanni and Vittorio stood together watching the race and discussing lap times and refueling procedures. They decided that to gain more time they would have the drivers go a few more laps between refueling if that was possible.

Giovanni timed Giuseppe's next lap, then shouted out in ecstasy, "Beniamino! Beniamino! Looks like your team fixed it! Giuseppe is back to top speed!" He hugged Beniamino, who grinned with pleasure. Enzo and Vittorio relaxed then, and went off to the cafeteria for a cappuccino and to discuss old times.

The race went on and the incredibly fast Ferrari F40's gradually outpaced the McLaren and the Porsche until they were again in the first three positions. Flashing by the pits, the F40's were unstoppable, their brilliant red color standing out magnificently against the other duller racing car colors. The crowd rose to their feet and cheered in a frenzy each time the F40's passed the stands, Stefano now in the lead with Pietro and Lucia, neck in neck, thundering down the track towards the Dunlop Bridge.

Giuseppe was really pushing his car to the limit and soon his initial five minute loss stood at three minutes and twenty seconds, so unbelievably fast were his lap times.

The announcer, overcome with emotion, reeled off the place positions, and every time he said the name Ferrari, the spectators in the stands and alongside the track erupted in loud cheers and shouts of "Bravo! Bravo!"

Darkness fell around 9:30 and the drivers turned their headlights on in order to see the track. Lucia experienced a whole new challenge, driving the circuit at top speed at night. Distances that she had measured in her mind, from one bend to the next, had been easy during the daylight, but now, even with the powerful headlights of the F40, she had to concentrate especially hard to avoid getting too close to a fence as she made her turns. At the same time she had to negotiate around slower cars and sometimes she would come up on them so fast on the Mulsanne Straight that only at the last second would she make out their red tail lights and swing over to the left lane to overtake. She was determined not to slow down and let the McLaren or the Porsche pass her, although she could see them in her rear view mirror, ever present and waiting for their chance to get past her and Pietro.

At a little after ten, the sign went up in the pits for Lucia to come in for a driver swap. Knowing this was her last lap before a two hour break, she took the F40 to its extremes, reaching 7700 revs in each gear, increasing her lead over the McLaren and the Porsche so that Lorenzo would have a good start when they changed drivers. She went through the Esses at well over 140 mph, steering the F40 around the curves, the tires squealing to gain adhesion and the engine roaring in third gear.

Pietro quite liked driving in the dark with the headlights on, and during most of the laps he would come up level with Lucia. Their tremendously powerful dual headlights would light up the track, making seeing ahead easier. But on the curves he or Lucia would back off and enter the curves one after the other in case a slower car was ahead of them.

Lucia and Pietro exited the Tetre Rouge Corner at 160 mph and gunned their F40's up to 200 mph, 210 mph, then 215 mph! The spectators watched as the beautiful Ferraris screamed down the track, their headlights glaring side by side. Then, as suddenly as they had been there, they disappeared in a roar of power that made the spectators shake their heads in wonder at the iron nerves of these drivers who dared to race at such speed for hour after hour in the dark night.

Lucia came into the pits and swapped with Lorenzo, who took off like a scalded cat when Giovanni banged on his roof to give him the signal. She took off her helmet and walked over to the pit door where Anna was waiting with Sheba.

The two young women embraced and Anna said, "Oh, Lucia, it's good to see you. You are so brave to drive so fast at night. I get lonely waiting for the two hours to end. How is it out there?"

"Very fast, my love, and very dark, but I think I can make it through the night. I only have to drive from twelve to two in the dark. Then when I drive from four to six it will be getting light around five thirty."

Pietro came in, followed by Stefano, and the foursome went off to the trailers with Sheba. "Come in our trailer," said Anna. "I'll make coffee and sandwiches for you." They went in and Lucia, Stefano and Pietro collapsed on the sofas. Anna put on the coffee and began to make the sandwiches.

"Whoa! I still see headlights in my head," said Pietro. He got up and gave Anna a hug and a kiss and she kissed him back ferociously.

"Oh, my love, I missed you this time. I was telling Lucia how lonely it is watching the race at night, but Sheba keeps me company.

Thank God for her, she is such a sweetheart!" Sheba, on hearing her name, lifted her head and looked inquisitively at Anna. Anna gently broke loose from Pietro's embrace and got two big dog biscuits from the cupboard and gave them to Sheba, who took them in her jaws and crunched them down in a few seconds then looked up for more.

Pietro went back to the sofa and stretched out. "This is comfortable. Come and lie down with me, Anna."

"After I make the coffee and sandwiches, then I'll come and hold you tight, Pietro." She poured the hot coffee into cups and put them on the table together with biscuits and a plate of tasty looking sandwiches.

Lucia and Stefano sat up, hearing the clink of the cups. "Thank you, Anna, that looks good. I am hungry too," said Lucia. She and Stefano tucked into the sandwiches and drank their coffee.

"Pietro, love, eat some sandwiches. You will need something inside you to keep your strength up if you are to drive again in two hours." Anna sat next to Pietro, who groaned and put his head on her lap.

"I'm a little tired," he said. "I'll have a five minute nap, then I'll eat, I promise."

"No, eat first, than nap for an hour, Pietro."

Pietro cuddled into Anna's soft stomach and closed his eyes. She gave up and sat there stroking his thick black hair.

Lucia and Stefano finished eating and lay down again. "Wake us at 11:30 please, Anna. Then we'll take quick showers to wake up properly," said Stefano. The three drivers lay unmoving for over an hour, each half asleep and dreaming of the Le Mans Circuit, seeing the headlights in their rear view mirrors and listening to the symphony of valve gear, camshafts and exhaust boom.

Anna lay back against the sofa and looked down at Pietro. "Please, God, keep them all safe," she prayed. She sat there for an hour until 11:25, then gently woke Pietro with a kiss.

He opened his eyes and looked up at her. "You are my angel, Anna, my very own angel." He returned her kiss and sat up. "Now I'm hungry," he said, grabbing a sandwich and wolfing it down, then taking a long drink from his cold coffee. "Lucia! Oh, Lucia!" he called. "Time to wake up. Stefano, you too!"

Lucia and Stefano awoke from their dreams and slowly sat up. "I was just drifting off to sleep," said Stefano as he rubbed his eyes. He helped Lucia up and they both stumbled towards the shower, then undressed and got in together. Lucia shrieked as the cold water poured over them before finally turning warm.

Meanwhile Pietro splashed his face with cold water in the sink, then dunked his head under the tap. "Whoa! That feels good!" He rubbed himself down with a towel and gave Anna a soft kiss on the lips. "Eight hours down, sixteen go to!" he said, kissing Anna again. "I'm looking forward to coming back into your warm arms at two o'clock. Are you going to have a nap now, my love?"

"No, I couldn't sleep, Pietro. I'll walk down to the pit area with you and wave you all off."

The four arrived at the Ferrari pit area and Giovanni put the sign up to start calling the F40's in for the driver change and refuel. Stefano and Lucia were first to go and they took off in tremendous bursts of speed to get back into the race.

Then it was Pietro's turn. As his car came into the pits, he hugged Anna close to him. "Arrivederci. I love you, see you soon!" he shouted over the roar of the cars passing the pit area.

"I love you too, Pietro," said Anna, kissing his cheek. "Be safe."

Pietro nodded and jumped into the F40, buckled his four point safety harness and put on his helmet. He pushed down the clutch and selected first gear. Giovanni banged on the roof when the refuel was complete, and Pietro pushed down on the accelerator, raised the clutch and was gone like a bullet, the twin turbochargers whooshing, the exhaust booming as he sped away.

He joined the main track at a little over 100 mph, changing up at 7000 rpm. He was in third gear and approaching 140 mph, then changed again to fourth gear and zoomed through the curves leading to Dunlop Bridge. His driving style superb, he felt the adrenaline rush as he rocketed towards 180 mph at which point he changed to fifth gear, crossed the Dunlop Bridge, overtook two slower GT2 cars and literally flew down the track, enjoying himself in the incredibly fast red F40.

Pietro used every bit of skill that he had learned from Vittorio and took the curves as fast as humanly possible, the F40 holding the road as if it was glued. He entered the Mulsanne Straight at 150 mph and swiftly built his speed up to 180, 200, 210 mph. The spectators cheered as the F40 went by, its engine howling like a wicked Banshee at maximum revs in fifth gear. Pietro reached 220 mph and five seconds later the first Chicane came into his vision and he slowed, double declutching down to fourth gear. Entering the curve, he changed down to third and picked his line to round the bend. He was forced to slow again as a Porsche 911 came into view. Pietro waited till he saw a gap and accelerated past the 911. Back on the Mulsanne Straight again, he put his right foot to the floor and the F40 responded instantly, and within a few seconds he was back up to 200 mph trying to catch up with his friends.

Meanwhile, Lucia and Stefano were dueling with two private GT1 entries; a big Porsche and a six-liter Corvette. They both kept close behind the cars in front, and as they went into a bend, Stefano saw a small gap opening up. He sped through it, followed closely by Lucia, the F40 engines snarling and growling as they took the revs to the max and passed the Corvette and the Porsche on the left.

After two hours of concentrated high speed driving by headlights, the Ferrari team was mentally exhausted, and when it came time to pull into the pits to change drivers, they were ready for it. Lucia's muscles in her arms and legs were actually weak from changing gears and pushing on the clutch and brakes, and as she got out of the F40 she trembled slightly. Stefano, who had pulled in earlier, saw a distressed look in her eyes and ran to her side to steady her. Giovanni and Enzo came over and asked what was wrong. Lucia said that she was just a little tired from the driving, but she would be all right again in a few hours.

Enzo, though very concerned, said it was really quite usual for the drivers of the midnight to two a.m. shift, because it is so tiring to both drive incredibly fast and have to judge the distances to the guard rail on curves and when overtaking. "I'm surprised that Stefano, Pietro and Giuseppe don't feel the same way. Or maybe they do, but they hide it well. Is that how it is, Stefano?"

"I must admit I am a little tired," replied Stefano. "But it is only after I got out of the car. While I was driving there was so much to concentrate on that I didn't have time to feel tired. It's such a fantastic feeling to drive on the track with the power of the F40. It seems more like flying a jet plane, it goes so fast!"

Pietro nodded in agreement. "I feel the same as Stefano, but now we will go with Lucia and Anna to the trailers and see that Lucia gets some rest."

Lucia listened to Stefano and Pietro, but when they finished speaking she said quietly, "While I was driving I, too was perfectly in control. It was only after I came into the pit area and stopped the engine that this strange tired feeling came over me. I'll be all right to drive at four o'clock." She went to the back of the trailer, unzipped her racing suit, took it off and lay on the bed.

Stefano went in and asked if there was anything he could get her to eat or drink. Lucia shook her head and said, "Just wake me at 3:30 and after I shower I will be fine." She smiled up at Stefano. "Please, Stefano, don't worry about me. You go and have a rest, too." She raised her hand palm upwards, blew him a kiss, closed her eyes and went to sleep.

Stefano went to join Pietro and Anna, who were discussing whether Pietro should sleep for an hour or stay awake and play cards. A soft tap sounded at the door. Stefano opened it and there stood Enzo and Vittorio.

"Hello, Stefano, we just thought we would drop by and see how things are," Enzo said. "Is Lucia awake?"

"No, Enzo, she's sleeping for an hour. Hopefully she'll be all right after that."

"Vittorio had an idea that might have helped, but if she is already asleep I guess we are too late."

"I tell you anyway," said Vittorio.

"Please, come in," said Stefano. Enzo and Vittorio came inside and sat on the sofa. Stefano closed the door. Anna and Pietro were sitting on the other sofa.

"Is anything wrong?" asked Anna.

"No, Anna, everything is fine. We just came to tell you an idea of Vittorio's. Tell them, Vittorio," said Enzo.

"Many years ago when I drove the Le Mans year after year, I got very tired at two in the morning. I would sleep and sometimes it helped, but a few times I would wake up even more tired because I'd gone into such a deep sleep my mind and body wanted to keep sleeping. And when it was time to drive again I was even more tired. So one time I went for a long walk and I found it helped. After that I found the best thing for me was to sleep on one off shift and walk on the next one. That way I could move muscles walking that I didn't use when driving, and I always felt better…much better than when I slept every time. So I thought I would pass on this idea and maybe it would help Lucia, but if she is already sleeping then she should sleep. But maybe you boys would do better to walk then sleep. It's just a thought," said Vittorio.

"A good idea, Vittorio!" said Anna. "Pietro and I can take Sheba for a walk now. Stefano and Lucia can sleep. And next time we will sleep and Stefano and Lucia can take Sheba for a walk. Come, Pietro, you lazy bones, let's go."

Pietro shrugged his shoulders. "All right by me. Let's try it!" He got up and took Sheba's leash from the counter. "Come on, Sheba, time to go for a walk." Sheba, willing as ever, rose up from the floor and stretched. "See you at 3:30, Stefano," said Pietro. Stefano nodded and went to lie on the bed next to Lucia in the back of the trailer.

Anna, Pietro, Enzo and Vittorio filed out of the trailer with Sheba. Pietro put Sheba's chain around her neck. "Come on, big girl, let's go," he said.

Enzo and Vittorio said 'Arrivederci' and went back to the pit area.

Anna, Pietro and Sheba set off to walk part way around the circuit.

"We will go to Tetre Rouge Corner, Pietro. The view is really good from there. And you will see how fast the F40's come out of the curve and onto the straight. You will be amazed at the power and all the noise." She took his hand and they set off.

They walked through the pit security where the guard, seeing the Ferrari insignia on their overalls, asked for their autographs. He smiled as Pietro scribbled his name on the Le Mans program cover. "M'sieur, qu'estce que l'numero de la auto?"

Pietro, whose knowledge of French was limited to merci and sil vous plait, thought about what the guard had said and turned to Anna. "I think he wants the car number? I caught the words auto and numero."

"Yes," said Anna, "You're right, Pietro. Write the number of your F40 on the program too." Pietro wrote under his signature the words, "Ferrari F40 numero 12." And handed it back to the guard.

"Merci, M'sieur, merci bien!" He offered the program to Anna, thinking she was driving too, as she had on her Ferrari racing overalls. She decided not to try and explain, so she signed her name under Pietro's and gave it back to the guard who thanked her profusely in French and went into what seemed to be a lengthy explanation of how he loved to see Ferraris racing in the Le Mans.

"Merci, M'sieur," said Anna, trying to sound as if they understood. They left the guard in his little booth and continued walking around the circuit, up the hill to the top of the Dunlop Bridge where the racing engines screamed in third gear at high revs, a beautiful noise, unlike any other in the world. Standing by the fence, they watched as the cars streaked over the hill at 160 mph, picking up more speed as they went downhill. Corvettes, Porsches, Ferraris, McLarens, Jaguars and Williams Renaults, all doing their utmost to win this tremendous endurance race of men, women and machines. They carried on past the incredible curves of the Esses, where real skill and split second timing shot the cars around one bend into the next. The roar of the engines and the bright headlights were hypnotic as the cars flashed by with incredible power.

Pietro and Anna, with Sheba on her leash, made their way along the track fence until they came to Tetre Rouge. They found a little spot on the grass and sat and watched the cars accelerating out of the turn and beginning the high speed run down the Mulsanne Straight. The sight was unbelievable! Race car after race car entered the curve at around 160 mph. As they reached the end of the curve, they would lunge forward, engines revving to the maximum in third gear, then a quick change up to fourth taking them onto the Mulsanne Straight at

185 mph. Another change to fifth gear had them flying down the straight at 200 mph, steadily increasing speed until they were a red tail light speck in the distance.

Anna looked around at all the people sitting on the grass watching the race cars roar by just a few feet away. She squeezed Pietro's arm and he looked at her in the glare of the headlights. "It is beautiful in a way, to see so many people watching the race in the middle of the night; to see the cars racing around the track," she shouted into Pietro's ear.

"Yes, it is part of history," Pietro shouted back. "The fastest production road cars with the finest engines, all competing at maximum speed to see who can come in first and win the glory for their team."

Anna suddenly jumped up and down in excitement. "Look, Pietro, there is your car, number 12 with Antonio driving!" They watched as Antonio came around the curve, the low red F40 with its extremely bright headlights was just overtaking a white McLaren. Antonio was in third at 7750 rpm and doing at least 170 as he passed the slower McLaren. Then, out of the curve, he changed up to fourth and was gone, flashing by the fence and hurtling down the Mulsanne Straight, going faster and faster.

Pietro listened to the multiple layers of sound from the Ferrari as it passed them; its twin turbochargers whooshing like a jet engine, its camshafts whining and its exhaust bellowing. Such engineering perfection, he thought. And I was so lucky to have been chosen by the great Enzo himself to drive his magnificent machine!

Anna and Pietro watched for a while longer as each of the four F40's entered the curve and accelerated down the Straight. Then they got up, and with Sheba on her leash, walked slowly back to the pit area, through the masses of spectators. The constant roar of the high performance engines and the bright headlights mesmerized the crowd as though a magic spell had been cast. Men, women and children, watched each car intently as it passed by, wondering perhaps what it would be like to drive the Le Mans Circuit in the middle of the night.

By the time Anna and Pietro got back to the trailer it was 3:30 a.m. Lucia and Stefano were up, drinking coffee and eating toast and marmalade. Lucia was obviously feeling much better as she greeted Anna and Pietro with a smile and a cheerful hello. "Did you two have a good walk? What's the world like out there?" she asked.

Lucia's tone was infectious and Anna laughed out loud in sheer happiness. "Lucia, it's wonderful. There are thousands of people all around the track and they all cheer when any Ferrari goes past. They all love Ferraris like we do!"

"I had a dream," said Lucia. "It was so vivid, Anna, you and I and Pietro and Stefano were on a boat somewhere. The sun was shining and we were drinking champagne. My mother was sitting on the deck and she spoke to me. She said, 'Lucia, you can do it. You must continue.' I asked her 'continue what?' and she replied, 'the race of course!' And I said I would. Then I woke up to find myself cuddled against Stefano. I woke him and we decided to make some coffee and toast. I feel really fine now!"

"Well, thank goodness for the dream!" said Anna. "That hot toast looks tasty. May we join you?"

"Plenty more bread in the cupboard and the coffee in the pot is still hot, so please do," said Lucia.

Pietro and Anna made slices of toast in the grill and covered them with butter and marmalade. They washed the toast down with strong hot coffee.

"Ah, that was good!" said Pietro. "I feel like a new man now!" He glanced at the clock. "Ten minutes to four. Have to get mentally stimulated." He playfully grabbed Anna and gave her a big cuddle, kissing her nose, eyes, ears and lips.

Anna was in the mood and kissed him back in return. Then hugging him to her, said "Go on, then, you Romeo. Go and win that race for me."

Back to the pits they went, all in high spirits. Giovanni was pleased to see Lucia looking her old self but said nothing, just gave her a hug. The sign went up to call Lorenzo in. As soon as he jumped out of the F40, Lucia gave Stefano a quick kiss on the lips and whispered, "Mia Amore," and got into the car. Stefano had not heard because of the track noise, but he knew instinctively what she had said and he blew her a kiss.

When the refuel was complete Giovanni banged on the roof and Lucia took off with her usual gusto. The F40 rocketed towards the track and was gone from view in a matter of seconds. Pietro and Stefano's cars came in and they were gone also. Anna stood waving cheerfully as they took off. She patted Sheba who stood faithfully by her side.

The race continued hour after hour. At 5:30 a.m. the dawn broke and by 5:45 the sun was in full view, promising another warm, cloudless day. Lucia, Pietro and Stefano drove at full speed from 4 to 6 a.m., 8 to 10 a.m. and noon to 2 p.m. All four F40's were still going strong as ever, with no mechanical problems.

At three o'clock, with one hour left in the race, Enzo and Giovanni decided that Lucia, Pietro, Stefano and Giuseppe would drive the final hour. Positions at that point were Roberto #8 in the lead, with Porsche #28 in second place, followed by McLaren #32 in third. Right behind them were Lorenzo in #6, Antonio in #12 and Enrico in #14. These were closely followed by a second McLaren, a Jaguar and a Corvette. The rest of the cars were over half a lap or more behind, but each one still had a chance to win the race.

Enzo took Lucia, Stefano, Pietro and Giuseppe into the pit office. Smiling, he told them, "Here is your chance, my young friends. Giovanni is calling in the cars now and you four are to drive the last hour. So good luck to each of you!" He hugged them one by one and to Lucia he gave a second hug. "Lucia, today you are going to make history. You are one very courageous young lady." Enzo kissed her on each cheek. "Go now," he said, "Lorenzo will be coming into the pit in a few seconds."

Ferrari F40 #6 with Lorenzo driving came into the pits. He jumped out of the car, visibly sad to turn over the car for the final hour. He gave Lucia a hug and told her to go win the race. Lucia got into the car and put on her helmet. Stefano came to the side, looked in and gave her the thumbs up sign, put his hand over his heart then lifted his hand and blew her a kiss. Lucia smiled and pursed her lips together to form a kiss in return.

Giovanni waited till the refuel was complete then gave his usual bang on the roof signaling Lucia to go. Lucia breathed deeply, revved the engine and let in the clutch. The F40 barked and howled as the drive shafts took up the massive torque of 760 bhp. The wheels spun, gripped and the F40 took off like an express train traveling at subsonic speed. Within three seconds Lucia was at 70 mph and at six seconds she closed in on 100 mph and joined the main track, accelerating magnificently until she was out of sight.

Next in came Roberto in F40 #8. He jumped out and clapped Stefano on the back as he climbed into the F40. When Giovanni gave the signal, Stefano took off in hot pursuit of Lucia, vowing to himself that he must drive like the wind, make every gear change at the highest revs and take every curve at maximum speed. He disappeared from view blasting onto the track and using all of the power in each gear to go as fast as possible. He was determined to win this race for Enzo. He had to see the great man achieve victory with this brilliant machine. Stefano drove faster than ever before, consistently defying the laws of gravity as he screamed into the curves and exploded out of them to gain maximum torque and get to the front of the race. He was determined to beat the Porsche #28 and the McClarens and prove to the world that the Ferrari F40 was the most powerful car in the racing world. Stefano forged ahead and began to pass car after car, the fabulous F40 engine executing faultlessly, giving its all after twenty-three hours of sustained high speed.

Enrico came into the pits in F40 #14 and swapped with Giuseppe who felt, as did Stefano, that he must win the race at any cost. When the signal came for him to go, he was mentally and physically ready, every nerve in his body straining to obey his brain signals. Giuseppe put his foot flat on the accelerator when it was time to go and the F40 roared down the pit lane, bucking and weaving as the rear wheelshafts attempted to deal with the tremendous power. Coming onto the track,

Giuseppe came close to hitting a slow Porsche 911, but at the last instant before contact, he veered sharply to the left, missing the Porsche by a hairbreadth.

Giuseppe gulped air at the shock of what had nearly been a tragic accident, but he recovered immediately and spun the steering wheel to the right, missing the spectator wall by an inch and accelerating back in a straight line off towards Dunlop Bridge. Hastily crossing himself, he muttered a prayer to Holy Mary Mother of God and breathed a tremendous sigh of relief.

Giuseppe's F40 took the Dunlop Bridge at 180 mph, the fastest so far, the V-8 's twin turbochargers spinning at maximum revolutions, forcing fuel into the injection system at a tremendous rate, feeding the hungry F40's engine as it hurtled down the track. His confidence restored after the near miss and his adrenaline high, Giuseppe felt supremely confident of his ability to guide the F40 through the curves as he came closer and closer, to the Tetre Rouge Corner with his engine revving to the limit in each gear.

He listened to the thundering of the engine at each gear change, and marveled at how the Ferrari design engineers could build an engine that could take such brutal punishment hour after hour. Giuseppe took the Tetre Rouge Corner at over 165 mph and came out of it at 185 mph in an incredible burst of power. He started down the Mulsanne Straight and again pressed his foot flat on the accelerator, overtaking a McLaren and then a Porsche. He saw the beautiful sight of Stefano's F40 #8 ahead of him. Giuseppe tried to gain on Stefano, but both cars were in fifth gear at 7000 rpm with 220 mph on the speedometer, so on this lap at least, Giuseppe would have to be content to sit behind Stefano and wait for his chance to take him on a bend.

Meanwhile Antonio, in F40 #12, came to a stop in the pit area to change drivers. Pietro came up to the car as Antonio jumped out. Pietro was about to get in when he turned, walked to the front of the F40 and took off his scarf. He rubbed the scarf gently against the Ferrari emblem on the bonnet. He rubbed again and again until the emblem's colors shone brightly. The Ferrari mechanics, their refueling finished, gathered around to watch him, unaware that he was repeating the ritual that Vittorio had executed thirty years before with the same scarf.

Giovanni shouted at him to get in the car and join the race, but Pietro paid him no attention. As Enzo and Vittorio also watched, Pietro knelt in front of the massive bonnet and kissed the Ferrari emblem with pursed lips. The crowd of spectators roared with delight. Pietro stood up, put the scarf back around his neck with the ends hanging over his shoulders, ran to the driver's side, jumped in and Giovanni banged hard on the roof, signaling him to go.

Pietro put in the clutch, selected first gear, revved the V-8 engine hard, let his foot up off the clutch and accelerated away with a stupendous burst of speed. The F40 shot out of the pit area onto the main track, gathering more and more speed as Pietro took it deftly through the gears until he was close to 8000 revs in third doing 150 mph. He steeled himself to take the car to its maximum limits, rounded the curve towards Dunlop Bridge and changed up to fourth gear. The F40 leapt forward as Pietro floored the accelerator, taking the bridge at 170 mph, almost flying over the top, then increasing speed down to the

Esses where he made a magnificent set of turns, overtaking two Porsches on the inside while they were scrubbing tires on the outside.

He built up speed again and took the Tetre Rouge right-handed at 175 mph, then careened down the Mulsanne Straight until he was neck and neck with a white McLaren. Pietro passed it on the left, rocketing away at 225 mph, the F40 singing to him with its camshafts and valves in perfect tune with the twin turbochargers bellowing at 8000 rpm. Pietro took the first Chicane at 200 mph, the tires screaming in anguish as he steered the car right into the curves, and at the last second, braked gently, spun the wheel to the left and roared out of the curve back onto the Mulsanne Straight. He changed up to fifth gear, floored the accelerator again and came up behind a Porsche. He pulled over to the left to overtake, but the Porsche also pulled over, trying to block Pietro. Without blinking an eyelid, Pietro swiftly turned to the right and overtook the Porsche which tried to block Pietro again, but Pietro was already too far ahead and the Porsche driver gave up in disgust. Pietro went on, going ever faster, passing car after car on lap after lap. He drove as fast as he dared until he was coming up on Lucia and Stefano, who were battling with a white McLaren and the ever dangerous Porsche #28.

The announcer reeled off the position in an excited voice: "Ladies and Gentlemen, the time is now twenty minutes to four, and there are five laps to go. In the lead is Porsche #28 driven by Heinrich Kleiber, followed by McLaren #32 driven by Jimmy Blue, then comes Ferrari #6 driven by Lucia Gapucci, followed by Ferrari #8 driven by Stefano Gapucci. Next is Ferrari #12 driven by Pietro Venini, then Ferrari #14 driven by Giuseppe Varzi." The announcer went on to describe the next five cars in the race, but the spectators were all concentrating on seeing if the Ferraris could regain the lead. Many people were now standing around the track, watching the duel of the fastest road-going prototypes in the world.

Lucia kept her foot on the accelerator, waiting for a chance to take the McLaren and the Porsche. She knew they would have to slow down significantly to take the acute right hand curve coming up. She positioned herself as close to the right fence as possible. The three cars were all running at 220 mph as they approached the corner. The Porsche #28 braked and threw itself into the right lane to take the curve as tight as possible, changing down swiftly from fifth to third gear causing the Porsche engine to scream as the engine braked the car. Taking the revs well beyond the red line was a risk, but the engine held together and the Porsche accelerated out of the curve with no engine damage and still in the lead.

The McLaren driver was more cautious braking much harder than the Porsche. Lucia saw her chance and turned into the corner with only a light tap on the brakes to keep her line. The McLaren crossed into the left lane and Lucia changed down from fifth to third and tore into the tiny gap between the fence on the right side and the McLaren on her left. The F40's engine took up the strain of the lower gear at 200 mph, the revs mounting to 8100. Lucia steered through the curve praying that the McLaren driver would keep his line and not come back in the right lane without looking. She concentrated on getting around the corner, then pushed the accelerator to the floor and the F40 surged past the McLaren, its driver surprised to see the Ferrari come out of nowhere and overtake him. He tried in vain to regain speed as fast as he could, but the sheer power of the F40's V-8 engine left him standing, and getting further and further behind.

Stefano, Pietro and Giuseppe cheered as they saw Lucia take the McLaren, and each vowed to do the same before this lap was complete. Each one also swore to himself that he would take the Porsche #28. The long run between Mulsanne and Indianapolis Corner gave Stefano and Pietro their chances. They roared along in fourth gear at 8000 revs until they were within five feet of the McLaren. They changed up to fifth, floored their accelerators and screamed past the McLaren, their F40 engines' 760 bhp showing its true spirit as they thundered past, tearing into the acute bend of Indianapolis Corner. Changing down to fourth, then third, hugging the left lane as they hurtled around the curve and accelerated away, leaving the McLaren a long way behind.

Meanwhile, Lucia accelerated out of the Armage Curve, thirty feet behind the Porsche #28. In third gear at 7750 revs, and keeping the power on, she waited until she was at 8000 rpm before changing up, the raw power of the F40's V-8 in fourth gear causing the red Ferrari to lunge forward, but the Porsche driver read her thoughts and straddled both lanes, preventing her from overtaking.

Lucia flashed her lights, but the Porsche refused to allow her to pass. She backed off a few feet to avoid hitting the Porsche in the rear, keeping her revs around 7500. She sat on the Porsche's tail awaiting her chance, knowing that she had the faster car, and if she was careful, it was only a matter of time before she would find a gap on one of the bends and take the lead from the Porsche.

The Porsche and the three F40's streaked around the track through Porsche Curve onto the White House Corner and down into

Ford Corner. No gap showed up on these turns as there were slower cars in front that were being lapped, and as each of the four leading cars negotiated past the slower ones, the pace of the race grew slower.

They passed the stands and the pit area and Lucia saw the sign held up by Giovanni: "Four laps to go, you can do it!" Lucia smiled and thought out a plan. She would take the Porsche on the wide stretch on the other side of the Dunlop Bridge where, even though there were still only two lanes, it was nearly wide enough for three cars to run side by side. She drifted back to ten feet behind the Porsche and readied herself mentally; her whole body on fire, every nerve in her body taut with concentration. The Porsche entered the steep approach to Dunlop Bridge in third gear, over revving the engine to try and out accelerate Lucia; knowing that if he could not put some significant distance between them she would pass him at some point and his chance at victory would be in ruins.

Even as the Porsche climbed the hill at an incredible 175 mph, Lucia stayed with him, ten feet behind, waiting her chance. Behind Lucia, Stefano and Pietro were racing neck and neck up towards Dunlop Bridge, their V-8 engines screaming at maximum revolution.

The Porsche crested the peak and changed up to fourth gear. Lucia stayed in third gear, her rev counter needle well into the red zone. She saw the wide area open up, changed up to fourth gear and turned to take the Porsche on the left. The Porsche driver saw her starting to pull to the left in his rear view mirror and instantly swung his steering wheel over trying to block her. But Lucia was ready for him and even as he steered to the left she swung to the right and surged forward, her right foot pressed hard on the accelerator pedal urging the F40 to go even faster. The maneuver completely surprised the driver of Porsche #28 as he watched the F40 pass him. Gaining more and more ground, she took the powerful F40 to its absolute maximum in fourth gear and, with the engine screaming louder than ever before, changed up to fifth at 8200 rpm. The F40 catapulted forward, leaving the Porsche a distant speck in her rear view mirror.

Lucia felt a tremendous sense of relief as she realized she was now past the Porsche and in the lead, with only three and three quarter laps to go. She kept up her high speed through the Esses, taking a line right down the middle, charging into the curves at 160 mph in third gear. Defying the laws of gravity, she flung the F40 into turn after turn, exiting at 170 mph. She confidently sped up to 200 mph as she came up to the Tetre Rouge Corner. Changing down to third, she held an aggressively tight line on the right-hander. She roared out of the corner onto the Mulsanne Straight, changing to fourth then fifth gear to reach 220 mph.

Lucia looked in her rearview mirror to see Pietro and Stefano passing the Porsche as they too pulled onto the Mulsanne Straight. The two red F40's grew in her mirror and she suddenly realized that the Ferrari team was now in first, second and third places with only Giuseppe behind the Porsche.

Lucia sped down the straight and came to the first Chicane where she was forced to slow as an Aston Martin and a Corvette were dueling on the curve side by side. She smiled, even though she was a little disappointed. Pietro was now in the lead, having taken advantage of the slowdown caused by the battle of the two slower cars. Lucia followed Pietro through the curve and accelerated her way back onto the

Mulsanne Straight. She looked in her rearview mirror to determine where Stefano was, but he was not in sight. Concerned, Lucia slowed automatically only to see Stefano blast past her, his engine revving to the maximum. Accelerating to 225 mph, he left Lucia behind as she realized he must have been in her blind spot on the rear quarter when she checked the mirror. Lucia chuckled. To think that Stefano would outrun her because she had been worried about him and had naturally slowed down. 'C'est la vie, thought Lucia. If fate decides she would be third, then third she would be. At least she must not let that Porsche get near her!

The three leading Ferraris charged around the track, ever increasing their lead over the Porsche and the McLaren. The crowd was cheering and waving all around the circuit. Some chanted, "Ferrari! Ferrari!" proud to see the spirit of Ferrari in the leading three positions. They continued racing around the track. The "Two Laps" sign went up, then finally the sign they all wanted to see: "Last Lap!"

21: EXTRA COURAGE REQUIRED! IT'S THE LAST LAP.

Giuseppe saw the Last Lap sign as he passed the pit area. He had passed the white McLaren on the last turn in the Esses and now he was coming up fast on Porsche #28. He felt the F40 telling him to change up to fourth as he screamed up towards Dunlop Bridge, but instead he made the sign of the cross and prayed out loud with no one to hear him but the beating engine of the F40. "Holy Mary, Mother of God, help me to pass that Porsche!" The F40 soared up the Dunlop Bridge in hot pursuit of the Porsche, the engine thundering at 8500 rpm, the twin turbochargers bellowing and the wind noise beating off the side windows. The noise in the car was deafening as the pistons detonated now at 8600 rpm. The red beast surged forward and as Giuseppe burst over the peak, he changed into fourth gear and lunged forward. The revs dropped in the higher gear but the torque flow was tremendous and the red beast had nearly caught the elusive Porsche.

Heinrich Kleiber in Porsche #28 saw Giuseppe's Ferrari coming down at him from Dunlop Bridge. He roared into the Esses at 180 mph, changed down to third gear and hurtled around the curves, the track fence barely a foot away as he used all of his skill to try and outrun the Ferrari. Giuseppe followed Heinrich through the Esses, inching his way closer and closer until he was a single car length from the Porsche's rear end.

Heinrich pressed his foot to the floor on the accelerator pedal in third gear, waiting till the rev counter went completely into the red danger zone, then changed up to fourth with a really fast gear change. The Porsche's transmission reacted perfectly and Heinrich came out of the Esses bend at 185 mph onto the short curve leading up to Tetre Rouge Corner.

Giuseppe kept right behind the Porsche, looking for the right moment to make his attempt to get past. He prayed out loud again, this time an "Our Father who art in heaven," followed by "Hail Mary."

The two cars entered Tetre Rouge, Heinrich on the inside right lane and Giuseppe level with him in the left lane. Heinrich didn't dare try and block Giuseppe. He knew that if he didn't maintain his line he would kill the pair of them. He changed down to third gear and floored the accelerator in a desperate attempt to outrun Giuseppe, using sheer engine power by over revving the Porsche engine. But all his attempts were useless as the F40 started to gain on the Porsche.

As both cars came out of Tetre Rouge, Giuseppe changed up to fourth gear and began the fastest race of his life. He pressed the accelerator so hard into the floor that his foot hurt, but he took no notice. Watching the rev counter as it again climbed into the red zone, he executed a superb gear change from fourth to fifth and the F40 responded perfectly, surging away from the Porsche.

Heinrich made his change from third to fourth to fifth gear, but knew even as he completed the changes that he was a beaten man. He watched the Ferrari speeding away from him. He floored the accelerator and the revs climbed to 8000. His speedometer showed 220 mph, but the Ferrari was still accelerating away from him. Ten yards, twenty yards…soon Giuseppe was fifty yards ahead of the Porsche with 230 mph on the speedometer, gaining more yards with every second.

Giuseppe cried aloud, "Grazie mille!" Thanking Mary a thousand times as his F40 screamed down the Mulsanne Straight, the Porsche #28 one hundred yards behind. Giuseppe breathed a high sigh of relief then prepared himself for the first Chicane and thundered into it at 210 mph. Braking ever so slightly, he took an abrupt right hand curve, changed to fourth, swung left to come out of the Chicane and accelerated out of the curve with a beautiful symphonic roar from his F8.

Back on the Mulsanne Straight, he took the F40 back up to 230 mph, looked in the mirror and saw a grey spot a long way back. The Porsche was beaten, if only Giuseppe could keep up the pace for the remainder of the lap. At 230 mph, Giuseppe was running 5 mph faster than his colleagues Lucia, Stefano and Pietro. On the next Chicane he saw them some 300 yards ahead.

Pietro exited the second Chicane with a glorious burst of power and headed for Mulsanne Corner, his F40 running superbly at 225 mph. He pushed the accelerator to the floor and the F40 reached 231 mph at 8000 rpm. He took Mulsanne Corner at 160 mph, changing from fifth to third gear, skipping fourth gear altogether. The rev counter needle vanished into the red zone and a tremendous vibration rocked the F40. Pietro was worried he had broken something, but the F40 engine and transmission took up the challenge, the engine did the braking and Pietro slid around the sharp corner, rear wheels spinning as they tried to grip the tarmac and turn at the same time.

Pietro gunned the F40 out of the turn and screamed onto the lower approach to Indianapolis Corner, back into third gear at 160 mph, then entered the Armage Corner at 170 mph, very, very close to the fence and narrowly missing a slower Williams-Renault. Coming out of Armage, Pietro glanced in his mirror to see three bright red Ferraris only one hundred yards behind him. My God! He thought. Giuseppe made it! We're going to take the first four positions! He took his F40 up to maximum revs in fourth gear and hurtled on towards the final two corners before the finish line. He took Porsche Curve at 190 mph, stayed in fourth gear for a quick burst to Ford Corner, then changed down to third gear and went into the sharp bend. He eased off on the accelerator and waited until he started out of the curve, then pressed the accelerator to the floor for the final run to the finish.

Pietro in F40 #12 came screaming across the finish line at 200 mph at approximately four p.m. to take the black and white checkered flag. He raised his right arm in salute as a huge roar came from the crowd. Next came Stefano, Lucia and Giuseppe as the crowd went wild with shouts of "Bravo! Bravo!" echoing through the stands.

Pietro braked heavily, pulled into the pit area and jumped out of the F40 and into Anna's waiting arms. She smothered him with kisses even as he asked Lorenzo to lend his helmet to Anna. Lorenzo gave her the helmet and Pietro bent down to give Sheba a huge kiss on the muzzle, then took the leash from Anna and handed it to Enzo, who took it in surprise. Pietro walked Anna to the F40 and opened the door for her. Anna got in and put the helmet on while Pietro helped her buckle on the four point seat belt. He ran around to the passenger side and got in quickly.

"Let's go, my love! One victory lap for you," said Pietro, leaning over and kissing Anna on her pretty nose. Anna laughed and pressed the clutch down, putting the F40 into first gear. She let the clutch up and accelerated gently down the pit area, changing neatly up to second and third gears. She joined the main circuit at about 80 mph and held that speed for the entire victory lap.

"That's about my limit, Pietro," said Anna.

"Darling, that's quite fast enough for me. Just so you are enjoying yourself."

They cruised the lap and the crowd cheered wildly and waved their congratulations as F40 #12 came around the track. Anna made one complete circuit then pulled into the pit area where the car was mobbed by the Ferrari mechanics. Anna and Pietro got out of the F40 and the young mechanics lifted them both high on their shoulders and made their way over to where Enzo, Giovanni and Vittorio were standing.

As the Paparazzi and television crews were taking pictures of the Ferrari F40s and all of the Ferrari team, the mechanics put Anna and Pietro down in front of Enzo, who stood there magnificent in his impeccably tailored gray suit. Enzo took Pietro by the shoulders and looked at him for a long time, impervious to the commotion going on around them. Finally he spoke in a quiet voice, almost a whisper, but Pietro heard every word. "You have shown tremendous courage for the second time in your life. You'll do well in whatever you do, of that I am sure. Thank you for winning the Le Mans in the Ferrari F40. You made an old man's dream come true." Enzo embraced Pietro and kissed him solemnly, first on one cheek and then on the other.

Pietro felt elated and sad at the same time, to hear this great man, Il Comendatore himself, thanking Pietro for making him happy. It was such an honor, Pietro's eyes filled with tears. Blinking them back, he spoke slowly and clearly, "I thank you, Signore Enzo Ferrari for trusting me to drive your F40. It is that great car, La Bella Macchina, that won the race; it is your great knowledge of design and engineering and your engineers and mechanics that won the race."

Enzo smiled and hugged Pietro to him. He whispered in Pietro's ear, "Take care, my boy, of yourself and your beautiful wife. If ever you need anything, call me." Pietro nodded, still unable to believe that the great Enzo had bestowed such compliments on him.

Enzo turned to Anna and hugged her close, whispering something in her ear at which Anna laughed. "Yes, Enzo, we plan to have lots of children, all boys!" she said, turning to Pietro and giving him a kiss on the cheek.

Pietro's face flushed red, then regaining his composure he said sincerely, "We will call our first son Enzo."

Now it was Enzo's turn to laugh. He thanked Pietro and Anna once again then said, "Now I must congratulate the rest of the team before the Paparazzi engulfs them with questions." He handed Sheba's leash to Anna and patted the wolf gently on the head. "Our lucky mascot, such a beautiful silver wolf!"

Sheba pawed Anna in a gesture of affection, then let out a magnificent howl, which frightened the photographers who were close by. Enzo chuckled. "Sheba makes the same sound as an F40. No wonder she brought us luck!"

Enzo went over to congratulate the other Ferrari drivers and the Ferrari Racing Team of engineers and mechanics, telling them how proud he was of their skill and determination. He thanked each one personally with a good Italian hug and a kiss on each cheek.

When he had gone the whole round, Giovanni held his hand up for silence. "I would like to say on behalf of everybody in the Ferrari Racing Team that it is we who are proud to see the great Ferrari name win the Le Mans. We thank you, Signore Enzo Ferrari, for letting us be a part of the Ferrari legend, and most of all we want to say we love you. Viva Ferrari! Viva L'Italia!" he shouted. The whole team shouted the theme. "Viva! Viva! Enzo Ferrari!"

Enzo stood tall and solemn, then he smiled and shook his head. "It is I who thank you, my friends. You make it all work and each of you is responsible for our great win today. Grazie, tanto!" The team whistled and shouted, hugging each other in the euphoria of winning the single most important endurance race in the world.

Lucia hugged Anna and Pietro. Stefano joined in and all four hugged each other, glad in a way that the race was over and they could relax and celebrate. Giovanni had the whole team line up in a tight group with Enzo in the middle for the press and television. The cameras flashed and the TV cameras recorded a piece of automotive history.

After that there were formal ceremonies to present the Le Mans plaque to Enzo as the winning manufacturing team. Champagne corks popped and the whole team drank a toast to Enzo. The tremendous excitement of achievement was in the air and the press and television crews loved it, taking picture after picture of the Ferrari team.

Pietro, Anna, Stefano and Lucia decided it was time to leave, but Pietro said he had two things to do first. He searched out and found Vittorio, sitting on his own by the pit area, a tall glass of champagne in his hand. "Come, Vittorio!" beckoned Pietro. The old man stood up and followed Pietro down to the track. Pietro stood in front of Ferrari F40 #12. He took the scarf from around his neck and gently cleaned the Ferrari emblem on the wide bonnet. He knelt down, stretched his arms wide, leaned forward and kissed the Ferrari emblem.

Vittorio chuckled. "You learned well, my boy. I am very proud of you. I know it takes skill and courage to win in the Le Mans."

Pietro walked over to Vittorio and gave the old man a hug. "Thank you for taking the time to teach me, Vittorio. I owe the win to you and to this fine racing car."

Vittorio raised his champagne glass to Pietro. "Salute!" he said, taking a sip of the champagne. "Now you must go. Your friends are waiting. Come and see me when you get back to Maranello. You can tell me about the race."

"I will, Vittorio, I will. Arrivederci!" said Pietro.

"Arrivederci, Pietro. Buona Fortuna," replied Vittorio.

Pietro turned and walked across the pit area to where Anna, Lucia and Stefano waited for him. He stopped in his stride, turned full circle and looked lovingly at the magnificent F40. He raised his hand palm up and blew a kiss to the F40.

"Ciao, mi amore," said Pietro. "Ciao, La Bella Macchina!"

THE END